"Susan Krinard has set the standard for today's fantasy romance."
—*Affaire de Coeur*

"The reading world would be a happier place if more paranormal romance writers wrote as well as Krinard."
—*Contra Costa Sunday Times*

"Susan Krinard is a vivid, talented writer with a sparkling imagination."
—Anne Stuart

PRAISE FOR THE NOVELS OF
SUSAN KRINARD . . .

"Krinard uses her lyrical prose to weave a fascinating tale of reincarnation and redemption." —*Library Journal*

"Rising superstar Susan Krinard dishes up yet another mind-blowing reading experience . . . explosive . . . [This] daring innovator and extraordinary storyteller . . . creates another towering landmark in imaginative fiction."
—*Romantic Times*

"Ms. Krinard brilliantly delivers a gripping romance, turning every emotion inside out . . . She holds you spellbound with her magic." —*Rendezvous*

"Written with tremendous energy, it exhilarates the senses and intoxicates the soul." —*Affaire de Coeur*

continued on next page . . .

SECRET
of the WOLF

Susan Krinard

BERKLEY BOOKS, NEW YORK

SECRET OF THE WOLF

A Berkley Book / published by arrangement with the author

ISBN: 0-7394-2169-7

BERKLEY®
Berkley Books are published by The Berkley Publishing Group,
a division of Penguin Putnam Inc.,
375 Hudson Street, New York, New York 10014.
BERKLEY and the "B" design
are trademarks belonging to Penguin Putnam Inc.

PRINTED IN THE UNITED STATES OF AMERICA

This book is dedicated to every man, woman, and child who has ever suffered the devastating effects of mental illness—those who have faced its challenges and have never given up hope of ultimate victory. It is also dedicated to the courageous men and women who have never ceased to search for cures, and to understand the mysteries of the human heart, mind, and soul.

—Susan Krinard, 2001

ACKNOWLEDGMENTS

I wish to thank Fred Larimore for his assistance with information about nineteenth-century Indian Army regiments, officers, and campaigns. His Web page on this subject is http://pobox.upenn.edu/~fbl/. Any mistakes regarding the British Army are my own.

I am also grateful for the ongoing encouragement, support, and feedback from my friend Eugenia Riley.

Chapter 1

SOUTH VALLEJO, CALIFORNIA, 1880

"*Stop!*"

The vicious drunkard who bent over the cringing boy paused, his fist in midair, as if he had heard the voice of God Himself. Or, at the very least, a policeman with a club.

But if any policeman was to be found in this shabby excuse for a town, he was otherwise engaged. Johanna Schell had no faith in police.

Nor did she have any delusions of divinity. But she trusted in the air of authority she'd cultivated for so many years, and in the strength of her voice.

She crossed the muddy road to the haphazard line of shacks crouched along the docks near the railway station. In the gathering dusk, she could just make out the man's unshaven face, the scar slashing his chin, the filthy clothing. He reeked of cheap liquor. The boy was pitifully thin, bruised, with the hollow, haunted eyes of one who had endured many such beatings. Johanna had seen that look before.

The man squinted at Johanna and produced an expression somewhere between a leer and a smirk. She saw the way he appraised her, judged her, dismissed her with the dubious aid of his diseased brain.

"You talkin' to me?" he demanded, swinging toward her.

"I am." She set down her doctor's bag, took a firmer grip on her valise, and drew up to her full height, almost the equal of his. "You will cease beating that boy, immediately, or I shall summon the authorities."

"The . . . ath-or . . ." He laughed. His young victim shrank in on himself, as if the laughter were only another sign of worse to come. "Who the hell you thin' you are, Miss High-'n'-Mighty Bitch?"

"I am a doctor. I've seen what you're doing to that boy."

"Boy?" He grabbed a handful of the boy's frayed collar and jerked him up. "This boy's m'son. I c'n do whatever I want wi' him. No *ath-or-tee's* gonna stop me. No woman, neither." He spat. "Doctor, huh. How good're you at healin' yerself?"

Johanna ignored his threat. "What has your son done to deserve this?"

The man's dull eyes grew confused. He couldn't answer, of course. There was no reason for the punishment, save for his drunkenness and a natural depravity. But his confusion quickly gave way to resentment. He yanked the boy this way and that, until the lad squeezed his eyes shut and went limp.

"*You* ha' no right to question me!" he snarled. "He's useless! Should throw 'im in the Straits and be done with'm!" He dropped the boy and grinned at Johanna. "You, too. Throw you in the Straits—af'er I have a bit o' fun."

"I doubt that very much," she said. She tested the weight of the valise, grateful for the heavy books that had made carrying it so inconvenient during her visit to San Francisco. She turned to the boy. "Don't be afraid, *mein Junge*. I will help you."

A large, dirty fist thrust itself into the air before Johanna's face. "You better help yerself."

"I generally do," she said. "I've dealt with worse than you."

He stared at her, as if she'd gone quite mad. Most of the denizens of the surrounding neighborhood must run in terror of this bully; he wouldn't be used to defiance. He had surely never faced those cursed by true madness. She had. And though her heart was beating hard and her hands were sweaty inside her gloves, neither madman nor bully would see anything but calm competence in the visage of Dr. Johanna Schell.

Calm competence was usually enough. It reduced hostility in the vast majority of the patients she'd dealt with in her father's private asylum. Even the most unruly of the residents had learned she was no frail girl to be intimidated.

This man was not one of the majority. He stepped close enough that his breath washed over her face in a nauseating cloud. "Looks like I'm gonna have to teach you a lesson . . . *Doctor*," he sneered.

The weight of the books in the valise was much less comforting than it had been a few moments ago. Johanna calculated the best angle of attack. Striking at his face was out of the question. His genitals, however . . .

"Run, boy," she urged the cowering child. "Run for help."

"Run, an' I'll kill you," the man said. "You hear me, boy? Ye're gonna stay and watch." His attention turned to his son just long enough. Johanna swung the valise. It connected. The ruffian grunted in pain and shock. He staggered and flung out his arm, hitting Johanna across the temple. She fell, dazed, as he pulled a knife from the waistband of his trousers and lunged for her.

The knife never reached its goal. Out of the shadows of the nearest alleyway, a dark shape flashed in front of Johanna and seized the bully's wrist. Johanna pushed up onto her elbows, struggling to make sense of what she witnessed.

She couldn't. The shape—the man, whose face remained only a blur—moved too quickly. He flexed the drunkard's arm back at an impossible angle. The knife spun into the dirt.

Now it was the bully who crouched, mewling in fear. The boy had already fled. Johanna's deliverer bestowed as little mercy as the bully had shown his own son. His fist struck like a piston, driving the drunkard onto his back. A second blow followed, and then another.

"You'll kill him!" Johanna shouted, finding her voice. *"Bitte—"*

The avenging angel stopped. Johanna caught a glimpse of gentleman's clothing that had seen better days, a body lean and tall . . . and eyes, their color indistinguishable behind a glare of absolute hatred.

The bully had met his match. This phantom would kill him, without remorse. He reached down to finish the job.

Johanna scrambled to her feet. "Please," she repeated. "Don't kill him, not on my behalf. The boy is safe. Let him go."

She had no way of knowing why the phantom had attacked, if it were for her sake, or the boy's, or some unknown motive of his own. But he paused again, and in that moment Johanna heard the choked sobs of the child she'd thought safely gone. He watched from the corner of a shack, his fist in his mouth, his bruised face white as a beacon.

"For the boy's sake," Johanna said, holding out her hand in supplication. She backed away until she stood beside the boy, reached out to gather him against her side. "Please. *Go.*"

The man straightened. Again she glimpsed his eyes, enough of his face under a stubble of beard to recognize what might have been a kind of coarse handsomeness. Then he hunched over, blending into the shadows. His prey gave one last squeak of terror, a mouse left half-alive by the cat. And the avenger leaped back into the alley from which he'd come.

Johanna took the boy by his shoulders and held him steady. "Are you all right?" she asked, sweeping him with her experienced gaze. Nothing broken. The bruises would mend . . . if his spirit did. "What is your name?"

"Peter," the boy whispered. A tear tracked its way through the dirt on his face, but he straightened under her scrutiny. He looked toward the place where his father lay. "My pa—"

"Peter, I want you to stay right here," she said firmly. "I am a doctor. I'll see to him."

"Is he dead?"

She swallowed, wondering whether it was sadness or relief she heard in his voice. "I don't think he is. But I will not let him hurt you again."

Peter nodded and did as she asked. She returned to the site of the unequal battle and found the bully lying where her rescuer had left him. She knelt to count his pulse and feel for broken bones. The right wrist was fractured, at the very least; he would have swelling in his face and two black eyes in the morning. But he still lived, and she saw no signs of internal bleeding.

She rose and wiped off her skirts, as if she could so easily rid herself of this man's barbarous taint. Odd; she couldn't quite bring herself to apply the same judgment to her phantom, in spite of the harsh punishment he'd dealt out. Hadn't he given the bully a taste of his own medicine?

She shook her head, bemused by her own primitive response. *Her phantom.* He was nothing of the sort—merely another disturbed resident of this fetid dockside warren. He, like the man he'd attacked, undoubtedly had a history of violence dating back to his own childhood. He was likely beyond saving.

But Peter was not. She left his father where he lay, collected the boy, and went in search of a local doctor who could take charge of the case. She had to ask in several disreputable saloons before she got intelligible directions to the home of South Vallejo's physician. He was none too pleased to be called out at dinnertime, but Johanna convinced him that she had the boy's care to consider. Quite naturally, that was a woman's job.

She wasn't above using male prejudices when it suited her purpose.

Peter, it turned out, had no living mother; but an elder, married sister lived in the town of Napa City, a major stop on the Napa Valley Railroad's route north to Silverado Springs. Johanna had no intention of leaving him in his father's "care" another night. She doubted the father would pursue the lad once he was out of reach, and any life would be better than this.

By the time she and Peter reached the Frisby House, a ramshackle two-story frame building that passed for South Vallejo's best hotel, the night was dark and damp with fog. She bought Peter the hotel's plain dinner, which he ate with great appetite, and secured them a small, musty room with two narrow beds. She treated his bruises, checked under his dirty clothes for cuts or abrasions, and did her best to make him wash up with the use of the cracked bowl and pitcher the hotel's housekeeper provided. His youthful reluctance to obey was heartening, if bothersome; his spirit hadn't been broken. There was hope for him yet.

Afterward, he fell into an exhausted sleep. Johanna was left to make the best of her lumpy bed and threadbare blankets, listening to the constant din of frogs in the marshes about the town and remembering, again and again, the burning eyes of the phantom.

Gott in Himmel help any local scoundrel who ran afoul of him without a passerby to interfere. She was not much given to prayer, but she offered up a sincere plea that none of his future victims would be any less deserving than young Peter's father.

And that she, personally, should never see him again.

H*e knew exactly which room was hers.*
    As he watched from the ill-lit street across from the Frisby House, he could smell her scent, carried by the cool, wet winds from the Strait and the ocean thirty miles to the west. He'd memorized the smell instantly when he went to work on that cowardly piece of filth among the dockside shacks.

He knew the boy was with her—but now that the whelp was safe, he was of no further interest. The woman was. He could not have said why, for she wasn't the kind of female he sought when sexual hunger came upon him. She wasn't beautiful, though her figure, full of hip and breast, was enough to rouse him.

Maybe it was because she'd stood there, so calm, when the bully attacked her. Remained calm when *he* appeared. He wasn't used to such composure when he was around. He preferred to provoke different emotions.

Maybe he was curious. She was a doctor. A female doctor. Because of her, the bastard would live . . . at least for today. She'd robbed him of his vengeance. She owed him for that.

But it wasn't his way to ponder what could not be explained. He existed by instinct, and emotion, and whim. Now his whim said that he wanted this woman, in a way no weak human soul could understand.

He could go after her, of course. He moved like the fog itself, all but invisible to human senses. He could steal her from that room with no one the wiser. Satisfy himself with her, and be done with it.

No one would stop him, least of all the Other—the one

he wouldn't name. To name the Other gave him power. And he wasn't ready to surrender himself.

Someday, he would keep what was his, and damn the Other to darkness and silence forever.

He dug his bare toes into the earth of the street, indifferent to the loss of his shoes. He didn't need them. He shifted from foot to foot, staring at the darkened window.

A bellow of raucous laughter burst from the nearest saloon, distracting him. The smell of liquor and beer drowned out the woman's scent. His mouth felt dry, ready for another drink. *That* took far less effort than climbing into the woman's room. It was the swiftest escape from the memories, the burden the Other had given him.

And in the saloon there were men who would cross him. Ruffians who would see only a lean, oddly dressed tenderfoot with too much money, ripe for the plucking.

He loped to the entrance of the saloon, whose doors spilled light like pale blood into the street, and went in. The room was full of carousers, with a couple of whores for good measure. He sat at the bar, pulled a handful of coins from his pocket, and ordered a whiskey straight. Ten drinks later, even the bartender was staring in amazement. Still it wasn't enough. Not enough to drown the memories.

Someone kicked at his bare foot. He ignored the first blow. The second came harder, accompanied by a loud guffaw.

"Hey, boy. Someone steal yer shoes?"

Still he waited, taking another sip of his whiskey.

"You hear me, you scrawny li'l pissant? I'm talkin' to you." A blunt, dirty hand snatched at the coins. "Where'd ja get all that chickenfeed, eh? You gotta share it with the rest of us. Right, boys?"

He ordered another drink and downed it in one swallow.

"Wha' 'r' you . . . some kind o' freak? Or is that water y'er drinkin'?" The glass was plucked from his hand.

He turned slowly to the man leaning on the nicked

wooden bar beside him. Another drunk, of the belligerent variety. A brute, no longer young but massive from hard physical labor, the kind who found a little extra incentive for a quarrel in the contents of a bottle. Just like the one who'd been beating on the boy.

Just what he'd been waiting for.

He smiled with deliberate mockery. "What's it to you, you ugly son of a bitch?"

The drunk let fly after a moment's disbelieving pause. It was pathetically easy to dodge the blow and slip around behind.

He kicked the drunk's feet out from under him. The audience laughed and snickered as the brute went sprawling . . . until the man pulled a pistol from his trousers. His shot went wild and crashed into the stained mirror behind the bar.

Several onlookers jumped the shooter, disarmed him, and tossed him into the street. The bartender cursed over his shattered mirror, and the rest returned to their drinking and whoring.

But the "freak" wasn't satisfied. He stuffed the money back into his pockets and went in pursuit of his prey. He found the drunk on his knees in the street, swearing a blue streak and wiping hands on muddy trousers. Bloodshot eyes lifted to his, narrowed in hate.

"D'you really want to see a freak?" he asked pleasantly. When he had the drunk's full attention, he stripped and Changed. It hurt, the way it always did, but he didn't care. He reveled in the pain. He finished, every muscle and bone screaming in protest, and waited for his prey to realize what he saw.

The drunk's eyes nearly popped from their sockets. He tried to scream. He wet himself and fell into a dead faint.

Laughing with his wolf's grin, he raked his sharp foreclaws along the slack, pockmarked face. Let the drunk remember this encounter, as the previous bully would. Let him scare his fellows with mad tales of men who turned into beasts. No one would believe. They never believed.

He bent back his head and howled. The sound bounced off alley walls and floated on the fog like a banshee's wail. All noise from the saloon stopped; he could almost see the faces turned toward the door, the hasty gulping of whiskey, the furtive gestures made to appease God or the devil.

He belonged to neither. Let them listen and be afraid.

He Changed back, dressed quickly, and turned for the hotel . . . and the woman. But a vast weariness overtook him; curse it though he might, he knew what it portended. The more he fought, the greater the chance the Other would seize control.

He must rest. Find some quiet place where he wouldn't be disturbed, and he might wake still in possession of this body.

With the last of his strength, he began to search for a sleeping place. In the end, he found he could not leave the vicinity of the hotel, where *she* lay. He discovered an abandoned, fire-damaged cottage two blocks away, tore through the boards nailed across the door, and lay down close to a window, where he could still catch the merest whiff of her scent over the smell of burned wood and mouse droppings.

She's mine, he told the Other. *No matter how often you drive me out, I'll come back. I will have her in the end.*

And you will have nothing.

Chapter 2

Though she had made this journey several times since she and her "family" had come to live in California, Johanna never tired of the view she saw from her window as the Napa Valley Railroad made its way north into this little bit of paradise.

Once South Vallejo and the marshy delta were left behind, the valley began in earnest. At first one saw only wide fields of grain and cattle pastures, isolated farms and rolling, nearly bare hills in the distance on either side of the tracks. Majestic, isolated oaks stood sentry singly and in small stands, their branches twisted into fantastic shapes. The native grasses were golden brown, almost the color of caramel. It had taken Johanna several months, that first year, to get used to the arid summers of California. She had come to appreciate their beauty.

At the valley's entrance lay Napa City, the capital and largest town in the county. Its dusty streets boasted the usual assembly of shops, hotels, saloons, and even an opera house. Here the train made an extended stop, and Johanna disembarked to escort Peter to his elder sister's home on the outskirts of town.

He'd been a quiet, solemn companion since they'd left the hotel early this morning. And no wonder: His life had taken an abrupt change in course. Johanna understood the shock of that all too well.

Peter's sister was glad to take him in, though she lived humbly and had the careworn face of most countrywomen. But country folk could also be fiercely loyal to their own. Johanna returned to the train depot satisfied that she'd made the right decision.

It was important that something good had come of last night's confrontation. She hadn't really slept at all in that narrow bed, and it wasn't because of the discomfort. Even now, in the bright midmorning sunshine, she imagined herself back in that foggy alley with the phantom.

Be sensible, she told herself. *You are always sensible.*

She settled back into her seat on the northbound train and turned her attention to the landscape once more. Such openness and abundance refuted the very existence of shadowy avengers. And she was going home.

Home. *Der Haven,* she'd named it . . . the Haven. A simple farm backed up against a wooded hill at the very top of the valley, surrounded by the last of her uncle's vineyards. A place of refuge for the small collection of former patients she and her father had brought with them from Pennsylvania two years ago. They were all that remained of the inmates of Dr. Wilhelm Schell's unorthodox private asylum—the patients with nowhere to go, no one to trust but the physicians who'd cared for them.

Dr. Schell the elder was no longer capable of caring even for himself much of the time. The apoplexy that had struck him down so tragically had curtailed his vigorous movements and the sharp brilliance of his mind. He needed the Haven as much as the others did. It was Johanna's charge to keep the place functioning, its residents content.

And to heal them, if she could. The need to heal was an essential part of her nature, and it made the responsibility worthwhile.

The train left Napa City and passed several small villages, their tiny depots strung along the rail line and its parallel road like knots on a rope: Yountville and Oakville, Rutherford and St. Helena, Bale and Walnut Grove. Gradually the valley narrowed and the hills to either side grew higher, clothed now in brush and trees. The vineyards that were beginning to attract so much interest appeared more frequently, each gnarled grapevine was thick with green leaves and hung with ripening clusters of fruit.

The grapes were very much like people, Johanna thought. Each variety took its own time in ripening, and had to be coaxed along by the vintner. Some were simply more fragile than others.

She blinked at her romantic turn of mind. Quite impractical, such thoughts. But they kept her from thinking about last night, or Peter's ultimate fate, or how well Papa and the others had gotten along without her. If not for the chance to hear an eminent neurologist lecture in San Francisco, she could not have brought herself to leave. But Mrs. Daugherty could be relied upon to look after the Haven for a day or two. Of all the people in the town of Silverado Springs, she was least bothered by the "loonies" who lived with the crazy woman doctor. And she needed the money.

Money. Johanna clasped her hands in her lap. That, too, was never far from her thoughts. When she'd brought her father and the others to California, her uncle's inheritance had been a godsend. Upon his death, Rutger Schell had left his brother the greater portion of his unsold vineyards at the head of the valley, a sizeable house, a fruit orchard, and several acres of wooded hillside. It had seemed sufficient to keep them all comfortable for many years.

But Johanna had miscalculated. Without families paying for the support of patients, without her father's practice, the money went too quickly. First she had sold the outlying vineyards, then the ones closer to the house. Now only the orchard, two acres of vines, and the woods remained. She had little else to sell. They grew much of their own food, but some they had to buy. And there were other necessities.

She smoothed her worn skirts and rejected the self-pity of a sigh. She would simply have to find a solution to the money problem . . . or trust that one would appear in time, as Uncle Rutger's inheritance had come so providentially just after Papa's attack.

Finding the landscape an inadequate distraction, Johanna removed one of the European journals from her valise, unfolded her spectacles, and began to read. Charles Richet's work—quite fascinating, though she could see he was missing the profound healing potential in the new science of hypnosis . . .

A light touch on her shoulder woke her from her trance.

"Silverado Springs, ma'am," the conductor said, tipping his hat. "Last stop."

"Of course. Thank you." Johanna smiled and tucked the book back in her valise. She was the last passenger to leave the train. No one had evinced much interest in a plain, spinsterish woman absorbed in a massive volume, and that suited her very well.

Of course, the people in Silverado Springs itself knew somewhat more of her. Like all small towns, even one prone to the visits of the more worldly health-seeking patients from San Francisco, residents of the Springs made it their business to know the habits of everyone in the vicinity. A woman doctor was certainly a novelty wherever she went.

"That hen medic," was the worst she'd been called—within her hearing. As she descended the steps from the platform and entered Washington Street, the central avenue in Silverado Springs, she could feel the stares of the idlers hanging about Piccini & Son's general store and Taylor's livery stable.

There was scant harm in them. She had encountered much worse in medical school, both in Pennsylvania and in Europe. She had long ago dismissed any doubt that she should not be a physician merely because of her sex . . . let others think what they might. Her father's opinion alone was the one that mattered.

Had mattered.

She adjusted her grip on the valise, passing a family of well-dressed tourists in town to take the waters. Though Silverado Springs was past its prime as a resort, it still had its share of summer visitors, who set up temporary living quarters at the Silverado Springs Hotel. There they could enjoy the warm weather, bathe in mineral springs, and gaze up at the great, bald-topped bulk of Mount St. Helena looming to the east.

She strode north among the neat frame houses of the town's residential section. It was a brisk four-mile walk to Der Haven, one Johanna was well accustomed to. She made her way back to the main, unpaved road, which ended just a little north of Silverado Springs, then continued crosscountry along a wagon path that pointed the way to the small farms clustered where the hills came together to close off the valley.

The Haven was one of the most isolated houses. It was that isolation that made Johanna feel her patients were safe from the prying eyes of the townsfolk.

The very potent sunshine on this particularly warm day in July almost tempted Johanna to remove the pins from her hair and let it fall. No one was liable to see her. But she resisted the impulse and increased her pace.

Surely Papa would be fine. She'd be glad to see him, nonetheless, glad to be back in charge and with everything under her personal guidance. Irene had been on good behavior two days ago; she hadn't made May cry in a week.

Lewis, the former Reverend Andersen, was in the midst of one of his low periods, not likely to disrupt the household with his talk of sin and his devotion to excessive cleanliness. Oscar was seldom any trouble. And Harper was . . . Harper, silent and unresponsive as usual. She wasn't about to give up on him.

On any of them.

The toe of her scuffed boot connected with something long and solid lying in the grass. She caught her balance and looked down.

A man lay there, sprawled insensibly on his stomach, most of his body hidden by the tawny grass. It was his shoulder she'd kicked, but he wasn't apt to have felt it. His face was turned away, but she knew he was unconscious.

She knelt beside him and felt for his pulse. It was thready, but regular. The man himself had a lean, tall build and reddish-brown hair. His clothing was that of a gentleman and had seen hard wear; it was dirty and torn. It also stank of alcohol.

Another inebriate. She'd had her fill of that last night. Compressing her lips into a firm line, she carefully rolled the man over.

The first thing that struck her was his handsomeness. His face was the very epitome of an aristocrat's: clean, strong but finely drawn, as if designed by a sculptor bent on depicting the ideal male. His long-fingered hands were tanned from the sun. His lips had a mobile look, even in stillness; his eyelashes were long, his brows slightly darker than his hair, lending strength of character to his features.

Strength he clearly didn't possess, if he'd gotten drunk enough to be lying here. She didn't recognize him from any of the nearby farms or from town.

A stranger. A vagrant. A drunkard somewhat less brutish than the one in Vallejo. Someone who might possibly require her help.

If he'd accept it. And while he remained unconscious,

she had no way of transporting him to the Haven. She'd have to get home and harness Daisy to the buggy. If she were very fortunate, he might come to his senses and be gone before she returned.

Just as she was getting to her feet, he opened his eyes.

They were the color of cinnamon, a light reddish-brown to match his hair. They seemed to stare at nothing. His breath caught and shuddered, as if he'd forgotten how to breathe.

"Are you all right?" she asked. "Can you hear me?"

His body jerked, and he lifted his head with obvious effort. She could see his eyes focus on her, the blurred confusion gradually replaced by stunning clarity.

For an instant she thought she knew those eyes. Then the moment of familiarity passed, and he spoke.

"You . . ." he croaked. "You're . . . in danger."

It wasn't in Johanna's nature to laugh in such circumstances. She crouched beside him. "I?"

"Evil," he said. His eyes began to unfocus again. "Evil— you must . . . be careful—"

She touched his forehead. It was damp with sweat, warm but not feverish. If he were experiencing delirium tremens, his symptoms ought to be more extreme. His speech would imply some sort of hallucination . . .

He grabbed her wrist. His grip was paralyzing in its strength. "Listen—" he said. His eyes widened in terror, and abruptly his fingers loosened, freeing her hand and leaving it numb. She shook it several times, concentrating on bringing her own pulse back to a normal speed. Her brief fear was totally without justification; he was in no state to be a danger to anyone.

A quick evaluation of his condition indicated that he was unconscious once again. With a renewed sense of urgency, Johanna made him as comfortable as possible. She had nothing to put over him but the short mantle she'd taken with her to San Francisco. It barely covered his shoulders.

"I will come back for you," she said, knowing he couldn't hear. "It won't be long."

She strode the remaining mile to the Haven in record time. When the whitewashed fence that ran along the perimeter of the orchard came into view, she released the breath she hadn't realized she'd been holding. The branches of the trees, like the grapevines in their neat rows, were hung with ripening fruit, but she had little thought to spare for their bounty.

The Haven was a large, rambling one-story house, constructed of wood and stone with a broad porch bordering three sides. It looked exactly like the refuge she called it, friendly and inviting and lived-in. She half-expected several of the "family" to be waiting on the porch to greet her. But it was Oscar alone who rose from his seat on the stone steps, waving his big hand and grinning from ear to ear.

"Doc Jo!" he said, lumbering toward her. "You're back!"

She noticed at once that the young man's shirt was misbuttoned, and he'd forgotten to wear his braces, so that his trousers fell loosely about his hips. Otherwise he clearly hadn't suffered in her absence.

"Good day, Oscar," she said, taking his outstretched hand. "How is everyone?"

"Good," he said, nodding vigorously. "Only we missed you."

"As I missed you."

"What was the city like? Were there lots and lots of people?"

"A great many, Oscar. But I can't tell you all about it now. First I need your help."

Immediately his guileless face grew wide-eyed and solemn. "I'll help you, Doc. Just tell me what you want me to do."

She patted his arm. "We must go and rescue someone who is ill. I'll need your strength to lift him."

He puffed out his broad chest. "I can do it."

"I know you can. I'm going to harness Daisy to the buggy, and then we'll be on our way. Could you take my valise inside, and tell the others we'll be back shortly?"

Oscar took the valise, lifting it as if it were filled with nothing but air, and trotted back to the house. Johanna crossed the yard to the small pasture just beyond the barn and fetched placid, reliable old Daisy, who tossed her head in greeting and allowed herself to be harnessed without a single mild protest.

If only human beings were so cooperative.

Oscar was waiting for her by the gate, nearly bouncing in his eagerness. He handed her up into the driver's seat and plopped down beside her, jostling the carriage with his weight. Johanna urged Daisy into her fastest pace.

The man was still lying where she'd left him, but his condition was considerably worse. Instead of resting quietly, his lean body was shaking with unmistakable tremors. He'd flung her mantle off into the grass.

Delirium tremens. She had no doubt of it now. He could become very dangerous if he began to hallucinate again. She was profoundly grateful for Oscar's dependable strength.

"This man is very sick," she told him. "We have to take him to the Haven to get well."

Oscar wrinkled his nose. "He stinks!"

"Yes. We'll have to clean him up later." She knelt beside the stranger and took his pulse again. It was racing. He might come out of unconsciousness at any time.

Her hand brushed a bulge beneath his coat, and she felt underneath. A heavy leather pouch hung from a strap over his shoulder. She opened the flap at the top. The purse was bursting with coins, both gold and silver, and a tightly rolled wad of bills. A great deal of money indeed, especially for a man who should have been robbed long since.

She closed his coat. "We'll put him in the back of the

buggy," she said to Oscar. "Can you lift him gently, by the shoulders, while I take his feet?"

Oscar did as he was asked, taking great care to be gentle. The inebriate was heavier than his frame would suggest; there must be solid muscle behind it. Johanna had lifted or restrained her share of male patients in her time; she remembered Papa's indulgent pride in her sturdiness. "My Valkyrie," he'd called her.

She ignored the stab of pain at the recollection and helped Oscar maneuver their patient into the back of the buggy, where the rear seat had been removed for the carrying of supplies and patients. This time she'd come prepared. She adjusted blankets beneath and over him, made certain that he was breathing without difficulty, and took the reins again. Oscar twisted in his seat to stare at the man.

"Who is he?" he asked.

"I don't know. We'll find out when he wakes up." If he lived. Many patients didn't survive the delirium. But with a flash of the intuition she'd learned not to dismiss, she guessed that he wasn't one to lie down and die easily.

Remember . . . he's just another patient in need of medical attention—and a drunkard at that. They hadn't accepted inebriates at the old asylum in Pennsylvania. Could the treatment she and her father had developed be used to illuminate the causes of a drunkard's need for alcohol?

She shook her head. Papa had been the one for wild flights of theoretical fancy and unorthodox schemes. Her business now was to keep this man alive.

Careful to avoid the worst ruts in the path, Johanna guided Daisy at a walk back to the house. Most of the Haven's residents were watching for her return, alerted by Oscar's earlier warning.

Irene leaned on the porch railing, patting at her dyed red hair with a beringed hand and posing to display herself to what she considered her best advantage. God knew what she'd think when she saw the new patient.

May, the Haven's youngest at fourteen, hovered at the edge of the porch, ready to flee at a moment's notice. The former reverend, Lewis Andersen, stood like a rigid sentinel, his face set in its worn lines of disapproval and misery. Harper, of course, wasn't there. It took far more than this to awaken him from his inner world.

She and Oscar eased the man from the buggy and carried him to the porch. Lewis stared at the stranger's face and backed away as if he'd seen the devil himself.

"Stinking of damnation," he muttered. His gloved hands sketched out the meaningless, repetitive patterns he adopted when he was upset.

Irene gave a high-pitched giggle and angled for a better view. May peered at the newcomer and took a step closer, as if she felt real interest in him. Then, just as abruptly, she skittered out of sight around the corner of the house.

The spare room was at the very rear of the house, in a portion built of local stone. It was always cool in summer, and isolated from the rest. Johanna and Oscar set their patient down on the bed.

" 'Woe unto them that rise up early in the morning, that they may follow strong drink,' " Lewis said behind them.

"Reverend Andersen, if you would be so kind as to fetch a fresh pitcher of cold water, and a glass," Johanna suggested.

Lewis backed out of the room. He would probably feel the need to wash his hands ten or twenty times before returning with the water, but that would give her a chance to undress her stranger.

"He's very sick," Oscar said solemnly, towering behind her.

"I'm afraid so. I must undress and bathe him and put him to bed, while he is still quiet. He may become excited later on."

"Like Harper does sometimes?"

Oscar hadn't forgotten the last time Harper came out of

his cataleptic state in reaction to some waking nightmare, screaming and crying until Johanna could calm him. All the residents had been afraid.

"It is possible," she said. "That's why I want to be ready. Do you think we could borrow some of your clothes for this man when he wakes up?"

Oscar grinned. "I'll go pick some out." He lumbered into the hall, footsteps thundering in the direction of his room.

Left alone, Johanna concentrated on undressing the patient. His shoes were too fancy for extended walking, and she expected to find blisters on his feet. Surprisingly, there were none. The coat had come from a quality tailor, though one might not realize it now.

His liquor-stained shirt was held closed by a few remaining buttons; if he'd had a waistcoat, it was gone. She removed his purse and then the shirt, tucking the pouch and money into the drawer of the night table. No one here would steal it, except perhaps Irene—and she wouldn't think to look.

Stripped to the waist, the stranger confirmed Johanna's guess about a muscular frame beneath the leanness. The pectorals were well developed, as were the deltoids and biceps. His waist was firm and tapered, ridged with muscle. All just as any sculptor could wish. No indication of prolonged illness or injury; not a man who had gone so far in drink that his entire body was ready to fail him. For an inebriate, he appeared to be remarkably healthy.

After a moment's hesitation, she unbuttoned his trousers and tugged them down. He was, after all, just another patient. She had no personal interest in him . . . no matter what some prurient townsfolk might say about a woman doctor concerned with the intimacies of male clients.

She laid his trousers across the back of a chair and briskly discarded his underdrawers. His thighs and legs matched the muscular leanness of his upper body; his hips were well-formed. In fact, every major portion of his anatomy was a masculine ideal.

Johanna licked her lips, grateful the patient was still unconscious.

Leaving him lightly covered, she went into her room, the closest in the hall to this one, and retrieved her basin and a sponge. She drew the chair up beside the bed and gently washed away the sweat from his body.

It was a thing she'd done many, many times, but her hand was just a little unsteady as she guided the sponge from his neck and shoulders down the length of each arm, across his chest, his stomach, each long leg. She turned him gently and bathed his back, glancing once at his muscular buttocks and then away.

She felt tension drain from her body as she finished and replaced the sponge in the basin. He needed a much more thorough bath than this, but she couldn't risk it now. If he had delirium tremens, the chance of hallucinations and agitation was still very real. He would have to be—

He pushed up from the bed before she realized he'd wakened. Fingers clutched at the sheets, and his head tossed deliriously from side to side.

"Where—" He coughed, and his voice cleared. He turned to stare at her. "Who are you?"

"A doctor. Johanna Schell. You're safe here."

He began to shake, violently, his teeth chattering. "Not safe," he said. "No." Fresh sweat covered his forehead and upper lip. His face went white, and Johanna recognized his impending sickness.

Quickly she removed the sponge from the washbowl and offered the bowl to him. He twisted his body and heaved into the receptacle, as if trying to keep her from witnessing his illness. He kept his back turned to her until she gave him a cloth to wipe his face.

"You shouldn't . . . have brought me—" He gasped. He made a warding motion with his hand. "Go 'way."

"I can't do that." She reached for his flailing hand and held it firmly. "What is your name?"

His face went utterly blank. She watched him struggle to find that information, perceiving his panic when he couldn't.

"Don't remember," he said. "Oh, God."

"You are suffering from alcohol withdrawal," she said, keeping her grip on him. "You may experience unpleasant symptoms, but you will not be alone."

The door opened behind her, admitting Lewis with the pitcher of fresh water and a glass on a tray. He set it down on the table by the bed and retreated, holding his hands out from his body as if they had become contaminated. The stranger reared up, staring at Lewis with an almost feral intensity.

"Thank you, Reverend," Johanna said. "Would you be so kind as to close the door behind you?"

He left with alacrity, doubtless to wash his hands another dozen times. Johanna poured out a glass of water and pressed it into her patient's hand, holding it steady with her fingers around his. "You must drink. Your body is badly depleted."

He gazed at her with the driven intensity he'd shown Lewis. *Such remarkable eyes.* She shook herself and lifted the glass toward him. He let her put it to his lips and swallowed the water like a man dying of thirst. She refilled it, and he finished the second as promptly.

"Excellent," she said. "Now you must rest. Rest and proper diet, plenty of water and abstinence from drink are the only cures for your condition. When you are better, we can talk."

"No." He caught her wrist as he had by the wagon road, in that same unbreakable grip. "Can't—" His throat worked, and he spread his fingers around it as if to choke himself. He released her, pushing her away as he did so. He began to run his hands up and down the lengths of his arms, slowly at first and then more and more desperately, as if he were trying to rip something away from his flesh.

"Not me," he said hoarsely. "Not me!"

Here it began, then—the delusions and hallucinations. He might be seeing insects, or snakes, or some other loathsome object. The hallucinations might continue for hours. Calmly she reached down for her doctor's bag and opened it. She carried a very small vial of chloral hydrate, which she used as sparingly as possible. This time she'd probably have no choice.

Her patient was panting now, eyes wide and wild. "Get out," he cried. He clawed at his arms, leaving red streaks. Seriously hurting himself could be the next step.

"Listen to me, my friend. I can make you feel better, sleep until this has passed."

He stopped his frenzied movements. "Help," he whispered.

"Yes." She poured a few drops of the syrup into a small spoon. "If you will take this—"

She thought it might actually work, that he would take the medicine quietly before matters proceeded to a dangerous point. He reached—as much for her as the spoon—his face unyielding. Then he froze, fingers bending into claws. His eyes rolled back in his head.

Johanna flung herself toward the bed just as his seizure began. She half lay across him, holding him down with the weight of her body. He convulsed beneath her. His heart pounded frantically, drawing her own into a sympathetic rhythm. His head slammed back on the pillow, once, again. The rigidity of his body relaxed, every muscle gone limp simultaneously.

The seizure was over. She checked his pulse and his breathing. Not good, but not fatal. Disentangling herself, she retrieved the fallen spoon and poured out new medicine. She pried open his mouth and pushed the spoon between his teeth.

He swallowed normally. She hovered over him for several minutes to make sure it had gone down, and used a clean cloth to mop his wet forehead. With her thumbs she massaged his temples and the space above his eyes, willing him to surrender.

The sharply etched lines between his brows smoothed out under her ministrations. His breathing slowed, steadied. It would be an hour before the chloral hydrate took effect, but in this state sleep might come more quickly.

She permitted herself to draw away at last, dropping into the chair and closing her eyes. She was exhausted, a state she did not enjoy admitting even to herself. Where was Papa's Valkyrie now?

The door swung open with a faint creak. "Doctor Johanna!"

Bridget Daugherty stepped into the room, wiping her hands on her apron. "Well, I'll be! The others didn't even tell me you was home. I was out in the back with the wash—" She glanced at the patient. "You been busy, I see. New guest?"

"For the time being."

Mrs. Daugherty sniffed. "Likkered up. You never took one of them in before."

"The opportunity hadn't arisen," Johanna said crisply. Bridget was a naturally garrulous soul, curious about everything and completely uneducated, but she also felt she owed Johanna a great debt for delivering her eldest daughter's child safe and alive when the other local doctor had proclaimed the case hopeless. She was steady, trustworthy, and tolerant of the odd residents of the Haven. Johanna could ask for no more.

"I found him in the road," she said. "He might have died if I'd left him."

"An' you can't leave any poor soul in need, can you?" Bridget shook her head. "Well, looks like you might need a hand tonight, after supper."

"I would much appreciate it," Johanna said, daring to close her eyes again.

"You're plumb tuckered, Doc," Bridget said. "You ought to rest."

"Not now. He must be watched."

Bridget clucked. "Same old story. Well, at least the wash is done, and I didn't have no trouble from anyone. I'll fix you up a supper tray and feed the rest."

"Thank you, Bridget."

A broad, callused hand settled on her shoulder and squeezed. "There's a letter for you came in yesterday's mail, from that Mrs. Ingram. I put it on your desk." Mrs. Daugherty left the room.

Another letter from May's mother, a full four months after the last. This time it might contain good news, something other than vague hints of her plans to return for her daughter, and the usual questions about May's well-being. But Johanna couldn't count on that.

In any case, the letter could wait. Johanna got to her feet and lifted her new patient's trousers and coat from the back of the chair. They might be washed, mended, and saved, with a little effort. Irene might be persuaded to do it for such a handsome stranger.

She waited out the next hour until it was clear that her patient was sleeping deeply, unlikely to wake for some time. She tucked the sheets and blankets high about his shoulders, smoothing them down over the contours of his upper body.

How beautiful he was, even in sleep.

She stepped sharply away from the bed, barked her shin on the chair, and reached for the doorknob. *Papa.* She must see Papa. He would be waiting, and she'd left him alone so long. Papa would have advice—

No, he wouldn't. Sometimes, when she was very tired, she forgot about the attack and what it had done to him. She expected to walk into his room and feel his arms around her, hear his laugh and his chatter about his latest progress with a patient.

Not today. Not ever again.

But this man might recover. *This* was within her control. She would see that he was up on his feet and well again, whatever it took.

With a final backward glance, she left the room and closed the door behind her.

Chapter 3

He remembered his name.
Quentin. Quentin Forster. Born in Northumberland, England, thirty-two years ago.

And suffering from a throbbing headache, a mouth full of cotton, and eyes that all too slowly focused on the room in which he lay. He blinked against the spill of light from the lace-curtained window. Thank God the sun wasn't shining from that direction.

The window looked out on something green. Peaceful. He braced his arms beneath him and pushed up. Every muscle ached and protested the abuse. The sheets and blankets that had been tucked in at his chin slid down to his waist. He discovered that he was naked.

Instinctively he looked for his clothes. A shirt and trousers, of homely cut and fabric, lay neatly over the back of a chair not far from the bed. They didn't look like his clothes, but it wouldn't be the first time he'd awakened to find his clothing and belongings unfamiliar.

At the other side of the room was a dresser, a washstand

with a pitcher, basin and towels, and a three-legged stool painted a bright shade of pink. Something about the color made him want to laugh. It matched his current situation in absurdity.

His bed was wide enough for two, with heavy cast-iron head- and footboards. The mattress was comfortable, the sheets clean. If he'd gotten into this room and this bed under his own power, he had no memory of it.

So where was he? This was not a hotel room. It was too neat and modest: neither a run-down boardinghouse nor an expensive inn that catered to the rich. He'd spent his share of nights in both.

Cautiously he flipped the sheets back and swung his legs over the side of the bed. He endured a brief spell of dizziness, and then tested his weight on his legs. They supported him well enough. Cool air nipped at his skin. He'd been sweating sometime recently; a fever? Or just the aftereffects of another drunken binge?

That was the one thing he was sure of. He'd been drunk. The blank spots in his memory always came after such episodes.

He tottered with all the grace of a babe in leading strings, making his way to the window. It was open the merest crack. He smelled the growing things beyond it even before he looked out. The sweetness of fruit trees. Flowers. Vegetables . . . tomatoes, carrots, peas. Freshly turned earth. The complex mélange of woodland.

Trees and tangled bushes framed the window. A pine- and oak-covered hill rose steeply a few yards beyond. The air was fragrant, with a hint of dampness. He could smell people nearby, but not in the numbers that meant close-packed houses and smoke and waste from thousands of residents, rich and poor and in-between. The only sounds were the singing of birds, a muffled voice, the distant lowing of a cow, the rustle of leaves.

He wasn't still in the City, then. He leaned his forehead

against the cool glass, thinking hard. There'd been the saloon in San Francisco . . . gambling, winning . . . making
plans to move on, catch the ferry to Oakland across the bay.
It didn't really matter where he went, as long as he kept
moving.

That was where the latest blank spot in his memory
began. And ended here, in this room.

But there was something else. He returned to the bed
and grabbed a handful of sheet, lifting it to his nose.

Yes. A woman. He shivered at the memory of her touch,
his body's recollection more vague but every bit as real as
that of the mind.

A woman. He groaned. Was this some woman's bed
he'd shared last night? He couldn't even remember her
face, let alone the rest of her. He glanced down at himself.
His body wasn't telling him that it had enjoyed a woman recently.

A small mirror hung above the washstand. He looked
himself over: He obviously hadn't shaved in a couple of
days. Aside from a certain gauntness and the dark half-
circles under his eyes, his face was unmarked. No surprise
there, and no sign of violence in the vicinity, nothing to in-
dicate that his amnesia hid behavior or incidents he should
fear.

But he *was* afraid. This was happening more and more
often, his periods of amnesia increasing in length each time.
He always swore he wouldn't take another drink . . .

Until it happened again.

As he always did when he awoke this way, he searched
the room for other clues. No peculiar objects he didn't remember buying. The shoes beside the bed looked at least a
size too large—so, for that matter, did the clothes. In the
drawer of the night table lay a heavy pouch of coins and
bills; his winnings had been very good indeed, it seemed.
And no one had stolen it while he slept.

But something was missing. He emptied the pouch and sifted through the coins.

The ring was gone. His mother's ring, inherited from her own family, the Gévaudans, and given to him upon her death—the last tangible memory of his family. Had he used it as a stake in a game, or drunk it away, or lost it?

He shrugged, shutting off a twinge of pain. His mother had been dead for twenty-four years. She wouldn't know how low he'd sunk.

He reached for the trousers laid over the chair. He was still weak enough that it took rather longer than usual to put them on. The thud of footsteps outside the door found him balancing on one leg like a stork, trouser leg flapping.

The door creaked open slowly. A brown eye pressed up against the crack. Someone—male—was trying very hard not to breathe audibly, making even more noise in the process.

"Come in," Quentin said. His voice felt long-unused. "Come in, if you please."

His secret observer took immediate advantage of the invitation. A sandy-haired giant, near six and a half feet in height, barged into the room. He wore overalls several inches too short and a wide grin, as if he'd never seen anything quite so delightful as a half-dressed man struggling to put his leg into his trousers.

"You're awake!" he said. "Doc Jo will be glad." He pointed at the shirt Quentin hadn't yet tackled. "Them's *my* clothes," he said with an air of pride. "You can borrow them until you're better."

Quentin won his battle with the trousers and sat down. Now he knew the origin of the clothes, in any case. He hadn't thought his taste could suffer such a major lapse. But there'd been the time when he'd woken up in the desert without any clothes at all . . .

"Thank you," he said gravely. He grabbed the shirt, while the overgrown boy watched with fascination. "Boy" seemed the right word for him, in spite of his height and bulk. He couldn't be more than twenty, though he spoke like someone much younger. Simple-minded, perhaps. There were far worse lots in life.

And surely the boy could answer basic questions. "My name is Quentin," he said, buttoning the shirt. "Can you tell me where I am?"

"My name's Oscar," the boy said. "Doc said to go get her when you woke up."

"Doc?"

"Doc Johanna. I helped her bring you here."

So he *hadn't* come of his own volition. And Johanna was a woman's name. A woman doctor. That would explain his memory of a woman's touch.

But this wasn't a hospital. The good doctor's home, perhaps? Had he been so ill?

He stood up and offered his hand. "I'm very pleased to meet you, Oscar. Can you tell me how long I've been here?"

Oscar gazed at the man's hand and suddenly folded his own behind his back in a fit of shyness. "I don't know," he said. "You been very sick. I helped take care of you."

"You and Doc Johanna?" At the boy's nod, he asked, "Where is this place, Oscar?"

"The Haven." He shuffled from foot to foot. "I gotta go get Doc now." He backed away and was out the door with surprising swiftness.

Quentin dropped his hand. The Haven. A very peaceful sort of name, to match the feel of this room. *The Haven.*

To a man like him, it sounded like paradise. But for a man like him, there was no such place.

Aware of a powerful thirst, he went to the washstand and poured himself a glass of cool water from the pitcher. The water was clear, as if it had come from a spring, with a faint tang of minerals. It was the most wonderful thing he'd ever tasted. He was finishing the last of it when the door swung open again.

No giant this time. This one was most definitely female. His practiced gaze took her in with one appreciative sweep, noting the lush curves of a body matched with the height to carry it: a statue, a goddess, an Amazon. He noted and dismissed the black bag in her hand. Her dark, modest dress was almost severe, out of step with the modern fashion of close-fitting cuirass bodices and snug skirts, but it did more to enhance her generous figure than any fancy ball gown might have done.

And as for her face . . .

At first he thought it rather plain. Its shape was oval, with a very slight squareness to the chin, and broad, high cheekbones. Her hair was a common light brown, drawn close in a simple style at the back of her head. Her brows were straight, without the provocative arch that might have lent her greater feminine allure. Her lips were, at the moment, set in a prim line, though they might be full enough when relaxed. Her nose was quite ordinary. And her eyes— her eyes were blue, the brightest thing about her, sharp with intelligence and purpose.

The eyes alone made her attractive. That, and the way she carried herself. Like a queen. Rather like his own twin sister Rowena, in fact . . . except that this doctor was human, and Quentin doubted she carried an ounce of aristocratic blood in that sturdy frame.

She strode into the room and closed the door behind her.

"You should not be out of bed," she said immediately. "Sit down, please."

Quentin obeyed. Her voice—low, a little husky, with just the trace of an accent—demanded instant obedience, and he found himself intrigued. More intrigued by a human being than he'd been in a very long time.

She pulled the chair up beside the bed and laid her palm on his forehead. It was the touch he remembered—that his body remembered. He shivered as if with fever, the tremor radiating south from her hand to his extremities like an electric current. The charge gathered in his groin and lingered there, even when she withdrew her hand. His arousal was immediate and formidable. She might as well have bared her luxurious breasts, within such easy reach of his hands, and offered them up to his exploration.

He swallowed and closed his eyes. His mind was conjuring up these visions because he literally couldn't remember the last time he'd taken a woman to his bed. He was burning up with lust, and he was afraid.

"You aren't warm," Johanna said, as if to herself. She bent to her black bag and removed a gauze packet, unwrapping a glass thermometer. "Please open your mouth—"

If you'll open yours, he thought. Yes; make a joke out of it. That had always saved him before. "Don't you think we ought to be properly introduced before engaging in such intimacies?" he asked with a grin.

She paused as if genuinely surprised, her thermometer suspended in midair.

"My name," he said with a slight bow from the waist, "is Quentin Forster. You must be the famous Doctor Johanna. I understand that I have you to thank for my presence in this very comfortable bed."

She raised one straight eyebrow. "I am Doctor Schell," she said. "I am pleased to see that you remember who you are."

Quentin started. Did she know about his lapses in memory? Had he been here long enough for her to learn so much?

She set down the thermometer and placed her thumb and forefinger above and below his right eye, pulling open his lids. "Very good," she said. "Do you remember how you came to be here?"

He considered lying. No, not with this one. And why bother? He'd be gone soon enough.

"Unfortunately, I do not," he said. "I wish I did, considering the state in which I found myself when I woke up."

She must have understood his intimation, but her expression remained tranquil. It was really quite striking, that face—or would be, if it could be made to smile. Without any good reason at all, Quentin wanted to make her smile.

Maybe then she'd actually see *him*. Remind him that something of the old Quentin was still within him, unsullied—the devil-may-care rogue beloved by the Prince's set in England, the gambler, the jokester who never took anything seriously.

"Your state," she said, "was extremely poor when we brought you here. You're very lucky to be alive, young man."

Young man? He was entering his third decade, and she couldn't be so much as a year older than he was, if that. He laughed. It hurt his chest, but he let it go with abandon.

"Do you find that amusing, Mr. Forster?" she said coolly.

"I'm not an infant, Doctor, and you aren't a grandmother yet, unless I'm very much mistaken." He grabbed her hand and turned it palm up. The hand was lightly callused and strong, but her fingers were tapered and graceful. The fingers of an artist. Fingers that would heal a wound or stroke naked skin with equal skill . . .

"Ah, yes," he intoned with an air of dramatic mystery. "I see that you have a long life ahead of you. You let nothing get in the way of your ambitions. But unexpected adventure awaits. A great challenge. And romance." He drew his finger over the creases in her palm. "A man has come into your life."

She reclaimed her hand without haste. "If that is the best you can do, Mr. Forster, you need additional instruction in fortune-telling."

Was that a twinkle in her blue eyes? Did she have a sense of humor, after all?

"Alas, the gypsies who raised me are far away."

"Then you'd do better to read your own palm, Mr. Forster. You came very near death."

"I doubt it, Doctor. I'm not easy to kill."

Her face grew even more serious, and her voice reminded him of a professor at Oxford who he'd regarded as a personal gadfly. "The effects of inebriety are cumulative," she said. "How long have you been drinking?"

He hid a wince. It wasn't a subject he cared to discuss. "How long have you been a doctor?"

She gazed into his eyes, holding him with sheer will as another werewolf might do. "I do not think you understand, Mr. Forster. You were suffering from acute delirium tremens, a condition that is often fatal. You have been with us for four days, most of which time you have been unconscious or raving. I am frankly amazed to see you capable of rational communication."

Raving. "I suppose I made a nuisance of myself," he said. "What did I rave about?"

"Most of your words were incomprehensible." She cocked her head. "But there was a pattern. When I first found you in a field about a mile from here, you tried to speak to me. You warned me of some evil, that I was in danger."

He shivered. He didn't remember it. He didn't want to. "I'm sorry," he said. "I must have sounded quite mad."

"You have no recollection of this."

He shook his head. "Unfortunately not."

"What is the last thing you do remember?"

"I was staying in San Francisco. I won a bit of money in a game. I was planning to catch the ferry to Oakland."

"You are now near the town of Silverado Springs, in the Napa Valley, some miles north of either San Francisco or

Oakland," she said. "Do you often experience these periods of amnesia?"

"Sometimes." What did they say about confession being good for the soul? It certainly seemed to be helping now. "Generally when I have a bit too much to drink." *And half the time I don't even remember the drinking.*

"It seems I owe you a great deal," he said, smiling to charm her away from more questions. "It was kind of you to take me in and look after me. At least I can pay you for your care." He reached for the drawer.

"We can discuss fees later, Mr. Forster."

"Quentin, please."

"Quentin," she said, in that schoolmistress tone. "Make an attempt to grasp that you have been suffering a severe condition for nearly a week, that you have apparently lost any memory of a portion of your life, and that you may not survive another bout. Such a state is not to be taken lightly—"

"Do you take anything lightly, Johanna?"

"Not where a life is concerned. And you are fortunate I do not, or I should have left you in the field."

Beneath her dogged assertiveness he detected the one thing she didn't want him to see—a woman's inevitably soft heart. The sort of heart that had caused her to take in a drunken stranger and care for him with no promise of reward.

And he knew his own strength. If he'd been raving, he might have become dangerous. Dangerous to her and anyone around her.

Perhaps, this time, he'd been lucky.

"Is that why you call this place the Haven?" he asked, gesturing at the room. "You scrape unfortunate sots like me off the floor and minister to them until they're well again?"

"Not as a rule," she said with a twitch of her lips. Humor again—hidden, but there. "You are something of an exception."

He placed his hand over his heart. "I'm honored. But if this is not a Haven for vagabonds such as myself, who does it shelter besides a skilled and lovely lady doctor?"

His compliment seemed to go right over her head. "You have met Oscar," she said. "He is one of the patients here."

"Patients?"

"You might as well know where you are, Mr. Forster, since you are likely to be spending a few more days with us."

"But I'm well, I assure you—"

"I shall be the judge of that." Before he could speak another word, she picked up the thermometer and pushed it into his mouth. His teeth clicked on the glass.

"The Haven," she said, "is what I call our little farm. There are seven of us in residence: myself, my father, Doctor Wilhelm Schell, and five patients. We came to this valley two years ago, when we found it necessary to close our private asylum in Pennsylvania."

"Your—" Quentin tried to speak around the thermometer. Johanna snatched it from his mouth, examined it, and shook her head. "You are a very lucky man, Mr. Forster."

"Quentin," he reminded her. "Yes, I'm exceedingly lucky." He laughed under his breath. "Is this by any chance a madhouse?"

"We do not use that name here. The Haven is different. Our residents are only a few of those we treated in Pennsylvania. Those it seemed best to bring with us." Her voice softened. "They have become very much like family. This is what I want you to understand, Mr.—Quentin. You will be meeting them, and I do not wish you to disrupt our routines out of ignorance." She searched his face. "Does insanity frighten you? Does it disgust you? You will see behavior you may consider peculiar—"

"More peculiar than mine?"

"—and if you cannot treat the residents with the dignity

they require, I shall have to make other arrangements for your care."

Yes, there *was* fire in Johanna Schell. It sparked in her eyes when she spoke of her "residents," with all the ferocity of a lioness guarding her cubs. Passion existed in that curvaceous frame . . . not for romance and the usual women's fancies, but to protect those in her care. A woman who took on great responsibility, and relished it.

In that way she was the complete opposite of Quentin himself. Johanna Schell was not like the demimondaines he'd tended to run into during the past several years, nor did she bear any resemblance to the proper and well-bred aristocrats of England. She was something new to him—honest, straightforward, unselfish, with hidden emotions yet to be discovered. He couldn't assign her to a category and dismiss her as unimportant, as he did the other men and women he met briefly in his wanderings. That was what intrigued him most.

Ordinarily, he wouldn't linger long enough to indulge his curiosity. But he found himself admiring this cool, stern, and utterly sensible goddess. Not merely admiring—he was *drawn* to her, and by more than the erotic promise of her touch.

If she'd been *loup-garou*, the explanation would have been simple enough. There was always the possibility of a sudden and unbreakable bond forming between two of werewolf blood. But, even though he lacked his brother's broad mental powers and flawless ability to recognize others of their kind, he knew that Johanna was unmistakably human.

No matter. He couldn't trust himself to remain here longer than strictly necessary. His safety—his sanity—lay in constant motion. And if his worst, half-acknowledged fears were correct . . . if he left turmoil behind each and every time he lost his memory in drink . . .

Guilt was one of the emotions he'd learn to outrun. Sadness was another. And loneliness.

Johanna reminded him that he was lonely. She and her healer's touch.

"I am the last man to judge another's madness," he said at last, meeting her eyes. "You may trust me in that, if in nothing else."

"That sounds like a warning."

"Yes." He smiled crookedly. "But I shan't be the one to prove how unwise it is to bring strange, besotted men home as you would a wee lost puppy."

"I would bet that you are not a puppy, Quentin Forster."

"Ah, do you gamble?"

"Only when I have no other choice." She gathered her skirts and began to rise.

He stopped her, laying his hand on her knee. She had a perfect right to slap him for his forwardness. She went very still. Their gazes locked. He was a gambling man, and he would have wagered all his winnings that she felt his touch the way he felt hers.

Not that any such effect would show on that carefully schooled face.

"What is your opinion, Doctor?" he asked. "Can you help me?"

"If you refer to your dipsomania . . . it is possible, if you wish to change," she said. "If you do not, no one can help you."

"Can I expect a lecture on the evils of drink?"

"There are plenty of reformatory societies for that purpose. I have other techniques."

"I'm fascinated." He let his hand slide just a fraction of an inch. The muscles in her thigh tensed. "Just what are these techniques?"

"They were developed by my father, using the science of hypnosis he learned in Europe, where he was educated as a neurologist. Hypnosis enables a doctor to communicate with that part of the mind that is hidden from a patient's own conscious thoughts. Using this method, a trained physician can help the patient to fight mistaken ideas that create many of his problems." She made a gesture with her hands—controlled, but revealing her enthusiasm as much as her eyes and voice. "In your case, this would be the desire for strong drink. My father's method has proven most effective in a number of cases, where insanity is not too far advanced."

"I've heard of this hypnosis," Quentin said. "It's something like mesmerism—"

"Mesmerism became little more than superstitious nonsense, rejected by men of science. Hypnosis, as we employ it, is far more advanced, yet misconceptions remain. My father—" She stopped. Quentin noticed that one of her fists had clenched. She caught his glance and relaxed her fingers. "This is hardly the time for a lecture."

"Your father must be an interesting gentleman," Quentin said, watching her face. "I confess that I'm a bit surprised that he sent you to deal with a strange male patient."

The zealous light went out of her eyes. "My father is no longer seeing patients. I received a full medical education in the United States and Europe; you need have no fears about my competence."

"I'm not afraid." He let his lashes drop over his eyes and lowered his voice to a seductive purr. "I shan't mind your company in the least, fair Valkyrie."

She flinched. "Why do you call me that?"

Well, well, well. Something else she was sensitive about, along with her patients, and her father. Had she been mocked for her height and hardy frame in the past? What blind fools men could be.

"Because you remind me of those ancient Teutonic warrior maids," he said. "Girded for battle and prepared to sweep the wounded from the field. I suppose your hair ought to be blonde, but I quite like it just as it is."

She actually blushed. It was the first typically female behavior he'd seen in her.

"That was my father's pet name for me," she whispered. *Was,* as if her father were dead, though she'd said he was here.

"It suits you," he said. "I mean that as a compliment."

She scraped back her chair and stood, shaking off his hand. "If I am to be your physician, Mr. Forster, you had best realize that our relationship must remain strictly professional."

He feigned surprise. "Naturally. If I am to be your patient."

"We shall discuss that possibility at a more appropriate time," she said. "You will stay in bed for the remainder of the day; I shall bring you a healthy breakfast to restore your constitution. And put from your mind any thought of drinking while you remain in this house."

The mere thought of alcohol made Quentin's gorge rise. He crossed his heart. "I promise I'll be good."

That almost imperceptible smile flickered at the corners of her mouth. "I wonder." She turned briskly for the door.

"Doctor—Johanna—"

She stopped, hand on the doorknob.

"Thank you," he said, meaning it. "Thank you for helping me."

"I, too, took the Hippocratic oath," she said. "Rest well, Mr. Forster."

Quentin was very tempted to test her composure by inviting her to join him under the covers, but long training as a gentleman quelled the impulse. Her dignity was not impregnable, but there was no point in wasting all his ammunition at once.

"Until later, then," he said.

He remained seated at the edge of the bed long after she'd left, working out the thoughts and feelings she had provoked in him. They were a mass of uncomfortable contraditions—the very sort of thing he'd avoided by moving on before there was the slightest chance of developing a relationship with anyone, or feeling much of anything at all.

Reflecting deeply on his own emotions was hardly the sort of game at which he was expert. It led him too close to the shadows, like drink. He was more than a little alarmed at the intensity of his reaction to Johanna Schell.

He fell back on the bed, pillowing his head on crossed arms. The ceiling above was a soothing, blank white, luring him toward oblivion. Why not sleep, as the doctor recommended?

But sleep had never been his most reliable mistress— unless he was drunk. His thoughts chased round and round like a wolf after its own tail.

Why did she attract him, unlike so many other women? It wasn't merely her curvaceous body; he'd sampled plenty of those in his time. No; the physical was only a small part of it.

It was her strength—not so much of body as mind and purpose. She carried herself with all the confidence of a man, but no one could mistake her for anything but a woman. She knew who she was and lived in herself without shame or doubt. He couldn't imagine her confounded by any of the fears or petty cares that afflicted so many average lives.

Perhaps she wouldn't be daunted by his demons—those demons he could never quite see, who hovered at the very edges of his consciousness. The ones who reduced him to a pathetic coward, terrified to look too deeply inside himself for fear of what he'd find.

Was Doctor Johanna Schell strong enough to match them? Could her science of hypnosis bring him to the end of his perpetual flight?

That was it. That was the heart of the subject, and of his sudden and half-unwelcome hope. Johanna Schell was like this place, this Haven . . . a sanctuary in the storm his life had become. Her touch not only moved and aroused him, it anchored him, drew him into a quiet place where his demons had no power.

He closed his eyes. God, how he longed for such a place. But to take the risk, to ask for her help and everything that might entail . . . had he any right? Even if she offered, with all her poise and faith in herself . . . what if that weren't enough?

Better to run. Better to spend one last day to be sure of his recovery, and leave this transient peace behind.

He laughed, as he always did on those rare occasions when his ruminations led him to a state of such maudlin self-pity. Laughter kept the tears at bay, and there was enough of an English gentleman left in him to disdain the ephemeral solace of weeping.

He wasn't that kind of drunk. He wished that he were. He wished that he could reconcile himself to a permanent ending.

But that was another thing a proper English gentleman simply didn't do. Not until there was no other choice.

Quentin covered his face with the soft feather pillow and laughed until no listener would have any doubt at all that he was quite insane.

Chapter 4

Whenever she was troubled, Johanna had always gone to her father.

In their life together, since her mother's death, she had been the sensible one. She'd kept the books and most of the asylum records, saw to her own handful of patients, reminded Papa to eat and helped him dress—each and every task carried out with the same single-minded efficiency.

Wilhelm Schell, for all his brilliance, had been the one with the touch of mischief, the ability to laugh even at the most serious moments. He could be annoyingly impractical. His mind made strange, unfathomable leaps from one concept to another, seemingly without logic. And he was the one who could explain and reassure on those rare occasions when her emotions got themselves in a tangle.

As they were now, due to Mr. Quentin Forster.

Despite all that had changed, Papa's presence still gave her comfort. She went directly from the guest room to her father's room, opening the door a crack to gauge his condition.

He was asleep. If she woke him, he'd only be more confused, and her trivial needs came a distant second to his. She closed the door. The patients had already eaten and were either outside, working in the garden, vineyard, or orchard, or resting in their rooms. She'd have time to make notes on the new patient.

Her office seemed very quiet as she sat down at her desk and took out a notebook. Quentin Forster must have his own set of notes and records of treatments and progress, to join the others neatly stacked in the desk drawer. This record, like May's, would be written entirely in her own hand, without any contribution from her father. The feel of the pen in her hand never failed to calm her thoughts on those rare occasions when they spun too fast for her to discipline.

Her heart gradually slowed from the rapid pace it had set ever since he touched her. Dipping her pen in the inkwell, she made a cool assessment of her new patient, point by logical point.

Quentin Forster. Age, estimated thirty years. Of English descent, probably aristocratic by his accent and general mien. Apparently in good health, in spite of his recent bout of delirium tremens. Clearly he was not the sort who drank constantly, or he could not be in such excellent condition.

In all likelihood he was here in the United States because he was the younger son of some wealthy landowning family, sent to make his fortune conveniently far from England. Such young men were hardly more than parasites, like the idle children of aristocrats everywhere.

Did he drink because he was in exile, or due to some personal weakness in his nature? No need to speculate; she'd learn that soon enough, during one of their first sessions of hypnosis. If she decided to take his case.

That was the question. He might very easily disrupt what they had here. Disturb the others.

Disturb her.

His laughing cinnamon eyes flashed in her mind. He was charming and handsome, of that there was no doubt. Intelligent, too. Proficient at reasonable conversation, if one discounted his jesting.

How long had it been since she'd had a truly rational conversation? One that lasted more than a few minutes and didn't leap wildly from subject to subject, or drift off into silence? She'd spoken to a few fellow doctors during the lecture in San Francisco, but they were apt to condescend to her because of her gender, if they paid any attention at all.

Quentin Forster didn't condescend. Except for his one inquiry about her father, he seemed completely unruffled at being attended to by a woman.

If anything, he seemed to relish the prospect.

And that was the challenge he presented. She must keep a professional distance from him, remain unmoved by his teasing and flirtation—something she could do easily enough with other men. Not so easy, perhaps, with him.

You are a woman, she told herself—something Papa had reminded her of on occasion, in the old days. *It is quite logical that you should find a man attractive, sooner or later.* In spite of what some male physicians and social arbiters claimed, she had always believed that women were sexual creatures. Even Johanna Schell.

Simple physical attraction explained much of her sense of discomposure. But why this man? Why now?

She shrugged and closed the notebook. There would be a day or two to decide; she certainly wouldn't turn him out so soon after his initial recovery. She'd make the correct decision . . .

"Well, what's he like?"

Irene came into the office—dramatically, as she always did, floating through the door in her silk dressing gown. Her faded red hair was loose in practiced disarray, and she wore enough face paint to be seen from the farthest rows of a large theater. She planted herself in front of Johanna and struck a provocative pose. "Come, now," she said in theatrical tones. "Don't even think of keeping him all to yourself."

"I suppose you mean the new patient," Johanna said dryly.

"Who else, in this dreadfully boring place?" Irene said with a sniff. "He's the most interesting thing to happen *here* in ages. Such a handsome one, too." Her eyes narrowed. "But you wouldn't notice that, with your withered spinsterish ways. You never notice anything important."

Johanna was used to Irene's narcissism and occasional vindictiveness. One didn't have a conversation with Irene unless it was entirely about Irene. "I noticed," she said. "But I have been somewhat more concerned with the state of his health."

"But he's better now, isn't he?" She stroked her hand—its delicacy marred by bitten fingernails—down her thigh. "You must introduce me to him as soon as possible. I can speed up his recovery."

"I'll introduce him to everyone once he's ready," Johanna said, her voice calm and authoritative. "For now, he needs rest."

"Don't try to fool me, Johanna," Irene said, tossing her head. "You just want to keep him away from *me*. You're afraid that when he sees me, he won't even notice you. Who would?" Her ravaged face took on a faraway look. "When I was on the stage, no man could take his eyes off me. I was the toast of New York and every city I visited. My dressing room was always filled with flowers and suitors on their knees." Her gaze sharpened and focused on Johanna. "It will be so again. Soon I'll have all the money I need to get me back, and then—" She broke off in confusion and hurried on. "But you want to keep me here, a prisoner, because you're jealous." She hissed for emphasis. "You're plain and dull and dried up as an . . . an old prune. You want to make me the same way—"

"I don't want to make you anything, Irene, but happy," Johanna said. Irene's delusion was such that she could not look in a mirror without seeing the promising young actress she'd been at twenty—the girl she'd left behind thirty years ago, sexually exploited and abandoned by a former "protector," lost to the stage and left to make her living through prostitution. She'd been declared mad and eventually found her way into the Schell's private asylum as a charity case. Now she was a part of the "family," if an occasionally difficult one.

Johanna opened another notebook and consulted the week's schedule. "I think we should have another session soon."

Irene primped and preened. "No time for that," she said. "I must go back to rehearsals. I'm to play Juliet, you know, with Edwin Booth himself."

She turned to go, swirling her dressing gown in a clumsy arc that was meant to be elegant. "Send the gentleman to me when he's rested. You'll rue the day if you deprive him of the opportunity to worship at my feet." She laughed girlishly and swept back out of the room.

Cherishing the renewed quiet, Johanna closed her eyes. Irene had relapsed over the past several weeks, convinced that she was in the midst of rehearsals for a play that would never open except in her own mind.

Though it might require many more months, Johanna intended to help Irene become capable of living in the world on her own, even if it was as something of an eccentric. Irene was a gifted seamstress. If she could be made to leave some of her delusions behind, she could put her skills to good use and earn a respectable living. And she could rediscover some measure of happiness in herself.

But that meant facing what she didn't want to face—the

fact that she was fifty years old and completely forgotten by her supposed hordes of one-time admirers. If she could only see that there was a different kind of worth that did not depend upon the transience of the flesh . . .

Johanna rose and went back into the hall. She paused to look in on Harper, who sat in his chair, unmoving and unaware of her fleeting presence. Then she continued on to Papa's room. He was awake now, and had pulled himself up into a half-sitting position, propped up on the layers of pillows at the head of his bed. Thank God he had regained some use of his left arm and leg, though they were still extremely unsteady.

Oscar had helped Johanna build the special bed rails that kept him from tumbling out at night. It looked like a cage— a cage such as his own body and brain had become.

"Papa," she said softly, closing the door behind her. "How are you feeling?"

He peered at her, his left eyelid slightly sagging over once-bright blue eyes. "Johanna?"

"I'm here." She sat on the stool beside the bed and took his left hand. It shook a little, the tendons and veins carved in sharp relief under the fragile, spotted skin. "Did you sleep well?"

"Hmmm," he said. He patted her hand with his right one. "You look tired, *mein Walkürchen.* Working too hard." His words were slurred, but comprehensible. That, too, had improved over time. "What day is it?"

"Wednesday, Papa."

"Good. Good." His bushy white brows drew together. "Where is my schedule, Johanna? I can't remember now if it's my day to see Andersen."

"Don't worry about that, Papa. I'll see to it."

"*Ja.* You always do." He chuckled hoarsely. "Where would I be without my girl . . ." His chin sank onto his chest. Johanna rose to adjust his pillows.

"Are you hungry, Papa? Some nice fresh eggs for breakfast?"

"I don't know." He moved his good hand irritably. "Have you any strudel?"

She smiled, swallowing. He'd always had a terrible sweet tooth. "Not today, Papa. But I can have Mrs. Daugherty bring some from town, perhaps, tomorrow morning."

"Don't bother. I can get it myself—" He struggled to rise, found the bed rails in his way, and tried to move them. The effort exhausted him. "Where are my clothes?"

She fetched the loose, comfortable clothing she'd had made for him, removed the bed rail, and helped him dress. It was a slow process, though not as slow as the bathing, which would wait until this evening. She encouraged him to do as much dressing as he could on his own, but the buttons always defeated him. While his feet were still bare, she checked them for sores or swelling, then pulled on his stockings and his soft shoes.

Such painstaking care took several hours each day, time taken from the patients, but she could not pass it on to Mrs. Daugherty. Except for the housekeeping and cooking, which took all of Bridget's considerable energy, Johanna could trust no one but herself to do that which must be done at the Haven.

When she was finished with Papa's feet, she worked his left arm gently through a series of exercises, and did the same for his leg. He bore it passively, adrift in his own world.

"Send in my next patient, Johanna," he said. "It's Dieter Roth, isn't it? He's a difficult one, but we're coming along." He patted her arm. "We're coming along."

Dieter Roth was one of their former patients at the asylum, who had been helped enormously by Papa's techniques and gone home before their move to California. But Papa often lost track of time, confusing the past with the present.

"We've a new patient, Papa," she said, fetching a glass of water from the pitcher on the washstand. "He's a dipsomaniac, by all appearances. I haven't treated one like him before."

"There is no reason why inebriety can't be treated as well as any other form of insanity," he said with sudden clarity. "The influences that drive a man to drink are not as simple as some would have us think. I have never believed it is merely a weakness of character."

"Nor do I," Johanna said, her heart lightening. "I haven't taken on a new patient in some time, however. I'm not sure how much he can pay, or if we can afford another charity case."

"We are doctors. We can't turn away those who need our help." The old fire lit his eyes. "And our methods work, Johanna."

"Your methods, Papa," she said, holding the glass to his lips.

"They all laughed at me in Vienna," he said. "But I've proven them wrong—" He choked, and Johanna rubbed his back until he was breathing normally again. His face was very pale.

"I just heard quite an interesting lecture in San Francisco," Johanna said quickly. "The speaker presented some rather controversial theories, not unlike your own. Would you like to hear them?"

But her father wasn't listening. He'd drifted away, lost in some memory that, for him, might be taking place at this very moment.

"Papa?" He didn't respond. She rose and replaced the glass on the washstand, blinking dry eyes.

He couldn't advise her. The decisions were all hers now. She knelt by the bed and rested her head on his lap. He touched her hair, tenderly, as if she were a child again.

"Don't cry, Johanna," he murmured. "Your mother will get well. You'll see."

"Yes, Papa." His hand stroked her head and went still. He had fallen asleep again, as he so often did.

"You're right, Papa," she whispered. "We can't turn away those who need our help. But things . . . are not as they once were." She paused to listen to his steady breathing. Yes, he was asleep, and wouldn't be disturbed by her worry. "We are coming near the end of our funds, Papa. I've sold all the land we can spare; I can't sell the orchard or the last acre of grapevines; they make this place what it is. I don't want the world too close—and it isn't what Uncle Rutger would have wished." She sighed. "I must have Mrs. Daugherty's help with the washing and cooking, and she must be paid a fair wage."

Her father shifted and gave a soft snore.

"We must have medicine, and clothing, the necessities of life—" She smiled wryly to herself. "I can do well enough without luxuries. You know I don't much care for fripperies in any case. I remember when it used to worry you, that I never sought such things. But I would be happy, Papa, if I can continue to carry on in your footsteps."

She raised her head and gazed at his placid face. "*Ach,* Papa. I'll complain no longer. I *will* find a way to continue, you can rest assured of that."

"I hope you'll allow me to help, Dr. Schell."

For just an instant she thought Papa had spoken. But no, the voice was wrong—the timbre a little deeper, the tone lighter, the accent English rather than German.

She spun about to face the door. Quentin Forster stood there, leaning against the doorframe with arms folded and one ankle crossing the other. Except for the faint circles under his eyes, he showed no evidence of his recent ordeal. Oscar's shirt and trousers did not look as oversized on his lanky frame as she'd expected, nor did they detract from his naturally elegant bearing.

Or his handsomeness—though he was in need of a good shave. And a haircut. But the longer hair and the reddish beard starting on his chin only gave his features a more roguish appeal. That slight roughness, combined with his aristocratic air, created a most intriguing combination . . .

She cleared her throat sharply.

"What are you doing out of bed?" she demanded. "I do not remember giving you permission to wander about the house."

He uncrossed his arms and stepped into the room. "You never did arrive with my breakfast."

"I am sorry. I shall see to it shortly."

"I can manage it myself, if you'll point the way to the kitchen." He glanced at her father. "I didn't mean to intrude, but I couldn't help overhearing . . . This is the elder Dr. Schell, I presume?"

Positioning herself to block his view, Johanna stood protectively by Papa's bedside. "Yes. Now, if you will kindly go back to your room—"

With flagrant disobedience he came closer, gazing at her father's face. "I'm very sorry," he said. His expression was serious, as if he truly meant it. "It must have been a terrible loss for you."

Was it possible that he had experienced such losses? Something had driven him to drink. Every one of their patients had suffered; such suffering could lead to madness, or make a mild case of insanity worse.

"He is not dead," she said stiffly.

"But he needs care, and you have the other patients." Quentin looked past the bed to the window, with its view of the small vineyard. "This place has a certain serenity that must benefit your residents a great deal. It would be a pity if you had to sell any more of it."

He'd come just a bit too close—close enough for the small hairs to rise on the back of her neck. She moved nearer to the bed.

"Eavesdropping is not the act of a gentleman, Mr.

Forster." She lifted her chin. "How much did you over-hear?"

"Enough to know that you could benefit by an influx of capital." He looked about for a chair and, finding none, leaned against the wall. "Earlier, we were discussing the possibility of your treating my . . . propensity for excessive drinking. As it happens, I can pay you well for such treatment. Enough, I believe, to help in your current circumstances."

Johanna's skin grew hot. So he had overheard something she'd meant no one, not even her father, to know. And he spoke with such . . . such presumption, as if he couldn't imagine her refusing his offer.

"We are doctors. We can't turn away those who need our help." Papa had been completely lucid when he spoke those words. He'd lived by them, and she believed in them as much as he did. Even if Forster had been unable to pay, she would have considered attempting treatment. But she hadn't decided. Now he was forcing her hand.

"If you've any doubts," Quentin Forster said, "the money is in my room. Over one thousand dollars in cash and coin."

So much? She'd never counted it, of course. The sum was considerable from her current perspective.

"I won it quite honestly, in a game of cards." He looked up at her from beneath his auburn lashes, unconsciously—or consciously—seductive.

She turned her back on him and gazed out the window. He had made it extraordinarily difficult for her to say no. The need for money was very real, for the sake of the Haven's residents. With such an incentive, she could think of only one reason to turn him down.

A personal reason. He made her uncomfortable, uncertain. In his presence, she felt a little of her normally un-shakable confidence waver. And, at the same time, she was drawn to him, woman to man. He unsettled her, and nothing was nearly so dangerous to a woman of science.

It would not do, not if she was to be his doctor. That would have to be made very clear.

"I could not charge you so much," she said, "nor promise a cure without further consultation."

"You haven't dealt with my particular brand of insanity."

She glanced over her shoulder. "Inebriety is not always equivalent to insanity," she said. "Do you claim another affliction?"

His face closed up, all the easy poise vanished. She'd seen that look before: Panic. Denial. Fear. The sudden realization that he did not wish to uncover the secrets in his own mind and heart—secrets he was not even aware existed.

But no one was forcing him to stay. He was not, like the other residents, incapable of living in the world. He might be at considerable risk to his health—even of death—but if he chose to leave, she could not stop him.

"I have treated many forms of insanity," she said. "Very seldom have we failed to see some improvement. But the rules of conduct here are strict. No alcohol. You must get along with the others. And you must also contribute to the daily work of the farm."

You make it easy on yourself, Johanna, she thought. *He's not the sort to remain steadfast in the face of a challenge. Frighten him enough, and he will leave. He will not be able to unsettle you any longer.*

Repulsed by her own cowardice, she faced him again. "Do you understand, Mr. Forster? I will do my best to help you, but I can make no guarantees. I must retain the right to decide if the treatment is not working. But I will not demand an unreasonable fee—no matter how much I may be in need of funds. I do not ask for charity."

The pinched look on his face cleared, and the tension of his mouth eased into a wry smile. "You wouldn't. But you nearly have me fleeing in terror, Dr. Johanna. I wonder if I'd rather face a herd of charging elephants."

She found herself relaxing as well. "Have you ever faced a herd of elephants, Mr. Forster?"

"Quentin," he corrected. "I've seen my share of elephants. Some were even real." He stood up straight. "Are you afraid of me, Johanna?"

The question was startlingly direct and perfectly sober. He'd sensed her unease. Or perhaps it was another warning . . .

"Aside from the fact that you are a stranger, which in itself calls for caution, I've seen nothing to fear in you."

She didn't think she'd ever seen eyes so compelling. Beneath their veneer of laughter was layer upon layer of ambiguity, a guardedness that might conceal any number of darker emotions, just as he hid his fear.

Finding and healing the source of that fear would be further proof of the Schell technique's validity—possibly even substantiation of her own theory, if the opportunity to test it presented itself in the course of his treatment. She could finally complete the paper she and Papa had begun . . . and the payment she received from Quentin would keep the Haven going for another few months, at least.

"Well?" he asked. "Will you take on my case, Johanna?"

She folded her hands at the level of her waist and nodded briskly, as much to convince herself as to answer him. "We shall begin work as soon as you've been introduced to the others and it's been established that you will—"

"Fit in?" He grinned. "You'd be surprised just how adaptable I am."

Somehow she wasn't in the least surprised. He seemed so at ease, in spite of his obvious problems and the way he'd raved in the throes of his delirium tremens. It was sometimes difficult to remember how very ill he'd been.

He was a mystery, and like all scientists she could not resist such a paradox.

"I would introduce you to my father, but as you see he is sleeping. He will not be very communicative; it is a result of his attack."

"I understand." Quentin came to the side of the bed and looked down at her father. His mobile expression changed again—to one of real compassion. Of knowing.

"I lost my own parents when I was fairly young," he said. "My grandfather raised me, my twin sister, and my elder brother." His mouth twitched. "He was something of a tyrant. Very strict."

Johanna hadn't grown up under such conditions, but she'd seen the damage that could be done to children in such households. "I'm sorry," she said.

He shrugged. "Long ago. And I gave Grandfather as good as I got."

"Were you often in trouble?"

"I'm that transparent, am I?" He chuckled. "Frequently. I was incorrigible, in fact. I doubt that any figure in authority would be tempted to spare the rod in my case."

Had he been beaten, then? "You were not . . . unloved."

"I had my brother and my sister. They could be jolly good companions—but they were a little more conventional. Braden often lectured me to be more upright and dependable." He pulled a face. "Elder brothers, you know."

She didn't; she'd been an only child, and often wondered what it would be like to have siblings. But Quentin didn't speak as though his childhood experiences had contributed to his drinking. That was something she wouldn't be able to determine until she put him under hypnosis.

Yes. She wanted quite urgently to know more about Quentin Forster, childhood and all.

"Well," she said, "the others should be coming in from the garden and vineyard in an hour or so. We generally do outside work in the mornings and early evenings." She examined him critically. "Since you seem steady enough, I'll give you a brief tour of the house, and then introduce you all around."

"I look forward to it," he said. But the twinkle in his cinnamon eyes suggested that he was much less interested in the other patients than he was in her.

That was very likely to change soon enough.

Chapter 5

Whatever possessed you?

Quentin had asked himself that question several times since he'd made the impulsive and reckless decision to remain at the Haven.

The deed was done now. And when he looked at Johanna, with that serious and oddly attractive face that hid so much from the world, he remembered what had driven him to it.

Yes, driven. It certainly hadn't been an act of logic. But then again, so little of what he did could be attributed to anything remotely like common sense.

He'd told himself he should leave. He still could, none the worse for wear, if things became complicated. But he believed that Johanna, alone of all people in the world, had the ability to keep him away from the bottle—and from the consequences that he feared came with it. As long as he didn't drink, he was in control.

At the very least, Johanna would have his money for her good works. She deserved it far more than he did.

He sat on one of the two ancient horsehair armchairs in the room Johanna called the parlor. It was the largest chamber in the house, scattered with mismatched chairs of every size and design, a large central table and several smaller ones, shelves of books, ancient daguerreotypes, an antique mirror that might have survived from better times, and well-worn rugs on the wooden floor. He'd noticed at once that there were no real breakables or fragile items on the shelves or tables—no china figurines, nor decorative plates and delicate china—nothing that a patient of uncertain temperament might smash or use as a weapon. The house, as embodied in this room, was worn, snug, and well lived-in, with nothing of luxury but much of safety.

The house matched Johanna herself. She was not beautiful, and her clothes were plain and much-mended, but no one could doubt her sincerity or her complete acceptance of herself and the world around her.

He'd already toured the roomy kitchen, where he'd been offered a late breakfast of coffee, bread, and eggs, left by the housekeeper, Mrs. Daugherty. After the meal, Johanna had shown him the smaller room she called her office. The remaining rooms were the patients' chambers, and Johanna respected their privacy. She did, indeed, seem to regard them more as family than men and women afflicted with madness.

"You've met Oscar," Johanna said from her chair opposite his across the parlor. "He is what many call an idiot—his level of intelligence is that of a young child. He is prone to a child's outbursts, but in general he is a gentle soul who asks only to be treated kindly."

"But he cannot be cured of such an affliction, surely," Quentin said.

"No." She leaned forward, her hands clasped at her knees in a posture completely free of feminine self-consciousness. "You see, he was born to a family in which his mother contracted a serious illness during her pregnancy. She died soon after his birth. I know little of his early life, but he was left much on his own as a child, and suffered for it. His father was himself a dying man, and begged my father to take the boy in." She smiled with a touch of sadness. "Oscar has been with us since the age of twelve. The world is not kind to those with his defect."

"As it isn't kind to any who are different," Quentin said. Johanna looked at him with such unexpected warmth that he found his heart beating faster. Good God, was he so much in need of approval, of any meager sign of esteem?

Or was it just Johanna herself?

She blinked, as if she'd caught him staring. Perhaps he had been. "I'm glad you understand," she said, and lapsed into silence.

He was trying to find something intelligent to say—something that might impress her with his wit and breadth of knowledge—when a woman flounced into the room from the hallway.

Never had Quentin seen a more vivid contrast to Johanna, except among the prostitutes who so often became his unsought companions. The woman was near fifty but dressed several decades younger, in flowing clothes that hinted of Bohemian affectation. She wore as much paint as any lady of the evening, but she carried herself like a queen. Once, she might have been pretty. She clearly believed she still was.

Quentin rose. The woman came to stand directly before his chair and assumed a pose. "At last," she said. Her dyed red hair was piled fashionably on top of her head, but a few stray wisps gave her an air of slight dishabille. Her colorless eyes glinted with predatory intent. "Johanna, introduce us at once."

Johanna sighed, so softly that none but Quentin could hear. "Irene—"

"Miss DuBois." The woman sniffed.

"—I would like you to meet Mr. Forster—"

"Quentin," he put in.

Johanna's mouth stiffened. "Quentin, please be acquainted with Miss Irene DuBois, one of our residents." She pronounced the name in the English way, vocalizing the final "e." "Irene, Quentin will be staying with us for a time."

Miss DuBois batted her eyelashes at Quentin. "Delighted, Mr. Forster. I am so glad you have come to see me. I had almost feared that all my admirers had forgotten about me." She extended a beringed hand.

Quentin did the expected and kissed the air above her knuckles. "How could anyone forget you, Miss DuBois?"

"Of course." She laughed, and the sound, much like her face, might once have been beautiful. "I knew at once that you were a man of taste and discretion. You could not have failed to see my performances on the stage on Broadway. I acted at the National Theater, Niblo's Garden, and the Winter Garden; everyone who was anyone came to watch me. When I trod the boards, no other actress was worth seeing."

Careful not to allow the slightest trace of amusement to cross his face, Quentin released her hand. He was beginning to guess what her particular form of madness might be. "The stage lost a great talent when you left it."

"Yes. You see, my doctors told me that I had worked much too hard, out of love for my devotees and my dedication to my art. They insisted that I sit out a season to rest. But I shall be returning very soon, and then the New York stage will be restored to its former glory."

"I'm certain that you shall dazzle your audiences," Quentin said. He glanced beyond her to Johanna, whose expression was unreadable. Did she approve of his playing along? He couldn't tell. "You haven't been here long, I gather?"

"Just for this season," she said. She threw Johanna a disdainful look. "Johanna would like to confine me here forever. This place is so drab without me, and the others simply couldn't get along without a little beauty and culture in their lives. Of course *she* didn't want you to see me. She knew what would happen."

Quentin recognized another cue when he heard it. He felt a profound pity for this woman, who lived in a past that might or might not have been as glorious as she painted it— a past that could never be restored. But he wouldn't be the one to shatter her illusions, even if Johanna's ultimate intent was to do so.

"I doubt very much that the doctor compares herself to you," he said.

Irene fluttered. "I should warn you, Quentin—do not fall in love with me. It is simply too dangerous. I am devoted to my art. But I will receive your homage."

"I shall be glad to give it." He bowed.

"I know it is cruel of me to forsake you," she said, "but I must have my rest." With that, she made her exit stage left.

Johanna was regarding him with a slightly raised eyebrow. "Now you have met Irene," she said.

"And I'm not likely to forget her." He sat down and crossed his legs. "She actually was an actress, wasn't she?"

"Yes. I believe she had a brief career with some modest potential. But she chose to accept the protection of an admirer who promised great things and delivered none of them." She hesitated, obviously thinking better of confiding further in him. "He abandoned her. Eventually, she became as you see her now. She has been with us, here and in the east, for ten years—one of my father's more recalcitrant cases. She does not truly wish to emerge from her delusional world."

"And one must *want* to be healed," Quentin said.

His insight surprised her. It was not what she'd have expected in his sort. "My father believed so."

"Her behavior doesn't trouble you?"

"Because she insults me?" Johanna smiled. "She can't

hurt me, Mr. Quentin. I am her doctor. My only concern is for her welfare. And she is by no means the most ill of our residents."

The sound of water rushing from the pump in the kitchen interrupted her words. "Ah. I believe that the Reverend Andersen has come in from the garden. Shall we go see him?"

Quentin followed her into the kitchen, where a thin, raw-boned man with sandy hair bent over the washbasin, furiously pumping water over his hands. As they watched, he picked up a bar of soap and lathered his hands until they were completely submerged in suds, and then rinsed them off again. He repeated the action five more times before Johanna spoke to him.

"Lewis," she said. "May we have a moment of your time?"

He spun about as if startled, hands dripping with soapy water. His gaze twitched from her to Quentin.

"Pardon me," he said. He returned to the basin, reached for the soap, stopped, and rinsed his hands instead. He dried them thoroughly on a towel hung beside the basin and pulled on a pair of white gloves. Only then did he turn his attention to Quentin and Johanna.

"I was working in the garden," he said in a clipped, irritable voice, not meeting their eyes. He lifted his hands and stared at them, as if he could still see specks of dirt invisible to anyone else. Quentin couldn't smell anything on him but the residue of soap, the cloth of the gloves, and well-washed human skin. The man's spotless clothing bore the faint scent of growing things, but no telltale earth. If he had been in the garden, Quentin doubted that he'd touched the ground with anything but the soles of his shoes.

"I am sure the garden is in much better condition for your labors," Johanna said. "Lewis, this is our new resident, Quentin Forster. Quentin, this is the Reverend Lewis Andersen."

"Not now," Andersen muttered. "I must cleanse—" He held his arms out from his sides and looked down the length of his body. "So much sin, filth . . ."

Johanna didn't react to his curious pronouncements. "Would you care to join us for tea in the parlor?"

"The china . . . it is not clean."

"I assure you that it is," Johanna said gently. "Please trust me, Lewis. You have nothing to fear."

He finally looked at her, hunching his bony shoulders. "Very well. A few moments." He started for the door just as Quentin turned to follow Johanna, and their sleeves brushed in passing. Andersen flinched as if he'd been struck.

"Pardon me," Quentin said. Andersen scuttled past him into the parlor and up to the vast stone fireplace at the end of the room, where he stared with horrified fascination into its dark recesses. He shuddered, backed away, and sat down in a chair in the farthest corner. He no longer seemed to notice the presence of anyone else in the room.

"Mr. Andersen has been with us for five years," Johanna said quietly. "Lewis, what do you think of the roses this summer?"

He huddled in his chair, turning his hands back and forth in front of his face. "I have tried and tried to make them perfect, but I fail. I fail."

"If you'll forgive me, Mr. Andersen," Quentin said, "I caught a glimpse of the roses. I've never seen any so beautiful. Your cultivation of them is quite extraordinary."

Andersen stared at Quentin. "You are British." His thin lips stretched in an expression of aversion, and Quentin felt as though he were being judged from the high pulpit of some vast London cathedral.

"You are a sinner," Andersen said abruptly. His eyes bore a hint of fanaticism, but it was more distressed than threatening. "What is your sin?"

The jokes that came so naturally to Quentin's mind

seemed very wrong under the circumstances. This man wouldn't understand his levity. "All men sin," he said. "I'm no exception."

"You run from them, but you cannot escape. I know." He locked his fingers together in a grip that must have been painful. "You cannot run from God."

"I doubt very much that God wants to find me," Quentin said, biting his tongue on the impulse to ask the reverend why he'd left his calling. "But I don't pretend to know His mind."

"He will find you. He found me. He found me." He cast a wild look at Johanna and jumped up from his chair. "I must go."

"We'll talk again," Johanna said.

Andersen fled the room with his hands pulled close to his body, careful not to touch any object in his passing.

Quentin blew a breath from puffed cheeks and sank lower in his chair. "If one looks beyond his affliction, he puts me in mind of a vicar I once knew. He wasn't terribly fond of me."

"Lewis has much improved from the early days in Pennsylvania," Johanna said. "When he was brought to our asylum by his family, he was unable to function normally. He spent half of each day washing himself, refusing to touch or be touched. He ate almost nothing. He was no longer able to attend his congregation or give sermons. And he spoke constantly of God's condemnation, of his own sin and worthlessness. He was determined to wash his sin away."

As if that were possible, Quentin thought with a bleak inner laugh. Aloud, he said, "But you've helped him."

"His washing is much less extreme, and on good days he is able to hold rational conversations. His distorted ideas have gradually lessened in their influence. In fact, he curtailed his usual cleansing ritual when we interrupted him— something he would not have done a year ago."

If Andersen had been worse before, Quentin could

scarcely imagine his state upon arrival. "What causes him to . . . act as he does?"

"I have come to believe that certain elements of his past experiences caused his mental collapse some years ago. By uncovering them through hypnosis, we have begun to confront them. By confronting them, we cause them to lose their power."

Uncovering the past. A deep chill penetrated his heart. "Another of your father's theories?"

"One of my own." She met his gaze without false modesty. "I am still developing this method of treatment."

He forced the fear aside. "I look forward to observing your technique."

"You shall have your opportunity very soon." She looked in the direction of the hallway. "There are only two others you must meet—May, our youngest, and Harper Lawson. I've seen little of May since you arrived, and she may still be in hiding."

"She's afraid of me?"

"She fears many things. In some ways, she is younger than her age. She came to us two years ago, in a state of hysteria. Her mother left her with us for treatment. Only Oscar and I have been permitted to come close to her. She has greatly improved but, as with the others, progress can be slow."

"What caused her hysteria?"

Once more Johanna hesitated. "I cannot give you details—that must remain confidential between physician and patient. Suffice it to say that her home life was not a happy one."

A leap of intuition, and a subtle change in Johanna's expression, told Quentin what he wished to know. His lip curled over his teeth, almost without his realizing it. "A child who has suffered at the hands of those who should have cared for her," he guessed. "Like Oscar."

Johanna looked down at her folded hands. "This is why

my father and I believe so strongly in what we do. To abandon such people to life in an asylum, or as prisoners in their own homes, is unconscionable if there is any way to help."

Under Johanna's dry tones and scholarly speech Quentin heard the ardor that made him so powerfully aware of her. She was devoted to these people, odd as they were. She accepted them. As she might accept *him.*

"You have a very generous spirit," he said with complete sincerity. "The world is fortunate that you chose this profession."

The palest stain of pink touched her high cheekbones. "Some members of the medical community might disagree. Our methods and ideas are controversial among neurologists and asylum directors." She rose and smoothed her skirts. "Come."

He was about to follow her from the room when he heard a muted sound outside the window overlooking the garden. He pushed back the lace curtains just in time to see a girl with short, dark hair tumbled about her face and a book clutched in her arms, dart behind a vine-covered trellis. She held very still, but he could see her brown eyes, wide with alarm.

May. She reminded him very much of a wild creature, not unlike his elder brother Braden's young American wife, Cassidy. But Cassidy hadn't been afraid of anything. This one would bound away like a fawn at the first perception of danger.

Johanna appeared at his shoulder. "You've found her," she said. "May spends most of her time in her room, reading, or in the woods. I don't deny her that freedom. She always remains close to home."

"I have some acquaintance with wild things and places," Quentin said.

"Do you?" Johanna tilted her head to search his eyes. "Perhaps, then, you will understand May."

"I am always in favor of understanding." He lifted his

hand, allowing it to graze hers. Unobtrusively she swept her hand behind her skirts and made haste to walk away.

What game are you playing? he asked himself. *What will you do if she begins to respond to your advances?*

He shrugged off the question as he did so many others and trailed after her into the hallway.

She paused outside a closed door. "This is Harper Lawson's room. He seldom leaves it, even for meals." She drew a breath. "Harper was a soldier in the War, fighting with an Indiana regiment. My father had only begun to work with him when he suffered his apoplectic attack. I have since determined that Harper's insanity has its origins in his service, though he was able to live a normal life for some time following the war. I have read other cases in which soldiers such as Harper . . ."

A soldier. Quentin lost the thread of her words, gripped by a sudden wave of dizziness. She'd said the War had made this man insane.

War.

He clutched at the wall, fingers curved into claws. A choking fear rose in his throat. His nostrils flared to the rank smell of smoke, of blood, of sweat and unwashed bodies. The hammering of gunfire reverberated in his ears until he could hear nothing else . . .

Bodies falling. Ambush. Captain Stokes collapsed beside him in midshout, missing part of his face. Blood drenched Quentin's uniform. Young Beringer's legs were shot out from under him. He screamed in a high-pitched wail of pain and terror.

Quentin's vision clouded, narrowed, fixed on the enemy among the rocks above. He could smell the outlaws in their hiding places, carrying out the slaughter from complete safety. There weren't enough men to take them on. This was supposed to have been a simple police action, to capture a

minor Pathan bandit who'd been harassing the more ami-
cable Punjabi villagers. Lieutenant Colonel Jeffers couldn't
have known that he'd sent them into a trap.

Untouched by the whizzing bullets, Quentin dropped his
pistol. He felt nothing. Nothing was the last thing he re-
membered, until he woke in the hospital tent . . .

"Are you ill?"

He sprang back, heart pounding, before he recognized Johanna's voice. He focused on her grave blue eyes until the trembling had passed.

Blue eyes like still, deep water. Calming. He floated away with them, into a land of peace. *Nirvana*, the Buddhists called it.

"Quentin," she said, drifting somewhere alongside him. "Do you hear me?"

He heard, but he couldn't speak. He didn't know what caused his pulse to beat so high, or why she thought him ill. She had been speaking of Harper, and then . . .

Nothing. Blankness. Moments and words lost to him—then Johanna's voice, her eyes. That was all.

Another one. Another episode of "disappearing," though he hadn't touched a drop of alcohol.

"You were somewhere else just a moment ago," she said. "Do you remember?"

Somewhere else. A place of blood and heat and fear. A narrow defile between jagged cliffs—a trap. Rocky walls closing in; a room of damp stones. Darkness. Hours and hours of darkness, and hunger, and pain. The images bled together in confusion.

And then the orders. Orders that came as hard and deadly as bullets. He threw up his arms, casting the images away. Staggering. Falling.

He found his weight supported against a solid, sweetly curved body.

"You had better sit down," Johanna said. "You have pushed yourself too hard."

Her words pierced the fog in his brain. *Johanna.* She held him. Her arms were strong and sheltering, but soft as a woman's should be. Warm. Comforting.

He gave up all thought and allowed himself the sheer physical pleasure of feeling her body pressed to his. Snug bodice and underclothing couldn't disguise the fullness of breasts that so generously fit the crook of his arm. He rested one hand on her waist, just where it joined the flare of her hips. Her simple dress was a great advantage under the circumstances: no flounces and layers and furbelows to get in the way. Just a bit of cloth and the heat of flesh beneath.

And her scent. Clean, smelling slightly of soap. The scent of woman. A woman who wasn't indifferent to the man she held. Her body was becoming aroused, even if she didn't know it.

He settled his face into the cradle of her upper shoulder, his cheek brushing her neck and jaw. With just a slight tilt of his head, he could kiss the skin above the edge of her collar.

"We shall postpone your introduction to Mr. Lawson," she said, her words muffled in his hair. "I will help you back to bed—"

"Only if you join me in it," he whispered.

"I beg your pardon?"

"I still feel quite . . . dizzy," he said, tightening his hold about her waist.

"We shall take small steps," she said, and began moving him firmly in the direction of his room at the end of the hall. The movement felt very much like an extremely intimate waltz.

"Do you dance, Johanna?" he asked, spreading his hand over the small of her back.

"Seldom, and not with my patients." Her pulse beat erratically, loud enough for Quentin to hear with no effort.

"Such a waste." He stumbled, and his hand slipped lower to cup her buttocks. There was no bustle to impede his progress.

She went stock-still and forcibly pushed him away, turned him about, and marched him with a soldier's tread through the door of his room. Without ceremony or excessive gentleness she let him fall to the bed.

"I had thought," she said, facing him with hands on hips, "that you might join us for dinner tonight. But I think, upon reflection, that you should remain in bed."

Quentin's protest died with the appearance of a rampaging headache. He might as well have been drunk, and earned it. He rolled sideways and stretched out, shielding his eyes from the light.

Johanna's hand settled on his forehead. "You are not feverish," she said. "Good."

Along with the pain in his head had come a very prominent swelling in his nether regions—which Johanna, doctor that she was, could not have failed to observe. Unfortunately, she didn't offer to lay her healing hands on his aching member.

"Do you know what happened to you outside Harper's room?" she asked, dousing his less-than-idle fantasies.

"Nothing," he said. He patted the mattress beside him. "Care to join me? I should like to sample more of your bedside manner."

This time he couldn't even raise a blush in her. "I believe," she said, sitting down in the chair, "that you briefly entered a spontaneous hypnotic state. Quite unusual, but not impossible. It bodes very well for our work together."

Their work. She meant the techniques she wanted to try on him, the cure for his drinking.

"Why did you ask me . . . if I was somewhere else?"

"I thought that you were reliving some episode in your past. As I mentioned before, this can happen in the hypnotic state—"

Reliving the past. His ribs seemed to contract around his heart, pressing down so that he couldn't breath. Was that how it would be, this hypnosis? Going back to the heat and blood and darkness, memories torn from some hidden place he hadn't visited in a decade?

Or worse, deliberately surrendering to the blankness, the nothingness?

"No," he rasped. "I think I . . . I don't think you can help me. I'm sorry, but I must leave." He began to sit up, but her hand stopped him. That capable, gentle hand, fingers spread as if she would capture his heart like some small wounded creature.

"I will not yet ask you what you saw there in the hallway," she said. "I have seen that look on Harper's face. But I can tell you that it is normal to be afraid." Her blue eyes were filled with compassion. "Every man has his reason for drinking. Perhaps your reason is not one you wish to face. But you have the strength and courage to do so."

"No." He laughed hoarsely. "I am a coward."

"No more than any other human being."

The irony of her words stopped his laughter. "And what if you're wrong? What if we start something we can't finish?"

"We will work together to find the answers, Quentin Forster."

Quentin closed his eyes. She'd won. Behind her gentle touch was the force of compulsion, *his* compulsion to remain and seek mending for the wounds even he didn't understand.

His compulsion to stay near her—his healing goddess. His Valkyrie.

For your sake, Johanna, I pray that the answers aren't more dangerous than the questions.

Chapter 6

Johanna loved the early morning, before any of the patients but May had left their rooms—when she had the garden and wood and orchard to herself, and plenty of time to think.

She walked out to the orchard while the dawn air was still lightly touched with mist and the old bantam rooster was completing his ritual welcome to the sun. The neatly pruned apple, peach, and walnut trees in their measured rows, like the vineyard on the other side of the house, contrasted sharply with the wild woods on the hillside beyond.

The vineyard and orchard were unmistakable emblems of man's imposition of order upon nature. Even in the short time Johanna had been in the Valley, she'd seen more fields put to the vine, more houses built for the men and women who worked this rich land. Yet it retained its loveliness.

Such order could be a very good thing, like a physician's aid when complications beset a woman's ordinary process of birth. Or when the mind turned upon itself and must be cured with the help of science.

Johanna leaned against the trunk of a mature apple tree, striving to arrange her thoughts in similar tidy ranks. She'd spent a restless night after yesterday's conversation with Quentin, her mind wholly taken up with the new patient, and not to any useful purpose. It wasn't at all like her to lose sleep just because she encountered the unexpected in her work.

But Quentin had managed to surprise her. His rapid and unprompted transition into an hypnotic state was startling enough, but then to witness what must surely have been a reliving of some great anguish in his past . . .

She pushed away from the tree and began to walk down the center of the row, hands clasped behind her back. It wasn't as if Quentin's capability for such retrogression was unique in Johanna's experience. He clearly hadn't known what he'd revealed during the incident outside Harper's room; amnesia for such episodes was typical. His ravings were those of a man trapped in a situation of great stress and suffering; he had been stricken with the kind of grief and horror she had seen in another of her patients. But Harper was seldom so lucid.

She remembered how Quentin had slipped with equal swiftness from an embattled state to one quite different, behaving in such a way that she hadn't been able to tell if he were genuinely enervated or playing the rake. His "affectionate" conduct had certainly suggested the latter.

Her cheeks felt warm, in spite of the morning coolness. She was beginning to see that Quentin's ready laughter and flirtatious speech were all part of the way he protected himself, his kind of defense against what was too terrible to bear, like Lewis's washing and Irene's delusions.

But what *had* he borne? Had Quentin Forster been a soldier? His words and expression during the episode implied it. Many former soldiers had turned to drink to blot out memories they couldn't tolerate. She had visited asylums housing men driven insane by the War. Most could not be cured.

Not by conventional methods. Not while so many asylum superintendents and neurologists believed that all madness was hereditary or came from physical lesions in the brain. Papa had never subscribed to that conventional belief. "Insanity," he had said, "is never simple."

Johanna turned at the end of the row and moved to the next, plucking a leaf from a dangling branch. Insanity was never simple, nor was her as-yet-unproven theory. It was still new, tested only by the smallest increments for the safety of her patients. But she'd begun to see results.

The first time she and Papa had witnessed what she called "mental retrogression," she'd been treating Andersen under Papa's supervision. While Andersen was hypnotized, he began to speak, spontaneously and unpredictably, of events that had occurred in his past—events that had clearly contributed to his illness.

Papa had been fascinated, ready to pursue this new avenue with his customary impetuosity. But Andersen had come out of his trance, and they'd had to postpone a second attempt. Papa's attack stopped any further exploration of their discovery.

But Johanna had never forgotten. During the past year she had taken it up again. She began cautiously, meticulously guiding Andersen into a past he was unwilling to speak of outside the hypnotic state. She walked with him through the very ordeals that had twisted his mind into its present illness.

And the treatment was working. Slowly, step by painfully slow step, it was working. Lewis had improved. Her tentative theory came into being, fragile as a new grape in spring.

The mind hid from itself. It was able to conceal its own darkest desires, its greatest fears, those most unpleasant memories it did not want to remember. And when it did so, it inevitably warped the personality out of its proper channels. Until those thoughts and memories were exposed to the light of the conscious mind.

Johanna had become more and more certain that her new method, based upon Papa's work, was the right one to pursue. Why, then, did she question herself when she thought of treating Quentin Forster with that same method? As if by fate, he had appeared on her doorstep—a man who might prove to be the perfect subject: easily hypnotized, suffering from unbearable memories of his past, but clear-minded enough to cooperate. And to wish for healing.

But he was *not* a "subject." He was as real and important to her as any of the others, for all the briefness of their acquaintance.

Johanna unclenched her fingers and let the crushed leaf fall. This idle speculation was unproductive; she'd already made the decision. She'd assured Quentin that she would help him, tried to allay his natural fears. She must not doubt herself if she was to succeed.

She went back to the house, pausing to throw feed to the chickens. That was usually May's job, as was collecting the eggs, but the girl had neglected her duties this morning.

Reminded of the letter in her pocket, Johanna drew it out and opened the envelope. Mrs. Ingram's missives from Europe were infrequent, always sent general delivery and without a return address, but at least the woman made some inquiries after her daughter's welfare, and expressed the intention to come for her eventually. What she did across the ocean she kept to herself, except for her occasional hints about working to make sure that she and May need never live in fear again.

Johanna kept the letters hidden from May. Until Mrs. Ingram actually arrived, there was no point in getting the girl's hopes up. Two years had passed; many more might do so before May's mother saw fit to come for her.

She scanned the first lines of the letter and inadvertently

crumpled the edge of the paper. The promises in this one were much more explicit than any before. "Please keep my daughter safe," the last lines said. "I will return for her very soon."

The statement might even be true. But if it were not, Mrs. Ingram need have no fear for May's safety.

She pushed the letter back in her pocket and looked up to find the subject of her musings only a few yards away. May was standing at the border of the garden in her plain, loose-fitting dress, poised on the edge of flight. The object of her riveted attention was Quentin Forster.

He stood as still as she, with the absolute motionlessness of a wild animal. He and May regarded each other minute by minute, as if in silent communication. Then Quentin held out his hand and spoke. Johanna couldn't hear his words, but the tones were low and soothing. He smiled. May flinched, eyes wide, and stared at his hand.

Of course Quentin didn't know any better; she'd failed to properly warn him. May was terrified of strangers, men especially, and Quentin was, in spite of his leanness, an imposing figure. Johanna felt an instinctive need to protect May from any discomfort he might inadvertently cause her. She prepared to go to the girl's rescue.

Then a miracle happened. May reached out to brush Quentin's fingers with hers, withdrew her hand, repeated the gesture. Quentin spoke again, and her piquant, heart-shaped face broke out in a tremulous smile. She answered him, her voice hardly more than a whisper.

The magical moment passed, as it must. May remembered her fear and backed away. Quentin didn't try to hold her. He watched her run off, a faint frown between his brows. Concern. Why should he care about a girl who was a stranger to him?

Why should he not, if he were a decent man? Inebriety, even insanity, did not always destroy what was fundamentally good in a human being.

She strode along the graveled path to join him on the other side of the garden. His engaging smile was back in place by the time she reached him.

"I've finally met your May," he said.

"So I see." She looked him over severely. "You ought to have remained in bed."

"But I had so little incentive. I've always felt that sleeping was a very poor use for a good bed."

This time she managed to control her blush. "A return of your illness will be incentive enough." But he hardly looked as though he needed more time to rest. He'd thrown off his debilitation as if it had never existed. "You have no lingering weakness, no distress?"

"Nothing that a dose of your healing touch wouldn't cure."

"I am surprised, Mr.— Quentin." She must not treat him differently than any of the others. Using first rather than surnames and formal address helped build trust, and she could not abandon the practice simply because it smacked of a greater intimacy when used with this man. "May generally refuses to go anywhere near strangers. She seldom even approaches any of the other patients, except for Oscar. What did you say to her?"

He lowered his voice conspiratorially. "I told her a secret."

What sort of secret? she almost blurted out. Instead, she considered how much she was prepared to trust him with May's well-being.

"I have no objection to you speaking with her . . . *if* you are very careful. It might help her to realize that not all men are—" She stopped herself from revealing too much. "Just remember that she is fragile, and cannot be pushed."

He glanced the way she'd gone. "Poor child. But you are helping her."

"I do what I can," she said coolly. Within the unconstraint and surprising rapport of their conversation lay a trap—that of treating Quentin more like a colleague or sympathetic friend than a patient.

"Breakfast should be ready soon," she said, starting for the house. "Let us go in."

He raised his head to sniff the air. "I thought I smelled cooking." His stomach rumbled audibly.

"I see that you have a healthy appetite," she said dryly. "Mrs. Daugherty arrives early five days a week to cook breakfast, so we shall have something substantial this morning."

Together they went in the back door of the house, passing the patients' rooms. Johanna sent Quentin ahead to the kitchen and looked in on Harper. He sat by the window, staring at the drawn curtains. No change.

If she could succeed in helping Quentin, there might be hope for Harper as well.

The others, with the exception of May, were already gathered about the large oak table in the center of the kitchen. Laid out on the cheerful gingham tablecloth were plates of sliced bread, a crock of fresh butter, a pitcher of milk, and a wedge of cheese.

Irene, at the head of the table, was dressed in a gown Johanna hadn't seen before, smelling of crisp, new fabric and cut along much more fashionable lines than most of the actresses's years-old wardrobe. The dress was somewhat vulgar and far more suitable for an evening at the theater than a country breakfast, but Johanna was most interested in its origin. Irene had no income to afford such a gown, nor had she any source for purchasing it.

Unless she had gone into Silverado Springs. Johanna had felt safe in assuming that Irene wouldn't do so, after the first time when she'd crept out to town one night only to be mocked and reviled as a woman both soiled and mad. She had too much pride to risk humiliation again.

Still, it would be wise to speak to her about the dress after breakfast. Irene was not above stealing.

Lewis Andersen, scrupulously honest, wore his habitual unrelieved black and was engaged in carefully refolding his napkin. Oscar eagerly watched Mrs. Daugherty as she put slices of bacon in the frying pan on the great cast-iron stove.

"Good morning, Mrs. Daugherty," Johanna said.

"Mornin', Doc Jo," the older woman said. "Take a seat. I've got bacon today, and fresh milk and butter." She glanced past Johanna to Quentin, never slackening in her preparations. "You must be the new feller. Feelin' better now, I take it?"

Quentin stepped around the table, caught Mrs. Daugherty's broad, chapped hand in his, and kissed it. "Quentin Forster, at your service. And I shall certainly be your most willing slave if that bacon tastes as fine as it smells."

She beamed. "Well, I'll be. A real gen'l'man. Haven't heard your like in some time." She lifted a brow at Johanna. "Can't believe this feller was ever sick."

"I had the best of care," he said, following her glance.

"You can't do better than having Doc Jo to tend you," Mrs. Daugherty said with a vigorous nod. "She wouldn't hear of leavin' your side, not even when she was near fallin' down exhausted. That's the kind of lady she is. She saved my daughter and grandchild. Never will forget."

Johanna longed for a useful task to keep herself occupied, but Mrs. Daugherty had matters well in hand. She'd learned on Mrs. Daugherty's first day at the Haven that the woman found her more of a nuisance than a help in the kitchen. "You keep them hands fer healin'," she'd said. "They ain't no good for cookery."

"Would you sit down, Quentin?" Johanna asked, indicating the chair next to Lewis.

"But I've saved a chair for you, right here," Irene said, ignoring Johanna.

Quentin flashed Johanna an apologetic grin and seated himself next to Irene. She latched on to him immediately, beginning her usual monologue about the theater, how desperate the New York producers were for her return, and how she would fight off her hordes of admirers when she went back. Lewis emerged from absorption with his own sin to stare at her with thin-mouthed condemnation.

"Only the devil waits for you," he said. "Beware, Jezebel—"

Irene sneered. "Pay no attention to *him*. He's crazy."

"Let us try to have a pleasant breakfast," Johanna said. Irene stopped talking with a pout, clinging to Quentin's arm. He made no effort to disentangle himself. Oscar wrenched his gaze from the frying pan to smile shyly at the newcomer.

"Hullo," he said. "I'm glad you're better."

"So am I," Quentin said. He plucked at his shirt. "Thank you for the use of the clothes."

"Do you like them?"

"Very much."

Oscar rewarded him with a gap-toothed grin. "Good." He turned back to Mrs. Daugherty. "Is the bacon done yet?"

"If I ain't careful, you'll eat all of it." She took the pan off the stove and laid the bacon on a serving platter, then took it around the table, beginning with Quentin, who made as if to swoon with joy.

"Wonderful," he said. He waited until the others were served, and offered Irene the plate of bread. Mrs. Daugherty cooked up a dozen eggs while everyone helped themselves to what was on the table.

Johanna seldom had a problem with her appetite, since she firmly believed in the value of hearty eating and good nutrition, but she found herself merely picking at her food. Again and again her gaze turned to Quentin. He was cordial and sympathetic to Irene, but there was a slight remoteness to his speech and manner, as if he were merely indulging her. He seemed to make no judgment of either Lewis or Oscar. Mrs. Daugherty had certainly fallen for his charm.

No grounds, then, to be concerned about his fitting in with the group—at least thus far. The thought made her feel unaccountably breathless. After all, he was hardly likely to remain beyond a few weeks or months. He was not like the other three men, who could not live elsewhere.

As if he'd noticed her preoccupation, he looked directly at her and smiled. "This is the most enjoyable meal I've had in a long time. How grateful I am that you rescued me, Doc Jo."

She winced inwardly at the nickname Mrs. Daugherty had given her. "I'm glad you find the food to your liking."

"More eggs, young man?" Mrs. Daugherty asked, hovering behind his chair with pan and serving spoon in hand. Irene grabbed his arm and glared at the older woman.

Quentin patted his flat stomach. "You've quite filled me up, madam. I think I must reluctantly forgo a third helping. But I have only the highest praise for your culinary expertise."

"Don't he talk fancy," Mrs. Daugherty said, winking at Johanna. "Just 'bout the same as you." She studied Johanna with a speculative eye. "You two could have some pretty edjercated conversations, I s'pose."

Mrs. Daugherty was too perspicacious for Johanna's comfort. She had learned long ago not to mistake a lack of education for a dearth of intelligence.

"Mrs. Daugherty," she said, "would you please prepare trays for Harper and my father? I'd like to deliver their meals."

The older woman shook her head. "Poor feller," she said to Quentin. "Harper's the lad who fought in the War. Never right in the head after that—" She caught herself at Johanna's pointed look and went back to her stove.

Johanna had just about given up on her breakfast when the back door to the kitchen swung open on squeaking hinges, banging against the wall. May rushed in, a sprite in calico, and dashed toward the table. With a darting glance at the others, she stopped by Quentin's chair and laid a bunch of wildflowers across his empty plate. Almost without pause, she snatched a slice of bread from the table and skittered out the door again.

"Well, I'll be," Mrs. Daughtery said. "I never seen her do that before."

Nor had Johanna. Quentin gathered up the flowers and bent his head to appreciate their scent. Irene simmered.

"Why do you let that . . . guttersnipe run wild through the place?" she snapped at Johanna.

"She does no harm," Lewis said, breaking his customary silence for the second time that morning. "Leave her be."

"Oh, is she without sin?" Irene asked with a trilling laugh.

Johanna rose. "Irene, Lewis, I believe it's time for your midmorning chores. If you'd be so kind, Irene, I have a few of Quentin's garments that need repair. Your skill with a needle is unmatched."

"I'll do it . . . for you, Quentin," Irene said, leaning into him. "Ordinarily I don't sully my hands with a seamstress's work."

"I shall be honored," Quentin said.

Lewis, who'd eaten little more than Johanna, scraped back his chair and walked out the back door, tugging repeatedly at the fingers of his gloves.

"I'm gonna see the new calf," Oscar announced.

"Best you all get along," Mrs. Daughtery said, wiping her hands on her stained apron. "I got cleanin' to do. Here's yer trays, Doc Jo."

"Come walk with me in the garden, Quentin," Irene said with a seductive smile. "I have so much more to tell you."

"I regret the necessity of refusing such a flattering invitation, but I believe I must consult with the doctor," Quentin said, slipping free of her hold. "Later, perhaps?"

"I'll leave the clothing in your room, Irene," Johanna said.

The long habit of deferring to Johanna's authority finally sent Irene flouncing off to her room. Oscar marched outside in search of Gertrude's calf. Johanna fetched Harper's tray, but Quentin intercepted her.

"Allow me," he said. "I think it's time I met Mr. Lawson."

"He is unlikely to notice you," she warned. "Harper suffers from severe melancholia and episodes of mania. The former has been much more frequent. He reacts to very few stimuli." After what had happened yesterday with Quentin, she had reason to be cautious. "If you feel ready—"

"I'm fine."

She took leave to doubt it, but this was as good a way as any to see if that episode would be repeated.

"Very well," she said. She led him to Harper's door and opened it. He was where she'd left him, still gazing at drawn curtains as if he could see through them to the world beyond.

"Harper," she said, motioning Quentin to set the tray down on a small table beside Harper's chair, "I've brought your breakfast. I hope you'll try to eat."

Harper's left eyelid twitched. It was acknowledgment of a sort—more than she often received. His thin fingers stretched on the arm of his chair.

"We have a new guest staying with us," she said. "Quentin Forster. He'd very much like to meet you."

Harper turned his head. He looked at the tray, at Johanna, and at last toward Quentin.

"I am pleased to meet you," Quentin said, extending his hand.

Unmoving, Harper gazed at the offered hand while his own fingers continued to twitch. Then, slowly, he lifted his arm from the chair. His hand reached halfway to Quentin's and seemed to lose its purpose. But his gaze rose to meet the stranger's, clearing to lucidity for the first time in many days.

"Sol-jer," he said, his voice rough with disuse.

Quentin glanced at Johanna in surprise. "Yes," he said reluctantly. "Years ago."

Harper shuddered. When the shivers passed he sat still for a long moment, until Johanna was sure any further chance of communication was gone. But he surprised her. He reached clumsily for the spoon on the tray—she never left him any sharp implements, even for eating—and scooped up a helping of egg. Most of it made it to his mouth. He continued to eat, without Johanna's help.

She touched Quentin's arm and led him from the room, amazed and gratified. It appeared that his affinity with May was not a singular occurrence.

"How did you do it?" she asked when the door was closed again. "He has not responded so well in weeks. I have not seen him show such interest in anything since I brought a neighbor's dog to visit—he seems to have a great affection for dogs. But he seldom responds to people." She realized that her hand was still on his arm and let him go, striving to modulate her tone. "He actually acknowledged you, and spoke."

"I'm afraid I can't claim any miraculous technique," Quentin said. "I'm no doctor."

"I wonder how he knew that you were a soldier." She shook her head. "You have a way with people, Quentin— with those who are troubled. It is no small gift."

He half turned away. "Perhaps it's because I am one of them."

She had an almost overwhelming desire to touch him again, to embrace him as . . . yes, as a kindred spirit, like her father had been. More—as a man who desperately needed human companionship and affection.

Was that what she felt for him? Affection?

The truth stole into her heart as if it had been there all along. She *liked* Quentin Forster. She wasn't merely in- trigued by him and willing to treat him—not simply attracted to his charm and good looks on a purely physical level.

She liked him, and wanted him to like her.

It had never been vital, in the past, that a patient should like her. Indeed, such expectations were detrimental to treatment; her own feelings were quite unimportant. Quentin's appreciative behavior might not even survive what she had in mind for him. He might hate her in the end, if she made him relive what he wished to forget.

Better that he should hate her than the rest of the world.

"I believe that your insight will help our work together," she said, recovering herself. "I planned to begin this morning, if you feel ready."

He shrugged. "Why not? I am rather curious."

"It's no subject for levity," she said. "The treatment may not always be pleasant."

"Thank you for the warning." He caught her gaze. "And for your honesty, Johanna."

She backed away. "I shall take in my father's breakfast, and make sure the others are settled. Shall we meet in my office in one hour?"

"I'll count the minutes." At first she thought he was going to take her hand and kiss it as he had Mrs. Daugherty's, but he only gave her a shallow bow and turned for his room.

Well, then. It was all proceeding as smoothly as she could hope. Her judgment had proved sound. She had matters—and her own emotions—under firm control.

She took the tray to her father, and readied her mind for the battle ahead.

Chapter 7

If ever Quentin had doubted his cowardice, he was absolutely sure of it now.

He waited for Johanna in her office, perched on the edge of the faded chaise longue that sat across from her desk. He could see a little of the view outside the window opposite; he had a very strong desire to climb through that window.

Instead, he got up and paced a nervous circle about the room, ending at her desk. The polished oak surface was spotless, dust-free, and neatly laid out with a minimum of clutter: a stack of papers or notes, an inkstand and pen, a metronome, a pair of medical books taken from the alphabetized rows in the shelf against the nearest wall . . . and a small vase of wildflowers, similar to those May had brought him at breakfast.

The desk was like the woman herself: orderly, pragmatic, its seeming severity moderated by the homely beauty of a handful of flowers.

Quentin was tempted to upset the perfect balance of the desk: scatter a few papers out of order, or stick a wildflower stem in the inkwell. Just as he had been tempted, more than once, to loosen the tightly bound strands of Johanna's light brown hair.

It wasn't too late to do something just outrageous enough to make her toss him out on his ear, reject him as a patient. He didn't have to go through with this. If Johanna's hypnosis was what she claimed, he wasn't going to be able to hide himself. Not any part or portion.

He sat at Johanna's desk and picked up her pen. The scent of her hands lingered in the glossy wood of the handle. He drew it slowly along his upper lip, thinking through what he'd already debated with himself a hundred times or more.

He *was* crazy, as crazy as any of the other residents of the Haven.

Because he trusted Johanna. He trusted her to help him, she alone of all men or women in the world. He trusted her not only with his uncertain memories, but with the one fact she surely could not accept—she with her logical mind. What would she do with that secret, once she received it into her keeping?

She thought she could cure him of dipsomania. He hadn't told her the rest, the thing he feared, the shadow he never saw except in nightmares and cloudy recollections of conflict and violence. He wasn't even sure it existed except in his imagination.

If it did exist, Johanna would discover it.

The pen snapped between his fingers, driving a splinter into his thumb. He watched a tiny bead of blood well up from the wound. In a few minutes no one would be able to see that the flesh had been broken.

Would he be dead by now, if not for the healing power of his body? Lying in some alley, perhaps, poisoned by alcohol or murdered by cutthroats?

The point was moot. His flesh, his bones, his organs— they all mended in time, barring a fatal stroke to the heart, spine, or brain. Only his mind didn't heal. He understood his mind least of all.

His elder brother, Braden, Earl of Greyburn, had once told him that he'd wasted a good mind in the pursuit of pleasure and frivolity. Braden didn't know about the Punjab, or the shadow that followed Quentin, haunting him from the corner of his vision. The shadow had gone away while he'd lived a fast life in England, unable to match the frantic pace Quentin set. It had returned five years ago, at the Convocation, and ended the life Braden had so disparaged.

I ran out on you, brother—on you and Rowena. I had to. What would you think to see me now?

He glanced at his hand again. The skin was almost smooth where the splinter had pierced it. Yes, his flesh had mended, but what of Johanna's pen? Wasn't it a metaphor for what she was—sound enough in average hands, but so easily broken in the wrong ones . . .

"I see that you are ready to begin."

Johanna stepped into the room, her arms full of books. Quentin jumped up and took them from her, setting them down on the desk.

"I must apologize," he said. "I fear I broke your pen. I'll replace it, of course."

She glanced at the broken pen and then at his face. "It doesn't matter. The pen was of no great value, and I have others." She began to replace the books in their proper slots on the shelf. "Would you please close the door? We shall not be disturbed for the next two hours."

Quentin shut the door and leaned against it. "The other patients?"

"Each has his or her own schedule of chores and rest periods, and we generally have our exercise in the late afternoon, before dinner."

"All very . . . systematic."

She turned to him, propping her arms on the desk. "I

find it works best with the mentally afflicted. Order is soothing to the troubled mind."

And to yours, Quentin thought. At the moment, he'd gladly take a little of that soothing himself. He left the safety of the door as if he were walking into the mouth of hell. "How does one go about this hypnosis? Does it involve the laying on of hands?"

"No touching is necessary. It is not mesmerism, with the making of passes over the body."

"A pity." His hands dangled like useless things at his sides, and his mouth was cotton-dry. "What do you want me to do?"

"I have found that a subject is in the most receptive state when fully relaxed," she said, drawing the drapes at the window. The room dimmed to twilight. "Please make yourself comfortable on the chaise longue."

Quentin sat down, hesitated, and swung his legs along the length of the chaise. Johanna pulled her chair from behind her desk and set it a few feet away from the foot of the chaise.

"I will briefly explain what we are about to do." She sat in the chair as straight-backed as the most rigorous arbiter of propriety, hands folded in her lap. "The man who first recognized the science of hypnosis was a Scottish physician by the name of Braid, who wrote that the hypnotic trance, into which I am about to induct you, is the result of a mental state of concentration in which all external distractions are excluded. In this state, the mind is receptive to ideas, even memories, that are ignored or forgotten by the conscious mind. As I explained once before, my father learned that it is possible under these conditions for the physician to introduce corrective thoughts and suggestions the mind would not routinely accept." She drew in a deep breath and clasped her hands. "I shall guide you into that state with the use of specific techniques."

It sounded a trifle too much like the sort of thing Braden

had been known to do with the servants at Greyburn, the Forsters' ancestral estate in Northumberland. But that was no "science of hypnosis," not something an ordinary human could manage. A man like Braden could overcome the very will of another, force him to forget rather than remember— a werewolf skill Quentin had lost somewhere along the way.

"Hypnosis also requires a kind of partnership between the doctor and the patient," Johanna said. "There is nothing to fear in it."

"Do you mean that you can't order me to do something against my will?" Quentin asked lightly. "Perform Hamlet's soliloquy while standing on my head?"

She smiled. "That is correct, as far as I have observed. That is why you must wish to be helped. Not all can be hypnotized. But your ability to go into a spontaneous trance, as you did yesterday, is an excellent sign." Her smile faded. "If you trust me. You must trust me, and give yourself into my hands. Can you do that, Quentin?"

Wasn't that what he'd been asking himself all along?

He met her gaze, all levity gone from his voice and his thoughts. "Yes, Johanna. I believe I can."

She blinked, as if taken aback by his sincerity, and he let himself become just a little intoxicated by the remarkable clarity of her eyes. Like a quiet ocean, they were—never troubled by more than the gentlest of waves. How would a man go about awakening their first real storm?

Surely it wasn't his imagination that she looked back at him with the same expectant wonder . . .

"Very well, then," she said. "Have you any further questions?"

"What is your battle strategy, Johanna?"

"I beg your pardon?"

"Your plan to fight my demons of dipsomania."

"It is quite simple. Once I have put you into a hypnotic state, when your mind is open, I shall ask you a few basic questions to determine the depth of your trance. If that is sufficient, I shall ask you more specific questions that have a greater bearing on your condition."

"Such as what drives me to drink. Can't you ask me that without my being in a trance?"

"A part of your mind is in hiding, Quentin," she said slowly. "It protects you from those things you do not want to see . . . or remember."

Quentin gripped the sides of the chaise as if it were a flimsy raft floating in the midst of a sea of hungry sharks. "Perhaps there's a good reason I don't remember."

She gazed at him earnestly, the passion bright in her face. "Can the reason be good if it causes you pain and suffering? If it drives you to risk your life? No." She shook her head. "There is still so much we do not comprehend about the mind, and how the brain and body work together. But I believe that much insanity is created by a kind of . . . separation from one's own true self. If we could only make the self whole again, insanity would be cured. If a man can see himself clearly in the mirror of his own mind, and accept what he sees, he is free."

She spoke with such conviction, such utter certainty. "You'll . . . plunder my memory like an archeologist digging for ancient pot shards," he said with a laugh. "I hope my brain is filled with more than earth and fragments of crockery."

She didn't return his smile. "It contains more than you or I or anyone could ever know. But it may reveal, under hypnosis, what it cannot do when you are fully conscious."

Surely she couldn't perceive the depth of his fear, or hear the drumming of his heart? A woman of her strength would find little to admire in a coward, a man without the courage to overcome his weaknesses—no matter how tolerant she was of the truly mad.

Quentin widened his eyes in an absurd pantomime of

terror. "You'll know all my secrets," he whispered. "I shall be overcome with chagrin."

"As your doctor, I would never reveal what I learn to anyone. I shall be honest with you, always." She paused and looked down at her hands. "The choice must be yours. I might simply attempt to convince your mind that you have no need for drink, and go no further. My father was very successful with such techniques . . . in effect suggesting to the open mind that its incorrect assumptions are mistaken, and lead it to change the behavior of the body."

Quentin braced himself against a premature wave of relief. "But?"

"But even if I succeed, the thing that causes you to drink will still be there, untouched." She held his gaze. "Do you understand?"

He thought he understood all too well. He'd have to give up on himself, for Johanna never would. She was that generous, and that remarkable. But he'd recognized that from the beginning.

"If nothing else," he said with false bravado, "I can help you develop your new methods."

Her cheeks reddened. "I am sorry if you think my motives are—"

"No." Impulsively he slid from the chaise and went to her, knelt before her chair and took her hands in his. "I have nothing to lose, Johanna. I'll be your willing subject."

The color in her face remained high, and her hands tensed under his fingers. "Quentin—"

"Shhhh." He kissed first one hand and then the other. "You might as well turn my brain inside out. You've already done it to my heart."

She sucked in her breath. He could hear her heart hammering against her ribs, feel the pulse throb in her wrists, blood and body giving the lie to her mask of composure. "Quentin, you are my patient. We have known each other only a few days. It is not uncommon for patients to think themselves . . . fond of their physicians, particularly when they have come close to death."

There. She'd given him an easy way out. He could laugh it off and beat a prudent retreat, knowing he'd made too reckless a move in the game. A move even he hadn't expected.

Because he hadn't been speaking entirely in jest.

He looked up at her lips, slightly parted as if she'd thought better of further conversation. They were full, naturally rosy without a trace of paint. Had they been kissed before? Had she ever found time in the midst of her doctor's theories to let a man hold her in his arms? In that feminine brain, seething with frightening intelligence and devotion to the study of the mind, had she any conception at all of the pleasures of the flesh?

Once he had known such pleasures intimately and frequently. Women had come gladly to his bed, flattered by his attentions. He'd lived in a world of mutual gratification shared among a well-bred set of rakes, roués, and worldly married women who knew exactly what they were getting and giving away.

Brilliant as she was, Johanna was anything but worldly.

"Please go back to the chaise, Quentin," she said. "We should begin."

The rebuff was clear. She didn't take him seriously. Why should she? He'd become a bitter joke, even to himself. With a sigh he returned to the chaise, resting his head and shoulders on the pillows and wondering if he might not prefer to have various body parts removed without benefit of the new anesthesia.

Johanna rose from her chair and went to the desk. She started the metronome, setting it into a slow, steady *tick-tick*. From a drawer in the desk she produced a candle and matches, which she set down on a small table. She moved the table close to her chair and lit the candle.

"You need not be concerned," she said, resuming her

seat. "You will be safe at all times, in this room with me. We may not go beyond the very first stages of trance today, and nothing I do will harm you."

He laughed under his breath. "Fire away, Doctor."

"Relax, as much as you are able. Try to clear your mind of all thoughts and worries. Very good." She lifted her hand. From the end of a chain hung a multifaceted crystal, catching the candlelight as it spun in slow circles. "Do you see this crystal? Look upon it now. Notice its translucence, the quality of light, the gentle motion as it turns round and round."

Quentin looked. There was nothing particularly fascinating about the crystal. He'd much rather gaze at the face above it, glowing with reflected light.

Except she'd made very clear her sentiments regarding his attentions.

"As you watch the crystal," she said, "listen to the rhythm of the metronome. How even and steady it is, like a heartbeat. When you hear it, all your worries and fears leave your mind. You feel at peace."

How could he feel at peace with Johanna so near, her scent drifting across to him? He was like a boy in the schoolroom, fidgeting and impatient to get out into the free, fresh air and away from the useless knowledge they crammed into his head . . .

"You will notice, as you watch the crystal and listen to the beat, that your eyes are growing very heavy. You are sleepy, and yet your mind is clear. Look, Quentin. Look, and listen."

Perversely, he resisted. Johanna was confident of her ability, but she hadn't faced a werewolf subject. What if he chose to fight her? Would she still be so determined to keep at it until she found his "cure"?

"You're resisting, Quentin," she said. "You must let go."

You instruct me to do what you cannot. He set his jaw. *You must work a little harder, Valkyrie.*

"Come, come. This won't do." She gazed into his eyes.
"Trust me, Quentin. That is all I ask. Trust me." Her voice
softened to a low, soothing drone. "You want my help. I
want to help you. Be my ally, Quentin."

Such a cold word, *ally*. It didn't satisfy him, not in the
least. But after a few moments he realized that her peculiar
magic was working, if not as she expected. It was her voice
he listened to, not the metronome—her eyes he watched,
not the crystal. He felt himself falling, falling into ocean-
deep blue.

"Good," she said. "Very good. You are closing your eyes
now. You continue to hear my voice, but your mind is relaxed, open. You are able to answer questions put to you
without hesitation. Whatever you experience from now on,
it has no power to harm you."

Quentin closed his eyes. Johanna's face remained as a
pale shape against the darkness behind his lids. He felt his
heartbeat settle into a lazy, comfortable rhythm.

"How do you feel?" she said from a slight distance.

"Fine." And he did. Remarkably well, in fact.

"Excellent. You will notice that your right arm has lost
all weight. It is floating up of its own accord."

The sensation of his arm floating in midair felt agreeable
and not at all strange. The rest of him felt ready to join the
arm.

"What is your full name, Quentin?"

"Quentin . . . Octavius . . . Forster. The Honorable. That
means . . . I'm not the earl." He was aware of the oddness
of his speech, but it didn't trouble him.

"And who is the earl?"

"My brother, Braden."

"Have you other siblings?"

"My sister, Rowena." He felt a twinge of guilt, but it
passed into the same dream state as his other emotions. "I
think . . . she's in New York now."

"You have lost touch with her?"

"I . . . haven't written to her in over two years."

"When was the last time you saw her?"

"In England."

"When were you last in England?"

"In 1875. Autumn."

"Why did you leave?"

A darkness intruded upon his tranquillity, drawing him away from Johanna's voice. His arm grew heavy, began to fall.

"You're safe, Quentin," Johanna said. "We will return to that some other time. You may lower your arm now."

He obeyed, feeling the darkness recede again.

"Have you been in America since you left England?"

He nodded. That was an easy question.

"Please tell me what you've been doing since your arrival in this country."

What he'd been doing? He thought back to the first day he'd stepped from the steamer's gangplank onto the dock in New York. He'd gambled in some high-class saloon—winning as he always did, sleeping on a fine bed in a fine hotel, boarding a train heading west the next morning. No plans, no future.

"It isn't . . . very interesting," he said. "Can we talk about something else?"

"As you wish. I once asked you about periods of amnesia following consumption of alcohol. How often have you suffered this?"

"I haven't kept an account."

"What do you do when you wake from such an episode?"

His stomach tightened. "Go. To the next place."

"Why?"

He couldn't make sense of her question. She fell silent, and he allowed himself to drift in pleasant nothingness. This was much better than drinking.

"Think about what happened yesterday, outside of Harper's room," she said.

Yesterday. It came to him, sprung fully formed into his mind. Johanna speaking of soldiers and war. The stench and the blood and the rattling din of guns.

"India—" he began, shivering.

"You're safe, Quentin, calm and at ease. India is far away."

"Far away," he repeated. "I was . . . on the northwest frontier. A subaltern with the Punjab Frontier Force, 51st Sikhs."

"What did you do there?"

"We . . . tried to keep the peace on the borders. Skirmishes with the tribesmen, bandits. Never stopped."

"How many years did you serve in the army?"

"Three. I was nineteen when I got my commission. I requested India."

"What happened in India, Quentin?"

He was nineteen again, eager and itching for action. There hadn't been any major battles in India since the Mutiny, but there were still the hill bandits and the occasional rebellious tribal leader to defy British rule. Quentin had fallen in love with the place, with its scents and colors and exotic ways. It almost didn't matter that nothing seemed to happen except drills and exercises and the occasional punitive foray. He was away from England, from Greyburn and . . .

"You were in a battle," said Johanna.

His first real battle, and his last. It began as a chase, with his captain, a fellow subaltern, and the Indian troops, into the hills after a particularly daring and elusive raider. It ended in slaughter.

He heard his own voice speaking, cool and unmoved, as if it belonged to someone else. As if the things he'd seen had been witnessed by someone else.

"And then?"

"I . . . don't remember." His throat closed up, trying to lock the words inside. That had been the first of the blank times, the beginning of a life of constant motion, desperate escape. "I woke up in hospital at the post, barely hurt. They said most of the men had been saved, the rebels destroyed. They gave me a commendation, but I didn't know what I'd done to earn it. My friends wouldn't tell me. They avoided me, and I didn't know why. *I don't remember.*"

"What do you think happened?"

He shut her out, her and her ugly questions. He drifted back to that agreeable place of nothingness where he simply existed, free of ties and emotion.

"Quentin, are you listening to me?"

"Go away," he muttered.

"We won't talk more about India for now. I would like you to think about something else instead. Remember when you were a child, with Rowena and Braden, before you ever thought of becoming a soldier."

Like a relentless Pied Piper, Johanna seduced him out of hiding. He couldn't help but follow where she led—back to a past that felt less real than a dream.

"Where did you grow up, Quentin?"

His mind went vacant for a moment, and then the words came to him. "Greyburn. My brother's estate in Northumberland. Only it wasn't his then. It was my—my grandfather's."

"And your father?"

"He died when I was a child. So did my mother."

"I'm sorry. That must have been very difficult."

"I was . . . the black sheep." He tried to chuckle. "Always in trouble. The peals Braden rang over my head . . ."

"Your grandfather raised you?"

"He—" His throat closed up again. "He was the earl."

"Did you get along well with your brother and sister?"

"Ro— we were twins. Very close. She could tell . . . what I was feeling, sometimes." He recalled Rowena's fair, piquant face and plunged into a profound sense of loss. "Ah, Rowena—"

"And Braden?"

"He was my elder brother. He did his best, even when he didn't know—"

Seething darkness descended like a curtain over his thoughts, cutting off words, intention, memory.

"Didn't know what, Quentin?"

No. *No.* The answer wouldn't come. He caught at the first safe thing that came into his head.

"There's something you don't know about me," he said. "A secret."

"Can you tell me that secret, Quentin?"

"Of course. I *trust* you." He felt himself float up from the chaise and circle her chair like a disembodied spirit. "Have you ever heard of . . . werewolves?"

"Do you mean a . . . man who becomes a wolf?"

"Yes. Running about on all fours. Howling at the moon." He hummed under his breath. "That's exactly what I am. A werewolf."

Chapter 8

Johanna had thought that she was prepared for just about any sort of revelation. She certainly should have been; as she'd told Quentin, the human mind was an organ of great complexity, capable of almost anything the imagination could devise.

Even of believing its owner to be a creature out of myth and legend. A shape-shifter. A . . . werewolf.

The word she'd heard used for the delusion was lycanthropy, but she'd never encountered it herself, nor read of any contemporary doctor or neurologist who had done so.

Suppressing her reaction, she took stock of Quentin. He was still relaxed, in a deep trance. He'd responded to hypnotism with relative ease—one of those rare men who required virtually no groundwork. He'd already given her much to work with.

But this . . . this she truly hadn't expected.

"Let me make sure I understand," she said. "You are a werewolf."

"Or loup-garou. Some of us . . . prefer the French."

"Us?"

"You don't think I'm the only one, do you?"

"I see." She leaned back in her chair, steepling her fingers under her chin. "Then Braden and your sister are also of these loups-garous?"

"It . . . runs in families."

He spoke with complete confidence, at ease with his "secret" identity. If his belief in lycanthropy lay at the root of his drinking and other fears, he showed no indication of it.

The temptation was very great to pursue this extraordinary turn of events to its natural conclusion. What would he do, if asked to actually become a wolf? She'd read of men and women, under hypnosis, reacting to suggestions that they were something other than human, mimicking the sounds and actions of various animals. Would he do the same, howling and growling, perhaps turning savage?

She couldn't imagine such a thing. But it would be the height of folly to provoke Quentin now. His illness was not merely dipsomania, possibly derived from experiences in the army. His response when she'd asked about his childhood suggested memories he wished to avoid. And now this . . .

"As you say, Quentin," she said, postponing further speculation. "I think we've done enough for one meeting. We shall explore these claims tomorrow, after—"

A shrieking wail came from somewhere beyond the door, rising into a bellow and falling abruptly silent. Johanna shot up from her chair.

"Harper," she whispered. "Quentin, please continue to rest. I'll return shortly."

He didn't answer. She opened the door and strode out into the hallway. Irene, Oscar, and Mrs. Daugherty stood at one end, staring toward Harper's room. Lewis poked his head out from his own room and ducked in again, carefully shutting the door.

"It will be all right," Johanna said. "Mrs. Daugherty, please take Oscar and Irene into the parlor."

With the same care she'd use approaching a wild animal, Johanna opened Harper's door.

He was in his usual place by the window, as if nothing had happened. The only change was that he no longer sat still, but rocked gently, forward and back, with his hands clasped between his knees. She moved closer to study his face. A scream such as she'd heard normally meant he was entering a period of violent mania, as he'd done three times since coming to her and Papa.

If that was the case, handling him would become much more difficult. But he continued to rock, ignoring her. It seemed safe to leave him just long enough to bring Quentin from his trance and send him to luncheon with the others.

Quentin had consumed entirely too many of her thoughts since his arrival. It was almost a relief to have another patient take precedence.

But Quentin wasn't finished with her. When she reentered her office, he was sitting on the edge of the chaise, staring up at the ceiling. He looked toward her, his cinnamon eyes glazed and unfocused, as if still in the trance. Harper's cry hadn't brought him out as she would have expected.

"I like this room," he said dreamily. "It smells good. Like you."

It was definitely time to finish. "Quentin, listen to the sound of my voice. In a few moments I shall be bringing you out of your hypnotic state. Do you want to remember what we have discussed today?"

He swung his feet to the floor and strolled toward her. "I want to remember you." He lifted his hand to brush her face. "Johanna."

His touch was intimate. She felt a physical pang, as if he'd penetrated her flesh.

Her first impression was incorrect. Surely he was awake

now. Pretending to be otherwise, though why he should wish—

"I like being with you," he said. "More than any other woman."

"That is enough. Our session is finished, and—"

"You like *me*, Johanna," he said, circling the pad of his thumb around her chin. "More than any other man."

She opened her mouth to deny it and caught her breath. "Go back to the chaise, Quentin." If he were under hypnosis, he would do as she asked, and if he were deceiving her, he'd do the same or be forced to surrender his pretense. "Sit down."

He dropped his hand, began to obey and then stopped, clutching at his head. "You despise me," he said. He started clumsily for the far wall, banged his hip into her desk, and stumbled as if he hadn't seen the obstacle.

Somnambulism. Even he would not take the game so far. And if he were still entranced, he and his mind were at their most vulnerable.

She clenched her fists at her sides. "I do not despise you, Quentin."

He turned about, his gaze moving this way and that as if he couldn't find her. "You said . . . you would help me."

"I will. Have no fear, Quentin. I will."

He smiled, like a glorious sunrise. "Yes." He came to her slowly. His hand found its way to her shoulder, slid around to cup the back of her neck. "My Valkyrie," he said, staring at her mouth. "You're so beautiful."

Mein Gott. He must imagine that he saw someone else.

"Quentin," she said, trying to control the shaking in her voice. "I shall count backward from five to one. As I count, you will become more and more awake, until—"

He leaned so close that his breath caressed her lips. "If I'm asleep, don't wake me." He pulled her into his arms, the motion rife with purpose.

Suddenly she felt small and fragile in a way she hadn't

since childhood. Not weak, not disadvantaged, but some-how *protected.*

How could a man like Quentin protect anyone, least of all her? And from what? Her analytical mind, always so ready to examine a problem from all angles, fell strangely mute on the subject.

But it wasn't completely silent. She was still able to make a concise mental roster of her body's reactions to Quentin's embrace.

Heart pounding. Breath short. Skin sensitive to the slightest pressure. Spine thrumming as Quentin's hands stroked her back. Nipples hardening where they met Quentin's chest. And in the vicinity of her reproductive or-gans . . . an indescribable warmth she hadn't experienced in many, many years.

All the symptoms of physical desire.

There was no doubt of Quentin's.

His lips began the endless descent to meet hers. They made contact. Pressed. Demanded a response.

Her body answered, pushing intellect aside. She opened her mouth and felt Quentin's tongue tease the inner velvet of her lips. An urgent spike of need drove down into her womb. She wrapped her arms around Quentin's waist and let him bend her back as he deepencd the kiss, as if she were the veriest, most insubstantial nymph.

A nymph with a bacchante's appetites. And all the while it seemed that Quentin was somnambulating—acting upon the desires his conscious mind kept in check.

She had no such excuse. She kissed him in return, touch-ing her tongue to his, savoring the purely erotic sensations she'd known but once before. Her seat and then her back came to rest on the chaise. Quentin's hand found its way to the aching swell of her breasts, scorched her flesh even through the sturdy, sensible cotton.

"Quentin," she half-protested.

"Johanna," he paused to answer, resuming his kisses on the soft skin under her jaw. "I want you."

His weight came down beside her on the chaise. His erection—quite considerable in size, her dazed mind calculated—pressed into her hip. She generally wore a minimum of petticoats; they hampered her movements and were unhealthily restrictive. What she did wear was hardly a barrier for a determined male.

She was the only barrier. Her will. Her sense of professional ethics. Her reliable common sense, which had somehow fled.

It was definitely time to call it back.

"I will now count backward," she repeated breathlessly. "You will forget all that has happened since we began this hypnotic session. When I reach one, you will wake, alert and refreshed."

He licked the tip of her ear. "Hmmmm."

"Five."

He drew her earlobe into his mouth and suckled it.

"F-four."

His hand settled on the skirts bunched around her calves and began to push up.

"Th . . ." She gulped. "Three."

He searched out the buttons at the top of her high collar.

"Two—"

The first three buttons came undone in swift succession. *"One."*

She held her breath. His fingers paused in their relentless work. His lips released her earlobe. He drew back.

The glazed look fell away from his eyes, replaced by complete awareness . . . and confusion. He jumped from the chaise and shook his head like a dog casting water from its coat.

"What happened?" he demanded.

She sat up and unobtrusively rearranged her skirts. "You don't remember?"

"You were about to hypnotize me, weren't you?"

She rose unsteadily from the chaise, leaving the buttons at her collar undone. She was sure she didn't have the fine manual control necessary to do the job.

"I did hypnotize you," she said. "The session went very well."

"I'll be damned—your pardon." He gave her the by-now familiar wry grin. "We're already finished?"

"We are, for today." She had recovered enough to hide her relief. "Have you any idea at all of what took place?"

He frowned. "Was I talking? I seem to remember talking. The subject quite escapes me. I hope I wasn't too much of a bore?"

"Not at all. You were an excellent subject. Limited amnesia is not rare in such cases." She noted that her words emerged without the quaver she'd feared. If he wondered how he had wakened in such a compromising position, he was too much the gentleman to say so. He showed no indication of repeating his previous behavior, or any consciousness of his most amazing claims.

"Yes," she said, smoothing her bodice. "The groundwork has been laid. I understand more clearly how I might help you."

Unease appeared briefly in his eyes. "Just what did I say?"

"I am your doctor. All you said is held in confidence. I shall not judge you, Quentin."

"Then there was something to judge." He sighed. "I know my life has hardly been a model of rectitude . . ."

She was on firm ground again. "Sit down, Quentin. There is one thing I do wish to discuss. You must tell me if the subject distresses you."

He braced himself with his hands on the edge of the chaise. "Go on. I'm ready."

"Have you ever heard the word . . . *lycanthropy?*"

He burst into a laugh, and kept laughing for a full half-minute.

"Forgive me," he said, wiping tears from his eyes. "What exactly did I tell you?"

"You told me that you are a loup-garou. A werewolf."

He caught his laugh before it could break free again. "How very amusing. I appear to be quite imaginative while hypnotized. Do you think I missed my calling as a writer of Gothic tales for hot-blooded young ladies?"

Johanna stood and paced to her desk, as if movement alone could calm her racing thoughts. In her experience, subjects under hypnosis could not easily lie. Whatever her doubts about his state after Harper's interruption, she knew he'd been deeply entranced during the first period of questioning. His admission had been real . . . then.

Was this the delusion that led him to drink—one that consumed his unconscious but did not reach his waking mind? How had such a thing come about? What had brought so strange a belief into existence?

"What do you know of lycanthropy?" she asked, swinging to face him.

"As much as anyone, I suppose." He shrugged. "Tales of Gypsy curses and witches donning wolf skins." His eyes twinkled. "Do you wish to search my person for a wolf skin, Johanna?"

No, he certainly was not aware of what he'd said while hypnotized. The issue must be explored in future sessions. She felt sure it was important. Most important.

Legends of werewolves were filled with blood and death. Quentin was incapable of violence, but the image of the beast must have great symbolic meaning, the root of everything that troubled him.

"That will not be necessary," she said. "I believe our meeting is over for today, and I wish to consider the results of this session." *Including my own behavior.* "I did not deal directly with your desire for alcohol. Do you feel any need to drink?"

"Not unless it be from your sweet lips."

Was this simply more trifling gallantry, or had he some memory of his recent advances? She was not prepared to face the consequences of confronting him on the subject. Not while she was still so rattled by the experience. And so ashamed.

"Well, then," she said, ignoring his comment. "You may do as you like until luncheon. Harper requires my attention—"

"Is something wrong with him?"

"His illness may have entered a new phase, and I have neglected him." *Because of you.*

"Then I won't keep you."

The moment he was out of the room, Johanna let her rubbery legs give way and sat down, hard. She touched her lips. They still throbbed from Quentin's kisses. Her whole body throbbed. In spite of her thorough knowledge of the biological processes involved, she wouldn't soon be able to dismiss the experience as a mere consequence of her profession.

All the theorizing in the world, all the calm admissions of physical attraction, were no match for the reality.

She had violated the unwritten rules pronouncing that a physician must not become involved with a patient. She could easily have taken control by pushing him away and ending the session—making him understand that such contact between them was entirely inappropriate.

Instead, she'd learned something about herself that was difficult to face, a sign of personal weakness she couldn't afford.

Her disciplined mind had failed her. She'd given in to the desires of her body, as witless as any callow girl.

She rested her head in her hands. How ironic. For Quentin, who must find this sort of thing so easy, the dalliance was forgotten in posthypnotic amnesia. While she, who had abandoned all thought of courtship or love, found herself plunged into the maelstrom all over again.

She picked up her pen with a shaking hand and realized it was the one Quentin had broken. One edge was sharp enough to cut. She swept the pieces to the side of her desk, located another pen in a drawer, and laid out Quentin's casebook.

Initial observations after first hypnotic session:
Patient suffers from delusions of lycanthropy: conse-
quence of former experience in army and childhood?
Prognosis:

Her fingers ached from her fierce grip on the pen. She let it fall. No amount of staring at what she'd written could make Quentin Forster fit neatly between the lines.

Only curing him would bring an end to this . . . this madness. But cure him she must, no matter how long it took.

Only then could she cure herself.

Quentin *slipped out of the house on silent feet, bound* for the forest on the hill.

He passed through the garden and jumped the low whitewashed fence without meeting any of the other patients. For that he was grateful; his mouth felt as empty of words as a spring gone dry of water. The only thing it was good for now was kissing Johanna.

And *that* had been a mistake.

The land rose abruptly from the Haven's little niche of the Napa Valley. Live oaks and pines marched up the hills and into low mountains, another kind of haven for the wild creatures that made this sylvan paradise their home.

Quentin removed his shoes and stockings a few yards

into the woods. He sighed as his feet sank into the soil, made up of the memories of countless autumns and the richly scented dust of pine. He smelled some small animal nearby, a rabbit frozen in fear of a potential hunter. At the base of a massive, red-barked conifer, a larger animal had left its clawed mark.

Life was all around him—life other than human. A life he'd all but left behind. He needed to be reminded of it now.

He started up the steep hillside, drinking in the forest through his feet and with every breath. This country wasn't like Northumberland, with its bare, broad moors and patches of ancient woodland. But it would do. It would more than suffice.

If he could find the courage to Change.

A faint path stretched out before him, worn into the prosperous, sun-dappled earth. Deliberately he left it, breaking into a lope that was as natural to him as superhuman senses. He leaped a small, deep ravine that carried the scent of recent moisture. The steep incline beyond challenged him to a faster pace, and he went up and up until his muscles burned and his clothing was damp with perspiration.

At the top of the hill he paused. The Valley spread out below, a patchwork of vineyards and fields with another range of hills on the opposite side, dominated by the crag-topped Mount St. Helena. Civilization held in the arms of the wilderness.

The image made him groan. His mind was full of similar comparisons, every one having to do with tangled bodies and naked flesh.

His flesh. Johanna's body. A body made for loving. And a mouth . . .

Bloody hell. He still wasn't sure what had made him do it. The decision to kiss Johanna had been spur of the moment, sprung fully grown from a source unbound by reason. He tried to remember his chain of thought beforehand: had he meant it as a joke on the too-serious doctor, a pleasant experiment to test the full extent of his interest in her . . . and hers in him? To see just how far the Valkyrie would melt when she thought she was safe?

That he'd been in a trance for some time he had no doubt. But something had snapped him out of it, and he'd wakened to find Johanna gone. That was when the compulsion struck him, as if he'd temporarily become someone else. Someone who didn't let moral compunction stand in the way of his desires.

The mere recollection of what followed made him ache with wanting. She hadn't pushed him away. She'd responded. God, how she'd responded. And he might have pursued the encounter to its inevitable conclusion if his sense, and hers, hadn't returned just in time.

So he'd grabbed the way out she offered, pretending to be unaware of what he'd done. And she'd acted the same . . . except for the flush in her cheeks, the hesitation in her speech. And the ambrosial scent of a woman aroused.

Quentin pulled his hand through his hair. He'd never been one for celibacy, but getting close to a woman—to anyone—was dangerous the way his life was now. He felt it; he knew it, with all the instincts nature had provided his kind.

He'd gotten himself hopelessly tangled up in Johanna's world. No matter how readily she responded to him, she wouldn't take physical involvement lightly, even if her morals permitted it. She'd buried her own desires so that she could cater, undistracted, to the needs of others. For all her intellect, she was half-blind to the power of her femininity.

And that made her vulnerable.

He knew he could seduce her, awaken the sensual woman under the Valkyrie's armor. He was very good at seduction. She didn't have werewolf senses to give her a fighting chance—only the frank, unwavering gaze that so clearly saw everyone but herself.

But these fantasies that passed through his mind were constructions of air. He still clung to the shredded façade of a gentleman. There could be no passing relationship with Doctor Johanna Schell: Either she remained his doctor, or she became something more. Something no one, human or werewolf, had ever been to him. Could never be, as long as he didn't *remember.*

You got yourself into this, he thought. *You chose to stay and accept her help. You can just as easily get yourself out again.*

By moving on.

He closed his eyes and fought for a sliver of fortitude. He hadn't Changed in many months, at least not that he remembered. Even the thought of Changing awakened vague fears of those blank periods that sent him scurrying from one saloon to another, one town to the next. Always wondering what he might have done. Carrying with him only a foul taste of menace, and violence, and darkness.

He'd told Johanna, under hypnosis, that he was a werewolf. She, logical creature that she was, would safely assume that the outlandish claim was just another symptom of his illness.

She wouldn't believe that he was more than human.

Had he ceased to believe it himself?

Time to find out.

He unbuttoned his borrowed shirt and stripped it off, placing it neatly on a flat rock where it would remain unsoiled. A warm summer breeze caressed his skin, teasing the short hairs on his chest. Already he felt the old sense of blessed freedom that came with the Change.

His trousers were next, folded and laid atop the shirt, and then his drawers. Naked, he stretched until his spine cracked and his hands extended toward the sun as if to borrow its vast energy.

But a different kind of energy filled him, and he imagined Johanna there on the hill. Watching him. Waiting for evidence that he was not entirely mad.

His manhood leapt to life again, stirring with sexual hunger. It was all too easy to picture Johanna naked beside him, under him, her full breasts pushing against his chest, round hips cradling him, strong thighs clasped about his waist as he entered her.

Aching with unrequited lust, he forced physical longing into a more useful channel. He gave himself up to the Change.

It took no more than a few moments for his body to remember its other shape. He melted into an ether of formlessness, floating between two realities, and when his feet touched ground again they were four instead of two.

He shook his coat to test its weight, sucked in a deep lungful of air that was sharper and richer than any human could conceive. A mouse had passed this way an hour ago, leaving tiny droppings. He could hear the distant cry of a hawk in search of the mouse's unfortunate cousin. Wind soughed in the tops of the pines, carrying the scent of a bird's nest and a pair of quarreling squirrels.

Under his paws the earth spoke in a language known only to the beasts. It urged him to run as only his kind could run, able to outpace the swiftest deer and outlast even the ordinary wolves the loups-garous resembled.

There were no wolves left here. They'd long since been killed off by hunters and settlers, driven to more northerly climes. Quentin had the hills and the woods to himself.

He gave in to the call and burst into a dead run from the very place he stood. He plunged among the trees and raced west, higher into the hills. Hardly a branch stirred at his passing. His paws were silent as they struck the ground, curved nails biting deep and releasing. Muscles bunched and lengthened with the perfect efficiency of a machine, and with far more grace. He let his tongue loll between his teeth in a grin of sheer happiness.

This was the way he'd always lived before: for the present, driving away memory in the pursuit of pleasure, whether it came in the form of sex or drink or games of chance . . . or the Change itself. *This* was the only escape that held a trace of honor.

He ran until he reached the crest of the summit dividing one valley from the next. Napa lay behind him, and another cultivated land spread under his gaze from the foot of the range to the silver ocean miles away. Beyond that ocean were other lands, India among them . . .

Suddenly cold, he crouched low and whined in his throat. Fear was back. And it seemed that somewhere inside him a presence reached out, took him by the scruff of the neck, and shook him furiously back and forth, this way and that, until he began to slip out of his skin.

No.

He howled. He jumped to his feet, turned about, and fled as if that same dark presence were a thing he could evade.

Time lost its meaning. He only became sensible of it again when the last stain of sunset bled away behind the western range. He found himself at the foot of the hill beside the Haven's whitewashed fence.

Instinct had carried him to the nearest thing to home he possessed.

As a wolf he lacked the ability to laugh, but inwardly he roared. What was the use in contemplating flight—from his lust, from Johanna, from facing the secrets she might expose—if even his lupine self turned against him?

Exhausted, he circled the house to the back door, tail tucked and head low. He wouldn't go to Johanna. He wasn't ready to face her yet.

What he needed was a good stiff drink. If anything resembling one could be had in this place, he'd sniff it out.

The door was open a crack; it was easy for him to nose his way in. No one saw him. He crept down the hall until he reached Harper's room, and stopped at the sound of weeping from within. The door swung in at the tap of his forefoot.

Harper sat in his chair by the window, a tray of half-eaten food on the table beside him. Quentin entered the room, keeping to the shadows along the wall.

Harper didn't notice. Tears streaked his face and pooled in his beard. The rasping noises he made were too soft to be heard by anyone outside the room, unless the listener were more than human. Harper had sanity enough to wish to hide his shame.

Driven by a sense of kinship and pity he didn't fully understand, Quentin padded to Harper's side and touched his nose to the man's dangling fingers. Harper's hand twitched. He shifted in the chair and felt blindly, touching Quentin's muzzle, his forehead, his ears.

"Here, boy," he said, his voice little more than a rattle. "That's a good dog." He stroked Quentin's head with the utmost gentleness.

Quentin stood still, his heart tight in his chest. Hadn't Johanna said something about Harper responding to a dog she'd brought to visit? Harper thought that he was a dog. A natural assumption for a man so detached from the world.

But he'd spoken, to a creature he believed could not judge him. The contact was oddly comforting to them both. Quentin closed his eyes and sighed.

"Don't worry, boy. I'll—" The stroking stopped. Quentin opened his eyes to find Harper gazing down at him, the light from the lamp on the table picking out the gaunt features of his face. His breath came faster, and his hand clenched in the fur of Quentin's mane.

"You," he whispered. "What are you?" The empty, distant look in his eyes sloughed away like a snake's skin, leaving them clear and almost sane.

Quentin could have sworn that those eyes saw him for what he was—saw past the fur and recognized the soul beneath.

He slipped free of Harper's grip and backed away. Harper stared after him, hand poised in midair.

"Don't," he said.

Voices sounded from the hallway. Quentin scrambled out of the room and ran for the back door just ahead of them. He charged straight up the hill without stopping until he reached the place where he'd left his clothes.

Panting hard, he Changed. The air had grown cool, and his bare skin ran with goosebumps as he snatched up his drawers.

Harper *knew*. He wasn't gifted with a werewolf's powers, but there was something about him . . . something that made him different, an outsider among his own kind.

Perhaps they *were* kin, after all.

He started back down the hill, skidding on the matted pine needles.

"Are you running away?"

He spun around at the whispered words. The unexpected intruder resolved into a girl, slight as a doe, the usual book tucked under her arm. May.

"What are you doing out so late?" he demanded. "It isn't safe—"

His words came out more harshly than he'd intended, and she recoiled. He recognized that look. She was expecting to be berated, punished, struck, all because he'd raised his voice to her.

"I'm sorry," he said. "I'm a brute. Forgive me."

Her tightly coiled muscles loosened. "Are you angry with me?"

Damnation. As little as he knew of the child, in spite of the very few insignificant words they'd exchanged, he felt an unaccountably fierce desire to protect her. What had Johanna said? "I have no objection to your speaking with her . . . *if* you are very careful. It might help her to realize that not all men are—"

She hadn't finished the sentence, but he could fill in the

rest. He'd seen his share of cruelty in his wanderings. God help anyone who raised a hand to her in his presence.

"Of course I'm not angry," he said, crouching to her level. "I was only worried about you. Worried that you might be running away."

"Not from this place. I like it here. I like—" She bit her lip. "You aren't leaving, are you?"

A few moments past he couldn't have answered that question. Johanna had said that May's mother had left her at the Haven two years ago. Abandoned her, from the look of it. Had this girl known anything but maltreatment and neglect in her former life?

Even his cowardice had its limits. He'd be damned before he added to her pain.

"No, May," he said, "I'm not leaving." He offered his hand. "I seem to have forgotten my shoes. Will you help me find them?"

She smiled—a heartbreaking, elusive thing—and took his hand.

They returned to the house together. A woman stood in the back doorway, lantern held aloft, waiting to guide the errant strays back to safety.

Quentin stopped before her. "You can douse the lamp, my dear doctor," he said, grinning past the lump in his throat. "I'm here to stay."

Chapter 9

Johanna sat up in her bed, throwing off the covers with a jerk. She came to full wakefulness a moment later.

Only a dream. Odd; she so seldom remembered her dreams, and nightmares like this were rarer still. Something about running . . . away from a threat without solid shape, a creature that panted after her, never more than a step or two behind.

A wolf had run at her side. She had felt no fear of the beast, only a sense of companionship and well-being. She remembered arguing with it, about whether to stand and fight, or run; the wolf had won the argument. So they fled, to no avail. At the very last instant, when the thing had almost caught up with them, the wolf whirled about and crouched, a shield between her and their pursuer. And from the mouth of the amorphous shadow came Quentin's baritone, strangely altered: *"I'm here to stay."*

Considering the ridiculous nature of the dream, she ought not to have found it so disturbing.

She pushed her heavy hair away from her face and

swung her legs over the side of the bed. For the first time since adolescence she subjected her large, sturdy feet to a critical examination. Vanity was something she'd dispensed with long ago, as being of no use to a female physician in a world of men, and quite pointless in her particular case. She was not beautiful, nor of the dainty sort so many men preferred.

"You pretend to be a man," Rolf had said, all those years past. He had not meant it as a compliment. It was one of the last things Rolf ever said to her before they formally ended their engagement.

He had found her overwhelming, unwomanly. Quentin didn't. The fact that she was comparing the two men troubled her.

She went to the washbasin and bathed her face, neck, and arms with tepid water. A bath would be welcome this evening, if there was time. Mrs. Daugherty was off today, which meant that Johanna would be serving up the meals, conducting Irene and Lewis through their sessions, visiting with May, looking after Papa—he was very much in need of a walk outside in the fresh air—and supervising Oscar in his various activities and chores. She would spend an hour with Harper, hoping to get some further response from him. And then there was Quentin.

She stared at her face in the mirror above the basin. A plain, somewhat ruddy face with high cheekbones, full lips, a slightly snubbed nose—thoroughly Germanic. Serviceable. Honest. All she needed for her work, where trust and compassion mattered far more than beauty.

Quentin had kissed those lips. She touched her mouth. It didn't throb anymore.

Her threadbare cotton nightgown lay against her body like a second skin. She peeled it off and studied her figure with severe objectivity.

Broad shoulders—too broad for the current taste. Full breasts. They might be considered by some to be an asset.

Her waist was small enough in proportion, but her hips more than made up for what her waist lacked in inches. Childbearer's hips, in a woman who would almost certainly never bear a child.

Long, strong legs. Arms more like a washerwoman's than a lady's. Large hands.

They seemed small when she was with Quentin.

"Ha," she scoffed, shaking her head. *"Du kannst immer noch ein Dummkopf sein, Johanna."*

She dressed as efficiently as always in austere underdrawers, chemise, a single petticoat, and a mended but perfectly adequate dress several years out of date, meant to be worn with a bustle she didn't own. Homely but sensible shoes. She put up her hair in the regular, utilitarian style, taking no more time on it than she ever did.

Oscar was already at the breakfast table, while Irene lounged at the kitchen door in her wrap, looking out at the bright morning with infinite boredom. Lewis seated himself quietly in his corner. May peeped in the window and dropped from sight.

Quentin made no appearance. Sleeping late, as he was no doubt in the habit of doing.

She realized that she'd been holding her breath, wondering if there would be a lingering awkwardness in facing him. For her own part, she had strengthened her determination to forget yesterday's blunder.

Forget, and forgive herself.

She served up day-old bread, cheese from the pantry, Gertrude's fresh milk, and overcooked eggs, which only Irene complained about. During breakfast, she engaged each of the patients in conversation. Irene and Lewis seemed less inclined to trade their accustomed barbs, but Oscar was his usual irrepressible self, telling of a bird's nest he and May had found in the woods, and the big red dog he'd tried to chase up the hill.

"It was mighty purty," he said. "And big, too. I wanted to pet it."

"Stay away from stray dogs," Lewis said unexpectedly. "They may bite." He paused to divide his second egg into a precise grid of bite-sized pieces.

"Don't you like dogs, Mr. Andersen?" Oscar asked.

"He doesn't like anything." Irene sniffed.

Lewis looked up, his gray eyes bitter with animosity. " 'Judge not lest ye be judged.' "

"That's terribly amusing," Irene said. "Weren't you the kind of preacher who called fire and brimstone down on everyone else in the world?" She leaned on the table, her breasts spilling over the edge of her dressing gown. "I know your kind. People like you are so afraid of their own lusts that they see evil in everyone else."

Johanna looked sharply at Irene, hearing the ring of honesty in her voice. She remembered her resolve to speak to the actress about the new gown—one more thing she'd let slip because of her preoccupation with Quentin.

Lewis shot up from his chair, face pale. "You . . . you— I saw you sneak off into town last night, when you thought no one saw. 'As a jewel of gold in a swine's snout, so is a fair woman which is without discretion.' "

Johanna stood, demanding their attention with her silence. "This is not a place of judgment," she said. "We are here to help one another. Irene, I'll have a word with you after breakfast, in my office."

Irene pressed her lips together and seethed. Oscar, sensitive to arguments, hunched over his plate. Johanna patted his shoulder and reminded him of the game they were to play later that day. He brightened and finished his breakfast.

May didn't repeat yesterday's daring foray into the kitchen, so Johanna left a plate on the doorstep for her. The girl needed more attention than she'd had of late. Johanna planned to lure her into a talk with the promise of a new book she'd brought back from San Francisco, and took a breakfast tray to Harper.

Harper wasn't in his chair. He wasn't even in his room.

Alarmed, Johanna set down the tray and ran into the hall. The back door stood open. She stepped through the doorway and found Harper sitting on the wooden bench in the garden, his hands hanging between his knees.

"Harper," she said.

He turned his head. "Doc," he croaked. "Is that you?"

She closed her eyes and whispered a childhood prayer. "Good morning, Harper. How are you feeling?"

"Tired," he said. "Hungry. Like I've been asleep for a long, long time."

How long had it been since he'd said so many words, with such perfect rationality? It sometimes happened that patients spontaneously emerged from a deep melancholy or cataleptic state, but she hadn't envisioned such a favorable development with Harper.

She masked her excitement and smiled in encouragement. Keep the conversation casual. Let him take the lead.

"I was just about to bring you your breakfast," she said.

"Much obliged." He squinted at her, as if looking into the light. "Where's the dog?"

She felt another surge of hope. His memory must be functioning if he could recall not only her name, but also a brief visit that had occurred months before. "The dog I brought to the Haven in April?"

He shook his head. "Last night. It was last night."

You cannot afford to be overly optimistic, she warned herself. "I'm sorry, Harper. There was no dog here last night."

"It was in my room, right beside me," he said with soft-spoken conviction.

Was he hallucinating? If so, she must tread all the more carefully. "I've left a tray for you in your room," she said. "Would you care to come in?"

"Do you think I could eat out here?" He raised his face to the sky. "The sun's so warm."

"Yes, Harper, of course. I'll return directly."

She left Harper basking in the sunshine and hurried into the house to retrieve the tray. On the way out she noticed that Quentin's door was open, and paused to glance inside. The bed was neatly made, but he wasn't there.

Gott sei Dank. No distractions from that direction . . .

Her relief was short-lived. Harper wasn't alone in the garden. Quentin stood beside the bench, bare-chested, his freshly mended shirt draped over his shoulder. Johanna forgot the tray in her hands.

She gazed mutely at Quentin's back, wide through the shoulders and trim at the waist, and observed with fascination the flex of his muscles as he put on the shirt. Hot prickles stabbed at the base of her spine. Her mouth went dry.

He turned around, feigning surprise. "Johanna. I didn't see you there."

Disregarding the heat in her cheeks, she set the tray down on the bench beside Harper. The former soldier's gaunt face broke into a smile.

"Thank you, ma'am," he said. "It looks delicious."

"You may call me Johanna," she said. "I see you've met Quentin."

"I just got up myself," Quentin offered. "We've been talking."

Johanna looked from Quentin to Harper in concern. They seemed at ease with each other, though she couldn't imagine that Harper had done much of the talking. And while she knew Quentin to be kind, he hadn't her training in dealing with those who'd been seriously ill. He was ill himself.

Yet she had admitted that he had a way with people. Harper had reacted to his presence the first time Quentin visited him in his room. They shared an experience of war and conflict that she did not.

There was so much she had yet to learn, and needed to know, about both men. Would fellow soldiers confide in one another as they wouldn't with a civilian, even their physician?

Her instincts told her that this was an unorthodox but legitimate approach. Harper and Quentin might actually help each other.

It was worth considering, in due course.

"You mustn't tire yourself, Harper," she said. "When you're finished, I'd like you to return to your room and rest. Quentin—" She glanced at him, not permitting her gaze to drift to the open collar of his shirt. "Would you kindly locate May and ask her to come to the parlor? I'm sure she's somewhere about. I have something to give her. You and I shall meet for our next session in my office at three this afternoon."

"I am at your disposal, Doctor," he said, clicking his heels with a British soldier's precision. The gesture was uncharacteristically formal, as if he'd sensed the conflict in her mind and respected it.

"Harper," Quentin said, nodding to the other man. "We'll talk again."

"Yes," Harper said. He watched Quentin stride off toward the woods. Without intending to, Johanna did the same. She recalled Harper's presence only when he gave a low cough.

"A good man," he said.

"Yes." She didn't feel prepared to elaborate on that subject at the moment. She noted with pleasure that Harper had finished his meal; his appetite had returned along with his reason, "If you are still hungry, I can bring you more. Shall we go in?"

Harper struggled to his feet, and Johanna helped him regain his balance.

"Sorry . . . I'm not in better shape, ma'am," he said, flushing.

"You have been confined to your room for many months," she said. "You must be patient in recovering your previous strength." She let him take the next few steps on his own. "How much do you remember?"

He felt his beard, testing its neatly trimmed length. "I remember you, ma'am. The room, and the dog. I can't rightly say that I remember much else."

"That is not surprising. You came to stay with us—my father and me—some time ago. You've been ill, and we hoped to make you better."

"Am I?" He met her gaze with warm hazel eyes, so mild that it was difficult to believe that he'd ever had bouts of manic, even violent behavior.

Even the insane deserved as much honesty as possible. "It is too soon to be sure," she said. "But until this morning, you were not speaking. Now you are. I would like to talk more with you about what has happened, and how you feel."

Depending on how much he did remember, and how stable he seemed, she would gradually introduce the idea of hypnosis and gauge his reaction. In the meantime, she'd spend a few hours each day simply talking, and allowing him to do so.

And if Quentin's company seemed beneficial . . .

Be methodical, Johanna. One step at a time.

Harper was reachable, but far from well. Quentin seemed normal on the surface, but so much was locked away underneath.

There was no telling what might happen in the coming weeks.

Excited, even flustered in a way she considered most singular, she escorted Harper to his room to rest and threw herself into her daily routine. First she met Irene in her office and asked about the woman's new gown. Irene, unsurprisingly, was evasive; after steady questioning, she admitted that she had gone into town to buy the cloth and pattern, and made the gown herself. She pressed her lips together rebelliously when Johanna reminded her that she was not to leave the Haven grounds unescorted. Nothing could induce her to explain how she'd come by the money to purchase the rich fabric for such a garment.

Johanna dismissed Irene and considered the problem. Short of confining the actress to her room, she couldn't be sure that Irene wouldn't visit Silverado Springs again. If she took the woman into town with her more frequently, perhaps Irene's desire to "sneak out" might be lessened.

Satisfied with that temporary solution, Johanna dealt with her father's needs and visited with him for half an hour, pretending that she didn't miss his imperturbable good humor and wise council. Oscar was kept busy with a new puzzle Johanna had ordered, made especially for him by a craftsman in town—one just difficult enough to stretch his mind without causing tears and frustration.

Quentin was as good as his word, and delivered May to the parlor before making himself scarce again. May showed every inclination of wanting to trail after him, but her pallid face lit up when she saw the book Johanna had brought back from San Francisco. Books were the single topic of discussion in which May could become as eloquent as any young girl her age.

Or had been, until Quentin. Johanna suspected she could be encouraged to talk about him with very little effort. She trusted him. Could he be instrumental in helping the girl overcome her remaining fears?

If she continued to think this way, Johanna mused, she'd be forced to acknowledge Quentin as a colleague.

She buried that thought at the bottom of her mind.

Just after luncheon, she conducted a moderately successful meeting with Lewis. If he was not improving as rapidly as he had in the past, at least he was not losing ground. Irene, as usual, was utterly uncooperative and couldn't be drawn into more than the lightest of trances. She was still far from the breakthrough Johanna hoped for.

Quentin appeared at Johanna's office precisely at three o'clock, nonchalant and seemingly at ease about the coming session. Johanna waved him in and closed the door.

"Harper has made quite an improvement, I take it?" he asked.

"Indeed. I have never seen him so lucid, not since he came to us." She gathered the hypnotic paraphernalia and drew up her chair. "Now I will be able to begin working to heal the source of his madness."

Quentin moved toward her. She stood very still and waited, half afraid that he might touch her. He stopped well short of the chair and developed a sudden interest in the view out the window.

"He appears to enjoy your company," she said. "He would benefit from a friend of his own age and gender."

He looked at her. "His recovery means a great deal to you, doesn't it?"

"I have been unable to help him. Now—"

"Now there's a chance." His cinnamon eyes were darker than she remembered, filled with emotions she couldn't interpret. "I hope he knows how lucky he is."

"Science, discipline, and care will heal him, not luck."

"And you," he said softly. "The most essential factor."

She dropped her gaze. "What did you speak of, the two of you?"

"Not much. He briefly mentioned the War. I didn't press him."

"Did he show any signs of distress, or violence?"

"He displayed little feeling at all."

And neither, at this moment, did Quentin. "But he said something that troubled you," she guessed.

"No. No. He reminds me . . . of men I once knew."

And of himself. The hidden self she had yet to discover.

"If you're ready, Quentin," she said, "we will go ahead with the hypnosis."

He took up her suggestion with alacrity and settled on the chaise. She repeated the induction methods of the previous meeting, and Quentin fell into a trance with even less resistance than before.

Nothing else went as hoped. She was unable to coax from him a single new fact or memory about his time in the army, his drinking, his lycanthropy, or his childhood. Either he was not in as deep a trance as she surmised, or he had, since the last meeting, developed much stronger barriers. He might not even be aware he had done so.

At least he didn't resume his amorous advances. He remained detached and as far away as the moon.

She brought him out two hours later. He asked no questions; in fact, he seemed eager to be on his way. Johanna banished her doubts at the disappointing results of the session. She knew her own skill and worth as a doctor. Patience was the remedy for such setbacks—patience, and a firm grasp of a scientist's objectivity. Progress was merely delayed.

What she required was a greater distance from Quentin. He would benefit from the same. The most efficient way to achieve that goal was in the company of others. He should socialize with all the patients, become one of the group.

"I would like you to join us on our walk tonight," she said at the door. "We shall gather in the parlor in a few minutes."

His smile held the same outward amiability as always. "Of course, Doctor. I'll be there."

Just after five o'clock she assembled the patients—all but Harper—together in the parlor for their thrice-weekly evening stroll. Papa was strapped into his special wheelchair, showing some interest in the proceedings, and Oscar was openly eager for the excursion. Lewis wore the black overcoat and gloves he always donned no matter what the weather. Irene was defiantly dressed in a gown and shoes entirely inappropriate for the outing, her way of protesting the exercise, and possibly of showing off to Quentin. May waited outside the door, prepared to trail behind them—at a safe distance, as always.

"Please return to your room and put on more suitable shoes," Johanna told Irene. "You'll hurt your feet, and that is of no benefit to your health—or beauty."

It was an argument that generally worked with the former actress. She flounced back to her room and reappeared wearing low-heeled, button-top shoes that looked ridiculous with the gown.

They set out on the wagon path that led away from the house, south toward the road. Johanna took the lead, pushing her father's chair, followed by Oscar, Quentin, Lewis, Irene, and May.

The day's heat was dissipating at last. Birds darted from one tree to the next, absorbed in their evening songs, and the angled sunlight splashed the fields and trees and scattered farm buildings with liquid gold.

Quentin caught up with her after a quarter of a mile. Johanna took a firmer grip on her father's chair and fixed a neutral smile on her face.

"It's beautiful in this valley," he said, slowing his stride to match her pace. "I don't think I was able to appreciate it when I first arrived."

This was the perfect opportunity to set the tone of their future relationship. "It is lovely. The region where my father grew up, near Mainz, was not dissimilar."

"The Rheinhessen?"

"Yes. You have been there?"

"Once. I did some traveling in Europe now and then. I've even read a bit of German literature: *"Was vernünftig ist, das ist wirklich; und was virklich ist, das is vernünftig."*"

Her father looked up at Quentin and laughed. "That will

never do, my boy," he said. *"'Was vernünftig ist, das is wirklich; und was virklich ist, das ist vernünftig.'"*

Startled by his participation, Johanna saw that his eyes were clear and focused, his expression animated. Quentin executed a sideways bow.

"I stand corrected, *Herr Doktor.* Do you agree with Hegel's sentiments? 'What is reasonable is real; that which is real is reasonable.'"

"I would not dare argue with the great philosopher," Papa said, shaking his head. "I am but a simple physician."

"That I very much doubt. Hegel also said: 'It is easier to discover a deficiency in individuals, in states, and in Providence, than to see their real import and value.'"

Johanna felt a burst of happiness. The conversation was entirely rational, and Quentin talked to her father as if he were an equal, not an enfeebled old man.

"Ha!" Papa slapped his right hand down on the arm of his wheelchair. "Why did you never introduce me to this young man before, Johanna? He shows great promise." He squinted up at Quentin. "Are you the new doctor? Forgive me, my memory sometimes fails me. I believe you will do very well here. *Ja, sehr gut . . .*" He lapsed into silence, withdrawing into his own thoughts.

"You were expecting another doctor?" Quentin said to Johanna under his breath.

"We had been discussing finding a third doctor to join us at the Schell Asylum in Pennsylvania, in order to expand our practice." She touched her father's head lightly, smoothing his thin gray hair. "It was Papa's dream. He fell ill before we could complete it."

"I'm sorry. We have so little control over our destinies."

He spoke of himself as well as Papa, but she would not permit self-pity. "I do not believe that. There is much we can do to influence what some regard as fate."

"Yes. You'd do battle with the gods themselves, wouldn't you?"

She heard no mockery in his voice, only genuine admiration. It was in his face as well, in his eyes. She brought Papa's wheelchair to a stop and turned away from Quentin to check on the others.

Oscar galloped past on an invisible pony, hooting and kicking up dust. Lewis's coattails flapped like the wings of a great crow. Irene walked as if she were on the stage, each sway of her hips exaggerated. May stopped as soon as Johanna did, maintaining the same precise distance behind, but her gaze sought Quentin with visible longing.

"We will take a short rest," Johanna announced, "and then return to the house." She wheeled her father onto the tawny grass at the edge of the path. They were not far from the place where she'd first discovered Quentin. She wondered if he remembered.

He sat down on the ground beside the wheelchair, plucking a dry stalk and placing it between his teeth. "Our session today wasn't very successful, was it?"

She loosened the strap that held her father safely in the chair. "Progress is not always steady. It is necessary to be patient. At least you've shown no craving for drink."

"I haven't had the opportunity. I suppose I could go into town—"

"Not while you are in my care."

"Warning noted." He patted the ground beside him. "Sit. Even doctors are allowed to rest from time to time, you know."

To decline his invitation would imply that she found his nearness disquieting. She tucked up her skirts and sat down a few feet away. Irene, on the opposite side of the path, was searching fastidiously for a rock to serve as a chair. Oscar ran around and around the field.

"I wish I could be a more promising subject," Quentin said. He tossed the stalk of grass aside. "I fear my presence at the Haven contributes very little."

She opened her mouth on a vehement protest. *That is not*

true, she almost said. *You are important . . . important to Harper. To May.*

To—

"You have already agreed to pay," she said quickly.

"And you have yet to take any of my money," he countered. "You said that everyone here does his or her share of the work at the Haven, but you haven't asked me to do anything." His lids drifted half-shut over his eyes. "I'm not really as lazy as I look."

How could any man's voice be so . . . suggestive . . . even when it spoke the most innocuous words? "I shall think of something," she said. "Have you any skill in carpentry? The house needs repairs, as does the barn."

"You'll find I'm also very resourceful." He plucked a wildflower and twirled its stem between his fingers. "Tell me, Johanna—you've spoken of your father's dreams. What of yours?"

She wasn't prepared for the change of topic. "My dreams are the same as my father's. To help and heal those who suffer, using the techniques he developed—"

"I don't mean your goals as a doctor. What do you want as a woman, Johanna?"

The question was much too personal, but she wouldn't let him see how it affected her. "I do not see why the two should be different."

"Most women I've known long for a family. A marriage, children."

"I would hazard a guess that most of the women you knew in England were of your own class."

"You don't think of yourself as being in my class?"

"My father is of the *gebildete Stände,* the educated class, but hardly an aristocrat. My mother was a merchant's daughter."

"But you must confess that you are a woman, Johanna."

I have been told in no uncertain terms that I am not a normal woman at all. "I do not deny my biology."

"Science," he said. "It isn't the answer for everything."

" 'To him who looks upon the world rationally, the world in its turn presents a rational aspect,' " she quoted.

"More Hegel? I have another for you: 'We may affirm absolutely that nothing great in the world has been accomplished without passion.' "

He was playing with her again, and she could not simply dismiss it as she wished to. "My passion is for my work, as was my father's."

"Did he love your mother?"

She pushed to her feet, brushing off her skirt with more vigor than was strictly necessary. "Yes. As I loved her. You may rest assured that I have known love, Mr. Forster."

He stood up behind her, close enough that his breath teased her hair. "I never doubted that you've given love. I only wonder if you have kept enough for yourself."

His words had the unexpected effect of thrusting her into the past—her past. In an instant she was back in the parlor of the house in Philadelphia, and Rolf was the one standing behind her.

Chapter 10

"You must choose, Johanna: lock yourself away in this unwomanly profession or become what you were meant to be." His hands settled on her hips, molded themselves to her breasts. "This body was meant to be loved and bear children. Don't deny what you are—"

She turned to face him. "I cannot abandon what it is in me to be. Of course I wish to marry you, and to have children. But I am good at what I do. I can help others who desperately need it." She met his gaze steadily. "Why must I be the one to choose? Would you give up being a physician for my sake?"

He laughed. "Always so rational. You pretend to be a man. Do you have a heart like a normal woman, or is it a machine within your breast?"

His accusation hurt as little had done since Mama's death. She'd never believed it would come to this—that he, a doctor like herself, who'd once encouraged her in her studies, should betray her now and demand such a sacrifice.

"I wish only to be your equal, Rolf. Your partner—"

He pulled her roughly into his arms and kissed her: a hard, punishing kiss that bruised her mouth. It left her cold and dead inside. This was not the Rolf she knew.

Or had she simply been wrong from the start? Her skill was a threat to him. He did not want her to succeed. If she had used her vaunted intelligence, she should have seen the signs, the symptoms that had led to this moment.

"You will never be my equal, Johanna," Rolf said, pushing away from her, "or any man's, though you pretend to be one. And no other man will want what you are becoming. You'll be lonely the rest of your life, old and barren and dried up inside."

She understood then that he was right. She'd run into many obstacles during her years of study, confronted many men who thought she defied the very role God had intended for all of her sex.

Rolf had changed . . . and so had she.

So be it.

Her face felt stiff, a mask of marble without life. "If you and the world ask me to choose between my heart and my intellect, then I shall do so, Rolf. I will become the very thing you believe me to be. And I will live quite happily without the kind of love you offer."

"J*ohanna.*"

She jerked back to herself. Not Rolf's voice, but Quentin's. His hands rested on her shoulders.

"You were very far away," he said. "Who was he?"

Had she spoken aloud? "I don't know what you mean."

"You were thinking of a man. I can tell."

"It is unimportant." She tried to step free, but his grip tightened.

"Who was he?"

"The subject cannot matter to you, Quentin. You are my patient—"

"Did you love him?"

"Let me go."

He did so, but only after a long hesitation. His unwillingness was palpable.

A shiver of alarm raced down Johanna's spine. Even so small a change in Quentin—the tiniest hint of possessiveness—reminded her that she didn't truly know him.

"I am responsible for helping you," she said. "You are not responsible for me." She raised her voice. "We're returning to the house, everyone."

They answered with various degrees of enthusiasm and trooped back the way they'd come. Quentin had nothing to say, but kept to himself in a kind of brooding silence.

Once back home, Johanna bathed her father, prepared a light dinner for the group, and carried trays to Harper and Papa. Harper continued to exhibit more alertness than he had in the months before, but he was still very quiet. She resolved to set aside several uninterrupted hours tomorrow to spend with him.

After dinner the patients assembled in the parlor. Johanna opened the windows to let in the cooler evening air and made sure everyone was settled. She encouraged the evening gatherings, as she did the walks, so that none of the residents of the Haven lost touch with their own humanity.

Tonight Quentin would join them. Irene was dressed in her gaudiest gown and waiting impatiently for his appearance. Lewis hunched in his corner, whispering to himself. Oscar kept busy with his puzzle. May, much to Johanna's satisfaction, came all the way into the kitchen and hunkered down beside the door, watching for Quentin as attentively as Irene did.

He entered the room, every inch the genuine aristocrat in his brushed and mended suit, supplemented by a waistcoat borrowed from Papa. All eyes were drawn to him, even Johanna's. She couldn't help herself.

Irene sprang to her feet, collected her dignity, and sauntered over to take possession of his arm. "I'm so glad you could come to my little farewell party," she said. "I do apologize for the . . . mixed nature of the guest list."

"You look charming," he said with a slight bow. "As does everyone." He stared at Johanna, and behind his smile was an intensity reminiscent of his odd behavior during the walk.

"Come sit by me," Irene said, tugging him toward the old horsehair sofa. "We have so much to talk about."

Quentin allowed himself to be persuaded, but he continued to gaze at Johanna until he could no longer comfortably do so.

Johanna got up, too restless to continue with her medical journal. Oscar gave her a toothy welcome when she sat on the floor beside him.

"You wanna play, too?" he said, sliding the half-finished puzzle toward her.

"I'm glad you like the puzzle so much," she said. She fit a piece into its slot. He followed with another, pushing his tongue out as he struggled to make the edges match, and clapped his big hands when it slid into place.

Johanna beckoned May to join them, but she only sank down closer to the floor. Nonetheless, the very fact that she was in view was an excellent sign.

Irene alone was incorrigible. As tolerant as Quentin was with her, she couldn't be allowed to monopolize him and ignore the others.

"Irene," Johanna said, "I believe we need a little music. Would you sing for us, please?"

An opportunity to perform was something Irene could not pass up, but she cast Johanna a scornful glance. "Who'll play the piano? You are certainly no hand at it, Johanna— if you can bring yourself to get up off the floor."

"Don't be mean to Doc Jo," Oscar scolded. "It's not nice."

Irene laughed. "What would you know of 'nice,' you—"

Quentin clasped her hand. "Allow me to accompany you, Miss DuBois. My poor abilities may not do justice to your vocal talents, but I hope not to shame you."

She simpered. "You could not do anything badly, my lord."

He shared a conspiratorial look with Johanna. "You do me too much honor, Miss DuBois." He stood up and walked her to the old piano. It bore a fine coat of dust from long disuse. He had just pulled out the bench when Lewis sprang up, produced a handkerchief from his waistcoat pocket, and began to dust the piano with furious diligence. Finished with his work, he sidled past May into the kitchen to wash his hands.

"Thank you, Mr. Andersen," Quentin called after him. He sat down and ran his fingers gently over the keys. "Only a trifle out of tune," he remarked. "It's a fine old instrument." He leafed through the brown-edged sheet music moldering in a basket beside the piano.

Irene plucked a sheet from his hand. " 'Lilly Dale,' " she said. "It's frightfully old, but I shall do what I can." She returned the music to Quentin and assumed a theatrical air, more for his benefit than that of her audience.

"One moment." Quentin turned toward the kitchen door, where May waited so quietly, and held out his hand. "I'll need someone to turn the pages. Will you help me, May?"

The girl ducked her head, on the verge of flight. Then, slowly, she rose and crept into the room, hesitating every few steps like a nervous fawn. She laid her hand in his.

He positioned her on the other side of the piano, away from Irene, who was far from pleased. "I'll let you know when to turn the pages."

But May surprised everyone. "I can read music," she

whispered. Even Lewis, returning to the parlor, paused at the rarely heard sound of her voice.

Johanna resumed her seat, puzzled but gratified. May's behavior was truly exceptional, and all due to Quentin. She must actually regard him as a protector, to venture in among the others.

"Well, then," Quentin said. "Shall we begin?"

Anxious to reclaim his attention, Irene hardly waited for him to play the introduction.

> *"'Twas a calm still night, and the moon's pale light,*
> *Shone soft o'er hill and vale;*
> *When friends mute with grief stood around the*
>   *deathbed*
> *Of my poor lost Lilly Dale.*
> *Oh! Lilly, sweet Lilly,*
> *Dear Lilly Dale,*
> *Now the wild rose blossoms o'er her little green*
>   *grave,*
> *'Neath the trees in the flow'ry vale."*

Irene's voice cracked on the high notes, but she was heedless of her own imperfections.

> *"Her cheeks, that once glowed with the rose tint of*
>   *health,*
> *By the hand of disease had turned pale,*
> *And the death damp was on the pure white brow*
> *Of my poor lost Lilly Dale.*
> *Oh! Lilly, sweet—"*

"Stop!"

She broke off, staring at Lewis. He stood before his chair, fists clenched, face drained of color.

"What's wrong with you?" Irene snapped. "How dare you interrupt my performance. I'll have you thrown out."

Her painted lips curled, and her eyes narrowed with crude cunning. "Or does my song remind you of someone, Reverend dear? Is that why you don't like it?"

Lewis didn't move. May pressed back against the nearest wall.

"I think we should try a different song," Johanna said firmly. "Something more cheerful, perhaps."

"As you wish." Irene began to sing again without accompaniment.

"Forth from my dark and dismal cell,
Or from the dark abyss of Hell,
Mad Tom is come to view the world again,
To see if he can cure his distempered brain.
Fears and cares oppress my soul,
Hark how the angry furies howl,
Pluto laughs, and Proserpine is glad,
To see poor angry Tom of Bedlam mad."

Quentin rose from the piano bench. "Miss DuBois—"

She marched into the center of the room and sang directly to Johanna, no longer making any attempt to stay on key.

" 'Will you walk into my parlour?' said a spider to a fly,
' 'Tis the prettiest little parlour that ever you did spy;
You've only got to pop your head within side of the
    door,
You'll see so many curious things you never saw be-
    fore!' "

"That is quite enough, Irene," Johanna said. "You may retire to your room."

"Just so you can have him to yourself!" Irene shrieked. "You are the spider, weaving your treacherous webs, but I can weave webs of my own. Soon you won't be able to stop me from doing whatever I want to do. Just wait and see!"

Johanna stepped forward to grasp Irene's wrist. Irene raised her free hand and struck Johanna viciously. Johanna slapped her in return.

The room became a tableau, frozen in time. Johanna regarded her own treacherous hand with horror.

"You bitch," Irene hissed, holding her palm to her reddened cheek. "I'll make you sorry you did that. See if I don't."

Quentin took her arm. "I think you should lie down, Miss DuBois," he said. He was deadly serious, brooking no argument. "I'll escort you—"

"You whore—you harlot!" Lewis shouted. "Leave this house!"

"Be silent!"

Quentin's voice was hardly raised above normal speech, but he might as well have roared. Lewis sat down abruptly. Irene went white. May remained motionless, and Oscar began to wail.

"It's all right, Oscar," Quentin said. "No one is angry with you." Oscar sniffled and rubbed at his eyes. "May, you needn't be afraid. I'll speak to you in a few moments."

May slipped from the room. Quentin steered Irene toward the hall. She didn't resist.

Stunned, Johanna comforted Oscar and got him working on his puzzle again. She went after Quentin and found him emerging from Irene's room, his features devoid of expression. At almost the same instant, Harper stepped into the hallway. His movements were furtive, his posture crouched, as if he expected imminent attack. When he saw Johanna and Quentin, he straightened, though his gaze flicked this way and that, searching for some hidden threat.

"I heard yelling," he whispered. "What's going on?"

"Be at ease, my friend. Just a bit of a row in the parlor." Quentin grinned. "Women on the rampage. Nothing you need worry about."

Harper's shoulders relaxed. "If it's about ladies, I'd better stay out of it."

"Very wise." Quentin glanced at Johanna, who took his hint.

"I'd like to speak with you for a little while before you retire," Johanna said to Harper. "I'll come by within the hour, if that's agreeable."

"Yes," he said. He retreated into his room, and Johanna shut the door. She tested the door to Irene's room and found it barricaded, doubtless with a chair jammed against the inside knob. Well, there was no harm in leaving her alone for a while. It was probably the wisest thing to do.

Composing herself, she turned to Quentin. "What you said to Harper was inappropriate."

"Why? Because I made the comment about women? It wasn't so far from the truth."

She flinched. "I should never have struck Irene. I'm well aware of that. It was inexcusable."

"But understandable." He was as serious as he'd been in the parlor, almost grim.

"No," she said. "I am a doctor."

"And a woman with feelings that can be hurt, like anyone else. Whatever Irene's problems, she went too far."

"You don't understand. I haven't yet been able to reach her, and until I do—"

"She struck you. That cannot be permitted."

"The mistake—the misjudgment—was mine. In any case, you must not interfere."

His eyes lit, turning cinnamon to flame. "I'll always interfere if anyone tries to hurt you."

"*Not* with my patients—"

He took both her hands in a grip both painless and unbreakable. "You watch over your patients with such devotion. Who watches over you?"

"I have never needed anyone to watch over me."

"And what if it was not Irene but someone else who

struck you?" he said between his teeth. "A man, capable of doing real harm?"

"None of the men here would hurt me. Certainly not Oscar, or Lewis—"

"How can you be so sure? Do you really think you know everything, Johanna?"

She stared at him, trying to make sense of this change in him. There'd been an inkling of it on the walk, and again in the parlor. He was behaving subtly, but noticeably, out of character.

"I know what I'm doing," she said, in the calm tone she ordinarily used with distraught or manic patients. "Oscar has learned how to control his strength, and as you see he is not aggressive. Lewis reacted as he did because he lost his wife in a tragic manner; Irene's song reminded him of it. I've always taken care with Harper. Are you suggesting I should be concerned about you?"

His pupils constricted in shock, and he let her go. "You think I'd hurt you?"

"If I thought you were a danger to any of us, I'd never have allowed you to stay." She sighed and rubbed her wrists, though she'd hardly felt Quentin's grip—not, at any rate, as pain. "I've seen how well you get along with May, when she would never trust anyone but me. Oscar likes you, and Harper has improved since you came." She turned away, fighting a lump in her throat. "I should be very sorry to see you gone, but I must insist that you not attempt to interfere as you did in the parlor."

Quentin's breath sawed in and out like that of a large, angry beast. The small hairs prickled on the back of Johanna's neck. Her instincts screamed for her to turn around and face him as she would a dangerous animal. A wolf.

Ridiculous. She forced herself to remain where she was until Quentin's silence left her no choice but to speak. He leaned against the wall, his hands braced to either side of his head.

So lonely, Johanna thought. *So sad . . .* "Quentin, I know you mean well—"

In a blur of motion he snapped around, mouth contorted and hands raised as if to strike. She had a single, precisely delineated view of his face. Had she not known who stood before her, she might not have recognized it.

Rage. That was what she saw—rage, and a kind of vicious satisfaction. Quentin's features seemed coarser, more brutish than she could have imagined possible.

Involuntarily she took a step back. Quentin looked like a man ready to kill.

The moment passed instantly, but not before she realized where she'd seen such a thing before. Harper had behaved so from time to time, before he'd entered his long period of cataleptic depression a year ago. He had never hurt anyone, but he'd walked on the edge of violence and might easily have become dangerous. He'd relived his service in the War as though it had never ended, prepared to attack or be attacked, kill or be killed. And after the manic periods passed, he had shown no indication of remembering what he'd said and done.

Quentin had already revisited his own oppressive, half-forgotten memories of war. Was this another manifestation, far less benign than the other?

Sweat pooled on Quentin's brow, as if he had just emerged from a battle. He slumped against the wall with a rueful shake of his head.

"You're right," he said. "I went too far. I'll try to remember my proper place from now on." He smiled to take the sting from his words. Johanna knew at once that he was unaware of his sudden alteration.

"Very well," she said, wanting very much to consult her notes. "If you'll excuse me—"

"Let me prove I'm worthy of your trust," he said, stopping her. "I've been thinking—I know how much care your father requires. He believes I'm a doctor, and he likes me.

I'd be glad—honored—to see to his needs, so that you can spend more time with the others."

Time and again Quentin had pushed past the appropriate boundaries of the doctor-patient relationship, and she'd let him do it. With this offer, he reached into a part of her life that she'd kept completely private.

"I told you that my father died when I was very young," he said to her silence. "It would be as much for me as for him."

Did he mean it? And if he did, could she trust him with the only man who'd accepted her, and loved her, without question?

Just now Quentin had revealed a side of his nature utterly foreign to what she knew of him, a new face of his illness. Yet she had always intended that the Haven's residents should help each other, form friendships that would support them in their struggles. Quentin might set a good example. If she had assistance with her father, she'd be able to work more diligently with Irene, May, and Harper. With Quentin himself.

And she was touched. Deeply touched, as much as she'd been troubled a minute before.

"Perhaps you can join me when I visit with him," she said. "After that, we shall see."

"Thank you." He glanced toward Harper's room. "I've another favor to ask. I assume you'll be hypnotizing Harper, now that he's speaking?"

"When he's ready. I shall not rush him."

"I understand," he said. "I request that I be allowed to observe your meetings with him. It might improve my ability to respond when you hypnotize me. I'd like very much to be your model patient."

The mischief was back in his eyes, along with that devil-may-care grin. She found her doubts and concerns banished as if by magic.

"That must be up to Harper," she said. "If he seems competent to make the decision, I shall ask him."

"Fair enough. I promised to speak to May tonight—please give my best wishes to Lewis and Oscar, and apologize for any distress I may have caused." He took a step toward her, stopped. "I will prove myself worthy, Johanna."

He gave her no chance to reply, but swung around and strode out the back door.

A*fter she had seen the others to bed, Johanna went to* her father's room and sat with him awhile, watching him sleep.

"I believe him, Papa," she said softly. "I trust him." She set her jaw. "I am *not* losing my reason. It is possible to think and feel at the same time, is it not? It's only a matter of finding the proper balance. That is what I must concentrate on. Balance."

Her father murmured something in his sleep that she couldn't make out. She took comfort in it nonetheless. She kissed him on the forehead and left him to his sleep.

Chapter 11

Quentin clucked softly to the old mare, encouraging her on her slow, steady pace toward Silverado Springs. The summer morning was warm, the road not unbearably dusty, and he was remarkably content to be holding the reins of a nearly decrepit equipage as different from his old racing phaetons as Daisy was from the fine-blooded horses he'd once ridden in England.

Oscar perched on the seat at his side, face bright with anticipation. His weight lent a considerable tilt to the buggy, but Quentin was glad for his company.

He'd had much on his mind the past several days. The minor incident in the parlor earlier that week, which he ordinarily would have forgotten, continued to gnaw at his thoughts. It wasn't because Johanna had rightfully reminded him that he had no place in disciplining her patients, or even her vague hint that he might be forced to leave the Haven if he didn't conform to her rules.

No, nothing so simple. The thing that most disturbed him was the brief but very real gap in his memory immediately following her warnings—the familiar sense of losing himself and returning without knowledge of where he'd gone or what he'd done.

It was the second such blank period he'd experienced since awakening in the guest bedchamber. At the Haven, he'd been out of reach of the drink that had always preceded such spells in the past. But this time, as with the first, he hadn't been drinking.

Only an instant, this time. Only a few seconds of disappearing, and then all was normal again. Johanna hadn't shown any alarm. He couldn't have done anything . . . said anything . . . too intolerable.

But he couldn't be sure. And then there'd been the conversation with Johanna on their walk earlier that same day, when he'd been so possessed by jealousy that he'd felt separated from his own mind and body.

A jealousy to which he had no right whatsoever. Johanna had taken that in stride as well, but even she must have her limits.

All he could do was try to make up for his behavior by promising Johanna the full measure of his future support and cooperation.

He'd lived up to that promise, at least. Today he and Oscar were headed into town to pick up much-needed provisions that Mrs. Daugherty hadn't the means to bring with her to the Haven. Among those supplies was lumber to replace the rotten planks in the barn, which Quentin had begun to repair.

He generally had company during his daily chores. May was his second shadow more often than not, satisfied to watch him or, on rare occasions, speak shyly of the book she'd been reading. Oscar was eager to imitate his actions, an unlooked-for responsibility that he tried to treat with the seriousness it deserved. He'd never had to hold himself up as a standard for anyone else's behavior, and it was a daunting task.

As for the others, Lewis responded with guarded civility to his questions about the roses the former minister tended in the garden. Harper was often in Johanna's office or in his room, but Quentin suspected the two of them might eventually become friends.

Only Irene avoided him, and he was glad enough for the reprieve.

Johanna was too busy to spare much time for him outside of their so-far fruitless hypnotic sessions, but he was constantly aware of her—of her scent drifting out a window, the low, familiar sound of her voice, the firm tread of her step. His heart skipped the proverbial beat every time she came near. He hid his little vulnerabilities from her quite well.

And, gradually, she seemed to dismiss any remaining concerns she might have held about him. She permitted him to spend additional time with her father, providing meticulous instruction on Dr. Schell's care. He needed bathing, help with eating, exercise of his wasted limbs, trips into the garden, and company most of all.

Quentin had seen Johanna's doubt—doubt that he could seriously wish to take on such burdensome and tedious care for a stranger. Doubt even about his motives. But after the first two days, she had trusted Quentin with her father's morning bath and meal. She'd spent that time with the patients, Harper and May in particular, and thanked Quentin at the end of the day with real warmth and gratitude.

Johanna's gratitude. How ironic that it should mean so much to him. But looking after the elder Dr. Schell wasn't some scheme born of his inconvenient desire for one of her rare smiles. It felt almost like caring for his own father—a man he hardly remembered, dead when he was a boy. He caught glimpses, in talking to the old man, in watching him and Johanna together, of what it would have been like to grow up with such paternal love and support.

Dr. Schell's brilliance, spirit, and compassion lived on in

his daughter. And Wilhelm Schell bore no resemblance to the ruling figure in Quentin's childhood.

Tiberius Forster, the late Earl of Greyburn.

Quentin's mind slid away from the image like a raindrop on the skin of a perfect grape. Tiberius Forster was long dead. That was another life, another world.

"We're not moving!"

He came back to himself at Oscar's plaintive observation. Daisy had stopped to graze on the golden grasses at the side of the lane, taking advantage of Quentin's inattention.

Quentin shook his head. "She's a wily one, isn't she? Would you like to take the reins, Oscar?"

"You bet!" He reached for the lines eagerly, and Quentin carefully placed them in the boy's hands, covering the much larger fingers with his own.

"C'mon, Daisy!" Oscar crowed, and soon they were on their way again.

Quentin had seen Silverado Springs from a distance but had never entered the town. It was as Johanna had described it to him: neat, peaceful, respectable, and well-provisioned enough for the flocks of moneyed resort-goers who came to the hot and mineral springs to bathe and improve their health. Aside from the springs and the attached hotels and amusements, it was much like a thousand other such towns that Quentin had visited, in California and elsewhere.

Retrieving the reins from Oscar, Quentin followed Johanna's directions to the general store on the main street. It would have been impossible to miss. The usual idlers lounged, smoked, or talked on the wooden porch, looking for something to alleviate their perpetual boredom. Quentin was mindful of their stares as he tied Daisy to the hitching post.

Johanna had warned him to expect a certain amount of wariness from the local populace. He couldn't help but laugh to himself; these good people might have more reason to be wary if they knew what he really was.

Oscar was oblivious to anything but the prospect of tasting the licorice Quentin had promised him. He bounded up the stairs, nearly upsetting one of the lounger's chairs.

"Damned idiot," the man muttered to one of his fellows, aiming a chewed wad of tobacco through a hole in the planks of the porch. "Shouldn't let him run loose."

Quentin paused on his way up the stairs to glance at the man, an ill-shaven lout whose belly protruded from between his suspenders. "Did he do you any harm?" he asked.

"Damn near knocked me out've my chair," the man said. "Who're you?" He snickered. "Another one of them loonies? You sure don't look like it."

"You'd be surprised," Quentin said. "My name is Quentin Forster. Young Oscar there is my friend."

The man debated how best to reply and decided to err on the side of caution. "You some hired man of the doc's?"

"I am boarding at the Haven," he said.

Another man, at the end of the row, made a low sound. "I'll bet," he whispered to his nearest companion. "Wonder how many male 'boarders' the lady doctor takes on there? Wouldn't I like to find out. She sure ain't picky . . ."

Quentin's vision dimmed, and the blood pounded in his ears. He sucked in his breath. "I shall pretend I didn't hear that remark," he said.

Clearly the speaker hadn't intended it to be heard. He took a hasty swallow from his bottle.

Before he could be tempted to take more definitive action, Quentin followed Oscar into the store. The boy had his nose pressed to the glass of the candy counter, practically ready to devour the glass in order to reach the treats within. The counter creaked ominously under Oscar's weight.

The gray-haired storekeeper seemed relieved when Quentin paid for the licorice and Oscar scampered outside to enjoy it. Quentin looked at the door, wondering if he ought to leave the boy alone with the insolent loafers.

"Don't mind them," the storekeeper said, heaving a sack of flour onto the counter. "They're all bark and no bite."

"They seem to dislike Dr. Schell," Quentin said. "Why?"

"She doesn't come into town much, so no one's gotten to learn much about her. A bit of a mystery, so to speak. People around here only know that she has lunatics at her place who would usually be in the State Asylum. Worry they might scare off the tourists, or that her patients might run mad and hurt someone." He shrugged. "And there's some who just plain don't trust a woman doctor. But she's always paid her bills, and I've found her right pleasant, if the quiet sort. I've never heard any harm of her or the people up at old Schell's place." He regarded Quentin curiously. "You can't be one of her patients."

"Because I'm too normal?" Quentin smiled and shook his head. "We all have our oddities, Mr. Piccini. Some of us are simply better at hiding them than others."

"Can't argue with that." The storekeeper filled a wooden crate with the smaller items on Mrs. Daugherty's list, set it beside the sacks of flour and sugar, and wiped his hands on his apron. "I'll go ahead and take this out, and you can square up with me afterward."

"That would be most—" Quentin stopped in the act of lifting the sack of flour to his shoulder and cocked an ear toward the door. "Excuse me just a moment."

He stepped outside to find the loiterers crowded at the porch railing, watching a scene that bore all the earmarks of a disaster.

Oscar stood in the middle of the street, turning in a bewildered circle, while a pack of boys yelled taunts at him from every side. The gang, its members ranging in age from perhaps fourteen to twenty and too well-dressed to be vagrants, had already done some damage. Oscar's licorice lay trampled in the dirt at his feet.

It couldn't be the first time he'd been mocked for his childlike slowness, but the Haven sheltered and protected him from such abuse. His eyes swam with tears. He would have made two of any of the boys, but he was heavily outnumbered. He didn't know how to defend himself against such an assault.

"Come on, you big dummy!" one of the pack bellowed. "Can't you fight at all? Or is your brain the size of a walnut?" The others joined in his raucous laughter.

Quentin dropped the sack of flour and started down the stairs. The men on the porch made no move to interfere. If they had planned to incite the bullies in their game, they thought better of it now and remained silent.

One of the bullies feinted toward Oscar, shouting and whistling, while another played at bear-baiting with a stick. Oscar flailed with one big hand and knocked the stick away. A boy, watching for his chance, maneuvered behind him and landed a punch to Oscar's backside.

With a howl, Oscar spun around, lashing out at his attacker. By simple good fortune, his fist connected with the boy's face. Blood spurted, and an explosion of dust shot into the air as the bully landed on his bottom. Oscar staggered back, not understanding what he'd done. The boy screamed in pain and rolled on the ground, clutching his broken nose.

All at once the rest of the boys flung themselves on Oscar, wolves pulling down a great bull elk. But no wolf would behave as cruelly as these humans did. Dust rose in choking waves; the smell of blood from the bully's nose filled Quentin's nostrils. He waded into the melee and thrust the boys aside with measured swipes of his arms, making a deliberate effort to leash his strength. The ringleader had pummeled Oscar to his knees, his blows striking past Oscar's upraised arms.

It was Oscar's blood that spilled now. The odor was maddening. Quentin lifted the bully by his collar, dangling him in midair like a pup held by the scruff of its neck in its mother's jaws. The boy's contorted face was the last thing he saw clearly.

Rage. Searing, mindless rage filled him. It turned his vision red and his reason to utter chaos. Shouts came to him distantly—adult cries of alarm and warning and threat. He ignored them like the squawks of so many cowardly birds.

Vultures, waiting for the carcass. Scavengers ready to attack anything too weak to resist.

They'd hurt Oscar. Hurt him . . .

"Quen'in?" Someone tugged on his arm. His gaze focused on Oscar's tear-streaked, upturned face. "I'm scared. I want to go home!"

Something in that woebegone voice reached him as nothing else could. He opened his hand and let the bully boy fall. Like a terrified rodent, the boy scuttled away.

What is happening to me?

His mind cleared, and he realized that he hadn't lost himself. He *remembered*: the rage, the desire to hurt. He hadn't gone anywhere near the saloon.

Sick fear gathered in the pit of his belly. He took Oscar by the arm and pulled him toward the buggy. Motion surged at the edges of his sight, townspeople curious and angry and ready to blame Oscar for what their own children had done. Blame Quentin as well.

Oscar scrambled up into the seat, unable to hide his terror. "Come on!" he sobbed. "Quen'in—"

"Loonies!" a man yelled. "Go on back to the madhouse!"

Quentin climbed in and took the reins. He saw with a start that the buggy's boot already held the sacks and crate from the store. The storekeeper edged up to the buggy, one eye on the growing crowd.

"I saw how it happened," the storekeeper whispered.

"I've loaded up your supplies. I know the Doc's good for it. You'd better leave now."

"Thank you," Quentin said. "I'll remember your kindness."

"Don't judge us all by these few," Piccini said. His fleshy face grew sad. "My sister was never right after she had her last baby. Folks are too quick to cast out those who are different. But you might want to warn the Doc not to let that woman—Irene—come into town for a while, until things settle down."

Quentin nodded, withholding his hand for fear that he might bring the crowd's wrath down on a decent man. He slapped the reins across Daisy's flanks and turned the buggy for home.

"Don't judge us all by these few," the storekeeper had said. Quentin knew too much of men to believe they were all alike. But how was he to judge himself? He'd brought trouble on Johanna by trying to help her. How much more harshly would Silverado Springs regard her now?

And as for Irene . . . if she'd been visiting the town so frequently as to be noticed, Johanna must know.

He and Oscar were a solemn pair as they unharnessed Daisy and put the buggy away. In the privacy of the barn, Quentin looked over Oscar's injuries and found no worse than a few bruises and a small cut that would heal on its own. Oscar had done the greater damage without even trying.

Quentin shuddered. If Oscar hadn't stopped *him* . . .

Johanna would have to know of this, but not right away. Put it off as long as possible. "I think you should go and play, Oscar," Quentin said gently. "Forget about what happened in town. It wasn't your fault."

Oscar sat down on a bale of hay, head in his hands. "I was stupid."

"No. You're not—"

"I *am* stupid. I am!" He lumbered to his feet and charged

out of the barn. Quentin let him go. He had much to learn about children—or those who thought like children—and Oscar was not without pride.

The house was quiet when Quentin carried the provisions inside. Lewis was reading in his parlor corner. He looked up, searched Quentin's face, and seemed about to speak. Quentin slipped past him, through the hall, and out the back door. The peace of the woods beckoned.

He Changed, assuming his wolf form with relief. He shook the taint of anger from his red coat and ran up into the hills. After a span of time that his human side estimated as half an hour, he returned to the edge of the Haven's clearing and Changed back. He was just buttoning his shirt when he realized he was being watched.

The scent was that of dry, cool skin, leached of nearly all its natural odor, and an overabundance of soap. Lewis Andersen. Quentin turned his head to watch for the betrayal of movement. Leaves rustled, and a black-clad figure fled with a snapping of twigs and branches, noisily skirting the edge of the clearing until he was out of view.

Lewis Andersen. Quentin grimaced and finished dressing. He should have taken more care, but all he'd thought to do was Change and leave his human problems behind for a short, precious time.

Had Lewis seen him Change? He wasn't the kind to report such knowledge to the world at large, but given his state of mind, Quentin very much feared such a bizarre sight would only worsen his condition. He'd surely see a shapechanger as a creature of the devil—if he weren't convinced of his own madness.

Can you possibly make matters worse? he asked himself. He was very much afraid he knew the answer.

He walked back to the house, too preoccupied to sense Johanna until she met him on the garden path.

"Quentin! I'm glad you're back." She smiled—actually

smiled at him, oblivious to what he'd done. His heart lodged in his throat.

"The goods are in the kitchen," he said. "Oscar is somewhere about." He summoned up his courage. "Johanna, you and I must talk—"

"Yes, we will attempt another session this afternoon. But I wished to tell you that Harper has agreed to let you observe my work with him, and we are about to begin."

The timing could not have been worse. He was in no state to concentrate on Johanna's techniques, not when he had so much to explain.

She saw his reluctance and misinterpreted it. "I know that our meetings have not been as productive as we hoped, but I believe you may benefit from this. Harper is another excellent hypnotic subject. All our work thus far has been most promising. This is the first time I will ask him to talk of the War itself." She touched Quentin's arm lightly; the hairs stood up all over his body. "He trusts you, Quentin, and that is why he wishes to have you present."

"I wouldn't desert a comrade in arms," Quentin said with a humorless smile. "Lead on."

The chaise longue with which Quentin had become so familiar was now occupied by Harper, who looked fully relaxed, his hands folded across his chest and his eyes closed. Quentin knew that emotion seethed under Harper's skin; no human being could suffer as he had and mend so quickly.

Johanna insisted that the acceptance of one's past held the mind's true cure. Quentin's stomach knotted with dread more intense than any he'd experienced when he was Johanna's subject. God help him, he didn't want to visit Harper's past, see into Harper's soul.

But it was too late to back out now. He took a second chair behind Johanna and concentrated on her routines as she darkened the room and led Harper into a trance. Her voice was rich and persuasive, tender as a mother's.

The muscles in the former soldier's face went slack. His

breathing slowed, hands rising and falling with the steady motion of his chest.

"Harper," Johanna said. "Do you hear me?"

"Yes." Harper's voice was deeper than usual, slightly slurred but intelligible.

"Good. You will now remember all the things we discussed and practiced in our previous meetings. You know there is nothing to fear."

"Yes."

"As we agreed, I am now going to ask you to remember the days when you served with the Twenty-second Indiana Regiment. As you talk of this time, you will feel no distress, nor fear, no pain unless that is what you wish. You will be able to separate yourself from all you experience if you find it too difficult. Do you understand?"

"Yes."

"Then I would like you to think back to the time when you first volunteered to serve. How you felt when you joined, and why you made the decision to do so."

Harper was silent for several moments. "I didn't want to go, you know," he murmured. "I never was much of one for fighting. Everyone in town knew that. My friends—they were all ready to join up as soon as the first shot was fired. No one said anything to me, but they looked. I always felt them looking. And all I wanted was just to stay home and blacksmith like my pa." He sighed. "It was a good life, working with horses. I didn't think I'd like shooting people."

"That was quite natural," Johanna said. "Please go on, Harper."

"I was seventeen when I decided that I had to serve."

"What made you decide?"

"Jimmy Beebe came over to talk to me the day before. The regiment was forming up. He was all fired up to go and get him some Rebs. He gave me his pouch of tobacco and promised he'd share it with me, even-Steven, if I came along. That's when I knew."

"Knew what, Harper?"

"That if I didn't go along, he was going to die."

J*ohanna had no doubt that she'd heard him correctly.*
    She paused to consider her next question, listening to Quentin's muted breathing behind her.

She was glad to have him there, someone who understood what she was doing and could lend a measure of support. Not that she required such support. But she'd missed his company over the past few days, while she'd been so fully occupied with the other patients.

Yes; she could admit it, if only to herself. She'd *missed* Quentin. His conversation, his grin, his friendship. Oh, they saw each other at meals and during the walks and parlor gatherings, but only in passing. Not even long enough for Quentin to disquiet her with one of his vaguely salacious comments.

She'd recognized the need for distance between them, and had gotten what she wanted. Only it wasn't what she wanted after all.

What she wanted, and what was right, were two different things.

For Quentin had surprised her once again. He was very good with her father, as he was with May and Oscar. He accepted each of them for what he or she was, expecting no more. He asked nothing for himself, and if not for his complete lack of progress in their sessions, she could not have been more pleased. Pleased . . . and very much aware of her growing admiration for him.

At least the work that kept her away from Quentin also prevented any more uncomfortable scenes between them. But she couldn't forget those that had already occurred: the kiss; Quentin's strange possessiveness on their walk; his fierce, almost violent desire to protect her after the altercation with Irene in the parlor.

The consequences of those moments had not disappeared. They had simply gone dormant, as if waiting for some new spark to bring them back to the forefront of her mind. And emotions.

Emotions she couldn't afford to dwell on now, no matter how much her heartbeat accelerated at his mere proximity. This was another test of her discipline, and she would not fail it.

She coughed behind her hand. "Harper, you said you thought your friend was going to die."

"I *knew* he was going to die," the soldier said hoarsely. "I saw it in the pouch. It came on me suddenlike. I saw him lying dead on the ground, with the tobacco spilling out, all bloody. And some other boys I knew—they were there, too. All dead."

Though his voice remained calm, Johanna knew he maintained his self-command by the merest thread. "Remember," she said, "none of these memories can harm you now. You are safe. Would you describe this knowledge of your friend's death as a sort of vision?"

"Yes."

"Had you had such visions before?"

"Yes." Harper's throat worked. "Lots of times, but never like this. Small things. I could tell where a horse had been traveling when I shoed him. I knew who Katie Young was going to marry when I held the ring her mother gave her."

Johanna resisted the impulse to glance back at Quentin to gauge his reaction. "So you could see the past and predict the future."

"Not always. Never as strong as when I saw Jimmy die. So I signed up with the Twenty-second and went south with the boys."

"Did you think you could protect them?"

"I don't know. I just knew I had to go."

"And what was it like, Harper?"

His voice dropped to a whisper. "It was hell. At first, my friends all were full of pepper and ready to fight. But then we saw how it would be. The endless marching through the mud and freezing nights, no supplies, shoes wearing out. Never enough food. And the battles. The noise." He lifted his hands to his ears and squeezed his eyes tight. "It never stopped. Jimmy tried to run away. They would've shot him as a deserter. I stopped him. And then I knew he was still going to die."

All at once Johanna understood. "It didn't only happen with Jimmy, did it?" she asked gently.

"No." Tears spilled over onto his cheeks. "All I had to do was touch my friends' guns—or their blankets, or their tin cups—and I saw what would happen to them. I kept trying to stop it. I couldn't." He clenched his fists. "They kept dying. Blown apart. Legs gone. Faces. Oh, God—"

"You blame yourself for what happened."

"I was the one who couldn't be killed. The bullets and shells never hit me. I hardly got wounded. And I was the one who should have died. *I* was—"

"Listen to me, Harper," she interrupted. "You've done very well, but we have accomplished enough for today. Now you'll allow the past to fade, let go of the pain, and prepare to return to the present."

"But I-I deserved—"

"To die," Quentin said behind her. "I deserved to die."

She pivoted in astonishment. Quentin's face was blank, his eyes staring. He gave no indication of being aware of his baffling declaration.

Astonishing. Johanna momentarily lost her train of thought, shaken by the conviction in Quentin's voice. So deeply did he identify with Harper that he'd fallen into a trance himself, and what came so spontaneously from his unconscious mind was more distressing than she could have predicted.

But this wasn't Harper's pain he was experiencing. It was his own.

He needed her. He needed her *now.*

Johanna rose from her chair and moved quickly to Harper's side. "Harper, you did not deserve to die. You did what you could to help your friends. You served with honor and loyalty. In time, you will come to understand why your memories bring so much guilt and unhappiness, and realize that you need no longer carry these burdens."

"I won't do it," Quentin shouted. "You can't make me!"

Johanna flinched. Quentin's anguish reverberated through her body, but she could not comfort him yet. She grimly concentrated on finishing the task at hand. "Harper, I will count backward from five to one. You will awaken, peaceful and refreshed, and rest until you feel ready to rise. What you remember of the War cannot hurt you, and you will begin to believe that healing is possible. Because it is possible."

"Yes," Harper murmured.

Johanna brought him out, watching carefully to make sure that he was conscious and at peace.

She turned back to the man behind her. "Quentin—" She paused at the tortured expression on his face. "Quentin, it will be all right—"

"No!" he cried. "I don't care what you do, I won't—" He tumbled from the chair and crouched on the ground, arms flung around his head. "I won't kill them!"

Chapter 12

*G*ott in *Himmel.*

Johanna sank to her knees beside him, reaching out as if to hold him, letting her arms fall to her sides again. She could not, at such a crucial juncture, forget herself, no matter how much she wished to console him. He needed her to be strong.

"Quentin, it's Johanna. You hear my voice."

He pulled his head closer to his chest and whimpered, a lost, despairing sound.

She locked her arms rigidly in place. "You do hear me, Quentin."

"Yes," he gasped. "Don't let him—"

"No one will hurt you. I will not let them." She hugged herself. "To whom were you speaking?"

"I can't—"

"He is not here now. Tell me his name."

"Grandfather." He looked up, face wet with tears. "My grandfather."

His grandfather. *"He was something of a tyrant,"* Quentin had said. *"I gave as good as I got."*

Maybe he hadn't.

"Where are you now, Quentin?" she asked.

"In the cellar. At Greyburn."

She shivered with foreboding. "How old are you?"

"I'm . . . eleven. Almost twelve."

He was reliving his childhood—the hidden childhood she'd never gotten him to reveal in more than bits and pieces. For just a moment his glazed eyes shone with pride. "I can Change now."

"Change?"

"Into a wolf, of course. That's because I'm a man." The fear returned, wild with defiance. "That's why he wants me to—to—"

"I'm here with you, Quentin. You can talk to me. What did he want you to do?"

He chewed his lip so hard that she feared he'd tear through the skin. "The kittens. He brought the kittens from the barn." He hugged himself. "He says I have to learn. He says I should like it—"

She didn't have to ask him again what his grandfather had wanted him to do. He'd already told her. *"I won't kill them."*

What sort of monster would ask his grandchild to kill kittens on command?

"You don't have to like it, Quentin."

"If I don't do what he says—I *won't*—he locks me up in here. Sometimes I don't know how long. I get hungry. Not very cold—" He sniffed and wiped at his nose. "We don't get cold easy. But then Grandfather brings the ropes—" He broke off and crawled to lean against the wall, curling into himself.

It was enough. She wouldn't force him to experience more of this . . . this torture. For that was what it must be. The questions could wait for another time.

"It's all right, Quentin," she said. "You're going to be all right now."

"Don't tell Braden." He stared at her almost as if he really saw her. "Don't tell him. He'll do something and Grandfather will hurt him. Rowena doesn't know. I make sure she doesn't find out. Promise you won't tell!"

"I promise." She swallowed hard. "Take my hand."

He did so with such immediate trust that she felt dizzy.

"We're going to leave here, now," she said. "Can you do what I say?"

His eyes—those rich cinnamon eyes overlaid with pain—gazed right into hers. "Yes."

"Then I want you to remember another place, another time. The Napa Valley, and the Haven, and the room where I am talking to you. You've been here before."

"I . . . can't."

"You will. It's a restful place, where the sun shines and the air smells like green things. Here you cannot be hurt."

"There is no such place."

"At the Haven there are people who care for you."

His face was utterly open, all hope and gratitude. "Do you . . . care for me?" he whispered.

It had been possible until that moment to maintain some semblance of detachment. With that simple, guileless question, objectivity shattered along with her heart. She pulled him into her arms.

"Yes," she said. "I care for you, Quentin."

His mute sobs shook her body. He fought them, as any boy might fight such humiliating weakness, and yet he clung to her. His mind had journeyed back to his childhood, but his arms were still those of a man, strong and apt to wring the breath from her lungs.

She stroked damp hair away from his forehead and murmured in what she imagined must be a maternal fashion, but she felt anything but maternal. His cheek rested on her breast. His breath burned through the fabric of her bodice. Soon he'd wake, and no longer be a child. What then?

As if he heard her thoughts, he stiffened and pulled himself up. The child in his eyes still reached for her, but she could see it—him—fading away, subsumed by another presence. Quentin, coming out of the trance at last.

But he didn't let her go. "You care for me?" he said, his voice nearly a snarl. "Liar."

Her heart stopped. "Quentin—"

"Don't call me that!" He shook her, just enough so that she felt clearly how much he could hurt her if he chose. "You think you can *help* him?"

"I don't perceive your meaning," she said. She couldn't show any hesitation now, or uncertainty. "Please explain."

They were knee to knee, chest to chest. Each of his harsh breaths rocked her forward and back. "*He* explains. I don't have to." He jerked her against him. She turned her head just before his lips touched hers.

"Never again," he rasped. "It will never happen again. Do you hear me?"

"Yes. I hear you."

"He tries to shut me out, but I won't be buried." His fingers framed her face. "He won't take what he wants. But I will."

He was going to kiss her. Not gently, not lovingly, but with the merciless drive to dominate.

"No, Quentin," she said, planting her hands between them. "It's time for you to come back. I will count backward from five to one—"

"No." He pushed her away. *"No."* Leaping to his feet, he flung himself against the wall like a caged animal, raking at it with curved fingers. His nails bit deeply enough to tear the wallpaper.

"That's enough, my friend." A tall, lean shape passed between Johanna and the madman Quentin had become.

"The enemy is gone," Harper said. "The War is over."

Quentin swung about, teeth bared. He looked just as he had that night in the hall, more bestial than human, his features shifting into something almost unrecognizable. His eyes narrowed to slits, spewing hatred at the world.

This was the wolf he claimed to be, the dangerous lycanthrope Johanna had assumed was a product of Quentin's wounded mind. This was the transformation he spoke of, and she didn't for an instant believe that he controlled it.

She got to her feet and stood shoulder to shoulder with Harper.

"It's safe to return, Quentin," she said. "You're safe. Come back to us."

Whether it was because of her words, Harper's tranquil presence, or something within Quentin himself, he began at last to respond. The savage light left his eyes. His body went boneless, sliding along the wall to the ground.

Harper knelt beside him. "Are you all right, brother?"

Quentin squeezed his eyes shut and opened them again. "What?" He braced his hands on the floor. "Did I fall?"

"You could say that," Harper said. He glanced at Johanna with a faint frown.

She shook her head in warning. "How are you feeling, Quentin?"

"Dizzy." He pushed at the wall to regain his feet. His face was expressionless. "Something happened . . . like before, didn't it?"

Her memory made the leap to their first session, when he'd kissed her and promptly forgotten.

"I'm not sure," she said. "When I was working with Harper, you entered a spontaneous trance."

"Again?" He smiled raggedly at Harper. "Sorry about the interruption, old chap. I hope I didn't spoil it." He pressed his forehead with the heels of his hands. "I appear to be just a little too susceptible to the good doctor's expert technique."

"You are extraordinarily sensitive to hypnotic induction," Johanna said. "I had thought, given our last few sessions—"

"That I was safe?" He laughed. "My old friends in England would be amused to hear that I'm sensitive to much of anything." He looked from her to Harper and back again. "The way you're both staring at me, I suppose I must have stood on my head and recited Shakespeare. Or did I sing 'God Save the Queen' horribly off-key?"

His jokes failed to conceal the real fear in his eyes. He suspected something of what had happened. His gaze found the torn wallpaper, and his expression froze.

"I must have been very badly off-key." He yawned behind his hand. "It's all quite exhausting, really. I'm ready for a nap—if you'll both excuse me."

Johanna's stomach twisted with the realization that she was afraid. Not of Quentin, but *for* him. She'd seen him transform from hurting, vulnerable child to an angry, violent man. Neither was a part of the Quentin she knew. Both were somehow connected to terrible childhood pain—and either might be the means of destroying him.

The Quentin she knew would more likely harm himself than any other creature.

"I would like you to go straight to your room and rest," she told him. "Will you remain there until I come for you?"

"You'll be lucky if you can get me to wake up," he said. "Don't hold luncheon for me."

He gave her and Harper a choppy salute and left the room.

Harper let out a long breath and sat down on the edge of the chaise. "Was I like that when I was hypnotized?"

"No." She moved behind her desk, trying to regain a sense of calm. "Thank you for your assistance."

"What did happen, with him?"

"I cannot tell you, Harper. Not for the time being." She shuffled a pile of papers. "How do you feel?"

He cocked his head. "Better. Except that I don't really remember much of what we talked about."

"That's quite normal. You will begin to remember things as you are ready to do so. We'll continue to work toward that end."

He was silent long enough that she was forced to look up from her papers and meet his gaze.

"It's funny, isn't it," he said, "how we're all hiding, one way or another."

She searched for a response that wouldn't betray her. "It's the nature of the mind to hide from itself. But it is possible to come out of hiding, and find life again."

"You'd know best, Doc. You'd know best." He stopped at the door. "You'll let me know if you need help?"

With Quentin, he meant. With the unpredictable savage they had both confronted.

"Yes," she said. "Thank you, Harper."

Once he'd returned to his own room, she gave up all pretense of examining her notes and let the disordered tide of her thoughts wash through her.

She should be glad. Today Quentin had made definite progress—exceptional, in fact. She was now convinced that the delusions he suffered must arise out of his childhood.

But the complications of his condition only grew more formidable with every new discovery. She'd underestimated the extent of his illness. He'd illustrated his claims of lycanthropy by becoming someone—something—who possessed the ruthless ferocity of a wild beast, a barbarous taste for tyranny.

Yet there'd been the child: innocent, abused, begging for help. And the man she'd come to know, who so willingly gave of himself.

Where was the real Quentin?

Which one was the man she had sworn to cure?

An unfamiliar thread of panic lurked inside her—the very real fear that she wouldn't be able to handle his case.

She had been too careless. What if he should turn truly violent and threaten the others?

What if she were forced to remand his care to someone else, at a facility where he could be restrained . . .

Sickness filled her throat. Yes, she might betray him—to people who knew nothing of the work she and her father had done, who'd put his sanity in even greater jeopardy with their ignorance and primitive treatments.

She would not trust any traditional asylum with Quentin Forster. He mattered too much. As all her patients mattered. Until she had no other option, she would continue to treat him as best she knew how.

That best must be better than she'd ever done before. The time would come when she'd have to be honest with Quentin about the dangers of his condition. As soon as she had enough information to devise a theory, and explain . . .

"I must speak with you, Miss Schell."

Lewis walked into the room, moving very much like a man with an important secret he was half-afraid to reveal, but determined nevertheless to do his duty. His chin jerked up and down several times as he came to a halt before her desk.

"I must speak with you, Miss Schell," he said again.

"What is it, Lewis?" she asked. "You seem concerned."

He shuffled from foot to foot. Johanna noted the sweat beading his brow, and the fact that the long hair he kept so meticulously combed over his balding head hung loose and unkempt.

"I am concerned—most concerned," he said quickly. "I tell you this only to protect us all from evil." He would not meet her eyes. "You must believe me."

"Please, sit down—" she began, but he shook his head.

"That man—Quentin Forster—I saw him in the woods this morning."

She came fully alert. "Did you?"

"Yes. I saw him—" He swallowed. "He was . . . un-clothed."

Johanna bit back a wild laugh. Lewis's sense of righ-teousness would find such a thing appalling, though that begged the question of why Quentin would be . . .

Unclothed. She shivered. "Mr. Forster was in the woods, not wearing his clothing?"

"It's worse. Much worse." He closed his eyes. "He . . . undressed, and then I saw him . . . I saw him . . ."

"You may confide in me, Lewis."

He gulped. "I saw him change . . . into a wolf."

Mein Gott. At last Johanna remembered to breathe. "You saw Quentin turn into a wolf?"

"Yes. I'm not insane. I saw it with my own eyes." He clutched at the lapels of his coat. "Evil. He must be evil. The devil's work—"

Johanna stood, pressing her hands flat against the desk to quell her unsteadiness. How was it possible that Lewis had been pulled into Quentin's unconscious delusion of ly-canthropy, when he could have no knowledge of it? When Quentin himself spoke of it only under hypnosis?

"Quentin is not evil, Lewis," she said. "I do not disbe-lieve you, but perhaps there is some other explanation for what you saw."

"No. I know what it was."

"A dog—"

"No!" He lifted his chin and met her gaze. "I know I have not always been well. But this was no hallucination. We are all in terrible danger."

Johanna found herself bereft of answers. Lewis was not one to fabricate tales, like Irene. Had Quentin indeed been running naked in the woods? Had he gone down on all fours and howled and behaved in such a way to persuade Lewis that he had turned into a wolf? If so, she had seri-ously failed in her work on behalf of both men.

A werewolf would be an unmistakable symbol of the demonic to one such as Lewis. Sin—his own and the world's—was one of his great obsessions. One she'd hoped was diminishing.

As she'd hoped the worst of Quentin's illness had been revealed.

"If there is evil, we will deal with it," she said, summoning all her calm. "You must trust me, Lewis. Wickedness has no power over us if we keep our minds clear."

His bony, austere face was filled with the desire to believe her. "I had to tell you. To warn you. We can still cast him out."

"Give me a little time to observe and determine the safest course. I am not without resources. Do you think you can go to your room and rest, now that you've shared this with me?"

He wrung his gloved hands. "You will call me if you need my help? I know of the greatest iniquities—" She saw the start of tears in his eyes. "Do not trust him, Miss Schell."

"I promise to take no chances." She walked ahead of him and opened the door. He went meekly enough to his room, though his gaze darted about the hall until he was safely behind the door.

Alone, Johanna loosened the tight rein on her emotions. She paced the length of her office and back again several times, consulting her father's pocket watch at the final turn. Bridget should have been here hours ago; it was already after lunch. The patients must be fed.

And she'd have to call for Quentin again, no matter how much he'd so recently suffered.

The kitchen door swung open, its creaking audible across the house. Mrs. Daugherty, at last. Johanna went to meet her.

"Sorry I'm late," Mrs. Daugherty said. "M' grandson had the colic and my daughter needed a bit of help." She squinted at Johanna. "You seem a might peaked. That Irene been givin' you trouble?"

"No, not at all." Irene, in fact, had been exceptionally furtive over the past few days. "Thank you for your concern. Can you prepare luncheon? I am behind today."

"'Course. Just send 'em all out and I'll take care of 'em." She began to roll up her sleeves and paused, pursing her lips. "Before I forget, I have a message for you." She rummaged in her skirt pocket. "Here you are."

Johanna took the slightly damp envelope from Mrs. Daugherty's blunt fingers. "A message? From whom?"

"Young feller in town—a doctor, like you." She winked. "A right handsome one, at that."

A doctor? Johanna turned the envelope over. Her name was written out in an elegant hand, but the sender remained anonymous. "Did he give his name?"

"I can't rightly recall. It was some foreign name, at that. Something with a 'B.' But he was quite the gentleman. Said he'd heard of you and wanted to . . . 'consult with you.' Yes, that was the word." She grinned. "I'd best get to work while you go read your letter."

A doctor. A foreign doctor, who wished to consult with her. She hadn't realized that anyone outside the valley knew of her work; she hadn't had time to write papers or attend more than a handful of lectures, let alone speak at length with her peers—if any of them would regard her as such. Few would likely remember her father after three years and a move across the country, in spite of his controversial papers and reputation as an eccentric.

Her mind crowded with speculation, Johanna hurried back to her office and opened the envelope. The stationery was lightly scented, but the writing was indubitably masculine. it was addressed to Doctor Johanna Schell.

"Dear Dr. Schell," it began. *"I hope that you will grant me the honor and privilege of introducing myself to you: Feodor Bolkonsky, doctor of Neurology from the University*

of Berlin. I have recently had the great pleasure of becoming acquainted with the theories of your father, Dr. Wilhelm Schell, and your own work in the field of treatment of the insane. I am currently residing in the Silverado Springs Hotel, and would be most grateful if—"

Johanna finished the letter at breakneck speed and then read it through more slowly.

Dr. Feodor Bolkonsky. She'd never heard of him, but that was no surprise. Her life here had been meaningful but insular, set far apart from those theorists and physicians and asylum superintendents whose work was garnering recognition in the rest of the country and abroad.

This Dr. Bolkonsky knew of *her*. He knew she was a woman, and obviously didn't care. He was not only familiar with the Schells' practice, but had made the effort to find and read her father's scarce papers and was aware that she was carrying on in the wake of Wilhelm Schell's disability.

He wanted her to come into Silverado Springs to dine with him and review the hypnotic treatment that he himself had begun to explore, comparing his experiences with her own. And he asked as humbly as any student.

Only minutes ago she'd been mourning the lack of physicians who shared her ideas and passion for real cures of insanity. And here, as if sent by fate, was a man who might not only understand, but could conceivably provide her with advice in treating Quentin. Perhaps he, himself, was capable of taking on Quentin's care should she find her situation too . . .

Overwhelming, Johanna? When before have you turned coward, simply because a case became difficult?

And when, she answered herself, *was it ever so personal?*

She carefully refolded the letter and tucked it back in its envelope. She took a number of deep, rhythmic breaths to calm the too-rapid pace of her heartbeat. The prospect of losing Quentin to another doctor was a matter of professional necessity, not of personal needs. It might very well be in his best interest.

If it were possible at all.

"Sufficient to the day," Johanna thought. And today she must continue to present a tranquil and competent face to the rest of the patients. She went to the dining room to join the others for luncheon.

Half the Haven's residents were sitting down to lunch in their usual places. Neither Quentin nor Lewis was present. Harper had taken Lewis's chair, his hair neatly combed and his beard trimmed.

Irene's eyes gleamed with satisfaction, as if she harbored glorious secrets she delighted in concealing. Her attitude was markedly changed from her brooding conduct earlier in the week. May stood in the kitchen doorway, looking for Quentin. When she didn't see him, she grabbed a sandwich from a plate on the table and ran outside.

Johanna drew Mrs. Daugherty aside. "Do you think it might be possible for you to come back tomorrow and bring another girl from town? I have an appointment in the Springs and may be gone half the day and into the evening."

Mrs. Daugherty cocked her head. "Well, I do know of a girl or two who could use the work, if I can convince 'em not to be scairt. How much could you pay?"

Bless the woman for her bluntness. "If the girl is satisfactory and is willing to help you see to the patients, I'll abide with whatever you think is fair."

"Just the way you did when I first came here," Mrs. Daugherty said. "It's a good thing I'm an honest woman!"

"We couldn't get along without you. Do you think that you could go back into town this afternoon and let me know by dinnertime if you've found someone?"

"Don't see why not. If I have help, I can do all the washing tomorrow."

"Excellent."

"It's that doctor, ain't it?" Mrs. Daugherty asked. "The one who sent you the letter. Meeting him, are you?"

"He's asked to consult with me. I don't often get the opportunity."

"'Course." The older woman bustled back to the stove. "I'll get things settled up here and head back to town."

Too restless to eat, Johanna took a tray in to her father and found him clean, contented, and alert. He had a broad grin for her, and ate with real gusto.

"I've been neglecting you, Papa," she said, helping him cut a piece of cold roast beef into small pieces. "I am sorry."

He tasted a bite and rolled his eyes. *"Sehr gut."* After a moment he looked at her. "Don't worry, *meine Walkürchen.* The young man has been very good company."

Quentin. "He's been spending much time with you?"

"A fine lad. Knows how to tell a good joke."

"You like him very much, Papa."

"Don't you?"

That old, piercing gaze caught her unaware. "Of course I do. But he is a—" She'd almost said patient, and remembered that her father had thought him a doctor.

"We made a good choice, bringing him in," Papa said. "He has a healer's touch."

A healer's touch. Her father had always been a keen judge of character. Was he still? There could be no doubt that Quentin had done him only good, as he had May.

But then there was Lewis. And Irene, who was now avoiding him. And today's disconcerting revelations.

She put her father to bed and went to seek Quentin. He was already waiting for her in the hall.

"We must talk," he said.

Her mind's eye filled with a tantalizing vision of Quentin standing naked in the woods, then shifted to the image of his face, snarling and brutal. Suddenly she didn't want to be alone with him in her office, or anywhere inside four walls.

"Yes," she said. "Shall we go to the vineyard?"

*I*t *was a place of tidily spaced rows of vines pruned into* tortured shrubs, each standing alone, well-disciplined troops of obstinate old men laden with burdens of new grapes.

The kind of place where he and Johanna could be together yet totally apart.

Quentin paused to run his fingers over the plump, nearly ripe fruit on the nearest vine, pretending to be fascinated by them. All the while his senses were focused on the woman a few feet away.

Of the little he recalled from his latest memory lapse, one thing stood clear in his mind: Johanna's arms. Johanna's touch. Johanna, holding him, comforting him. Johanna's voice whispering, "I care for you, Quentin."

What had he done to provoke those words, that tenderness? And what had happened afterward to bring the wariness into her eyes, while Harper watched vigilantly beside her?

He crushed a grape between his fingers and let the pulp fall. "What did I do, Johanna?" he asked. "You told me that I entered another spontaneous trance, but I know very well that's not all." He sought her eyes. "Tell me the truth."

She paused in her own examination of an immature bunch of grapes and looked up. She was too restrained, too emotionless. Hiding something from him.

Something he wasn't going to like.

"As you know," she said, "our past few meetings have not been very successful. I haven't been able to fully hypnotize you, as I did at first. But this time—" Her body tensed as if to take a step toward him, but she reached for the nearest vine instead. "You underwent a sort of transformation. It was as if you were indeed a child again. A child who had suffered much."

He laughed, torn by mingled relief and dread. "Ah, the agonies of youth. I must have disgusted you."

"*Stop.*" She didn't touch him, but the sheer force of her determination silenced him. "You make light of it, but things happened in your childhood that must have affected you deeply. You told me about your grandfather—"

Her voice faded. Between one moment and the next, his mind went blank. Pictures, like photographs frozen in time, came to him one by one. Greyburn. Playing on the vast lawn with Rowena and Braden. The Great Hall hung with its swords and shields and immense wooden doors carved with images of wolves and men. His mother in bed, slowly dying. The room with the armor, where Grandfather dealt out punishment. And the cellar . . .

A swell of dizziness sent him grabbing a handful of leaves as if their frailty could support him. They tore from the vine and fluttered to the ground.

Johanna caught him in her arms. She held him until he could stand again, and let him go.

"I am sorry," she said. "I know this will not be easy for you, Quentin. But I believe what happened today is significant. You must not give up."

He clasped his hands behind his back to disguise their trembling. He wanted to give up. If not for the memory of Johanna's arms about him, protecting, caring . . . loving . . .

"Was that all I did? Behave like a child?" He clenched his teeth. "Did I become . . . aggressive?"

The minute alterations in her scent and her stance gave her away, though she hardly moved. "Have you reason to believe that you might?" she said, her voice unnaturally quiet.

She was sidestepping his questions with more of her own. How could he explain? How, when he didn't understand it himself? "There may have been times when I didn't behave quite properly."

"Times you don't remember, because of the gaps in your memory? Yes, you told me about them in our first session, but I assumed—" She broke off and looked away, her expression bleak. "Have you experienced such gaps since you came to the Haven?"

He went cold. "Yes."

"But you have not been drinking."

He shook his head.

"Do you remember *any* occasion when you became aggressive, here or in the past?"

Until this morning, he could have answered "yes" with perfect honesty. Until this morning, he'd had only the sense of wrongness following his many binges. He'd see wariness in the eyes of strangers, sometimes fear, even hatred. That was when he knew it was time to move on.

But this morning, in town, he had remembered: the anger, the wildness, the desire to hurt those who had bullied Oscar.

"You must be honest with me, Quentin." Her face had gone a little pale under its ruddiness.

"I've tried to be," he said, choking on the half-truth. His nails bit into his palms. "Did I attempt to hurt you, or Harper?"

"No." She wasn't lying, but she withheld something from him, and she wouldn't meet his eyes. The only solace he could find was in her nearness; she still trusted him enough to put herself within his easy reach. He was torn between the desire to weep and to catch her up in his arms and kiss her until she was breathless.

"I would never hurt you," he whispered. "Not you or anyone at the Haven. But there is something you must know." He gazed off across the rows of vines, and beyond to the fields and wooded hills. "Something happened this morning, when I went into town with Oscar."

He told her, slowly, of the incident in Silverado Springs, Oscar's predicament, and what he had done. She listened as dispassionately as if he were reciting a list of the provisions he'd brought back from town.

"You were trying to protect Oscar," she said after a long, charged silence. "You didn't hurt the boy."

"No."

"Then it seems to me that your reaction was not unwarranted." She spoke as if by rote, all passion quenched. "Oscar could not defend himself. It is in our desire to succor the weak and helpless that we rise above the beasts."

Was she creating excuses for him, or had he failed to make her understand? *You do a disservice to the beasts, Johanna. It is men who are the savages.*

"I fear," he said, "that I didn't improve the Haven's reputation in Silverado Springs."

"That does not concern me. It will take time to make people realize that insanity or mental deficiency is neither a shame nor a sin." She blinked several times, returning from a place inside herself, and finally looked at him.

"When you first came to us," she said, "I thought the drinking was the cause of your illness. I was wrong." She searched his eyes, piercing straight to the heart. "It's the shadows that haunt you. The shadows of your past. The ones that came to life in your childhood, and followed you into India. And led you finally to us."

Quentin felt as if she'd sifted his mind like one of the true loup-garou blood. She knew him better than he knew himself. But when had he ever really known himself?

She drew in a breath. "You do want help, Quentin. No matter what difficulties we may face."

God help him. "Yes."

"Even if it means—" She paused, and again he was left with the certainty that she had stopped herself from speaking frankly. But not because she was afraid of him. He hadn't yet driven her to that.

Did she fear *for* him?

"There is one more thing I must ask you now," she said.

He braced himself. "Ask."

"Lewis came to me today. He claimed to have seen you change into a wolf."

Quentin couldn't quite stifle a bitter laugh at the absurdity of it. "Oh, lord."

She simply stared at him. "Were you running in the woods unclothed, as Lewis claims?"

How could he answer? "I was in the woods. I did a bit of running."

"And did you feel the desire to become a wolf, Quentin?"

The quandary was most ironic: to let Johanna believe him even more insane than he was, or tell her the unvarnished truth.

If any human could be trusted with the facts of his nature, she could. But such knowledge would place more burdens upon her—the burden of belief in the face of all she knew, the burden of secrecy   and the burden of acceptance. If she *could* accept.

It was too great a risk. Their relationship hung in the balance.

And what relationship is that?

"A wolf, at least, very seldom doubts his own sanity," he said at last.

Her face revealed her thoughts as distinctly as chalk on a slate. "Is this all you have to tell me?"

"I wish I were not such a disappointment to you, Johanna."

Rare temper sparked in her eyes. "You did not mention any of this to Lewis?"

"No. I was trying for a little solitude."

She clearly had more to say, but held her tongue. "Lewis was very upset. It will be best for you to stay away from him. And if you feel any urge toward—"

"Running naked in the woods?"

"—any desire to turn into a wolf, you will come straight to me."

"I understand. The next time I feel the need to divest myself of my clothing, I will most certainly go straight to you."

Her fair skin caught fire. "We'll continue this conversation later. I shall be going into town for part of the day tomorrow, and have arrangements to make."

He caught her arm as she turned to go. "I have a question for you, Johanna."

She tilted her face to his, and his body tightened with desire.

"When I was in my trance . . . did I kiss you?"

The flush spread from her neckline to her forehead. It was all he needed to know. He bent just enough to fit his mouth to hers, and kissed her again. Lightly, a mere brush of the lips was all he dared to attempt. The shock that coursed through him was as powerful as anything he'd felt while buried deep in the aroused body of a woman in the throes of her passion.

Any woman but Johanna.

She didn't strike him, or stumble away. Her eyes lost their bright hue, leaving her cheeks with the only color in her face. Her lips parted and closed again without uttering a sound. If not for the heightened richness of her scent and the audible speeding of her heart, she might have seemed unmoved.

When he let her go she simply turned and walked back toward the house, her skirts trailing unheeded in the fecund earth.

Chapter 13

The thick limb of the old, blasted oak split in two at the first blow of Quentin's axe. It was only one of many such branches he planned to reduce to firewood this morning; no telling how long the pieces of the felled tree had lain at the side of the house, awaiting someone able and willing to make them useful.

Winter was far away, but Quentin had a clear choice of vigorous physical labor or going in search of a bottle.

He swung the axe again. The morning was hot, and his bare skin ran with sweat. May and Oscar had watched for a while, well out of the way of flying chips of wood, and then had gone off to the woods. Lewis was avoiding him, as expected, along with Irene. Mrs. Daugherty and a hired girl from town were busy with washing. And Johanna . . .

Johanna was gone to town. On business, she said. Something about meeting another doctor. Quentin felt her absence like a physical ache.

His entire body ached with wanting her.

A chunk of wood the size of a man's thigh flew a good

several yards and landed with a thud. Quentin let the axe slide from his grip and wiped his hands on his trousers.

Careful. He might find chopping up a tree satisfying given the scarcity of more pleasurable exercise, but not at the risk of doing real damage to the landscape or its denizens. He retrieved the axe, clamped his teeth together, and lifted it for another attack. He drove the head so deep in the wood that it stuck. He snorted in disgust.

"The tree's already dead, friend."

Quentin left the axe where it was and turned on his heel. Either Harper had approached with the silence of a loup-garou, or Quentin had gone deaf to the world. He thought the latter much more likely.

Harper raised his hands. "Sorry. Shouldn't have snuck up on you like that."

"No harm done," Quentin said, concealing his surprise. It wasn't that he and Harper hadn't talked, but this was the first time the man had sought him out.

And Harper was beginning to carry the look of a healthy man—healthy in body and spirit. His eyes were no longer sunk so deeply in his face; the etched lines between his brows and at the sides of his mouth had flattened. There was even a hint of greater fullness under his cheekbones, a little more flesh over his ribs.

That was how much good a few hypnotic treatments with Johanna had done him.

But it was the expression in Harper's eyes that had changed the most. They hadn't entirely lost their haunted look, but they were clear and sane. No more retreating into a world of his own. He was of *this* world now, and planned to remain in it.

He had more backbone than Quentin did.

Company was not what Quentin had in mind, but now that Harper was here he felt the tension drain from his muscles. Any distraction from thoughts of Johanna was welcome.

He sat down on the largest branch and stretched his legs. Harper joined him, turning his face up to the sun.

The quiet between them was comfortable, almost comforting. Quentin hadn't expected it. Harper had witnessed his spontaneous trance yesterday, and all that it entailed. It wasn't his business to withhold judgment, as Johanna did, and yet he seemed perfectly at ease.

Perhaps nothing so bad had happened after all. But if Johanna had failed to tell Quentin the whole truth about yesterday's incident, Harper might be persuaded to fill in the blanks.

"Thank you," he said. "For what you did yesterday."

Harper shrugged. "Just helping a comrade in need."

"Even though we didn't fight for the same country, or in the same war?"

The other man's gaze had an uncanny directness. "You sure about that?"

He was equally direct in his speech. Quentin bit back the impulse to ask him what he meant.

"I seem to remember," Quentin said, "you saying something about the enemy being gone, and the war over. I gather that I needed the reminder."

Harper didn't answer straight away. He stretched out his own legs—long enough to match Quentin's—and cracked his knuckles. Each movement he made was that of a man who felt joy in the simplest actions.

A simple man, Harper. Except that he claimed to see visions.

"You needed to be reminded, then," Harper said at last.

"Because the enemy isn't gone," Quentin said. "The war isn't over." He smiled bitterly. "Are you here about yesterday, Harper? Do you have something to tell me?" His mind raced with dire possibilities, matching the tempo of his heartbeat. "Did I do something to frighten Johanna?"

"Doc?" Harper chuckled, as if he found the notion of

Johanna afraid inconceivable. "No. Not in the way you mean."

Quentin released his breath. "What did I do, Harper?"

"Reckon she'll talk about that in her own time." Harper searched his pockets for something that wasn't there. "I don't remember very much of what I said. Must have talked about what happened during the War. Don't want to think of that yet. Not just yet." He shivered. "Doc says it'll come back to me when I'm ready. I reckon it's the same with you."

So Harper wouldn't discuss it as Quentin had hoped, not without further prompting. Still, his casual manner laid to rest Quentin's most immediate fears.

"Do you remember anything about the past few years, while you've been with the Schells?" he asked.

"Not much. Didn't want to come out. Not until . . ." He shot Quentin a keen look. "Why're you here, Mr. Forster?"

"We hardly need stand on formality." He offered his hand. "Quentin."

"You know my name." Harper gripped his hand with strong, thin fingers. "I don't remember when you first showed up, either."

Quentin rested his palms on the rough, peeling bark of the oak. "I . . . stumbled across the Haven two weeks ago."

"Seems longer."

"It *feels* longer." As if he'd known the people of the Haven forever. Wanted Johanna forever.

Harper closed his eyes. "My family sent me to the docs years ago. Guess I was too hard for them to care for, after I went back to Indiana. I know I was crazy. I owe whatever I've got now to Doc Schell."

Quentin shifted on the branch. He didn't want Harper's personal confidences. The man bared his heart for all the world to see.

As he'd bared *his* to Johanna.

"She is a remarkable woman," Quentin said stiffly.

"Is that what you think?" Harper nudged at the dirt with the toe of his boot. "I reckoned you had a slightly different opinion."

Quentin jumped up and paced away. "I don't understand you."

"You understand." Harper leaned back, clasping his hands behind his head. "You're pining after that woman, and she feels the same. It's just that neither one of you'll admit it."

Quentin clenched his fists. Was it that obvious, then? Or was Harper the only one sane, experienced, and observant enough to notice?

"One of your visions, Harper?" Quentin snapped without thinking.

"Guess I must have talked about that when I was hypnotized," Harper said. "Seeing things, and all. Don't blame you for doubting." He scratched his beard. "It's something I can't help. Every time I touch a thing that people have touched—well, it happens. It's just that for a long time I wasn't letting anything through."

Had Quentin been an ordinary man, he might have scoffed at Harper's words. Who, after all, believed in visions spawned from merely touching an object?

Who believed in werewolves?

"I reckon you need proof," Harper said.

"You have nothing to prove to me."

"No. It's always our own selves we have to prove to." Harper stood up and reached for the handle of the axe that stood almost perpendicular to the stout oak branch in which it was embedded.

"You've been working with this axe," he said. He tugged at the handle, but it wouldn't be moved. "You didn't work long, but you put a lot into it. Enough for me to see."

The short hairs stood up on the back of Quentin's neck. "See what, Harper?"

"A little of you." He frowned. "Isn't easy to explain.

Sometimes . . . I can feel something about a person from a thing they just touched. If they only used it a brief while, it doesn't linger. If it's a thing people have had for a long time, that's what makes the difference. Sometimes I see what a body's been doing, or where he's been in the past. Or I see what's going to happen to him." His prominent Adam's apple bobbed. "Right now, I can see what you intended to do—chop this tree to bits because you wanted to stop thinking about other things."

"Very good," Quentin said with heavy sarcasm.

"You think you can stop wanting the lady if you tucker yourself out. But you aren't going to finish what you started."

"Perhaps because I'm sitting here instead of working."

"I'm just telling you what I see. And what I don't see."

"Is that why you're here, then? To predict my future?"

Harper clasped his fingers together until his knuckles stood out from the flesh. "I wasn't able to help my friends when I saw what was coming for them. Maybe this time . . ." He sought Quentin's gaze, his own earnest and grave. "I see that you have many trials ahead. Someone is following you—someone you know. He'll hurt you if he can. You may find what you seek, but your fate depends on the decisions you make."

Quentin laughed. "Isn't that true of every man's fate?"

"No." Harper looked up at the bulk of Mount St. Helena rising to the east. "Or if it is, I can't always see it."

"That's fortunate, or you'd be very unpopular among your fellow men."

Pain flashed in Harper's eyes. "I found that out early on. That's why I never talked too much. People don't want to know. I didn't want to know, either."

Quentin felt something disagreeably like shame. Who was he to mock this man? Harper had his own tribulations, and he thought he was trying to help. He exposed himself out of a sense of friendship. He thought Quentin was worth the effort.

True friends had been a rare commodity in Quentin's life, through no one's fault but his own. He'd either driven them away or run from them, every one. Quentin Forster, the ever-popular, who made people laugh or gasp or shake their heads, but never left them bored.

And he always left.

"I'm sorry," he said. "Some secrets are best left unshared."

"And some have to be." Harper looked back at him. "You've been running a long time, my friend. Pretty soon you'll have to stop running and face what's after you. There's no other way."

"You received all this from an axe handle?"

"No." Harper dangled his hands between his knees. "No."

Quentin took the handle of the axe in both hands and jerked it free. "Thank you for your advice. Now, if you don't mind, I think I'll continue my work—"

Harper stood up. "You've come to the right place, Quentin. This is where you make a stand, and fight."

Quentin swung around, and Harper stepped away from his bared teeth. "Will Johanna come to harm by helping me? Will she?"

"Is that what you're most afraid of, or is it the way you feel about her?"

"*Will she?*"

"I don't see everything. I just know that you and the doc— " He sighed and shook his head. "I've told you all I can."

"You said someone was following me, someone I know. Who?"

Harper took another step back. "I have to rest now." His voice grew muffled, detached. "I'm tired."

"Harper—" Quentin reached out, but Harper was already walking back toward the house, stooped and weary. Quentin let him go.

"Your fate depends on the decisions you make," Harper had said. But it wasn't just Quentin's own fate at stake. Harper had told him little about himself he didn't already know. And as for the business about someone stalking him . . .

He thought about the many times he'd lost track of hours and events, and his frequent sense of wrongness following those times. Had he committed some reprehensible act that had won him enemies? If so, why hadn't he sensed pursuit? Loups-garous had too many advantages over humans, at the very least in the keenness of their senses. And he hadn't met another werewolf in all his journeying across America.

But he *was* running. Harper was right about that. The soldier had recognized a man running from himself.

The very thing that made him want to run from the Haven was the same element that kept him here, chained to this place by fragile dreams and desperate hunger.

Johanna.

"You're pining after that woman, and she feels the same. It's just that neither one of you'll admit it."

Hope had an insidious way of popping up in the most unexpected places. Deadly hope, that intensified desire to fever pitch.

Desire obliterated every other need, even the need for escape. The very idea of lying with Johanna was more than he could bear. It raised within him the rapacious predator that wasn't appeased with stolen kisses in vineyards, or a gentleman's restraint. It urged him, over and over, to let go. Take what he wanted.

Take Johanna.

She wants you.

He swore foully and slammed the axe into the branch.

Half of the branch spun into the air and flew like a cannon-ball to the edge of the woods. He could prove at least one of Harper's predictions false.

He raised the axe and brought it down on the branch with all his strength.

J*ohanna was already to the edge of Silverado Springs be-*fore she realized she'd driven the entire distance with no notion of how she'd made the trip.

She gave thanks to patient, reliable Daisy, who'd followed the path to town on her own. At the moment, the horse seemed to possess more intelligence than her owner.

The same scene kept repeating itself again and again in her mind, just as it had done all last night and this morning.

"When I was in my trance, did I kiss you, Johanna?"

She touched her lips. The kiss in the vineyard was nothing compared to the one he'd given her during his first hypnotic session, yet it had been all she could do to preserve her mask of indifference and walk away as if she remained unmoved.

Was he finally remembering that first kiss? Did he remember her uninhibited response?

She could only pray he did not. At least she'd given him no encouragement. And they would both have more vital concerns to explore in their next session.

If there was a next session.

She sat up straighter in the buggy's seat and patted the top of her hair. All pins were in place, and she wore her best dress—the only one really suitable for meeting a fellow physician. For the next few hours, she hoped to be thinking and speaking of nothing but professional matters.

Silverado Springs's main street was sleepy at this time of day, when luncheon was past and anyone who had no need to be working outside sought shelter from the heat. Even the usual loafers at the general store were absent. But as Johanna drove Daisy to the Silverado Springs Hotel, she passed a handful of townsfolk who looked at her askance and walked quickly away.

Quentin had warned her. He'd warned her about many things, if she'd had the common sense to listen.

She arrived at the hotel and gave Daisy into the keeping of the stable boy, providing the lad with enough coins to see to her comfort. There was no mirror to check her appearance, so she satisfied herself with a few more minor adjustments to her coiffure and brushing off the narrow skirt of her dress.

The Silverado Springs Hotel was no longer the fashionable place it had been a decade ago, but it did enough business to maintain the gardens, grounds, and mineral baths that were its claim to fame. The lobby was empty save for a tourist couple discussing possible local excursions with the concierge.

Johanna scanned the lobby a second time and sat down to wait in one of the slightly worn chairs. She was early, and it wouldn't do to seem overeager. This Dr. Bolkonsky might prove to be a disappointment, after all.

She picked up a magazine and was idly perusing an advertisement for women's hats when she smelled the strong and woody scent of expensive cologne.

Her gaze moved up from the man's highly polished black boots with white spats, snug gray trousers, single-breasted blue coat over a gray silk waistcoat, immaculate shirt and cravat to the face above his starched stand collar. There she stopped, catching her breath.

He was beautiful. No other word would suit. And though her head had never been easily turned by masculine beauty—at least not until two weeks ago—she found herself hardly able to believe this man was real.

Golden hair spilled in waves to his shoulders, framing a face made to inspire angels to flights of song. His features were strong enough to be completely male, but delicately carved, refined with the aesthetic appeal of a true intellectual. His eyebrows were several shades darker than his hair, lending his expression greater definition; his nose held an aristocratic arch. The sensitive mouth curved up in a charming smile.

Charming, beautiful, perfect. Too perfect, she decided. A man without flaw must inevitably grow tiresome. Quentin's face—attractive but humanly imperfect—hovered in the back of her mind.

"Dr. Schell, I presume?" the man asked, banishing Quentin's image. He tipped his top hat and clicked his heels. "I am Dr. Feodor Bolkonsky, at your service. *"Sehr erfreut, Sie kennenzulernen, Frau Doktor."*

"You speak German!" Johanna rose, offering her hand. He took it in a firm clasp that did not condescend to her gender. *"Sagten Sie nicht, Sie hätten in Deutschland studiert, Herr Doktor?"*

"Ja, in der Tat." He switched back to English, still smiling. "I have made it my business to learn everything possible about your work, and your father's. I have been looking forward to our meeting with great anticipation."

"As have I." She returned his smile, feeling foolish for no good reason. "There is so much I have been unable to discuss with others of like mind."

He extended his arm. "I think you will find me very much of a mind with you and your father, Dr. Schell. It was because of my interest in hypnosis that I first encountered the elder Dr. Schell's work, and realized that much I had been considering had already been taken up by you. I hope you do not mind my familiarity; I feel as if I know you."

"I am not one to stand upon formality," she answered. "To the contrary, it is excessive dedication to useless convention that all too often stands in the way of true progress."

"Ah! A woman after my own heart. I can already see that we think alike." He briefly rested his hand on her fingers.

"We both believe that what some consider irregular methods are often the only ones that bring results."

He led her to a small private room off the main dining salon, where he offered her a seat and ordered refreshments. "It is some hours until dinner, but I thought we might occupy them with no difficulty." He took the seat beside her. "I hope you brought some of your case notes and observations, Dr. Schell. I've heard something of the Haven since I arrived in town."

"I'm sure you didn't judge us on the rumors circulating here," she said, concealing her unexpected anxiety. "Many people have an unreasoning fear of madness, when so few of the insane pose any danger whatsoever."

"As you say. I am sure what you do here is the work of a pioneer who deserves far more recognition than she has received."

Johanna blushed as she hadn't done with anyone but Quentin. "You give me too much credit, *Herr Doktor*—"

"You will call me Feodor. No formalities, *verstehen sie?*"

"Yes." She sat forward in her chair. "I am not pursuing this work with an interest in fame. It was my father's hope that we might develop new techniques to ease the burden of insanity. I believe we have made real progress, and I am more than happy to share what we've discovered. If you have worked with hypnosis, I have no doubt that there is much I can learn from you . . . particularly if you have recently been in Europe. We are so out of touch, here."

"I hope to remedy that situation," he said. "I've brought texts from Germany and France, as well as some of my own notes." His smile warmed. "I feel sure this will not be our only meeting."

Johanna resisted the urge to clear her throat nervously. It was much too soon to bring up Quentin's case, but Feodor Bolkonsky seemed a most extraordinary man. He might very well be what she'd been hoping for.

"Will you be staying long?" she asked.

"I am currently residing in San Francisco, which is why it was possible for me to seek you out. To my great good fortune."

"I was recently in San Francisco for a lecture," she said, flattered by his compliment. "I don't recall seeing you there—"

"Sadly, I was out of town at the time." He lifted a brown leather satchel resting against the side of his chair and set it on the small table between them. He opened the satchel and pulled out a pair of new books. "I hope you'll accept these as a token of my esteem, Dr. Schell."

She touched the covers reverently. Both were texts by well-regarded neurologists in Europe whose works she had been unable to obtain in America. "Thank you . . . Feodor. You must call me Johanna."

"I will, with pleasure."

They spent a few more minutes in small talk, on subjects ranging from the comparative weather in San Francisco and the Napa Valley to the latest play Feodor had seen in the city. But then the real discussion began. Johanna swiftly lost track of time as they exchanged opinions on such fascinating topics as Wundt's *Principles of Physiological Psychology* and Charcot's theories on hysteria.

Feodor's knowledge of hypnosis was more thorough than that of any other doctor Johanna had met, even in the East. He agreed with her belief that insanity was not merely the result of lesions of the brain, but often stemmed from purely emotional causes. He shared her hope that hypnosis might prove an invaluable method to cure many types of madness, and possibly a number of physical illnesses as well. She couldn't wait to hear his thoughts on her theory that taking patients into their pasts, in search of inciting causes of insanity, was highly beneficial.

They hadn't yet reached the subject of specific cases when Feodor pulled out his watch and made a sound of surprise. "How quickly the hours have flown. I see it's time for dinner. I've arranged a private meal for us here. It will allow us to continue our talk."

"That sounds excellent." When he turned away to summon a waiter, she touched her cheek, wondering if it looked as warm as it felt. Her mouth was dry from the long conversation.

"A little wine before dinner?" Feodor asked. A waiter had already cleared and set the table, and was presenting a bottle of wine in a silver cooler.

"Please," Johanna said. The waiter poured, and Feodor tasted his wine with a connoisseur's deliberation.

"It will do." He signaled the waiter to pour for Johanna. In spite of her desire to be cautious, thirst made her take a much larger sip of the wine than was prudent.

"Bring water, as well," Feodor ordered the waiter, who hurried off. He leaned back in his chair and watched Johanna. She set down her glass, still strangely flustered at being the focus of his attention.

"I hope," she said, "that after our meal I may have an opportunity to consult with you about a particular patient. The situation is rather delicate—"

"You may, of course, rely on my complete discretion. I will be most interested to hear the details." He sipped his wine. "You said that you have four patients, I believe?"

"Five, now—I have a new case as of two weeks ago. And one of the original four is really not a patient in the strictest sense of the word. He, like the others, had few choices about where to go."

"But you and your father took all of them in."

"We have benefited as much as they have."

Feodor leaned toward her. "You are too modest, Johanna. These people are not merely medical subjects to you."

She couldn't argue with him in that. She wondered how well she would do in any argument with such a man.

And yet she wasn't disturbed at the idea of having met her equal, a male doctor who neither condescended to her nor betrayed resentment at her accomplishments.

He captured her gaze, drawing her out as surely as the summer sun brought the Valley's grapes to ripeness. "Who is your most intriguing patient, Johanna?"

"Quentin Forster," she answered, without thinking. She'd meant to discuss her cases in general terms before revealing names, and then only if she felt comfortable in doing so.

"Is he your newest one?" he asked.

Now that the subject was broached, her feelings were decidedly mixed. She was inclined to trust Bolkonsky, and he definitely had the necessary skills and approach to treat someone like Quentin. But to speak candidly about Quentin was going to be more difficult than she had imagined.

"Yes," she said. "A case of dipsomania, complicated by . . . delusions of lycanthropy."

"Fascinating." Feodor stroked his lower lip. "Was he brought to you by family members?"

"No. He found us."

"And have you had success in treating his condition?"

"I am . . . presently considering my options."

"Tell me about him," Bolkonsky said. "Perhaps you can benefit by a second opinion."

She took another quick sip of wine. "I was not being accurate when I said that Quentin was my most intriguing patient. Irene DuBois is also a considerable challenge— "

"Irene DuBois? The actress? I saw her once on Broadway. Very . . . interesting."

Surprised, Johanna glanced at his face and caught a faint shift in expression, as if he'd blurted out something he hadn't intended to say.

"My apologies for interrupting," he said, recovering smoothly. "You were speaking of Quentin Forster—?"

"Actually, my greatest progress has been with a former

soldier in the War, who has suffered intermittent mania and long periods of catalepsy and melancholy. Let me tell you a bit about him, instead."

Feodor listened, but she could have sworn that a flash of displeasure darkened his ice-blue eyes. That, she decided, must be the work of her overly sensitized imagination.

Soon enough dinner arrived to rescue her, and they ate in relative silence. The food was delicious, exquisitely prepared, and nothing like Mrs. Daugherty's plain but nutritious cooking. Johanna enjoyed it less than she'd expected. She deliberately avoided finishing her wine, even when Feodor offered more.

But after-dinner conversation returned to easier channels. She rose to leave, several hours later, in good charity with Feodor Bolkonsky and somewhat bemused by her earlier disquiet.

"Thank you so much for the dinner, and the excellent company," she said.

"You will come back tomorrow?" Feodor asked as he escorted her to the stable, where they waited for the stable boy to harness Daisy. "I realize that you have your own business to attend to, but I should very much like to continue our discussion of this intriguing patient of yours."

"Harper?"

"Quentin Forster. A lycanthrope is something I've never encountered before. And it's precisely the kind of case I feel is best suited to my particular skills."

How could she continue to demur, when Bolkonsky was so eager to help? She couldn't have been given a more advantageous opportunity.

"I look forward to it." She gave the well-fed horse a pat on the withers and accepted Feodor's help into the buggy. "Is two o'clock satisfactory?"

He took her hand and kissed the air above it. "More than satisfactory."

"Until tomorrow, then. *Auf Wiedersehen.*"

"*Auf Wedersehen,* my dear doctor."

Johanna hurried Daisy into a trot, following the path by the last light of day. Something like elation hummed through her body and filled her mind with a hundred new ideas. How much she'd missed, living here in the country! But surely there were few like Dr. Bolkonsky, who could understand and match the flow of her thoughts so perfectly.

Mrs. Daugherty was waiting up for her, concern evident in the set of her mouth. "Thought you'd never get back," she said. "My girl's gone home."

"I'm sorry. I shouldn't have stayed away so long." She had a powerful urge to hug Mrs. Daugherty, which would doubtless startle the old woman into believing she had run mad herself.

"I take it yer meetin' went well?"

"Very well, thank you." She caught the smells of left-over dinner in the kitchen. "Everyone has retired?"

"Far as I know. Since you weren't here, they all went to bed early. I checked up on your pa, but young Quentin has been takin' right good care of him."

"Yes." Her heart did a somersault at the thought of seeing him again. She felt so much hope.

And a very strong need for a long, hot soak. "I know it's late, Bridget, but could you help me prepare a bath?"

"I always keep water heatin' on the stove." The older woman squinted at Johanna and slowly smiled. "Well, well. You're in the mood for luxuriatin', I can see that. He is a handsome sort, your doctor."

Johanna pretended not to hear the innuendo. "If you're sure you don't mind—"

"Not at all. You just go to your room and I'll take care of the rest."

Tripping lightly down the hall, Johanna paused to listen, hearing only the quiet of a settled household. Papa was asleep. She went to her room and threw open the windows to the evening breeze.

Her bathtub, separate from the hip bath used by the others in the pantry off the kitchen, was set in a corner of her room behind a screen. It was a small, personal indulgence she wasn't able to use nearly often enough.

She hummed under her breath as she undressed. Mrs. Daugherty came in with a bucket of steaming water and emptied it into the tub, then brought in two more buckets of cool water to mix in. It made for a very shallow and lukewarm bath, but Johanna wasn't about to complain. She stepped behind the screen and shed the rest of her clothing.

"Will you take my dress for cleaning and brushing, Mrs. Daugherty? I may need it again soon."

"I will indeed."

"Also, can you bring your girl tomorrow? I may have another appointment in town."

The older woman chuckled. "Will you, now. Well, I s'pose my daughter can spare me an extra day or two this week. Good night, Doc Jo."

"And you." She waited until Mrs. Daugherty had closed the door, and sank into the tub. If only she had that wine now . . .

"Johanna."

She sat bolt upright in the tub, sending water splashing over the edge.

Quentin.

Chapter 14

She was quite naked.

Quentin knew that, had known before he walked through the door. The scent of her skin had carried into the hallway, a perfume of bare flesh tinged with the minerals in the water and a trace of perspiration that carried the unmistakable signature of arousal.

Not blatantly sexual, perhaps. But arousal just the same. And it had drawn Quentin to her with the force of a deadly compulsion.

He stopped at the sound of her indrawn breath. He'd given her warning. She was safe behind the screen. But he wasn't safe. He wasn't safe at all.

All day long he'd chopped at the fallen tree, trying to sweat her out of his system. It hadn't worked. Harper's words rang in his head with each blow of the axe, and he'd paced and listened and smelled the air for the first hint of her return to the Haven.

Now she was here, and he couldn't wait any longer.

"Quentin?" Her usually steady voice carried a quiver.

"This is not a good time. I will speak with you in the morning—"

"You were gone all day." His words sounded harsh even to his own ears.

"Please leave," she said. He heard the splashing of water, imagined her covering her full breasts with her arms in an instinctively protective gesture. He wet his lips.

"I won't hurt you." An absurd statement. Of course he wouldn't hurt her, wouldn't rush around the screen and scoop her from the water and lay her on the bed and ravish her . . .

"I would appreciate some privacy," she said.

So would I. With you. He struggled to rein in his unruly imagination. His mind was spinning wanton images of him and Johanna cavorting in her bed, of her uninhibited cries as he entered and rode her, of her skin flushed with passion.

He could see far more than just her face if he stepped around the screen. He wildly considered going back out to the yard, amid the stacks of newmade firewood, and resuming his attack on the fallen oak he had yet to defeat.

It wouldn't help. Nothing helped.

"Mrs. Daugherty told me you went to meet a doctor," he said. *A male doctor.*

"That is not your concern," she said sharply. Johanna was seldom angry.

Her indignation did nothing to quell his own helpless arousal. Nor did the heavy scent of a man's expensive cologne on her clothing, in the room—and underlying it, too faint to identify, the smell of a strange male.

He moved to her bed, where she'd laid out her undergarments. They smelled only of *her.* The chemise was of material too coarse to be of the best quality, but he stroked it against his face as if it were made of the finest silk. He inhaled her.

"What are you doing?" she demanded. "This is not appropriate behavior. Leave at once."

She spoke as if to a child. Or a madman. He laughed hoarsely. "What are you afraid of, Johanna? I just came in to say good-night."

Do what she asks, he told himself. *Leave.*

Why should you? another part answered. *Harper said she wants you. Make her admit it.*

He sat down on the edge of Johanna's bed, trapped between two conflicting forces. His mind was the battleground. He couldn't get a grip on his thoughts, let alone make them obey his will.

"Quentin?"

He didn't trust himself to answer. The ugly, lustful propensity within him ruled his voice. Another Quentin spoke in his mind, a second self, mocking his restraint—twisting in his brain until the agony made him reach for a bottle that wasn't there.

"I know you're still here, Quentin," Johanna said. Her voice had calmed, becoming that of the impersonal physician once more. Quentin nearly hated her for that self-possession.

He was consumed by darker compulsions.

Obsessed.

"I am getting out now," she said.

He could almost see her rising naked from the water. Lifting one long leg and then the other, water streaming over her soft, fair skin. Breasts glistening, each erect nipple crowned by clinging drops. Belly slightly rounded, full hips made to cradle a man's body, strong thighs with a secret thatch of brown curls between.

Quentin thrust his fingers into the bedcover, grabbing fistfuls of quilted cloth.

Johanna walked out from behind the screen. She didn't cower or try to cover herself, though she must have seen at once that he hadn't averted his gaze. She stood tall and defiant, her arms at her sides, only the rapid rise and fall of her breasts revealing her emotion.

"Is this what you wished to see?" she asked. "Look, then."

Oblivious to shame, Quentin complied. He devoured her with his eyes. Her face was flushed, as he'd imagined it; her hair fell in wanton disarray about her shoulders, an errant lock trailing over one full breast.

Her breasts were magnificent. Firm, lush, begging to be suckled. Her shoulders were broad enough to support them in perfect proportion. Her waist narrowed beneath them, flaring out into generous hips. She held her legs close together, but he glimpsed the blush of her sex behind the screen of curls.

And he smelled her. That body, such fertile ground for a man's seed, revealed her true desires, the ones she dared not show with her fearless blue gaze.

Arousal. Moisture that gathered and spilled over to ease a man's passage, perfume surely even a human male could scent.

His own body was more than ready. He ached. He throbbed. Satiation was only moments away. He could seize her now and she would hardly resist. On the floor, against the wall; lying beneath him or on her knees, again and again until he'd had enough . . .

He rose. He fumbled for the buttons of his trousers. She watched and didn't move, silently pleading with him to take her. Take her.

One step. Another. He dragged his gaze from her body to her face. Her eyes.

Johanna's eyes. Waiting for him to betray her trust.

No.

His feet sealed to the floor. His muscles spasmed. He managed to make them function at last, moving him back. Away from Johanna, one inch at a time, toward the door.

Howling. He heard howling, from somewhere in the center of his being. The rage of a thwarted monster. If Johanna spoke, he couldn't hear her. By touch alone he found the doorknob and turned it. The howling pursued him all the way back to his room.

J*ohanna's legs buckled.*
   She dropped to her knees on the floor, giving her trembling muscles a chance to recover. Never in her life had she felt so weak, or so confused.

Not afraid. That was the remarkable thing. She'd seen as soon as she stepped out from behind the screen what Quentin intended.

But Quentin would never commit rape. That certainty helped her to stand still and wait for Quentin to realize it himself.

Not before she had been driven nearly to the very edge of her faith and reason. Not before she'd realized that some part of her almost wished he had followed through with the impulses that ruled him.

Gott in Himmel. Self-disgust tightened her throat. She pushed herself to her feet and went to the door. The hallway was quiet and dark. Her door had a lock, like all the rooms in the house, but she hadn't felt the need to use it since taking up residence here.

If she turned the key now, would it be to protect herself from Quentin, or impose an artificial defense against her own emotions? She left the door unlocked and stumbled to the bed, feeling for her dressing gown. She had to concentrate to get the sleeves over her arms and the sash tied about her waist. By the time that simple task was finished, her sense was restored.

Sense, but not equilibrium. That would take a little more effort.

She sat on the edge of the bed, where Quentin had been. The spot was still warm from his body, but she didn't flinch away. This had to be faced, and squarely.

What had happened? She could only guess what had set

off Quentin's bizarre behavior—and her own equally aber-
rant response to it.

Revealing herself to Quentin had been the height of
folly. Had she actually believed it might help him?

She backed away from the painful thought of her own
lapse and tried to consider the causes for Quentin's conduct.

She'd been gone all day, true. She didn't know what
might have happened during her absence, except that Mrs.
Daugherty had nothing to report.

Quentin had acted as though intoxicated, but she hadn't
smelled alcohol. Something had gone very wrong.

The wrongness was the same she'd seen yesterday in
their last session, and in the parlor. In his eyes lurked a
shadow Quentin, a man-beast filled with lust, irrational
hunger, even a kind of cruelty. A creature who wanted her,
making no attempt to hide it. And Quentin wanted her just
as much.

That was the truth she had avoided, danced around, regarded with the sham of a scientist's detachment. Just as
she had failed to admit that Quentin might be far more afflicted than he appeared. The part of his mind that controlled the darkest human instincts had briefly lost some
interior battle, here in this room, a battle in which she was
the prize.

Hypnosis released the shadow Quentin. So, she suspected, did drink. Neither had been used tonight. What had
triggered it? Could it possibly be the kiss in the vineyard,
and jealousy the ordinary Quentin couldn't admit?

The only way to be sure was to hypnotize him again.
And she couldn't trust herself to do it. She'd come too close
to forsaking everything she believed in.

She wanted him.

There. It was said, admitted fully, if only in her mind.
She wanted to know what it would be like to lie in his arms,
feel his kisses all over her body, experience the joining of

flesh she had only read about. She wanted to explore the lean, honed muscles she had only glimpsed before, see those red-gold eyes alight with the pleasure she gave him, and know ecstasy in return.

Quentin would give her ecstasy. She had no doubt that he was a superb and experienced lover, as accomplished in that skill as he was articulate and charming. And even if the Quentin she wanted had been temporarily absent, replaced by someone feral and dangerous, her feelings had not vanished. She saw now that they were a permanent part of her being. She understood that she had stepped out from behind the screen, knowing he was waiting, *because* of them.

Mere modesty did not keep her from his bed. Society's conventions did not trouble her. A woman was physically capable of enjoying the act of love, and should be free to do so. She understood fully what was involved in the practice of sexual intercourse, in theory at least.

As long as she remained Quentin's doctor, that theory would never be tested. But if Bolkonsky were able to treat him . . .

Good God. Had she been fooling herself? She had assumed that sending Quentin to another doctor was best for him, because she had begun to lose both control and objectivity in his particular case. He was unable to regard her as a doctor, and she hadn't been successful in maintaining the necessary distance and authority. Better to send him away than fail him.

Oh, yes, she found him attractive, fascinating, impossible to ignore. She had reacted too strongly to his kisses. She was never so aware of being a woman as in his presence.

But she had not envisioned a lasting relationship between them, not even in her dreams. Now she saw the selfishness of her motives.

If Bolkonsky took Quentin's case, he wouldn't be her patient. He'd be able to get well, without distractions. And then . . .

Then he could come back to her, man to woman, and all would happen naturally as it was meant to. She'd have Quentin for herself.

Unless, when he was cured, he didn't want her. Unless his interest was a patient's preoccupation with his doctor, the desires of a man separated from the rest of humanity, bound to vanish when he was restored to health and sanity.

She laughed. *How you build castles of air, Johanna. Be careful, lest they send you smashing back to the earth.*

H*e waited for her in the hotel lobby as he had yester-* day, a little more serious and less inclined to light conversation than he'd previously been.

That suited Johanna very well. They had much ground to cover, not least of all the issue of Quentin's future care.

She refused to dwell on last night's dreams, or how she'd awakened drenched in perspiration and aching with unsated needs. Quentin Forster was at the center of those dreams: red, seething, burning. Feodor Bolkonsky was cool, collected, the consummate professional, and just being in his presence reminded her that she was first and foremost a doctor.

She'd momentarily considered discussing Bolkonsky with Quentin that morning, but Quentin was nowhere to be found. Harper mentioned seeing him heading for the woods, and he hadn't returned for luncheon.

Was he feeling chagrined about last night? Did he remember it at all? She was almost glad not to have to face him again so soon. Today's meeting with Bolkonsky would surely give her a much-needed sounding board.

"I am very glad to see you again, Feodor," she said when she and Bolkonsky were seated in the private room. "I have an important subject to discuss with you." She readied herself. "Yesterday I mentioned the case of Quentin Forster, and you seemed particularly—"

He held up a gloved hand. "I beg forgiveness for interrupting you, but there is an urgent matter I must bring up before we continue."

"Urgent?" She saw now that she had overestimated his tranquillity. His fair skin was flushed, and his lips were pressed tightly together. She determined that he was angry, though not with her. Someone—or something—else had upset him before her arrival.

"Of course," she said. "Please go on."

"You must understand, Johanna. I had not planned for it to be this way, or to introduce the topic in such unseemly haste, so soon after we met. I have no choice." He cleared his throat. "It concerns another patient of yours, one May Ingram."

May had been so far from Johanna's mind that at first she was certain she'd misunderstood. "May? You know of her?"

"Yes. You see, I have been retained by May's father, Chester Ingram, to consult with you about returning her to his care."

With one brief sentence, Feodor set Johanna's thoughts in complete disorder. May's *father.*

Caught between fear and anger, she got up from her chair and paced to the window. She'd hoped never to be put in this position, though she had always known it was a possibility, ever since that night two years ago when a frantic Mrs. Ingram had brought May to the Haven.

Rain. A mother and young girl on the doorstep, soaking wet, carrying a pair of small traveling bags as if they were on a weekend visit to friends in the country.

"You are Dr. Johanna Schell?" the woman had asked. "I need your help."

Johanna had let them in. In short bursts of speech, the woman—young, well-dressed, and with a haggard, careworn face, told Johanna why she'd come. Not very coherently, not in great detail, but enough to make clear the extremity of her errand.

May had confirmed the truth of her mother's words when she'd suffered an hysterical fit right there in the parlor, and Johanna made her decision. With it had come certain promises and assumptions. May's mother vanished into the night, and didn't return.

Now May's father had appeared out of the blue, a man whose role in her flight had only been hinted at in Mrs. Ingram's hushed narrative. Those hints had been enough, more than enough at the time . . .

"Johanna?" Feodor stood at her elbow, frowning in concern. "I have upset you."

"You have surprised me." She made her way back to the chair and sat down, willing her heartbeat to slow. "I did not expect such deception from you, Doctor. This is the real reason you sought me out, is it not?"

Feodor sighed. "I would have wished to find you in any case, Johanna, for the work you and your father have done. This simply provided an additional excuse. I was quite surprised to learn that the girl Mr. Ingram searched for was a patient of yours."

At the moment, Johanna had scant interest in sorting out his motives. "Perhaps you had better start from the beginning."

"Of course." He sat down and regarded her earnestly. "I had only recently come to San Francisco, with the intention of remaining a few months, when I met Mr. Ingram at a social occasion. You must have heard of him: He is a prominent banker in the city."

Yes, she knew that much. Mr. Chester Ingram was a powerful man of great influence, no doubt. "Go on," she said.

"While we were talking, I told Mr. Ingram of my theories involving hypnosis. Mr. Ingram expressed regret that I had not been on hand to look after his wife two years ago, when she ran off with their daughter and disappeared. It seemed that Mrs. Ingram, having become mentally unstable, had labored under the delusion that her life was in danger, though she'd had everything a woman could desire."

Everything of material goods, he meant. "Was her condition diagnosed as insanity?"

"You must know as well as anyone," Bolkonsky said gravely. "Did you not meet her yourself?"

"Yes." There was no point in denying it now. "I did not find her to be insane, merely frightened."

"Ah." Bolkonsky was a little less cool than before, which hardly rectified his less-than-honorable behavior. Johanna did not trust his cordiality. "Mr. Ingram deeply missed his wife and daughter, and since May was subject to hysterical fits, he was most worried that she would not be suitably cared for. During most of the past two years he had believed both of them unrecoverable. He but recently discovered that May might still be in the area, and was having the possibility investigated.

"A few days later, he informed me that his daughter was a patient at a small private clinic in the Napa Valley, one administrated by the daughter of Dr. Wilhelm Schell. Naturally, I told him what I knew of your family's spotless reputation. He asked me if I might approach you about releasing his daughter into his care, so as to minimize the girl's discomfort. It is his desire that I should continue any treatment that may be necessary in light of what she has suffered."

At least Bolkonsky was aware that some trauma might have been involved. He surely underestimated it.

"I see," she said. "I believe I understand." Coldness seeped into her stomach. "It is true that Mrs. Ingram came to me two years ago, in an extreme state of distress, and begged me to look after her daughter, who was indeed suffering from hysteria. She said she was running from great danger, and could not care for May under the circumstances. I took the girl in. Mrs. Ingram asked me to promise not to reveal May's location, or her true name, until such time as she returned."

"But she did not come back."

"No." Johanna wasn't giving Bolkonsky a whit more information than she had to, and that included news of Mrs. Ingram's recent letter hinting at an expeditious return from Europe.

Bolkonsky shook his head. "It is a measure of your good heart and devotion to our profession that you have maintained the child at your own expense. Now that is no longer necessary. I know that you must have accepted Mrs. Ingram's mad tales, or you would have contacted May's father long ago."

Mad tales. Her intuition had long since told her otherwise.

"She was May's mother. I had no reason to disbelieve her, and I fully expected her to come back within a few months."

"Of course." Bolkonsky smiled. "You could only offer help to those in need, and maintain your doctor's confidentiality. But now you can hear the truth. I have spoken at great length with May's father. His wife was profoundly disturbed, from a family with a history of madness. Mr. Ingram had her under a doctor's care, but he was unsuccessful in curing her madness. Due to the lapses of an inattentive servant, she escaped with May before dawn one morning."

And made her way, evidently, to the Napa Valley. "I have seen many patients with such delusions," Johanna said.

"And sometimes it is difficult to tell where delusion ends and reality begins. But May has been without a parent for two years. There is a certain fear that she might inherit her mother's madness, due to her tendency toward hysteria—"

"May is not mad." Johanna gathered her feet under her and thought better of it. *Be calm. Do not let him see your anger. He must believe you his ally, not his enemy.* "She has not suffered an hysterical episode for a year."

"If she is cured of hysteria, Mr. Ingram and I have you to thank."

"Perhaps. But she still suffers from extreme shyness and a fear of the outside world, particularly men. You propose to take her from the Haven at a very critical time."

Bolkonsky nodded with obvious sympathy. "I would prefer to leave her in your care and make the transition very slowly, but Mr. Ingram is eager to be reunited with the daughter he'd thought lost. I anticipated the awkwardness of this, and asked that we continue in consultation with you, and with all due caution, so as not to upset May unduly. Mr. Ingram has agreed."

Johanna bit the inside of her lip. In spite of Bolkonsky's mild words, she had no doubt that he meant what he said. A parent had legal rights to his child that she, as a doctor, did not.

Johanna had never known how Mrs. Ingram had heard of the Haven, then so newly founded in the Valley, or why she'd given a strange doctor so much trust. But Johanna had been determined not to betray that trust.

If even half of what Johanna suspected were true, she dared not allow May to go back to her father.

There was the chance, however slight, that she was wrong, and Mrs. Ingram was truly unstable. Johanna hadn't had time to assess the woman's condition properly. She'd taken action based upon her own experience of similar cases over the years upon that, and May's hysterical state.

She had no facts, only supposition. Bolkonsky believed Mr. Ingram—or so he said. Only yesterday she'd judged the foreign doctor of sound mind and good heart, but her opinion of him had sunk considerably in twenty-four hours. Her previous trust was out of the question.

That was grounds enough to proceed with extreme caution.

"I am glad to hear that Mr. Ingram recognizes the necessity of moving slowly, for May's sake," she said. "She has come to regard the Haven as her home. She will not do well if she is forced to leave abruptly."

"Quite understandable." Feodor had returned to his former elegant poise, leaving Johanna no doubt as to his confidence. "Between the two of us, I'm certain that we can achieve this in the best way possible." He reached for Johanna's hands. "Together, Johanna. You and I will work together to help May and reunite her with her loving father. I shall consider it a privilege."

Johanna withdrew her hand before he could make contact. "I think that it might be best if you come to the Haven to visit May before we proceed further. I feel certain that when you see her, you will—"

"That will not be advisable. As you said, the Haven has been her home for two years. Neutral ground would be better. I suggest that you bring May to me here at the hotel. I have large and comfortable rooms that can serve for any examination or necessary treatment."

Johanna gazed at him through narrowed eyes. He was prevaricating. May would be better off being evaluated at the Haven, but Johanna sensed that Bolkonsky did not wish to visit her home for reasons of his own. Still, this was not the time to raise objections. She must save her ammunition, and buy time.

"I will need to prepare her for coming into town. In a week—"

"I'm afraid her father will not be content to wait so long. He is exerting a certain pressure upon me to act promptly. It must be tomorrow."

Such coercion explained Bolkonsky's earlier signs of anger. No doubt he disliked being pressured by a client; he was a man who expected to get his own way. How foolish she'd been to be dazzled by him.

And this was the end of her hopes about finding Quentin a good, fully impartial doctor to continue his treatment. Transferring him to Bolkonsky was now out of the question.

"Tomorrow is too soon," she said. "I must insist—"

"I'm sorry, Johanna. You'll see the wisdom of this, I feel sure. I fear that if we do not do as he asks, Mr. Ingram may involve the law . . . and neither one of us wishes that."

Johanna recognized a threat when she heard one. "There is one thing I will not allow, and that is May being hurt. If at any time I feel that she is harmed by this, I will stop it."

Bolkonsky withdrew a step. "You do realize that her father has complete authority over his own child."

"I meant what I said."

"*You* could not do otherwise." He tossed back his golden hair in an arrogant gesture. "I continue to admire your professional devotion."

This Feodor Bolkonsky was fully capable of mockery. "May and I will meet with you, as you requested," she said, "but I shall expect to see Mr. Ingram privately for an examination of my own. Then I shall determine if and when she is fit to meet her father."

"Agreed. Shall I expect you and Miss Ingram here tomorrow at one o'clock?"

May's voluntary appearance was a preferable alternative to her seizure from the Haven by force. "We'll be here."

"Then I shall bid you adieu, so that you will have the time you need with Miss Ingram. I am sorry that our other business has been delayed, but I hope we shall have future opportunities to discuss your other patients." He tipped his hat, clicked his heels, and strode from the room.

He was annoyed, the polished Dr. Bolkonksy, that she had dared to argue with him. But he expected to prevail. Why should he not, in dealing with a woman?

He did not know her. And she was well aware that her most dangerous opponent was May's father, not this foppish physician who so excelled in manipulation and deception.

D*aisy seemed to sense Johanna's worry as they drove* back to the Haven. Half-formed plans were already hatching in Johanna's mind, ranging from the deliberate to the desperate. Finding solid proof of Ingram's alleged improprieties with his daughter and facing the influential businessman in a court of law was certainly one of the more desperate, if it came to that.

But deliberation won. The best scheme was to delay Bolkonsky and Ingram until firm arrangements could be made—arrangements for May's safety. Let Bolkonsky and Ingram believe she was cooperating. Resistance too soon would arouse their suspicions.

If there was even a grain of truth in Bolkonsky's claims of Mrs. Ingram's madness, Johanna much preferred to err on the side of caution. May could always be returned—if, against all Johanna's instincts, Ingram proved to be worthy of his daughter.

May was almost old enough to live on her own, but her mind was still that of a frightened girl. She was not ready for the world. She would do best residing with someone she could learn to trust, if she had to leave the Haven. Someone who could hide her as long as necessary.

May's precarious situation would consume all Johanna's time and effort from now until this matter of Mr. Ingram was satisfactorily resolved. The other patients would have to wait. And Quentin . . .

She had no choice but to put his treatment aside until she found another suitable doctor. That might take weeks, or months—every day a test of her will. She could only hope that his condition didn't worsen.

She unharnessed Daisy, gave her a measure of grain, and started toward the house. May was not in the garden or, as far as she could see, in the orchard or vineyard. In the full heat of the day, the patients were apt to be resting in their rooms.

Like a coward, she hoped Quentin remained in his. She wasn't to be so lucky. Quentin and May were together in the parlor, the girl reading to him in her light, hesitant voice. Mrs. Daugherty knitted on the sofa. All three looked up as Johanna entered.

Quentin blanched. He must remember at least some of what had happened last night. How much did he remember? . . . That was the question. But he collected himself, spoke softly to May, and rose from his chair.

"Good afternoon, Johanna," he said.

"Good afternoon."

"Back so soon?" Mrs. Daugherty asked. "Didn't expect you 'til evenin'."

"My plans have changed." She smiled at May. "May, I'd like to talk to you, in my office."

May glanced at Quentin, who nodded. "We can finish the book later," he said. "I do want to know what becomes of Avis."

"You won't read ahead?" May asked.

Quentin crossed his heart. "I promise."

May set the book down and went to Johanna. Quentin took the opportunity to slip from the room.

Relieved, Johanna took May into the office and shut the door. "You have had a good day?" she asked as the girl perched at the edge of the chaise longue.

"We spent the afternoon reading." May's tremulous smile lit up her face. "Quentin said I have a lovely voice."

"You enjoy Quentin's company, don't you?"

"Oh, yes. He is wonderful."

Wonderful. That was not the sort of word May was in the habit of using, when she spoke at all. And though she had

222 Susan Krinard

been the most relaxed in Johanna's company, something in her was always held in reserve. Even after she had overcome the more blatant symptoms of hysteria, she remained fearful and bereft of real trust for the world.

Today, May was happy. Genuinely happy, as she hadn't been since her mother's departure. Oh, there'd been moments of contentment and pleasure, but May had seldom reflected the joy of her name.

Johanna had seen enough of human character to postulate that May's happiness was due to more than Quentin's kindness and gentle attention. The girl was just old enough to fall in love. Quentin was agreeable and handsome. What could be more natural?

In other young girls, nothing at all. In May, it was a miracle.

Quentin, of course, would never take advantage of such tender emotions. He behaved toward her like an affectionate elder brother; he did May much good by teaching her that not all men were to be feared.

Those lessons were soon to be put to the test.

"Why don't you lie back and be comfortable," she instructed the girl. May did as she was told, her thoughts clearly on something—someone—else.

"May, this may be a difficult question, but I want you to answer it as best you can." She breathed in deeply. "Do you remember your father?"

The answer was very long in coming. So long, in fact, that Johanna finally realized May hadn't heard her. She repeated the question, and still May was silent.

"Tell me about Quentin," Johanna said.

May began to speak with enthusiasm, smiling up at the ceiling. Her hearing was not impaired, nor was her understanding. She simply did not want to hear or think or speak of her father.

She never had. But that was not the sort of proof that

would hold up in court. May had not yet reached the age of consent.

Johanna let May's monologue run its course, attempted without success to return to the subject of May's father, and then set her loose. May virtually skipped from the room. Doubtless she was going in search of Quentin.

She was free to seek him out.

After a half-hour of notations in her records, Johanna went to her father's room and sat with him a while. He slept peacefully on clean linens, hair combed and beard trimmed with loving attention. Quentin's work.

In the hour before dinner, she went out to her favorite place in the orchard to think. She caught a glimpse of something moving in the wood on the hill—a flash of motion and color, red amid the green. A while later Quentin emerged from the wood. He carried his head and shoulders set low, a man bearing a burden he wanted no one else to see.

She almost called out to him. In the end, her will—and her fear—were stronger than desire.

Chapter 15

The next afternoon, braced for the ordeal to come, Johanna took May into town.

She had finally given May half the truth about their reasons for going; she said that she wanted May to meet a doctor friend of hers, making sure that May understood that this "friend" was a man. She refused to be any less honest with her young patient. Had May reacted with a return to hysteria, or run off into the woods, Johanna would have postponed the meeting indefinitely and proceeded with the next move.

But May wasn't unduly disturbed. She didn't freeze in terror at the prospect of leaving the Haven or meeting a stranger. It was a vivid mark of her improvement that she went willingly, even with a touch of enthusiasm when Johanna promised to look for new books at the general store.

May had wanted Quentin to accompany them. But Quentin's presence would be a wild card in a very tenuous situation.

So she and May went alone, the girl outfitted in her

second-best dress, Johanna in her most sober gown. She found herself driving more slowly than usual, preparing herself for any eventuality and the absolute necessity of deceiving Bolkonsky, just as he'd deluded her.

All too soon they were in Silverado Springs. May seemed not to notice the sometimes hostile stares of the townspeople; she simply hunched in her seat beside Johanna. At the hotel, she took hold of Johanna's hand and clutched it so emphatically that her delicate bones seemed in danger of breaking.

"Don't leave me," she begged. "Don't leave me alone."

"I'll be here with you," Johanna said. She gave the girl a quick hug. "It will be all right." *No matter what I must do to make it so.*

A clerk in the lobby informed Johanna that Dr. Bolkonsky awaited their arrival in his suite of rooms, and offered to lead the way. Bolkonsky opened the door to her knock.

His blue gaze immediately fell on May. "Ah, Miss Ingram. I'm so glad you could come today."

May shrank behind Johanna. "I want to go home," she whispered.

Johanna and Bolkonsky exchanged a guarded look. "Of course you do," he said gently. "And you will, soon enough. In the meantime, ladies, won't you come in and take refreshments with me?" He smiled at May. "I have some delicious biscuits and jam and cakes."

May's wary expression matched Johanna's own feelings. She led May into the sitting room, unobtrusively keeping herself between the girl and Bolkonsky.

Bolkonsky's suite was undoubtedly the hotel's finest accommodation, its furnishings rich and only a little out of date. Bolkonsky's practice must be very successful indeed, if he were not heir to some fortune that allowed him to spend money so freely. Johanna realized that she'd never inquired about his family or background beyond his education. Now she wished she knew a great deal more about him.

"Please, sit down," he said, offering the women chairs near the window. He personally served the refreshments, but the biscuit May selected remained uneaten in her hand.

"Well, May," he said. "As I said, I'm glad you and Johanna could come to see me today. She has told me much about you."

May stared at him—openly, not with the brief, darting looks she ordinarily employed with strangers. "Why?" she asked.

Bolkonsky glanced at Johanna in surprise. It *was* unlike May to be so direct. Johanna was no less startled, but also proud of the girl's courage. This meeting might be endured without disaster.

"Johanna surely told you that I am a doctor, as she is," Bolkonsky said. "I know you've been staying at the Haven, and that you are familiar with Dr. Schell's methods. I had hoped you might talk with me, and perhaps allow me to hypnotize you. It would be a very great help to me, you see."

May crumbled her biscuit between her fingers. She looked at Johanna with pleading in her eyes.

"I would rather not," she said. "Johanna . . ."

"I know I am still a stranger to you," Bolkonsky said, "but I hope to remedy that situation." He picked up a book from a side table. "I understand that you enjoy reading. I've brought a book for you—"

"I don't want it." May bolted from her chair and moved behind Johanna's. "I don't like him," she whispered in Johanna's ear. "If Quentin were here—"

"Ah. Quentin," Bolkonsky said. "Is he a friend of yours?"

"Yes." May's face hardened into a mask of defiance. "*You* aren't my friend."

This went far beyond remarkable behavior for a girl who

feared nearly everyone and everything. Johanna hid a triumphant smile. This would not be such a one-sided battle after all.

"Is there a place where I might have a word with May?" she asked Bolkonsky.

"Certainly. Just through the door behind you." He smiled again at May. "Take your time."

Johanna took May's hand and led her into the bedchamber Bolkonsky indicated. She closed the connecting door between the rooms.

"May, I must ask you a question. Please answer honestly. Why do you dislike Dr. Bolkonsky so much?"

May stood rigidly against the wall, her fingers curled into fists. "Do we have to talk to him? I'd like to go home now."

Johanna rested her hand on May's dark head. "I know you would. Think of this as a sort of play, with you and me as the actors."

"Like Irene?"

"Perhaps not exactly like Irene. But I like Dr. Bolkonsky no more than you do." She smiled encouragement. "I need your help to make the doctor think that we are both happy to be here. I wouldn't ask you without good reason."

"He knows Quentin, doesn't he?"

The odd certainty in her voice took Johanna aback. "Only in the way he knows of you, as a resident of the Haven. Why?"

She began to shake. "I'm afraid."

It wasn't an answer, but Johanna could see that May had reached the end of her endurance. Damn Bolkonsky—and her own failure to find some alternative to bringing May to town.

"I'll speak to the doctor and tell him you are not well." She cupped May's cheek in her palm. "You remain here until I come for you."

For the first time May smiled. "Thank you, Johanna."

"You're welcome." She left Johanna in the room and opened the door to the sitting room.

Bolkonsky was no longer alone. Another man stood beside him, head bent toward the doctor in hushed conversation.

Johanna stopped, misgiving blooming into alarm. The man was tall, large-boned, and well, if loudly, dressed; his features were heavier than May's, the eyes a muddy gray rather than dark brown. But Johanna knew who he must be.

"Dr. Schell," Bolkonsky said, stepping in front of his co-conspirator. "I . . . something unexpected has happened. May I introduce Mr. Chester Ingram, May's father. Mr. Ingram, Dr. Johanna Schell."

Barely inclining her head to the intruder, Johanna fixed Bolkonsky with a cold stare. "I thought we had agreed—"

"Yes. But Mr. Ingram has expressed a reluctance to wait to meet his daughter again. It is understandable, after all . . ."

Understandable—or planned all along? Johanna turned her gaze on Ingram. "Mr. Ingram, May has been under my care for the past two years, as you know. She is subject to hysterical fits if exposed to upsetting conditions." She fortified herself for the unaccustomed lies. "I brought her today with the expectation that she would have the necessary time to adjust to the prospect of returning to your care. I was to speak with Dr. Bolkonsky, and arrange a later meeting between you and your daughter."

Ingram pushed past Bolkonsky. He carried himself with the air of a man who was used to command, and did not like being so addressed by a woman.

"So Dr. Bolkonsky told me . . . Miss . . . Dr. Schell," he said. "But I have been wrongfully separated from my daughter, whom I love, for two long years." His eyes narrowed in calculating assessment. "I know that my wife brought May to you with crazy stories born of her own madness. I don't blame you for believing her; she is very persuasive. But now it's time for May to come home, for us to be a family again. I will brook no needless delays."

"Needless?" Johanna fought to control her anger, and the instant hostility she felt for this man. Hostility, and fear—for May's sake. This was a man from whom a woman might flee in fear for her health. Or her life.

"You do want what is best for your daughter, Mr. Ingram?" She stepped closer to him, looking up into his face. "I have worked long with May to overcome her fears—the fears she has shown ever since she came to me. If you wish her to become hysterical again, then by all means proceed as you have been."

Ingram glanced at Bolkonsky in outraged amazement. "*This* is the doctor you told me was to be trusted? She—" He broke off, staring toward the door to the bedchamber. May stood on the threshold, utterly still. Her face had lost all color.

"May," her father said hoarsely. He opened his arms. "May, my darling—"

With a choking gasp, May bent backward at the waist, her spine forming a sharp curve. Johanna barely made it to her in time to catch her before she fell. The girl convulsed, her teeth clicking together.

Johanna yanked a curtain cord from the window, eased May to the ground, and pushed the cord into her mouth to prevent her from biting her tongue.

Bolkonsky dropped to his knees beside her and helped hold May down. In a few moments it was over. May's face was bathed in sweat; her body was limp. She kept her eyes tightly closed.

"*Gott in Himmel,*" Johanna whispered. One bout of hysteria, and all the progress of the past year was lost. She had been so sure that May was over the fits for good.

Arrogance on her own part. Sheer arrogance, hubris, stupidity . . .

May's father came toward them and crouched as if to

take May in his arms. Bolkonsky forestalled him and carried May into the bedchamber himself. Johanna sat beside May, shielding her from any further male intrusion.

"Move away at once. Let me be alone with her," Johanna said, adjusting the pillows under May's head. "She has not had such a fit in over a year; you will have to explain to Mr. Ingram the severity of her relapse. We expected too much of her, too soon."

"I must concur with your analysis," Bolkonsky said.

Johanna didn't allow him to see her surprise at his sudden cooperation. "Then make Mr. Ingram understand that he cannot take May with him until she has fully adjusted to the prospect, however much time that may require. Unless he wishes her to become even more ill." She twisted to meet Bolkonsky's gaze. "Surely you see that she fears her father. Do you still believe she belongs with him?"

The Russian doctor stroked his chin. "This is a setback, Johanna, but we can still find a satisfactory conclusion. I will see what I can do."

"And ask him to leave these rooms so that I can take May back to the buggy. I will not have her suffer again today."

Bolkonsky answered with a bow and retreated. The door remained opened a crack behind him.

"What the hell is going on?" Ingram demanded. "What's happened to my daughter? I thought you said this woman cured her."

"I have no cause to doubt—" Bolkonsky began.

"She's useless, a charlatan. I won't have May in her care one minute longer—"

The door closed, shutting off his words. May remained still and mute.

"All will be well," Johanna murmured, stroking damp hair away from the girl's face. "We'll be home very soon."

May opened her eyes. "Where am I?"

"Don't worry about that now. Just rest."

"I'm not tired." She reached for Johanna's hand. "Are we going now?"

Given what May had just experienced, that was a regular speech. She hardly seemed aware of what had set off her fit, or why she'd been afraid. Johanna cast up a wordless prayer of gratitude.

"Soon," Johanna assured her. Bolkonsky entered the room, hovering in the doorway. Johanna joined him out of May's hearing.

"He's gone," Bolkonsky said. "I'll keep you informed as to his decision regarding his daughter."

"*Sehr gut.* I think it best if we postpone any more meetings for at least a week. Mr. Ingram should return to San Francisco for the time being."

Bolkonsky didn't reply. His cool stare swept over May. "She seems recovered enough. I will send you a message at the Haven."

Nodding her agreement, Johanna helped May up from the bed and walked her slowly back to the stable. May showed no further reaction to what had happened, nor made any reference to Bolkonsky or her father. It was as if they had already ceased to exist for her.

And they would soon enough. The time for mere planning was past.

Oscar galloped out to meet them when they arrived at the Haven, and immediately took charge of Daisy. Johanna saw May to her room and made sure she was calm and comfortable, then visited her father and Harper. She made an appointment to talk with Irene and Lewis before dinner, and then took Mrs. Daugherty aside where they could not be overheard.

It was not a great leap of faith to trust the older woman with vital secrets, and Mrs. Daugherty was canny enough to have understood something of May's reasons for being at the Haven. She listened to Johanna's brief explanations with a furrowed brow and an increasingly dark expression.

"You were right to come to me," she said. "I know just what to do. I've a cousin over in Sacramento—she's got girls near May's age, and she'd take her in if I asked. Warm-hearted woman who never turned down a body in need."

"Like you," Johanna said, clasping Bridget's hands. "I have reason to believe that May's mother could return for her soon. If we can keep her safe until then—"

"How fast d' we have to get her away?"

"I think I've bought us a week. Time enough for a letter to reach your cousin."

"Then let me get to writin' it, an' I'll get it out in tomorrow's post."

Grateful and relieved, Johanna wandered about the house aimlessly for half an hour and finally found herself standing in front of Quentin's door.

Her feet had carried her there without her brain's participation. She knew why. Her mind was bursting with a thousand concerns she wanted to share with someone who would understand, her worries for May chief among them. She went to Quentin instinctively, as once she'd gone to her father.

He wasn't her father. How could she even consider it, after the events of two nights ago? If she couldn't treat him as a patient, far less could she confide in him as a peer. To do so would put them both in jeopardy.

Nor dared she tell him what had happened at the hotel, given his closeness to May. It was a grave shortcoming that she felt the need to confess her fears to him.

To what purpose? So that he might put his arms around her and tell her it would be all right, as she'd so glibly told May?

So that he might kiss her?

She shivered and rested her forehead against the wood of the door.

•　•　•

Johanna *stood just outside.*

Quentin could smell her, hear her breathing, sense her agitation through the flimsy barrier of wood. It was the first and only time she'd sought him out since he'd gone to her room the night before; he'd made himself scarce, and she'd been busy with May.

Visiting with that new male doctor in town.

The hair rose on the back of his neck, and he smoothed it down with one hand.

Jealousy. Wasn't that what had sent him to invade Johanna's most private sanctum? Johanna had returned from town that day with a spring in her step and eyes alight with pleasure. Quentin had watched her, reluctant to go too near because of the potency of his feelings. Afraid to trust himself around her.

Jealousy. Oh, he'd denied it vehemently to himself. He knew nothing of this Bolkonsky beyond his name and what little Mrs. Daugherty had told him. He was no physician to share Johanna's professional life and interests. He had no claim on her—none that extended beyond his imagination. But he had entered her room, uninvited, as no gentleman would do. That was where the memories became confused.

Just like before, as if some outside force had snatched control of his mind and body, he could recall only scraps of conversation—enough to know that he'd behaved badly. Enough to send him slinking from her room in shame, and avoid her thereafter.

What he remembered with painful intensity was arousal—overwhelming, single-minded lust—and the sight of Johanna's naked body.

All it took was that one memory, and he felt as he had then. He spread his hand against the door as if he could touch her flesh. Mold it between his hands. Kiss it in a thousand ways and a thousand places.

He groaned. At least he knew he hadn't attempted to ravish her, or he'd have been ejected from the house. Scant consolation.

No consolation at all.

It didn't help that he suspected the situation with Johanna, May, and the mysterious Dr. Bolkonsky had not turned out as Johanna hoped. Her manner had been considerably more sober yesterday, after her second meeting with the doctor. And today . . .

Today she'd taken May to town with her, an extraordinary occurrence in itself. She certainly hadn't confided in him, but he'd seen her face upon her return, when she was too preoccupied to notice his presence.

And May had come directly to him.

He'd tried to speak with May, to learn why she'd gone with Johanna and what had transpired, but she hadn't responded to his careful questions.

Quentin had never made a habit of studying human nature, but his werewolf blood made it relatively easy to know what humans were feeling. Johanna was no better than May at hiding her emotions. She was distracted and worried.

He had added to that burden.

What was he to Johanna Schell? A source of confusion, of apprehension, perhaps even of fear. He might be her patient, but he was not her lover, or her keeper.

He might become her obedient hound, awaiting his chance to roll on his back in abject apology. A woman might tell a dog what she wouldn't share with a wolf.

Should he hear that anyone or anything had hurt her or May, hound would become wolf in an instant.

And do what? he asked himself, laughing derisively at his own conceit. *This wolf's fangs have been pulled.*

"Quentin? Are you there?"

He leaned into the door, resting his forehead against the wood.

"I'm here."

"We'll be having dinner soon, and a gathering in the parlor afterward. I hope you'll join us."

It would be the first such gathering since things had gone so wrong a week ago. Johanna was striving for a sense of normality.

"I'll be there," he said. *And I'll behave myself—at least enough to learn what is troubling you and May.*

Her footsteps moved away from the door. So, she was dodging the chance to speak to him alone.

Wise, from her perspective. But two people could be alone even in a crowd, and he'd find a way.

Dinner was a tense, quiet affair. Even Mrs. Daugherty said little. Afterward, in the parlor, Lewis made exaggerated efforts to stay far away from Quentin. Irene claimed the entire sofa; she smiled like the idiomatic cat who'd eaten the canary. Harper took a chair by the empty hearth, his gaze shifting from Johanna to Quentin and back again. Wilhelm Schell nodded to himself from his wheelchair and Oscar played with his puzzle, while May sat cross-legged on the carpet at Quentin's feet. Johanna ensconced herself at the head of the room, separate from everyone else—especially Quentin.

She needn't have worried, when the two of them were accompanied by six potential chaperons.

Chaperons with no power to prevent a loup-garou from doing whatever he wished . . .

No. He forced out the savage, alien thoughts and concentrated on his objective. He had to get Johanna to himself, but not for the reasons his vivid imagination suggested. Casually, he picked up his chair and carried it close to Johanna's. May scrambled to follow him. From the sofa, Irene snickered.

Johanna concealed any hint of discomfort. "Quentin," she said, loudly enough for the others to hear. "How was your day?"

Such banalities were just another shield between them. "Better, I think, than yours," he said under his breath.

She pretended not to hear him. "You have such a handsome voice, Quentin. I thought you might read to us this evening, from one of May's books." She smiled down at the girl. "Would you like to choose one, May?"

"By all means," Quentin said, grasping the opportunity. "May, didn't you tell me the other day that you'd found an abandoned bird's nest? I'd very much like to see it, if you'll bring it along when you fetch your book."

The girl hesitated, sliding a glance at Johanna. "I'll get it," she said, and scurried into the hall.

Johanna sat very stiff and tall in her chair. Quentin smiled vaguely about the room for the benefit of the other patients, as if he had nothing at all on his mind.

"About the other night—" he began.

"There is something I must tell you—" Johanna said.

They stopped at the same moment and stared at each other.

"Ladies first, by all means," Quentin said.

"No. Please continue."

He lowered his voice to a hoarse whisper. "Johanna, I owe you a profound apology. I came into your room uninvited. I behaved like a cad. I am sorry."

She breathed in and out several times. "Do you remember what you said and did?"

"I remember . . . enough." He tried to capture her eyes. "I wasn't myself, Johanna. Will you accept my apologies?"

"Of course, Quentin. As a doctor, I understand such things. Let us speak no more of it."

His lip curled. There was his answer. It always came back to that, didn't it? Her professional detachment was her shield—maiden's armor, to protect her from unwanted intimacy or the chance of transgressing the patterns and accommodations of her life. She could still look at him and act as though he hadn't seen her naked body, never come close to—

He tried to stop the thoughts as they spilled, unchecked, from the dark reaches of his mind, but they were stronger than he was. "Shall we speak of Dr. Bolkonsky instead?"

She flinched, hardly more than a twitch of an eyebrow.

"You took May into town today," he said, "to see this Bolkonsky."

"Yes, I did."

"And something went wrong."

Johanna drew her legs under the chair. "May is not used to leaving the Haven."

"It was more than that. I saw both of you when you came back. She was terrified, and you were gravely upset."

"This is a personal matter."

"Personal? For you, or for May?" He leaned closer to her, and she angled away. "If it concerns May's well-being, it concerns me as well."

She straightened and met his gaze. "I appreciate your friendship for May, but she is my patient, not yours. And soon—" She broke off and visibly braced herself. "Given the complications that have attended my attempts to treat you, it seems best for everyone if I locate another doctor who can take over your case."

He felt not so much shock as anger—righteous, cleansing anger. He clenched his fists in his lap. "You mean you want to get rid of me."

Her eyes widened. "No, Quentin. It's for your own good."

"For *your* good, because you're afraid."

Her expression grew remote. "I wish only for you to receive the best of care. I may not be able to provide it . . . as I'd hoped." She swallowed. "You will not be leaving right away. There are few doctors to whom I'd entrust any of my patients, and the search will require diligence. In the meantime—"

"In the meantime, we'll go on like this, avoiding each other, avoiding the truth. Neither doctor and patient, nor friends, nor lovers."

She paled. "I would hope that we are friends, Quentin."

Her distress drained the unwonted anger from his body. What was he doing to her? It couldn't have been easy to admit that she no longer felt qualified to act as his doctor, even though he was the one to blame. How could he expect her to acknowledge anything else?

"Johanna—"

May chose that moment to return to the parlor, bearing the bird's nest in her cupped hands and a book tucked under her arm. She laid the nest at Quentin's feet. A porcelain fragment of a blue robin's egg rested at its center.

Quentin smiled for May's sake. "A treasure indeed," he said, lightly touching the nest. "Surprisingly sturdy, for all that it's made of twigs." He glanced at Johanna. "Very much like the human mind."

"And should it tear, it can be mended," she said with her usual composure. "If the desire is strong enough."

"Not so the egg inside." He tapped the broken shell with his fingertip. "No mending it once it breaks."

"Then we must take that much greater care to protect it. May, did you bring your book?"

With a little sigh of compliance, May began leafing through the book to find her favorite passage.

Irene, feeling neglected, arose from her royal seat and sauntered over to join Lewis. He ignored her, and so she turned her attentions to Harper. Quentin heard the murmur of their conversation, during which Irene strove in vain to attract Harper's interest. He responded with neutral courtesy, which offended Irene's sense of self-importance. She whirled about and set her sights on more familiar prey.

"I hear you have a new lover, Johanna."

Johanna blinked at the sudden attack. "I beg your pardon?"

"That handsome new doctor in town, Bolkonsky." Irene's smile was poisonous. "I don't know why you ever thought he would have an interest in *you.*"

May dropped her book on the carpet and stared at Irene. Quentin touched her shoulder. She was trembling.

"Why don't we go for a walk, May," he suggested. "You can show me where you found the nest."

The girl refused to budge. Johanna rose to take Irene's arm and steer her away from the others. Despite the low pitch of her voice, Quentin heard every word she spoke.

"How do you know about Dr. Bolkonsky, Irene?"

"You think I'm stupid, don't you? Just because I've been forced to live out here in this rural backwater with a house full of loonies and old maids—" She shook off Johanna's hand with a sneer. "Well, I do know about Feodor Bolkonsky. I know a lot more than you would ever guess. I still have admirers who have no intention of leaving me here to rot, and I—" She caught her painted lower lip between her teeth. "You might as well give up, Johanna." She pointed her chin toward Quentin. "Take *him* if you want. I don't."

She flounced back to the sofa, leaving Johanna to stare after her. Quentin wasn't in the least surprised that Irene DuBois had her own devious ways of tapping into the local gossip, even if the town considered her one of the "loonies" herself. She certainly wouldn't balk at prying into Johanna's personal and professional affairs.

She might even have already done what Quentin planned to do tonight. He hoped that Johanna didn't draw the same conclusion.

"Trust a woman like Irene to know the names of every eligible male within a hundred-mile radius," he joked when Johanna rejoined him. "I believe that I should pity the man."

"I do not." She sat down again, her expression shut to him. There'd be no further chance for conversation tonight.

Quentin did as he was asked and read May's passage

from *The Story of Avis.* The others made a pretense of listening, but he doubted they truly heard. When the gathering broke up an hour later, Harper made as if to speak to Quentin, only to fall silent. Quentin didn't encourage him. All his attention was centered on Johanna and May, the doctor and the innocent. They needed him, and, come the end of the world, he wasn't about to let them down.

J*ust after the stroke of midnight, when everyone was* tucked safely in his or her bed, Quentin slipped into Johanna's office. He knew exactly what he was looking for, and where to find it.

If he felt like a thief in the night, that was exactly what he was. Johanna kept her notes in the desk drawer, unlocked. She obviously hadn't expected any of her patients to go rifling through them. Not Irene, who might have already done so. Certainly not Quentin.

The recent entries about her meetings with Bolkonsky, and the visit with May, were tucked into the front of her notebook. Quentin sat down at her desk and read by the sliver of moonlight that shone through the office window. He sifted the lines of careful handwriting until he found the pertinent section.

The earlier notations rang with the confident satisfaction she'd shown after the first encounter with Bolkonsky. What she said of the man bordered on infatuation. Quentin's hair bristled, and he had to force his mouth to close over his teeth, which had a tendency to bare at every mention of Bolkonsky's name.

Fool, he told himself. *Concentrate.*

Concentration paid off. Yes, she thought very highly of the doctor at first. Enough to be flattered by his attention, to write glowingly of his knowledge of hypnosis and his study of her father's work. She even wrote of her hopes that Bolkonsky might become Quentin's new doctor.

But the next meeting's entry was different. *May's father,* he read, and stopped.

May's father. A Mr. Chester Ingram, a wealthy San Francisco magnate, a man Johanna had never mentioned. Bolkonsky had come to Silverado Springs to recover Ingram's daughter, lost to him two years ago. And he'd deceived Johanna in order to gain her trust before revealing his true motive for summoning her.

That was why she'd taken May into town.

Quentin set down the page and stared out the window. Johanna must have known of May's father, but she had deliberately not contacted him. She'd kept the child here, apart from Ingram, and was distressed at his appearance. Quentin remembered what she'd told him before he met May for the first time: "Her mother left her with us for treatment. I suspect her home life was not a happy one."

No reference to the mother here. Only a description of May's visit to town, where something had gone terribly wrong.

An hysterical fit. Terror. All because May's father had come into the room against Johanna's wishes and recommendations.

The terse sentences Johanna had written here hinted at so much more than they revealed. The one point made abundantly clear was that Johanna did not want to release May to her father . . . and had no intention of doing so.

Quentin swallowed the sourness in his throat and replaced the notes in their original order, then began a second search that took him to the bookshelves against the wall, and the boxes of older records.

The ink was faded on the original entries, made the night May came to the Haven. Quentin read them through without stopping, every line, until he understood the cause for Johanna's apprehension.

No proof, of course. Only speculation, the pleas of a frantic mother, the implications behind a young girl's bizarre behavior. Behavior that had changed when she was left alone to heal.

Only to be reawakened when she met her father face-to-face.

The sound of crumpling paper drew Quentin's unfocused stare to his hands. He'd crushed the sheets into balls in his fist. Releasing a shaky breath, he smoothed the paper flat on the desk.

No matter. Johanna would know someone had been rummaging about in her private papers, and it wouldn't take her long to determine the culprit.

Quentin reassembled the notes and restored them to their place in the box. The tight sickness in his chest was abating, replaced by the cold, metallic sting of compulsion. He left the room, and the house, in a body most would have mistakenly called human.

No one stirred on the grounds of the Silverado Springs Hotel. The staff had retired, the guests were asleep, and the night clerk was completely inattentive to werewolves on the prowl. Quentin easily slipped past him and found the register that listed Mr. Ingram's room.

He didn't know why he was here. He had ceased to think clearly from the moment he put Johanna's notes away. The fog in his mind had become so familiar that he hardly questioned it.

Tonight it drove him to the doors of the hotel's best suite. But the occupants behind these doors were not sleeping. He could hear the creaking of furniture, the whispers, the guttural laughter.

A man and a girl. He'd heard such whispers before.

His urge to kick down the door subsided as quickly as it came. He retraced his steps to the lobby and out into the night, circling the hotel until he located the suite's windows, open to the cool air.

Why should a man like Ingram bother to take precautions against intruders? What had he to fear? Quentin vaulted over the windowsill, avoiding the clutch of heavy draperies. He found himself in a darkened parlor only a room away from the voices—louder now, the man's whispering more insistent, the girl's strained.

He crept to the connecting doorway and looked through.

The girl could not have been more than fourteen, her maid's skirts bunched up around her thighs as she sat on Ingram's knee. She could have passed for much younger. She squirmed and leaned away from him as he nuzzled her cheek.

"Don't pretend you're innocent," he said, running his hand over her stocking. "I know you want it."

"Please, sir," she said. "I have to get home."

He chuckled. "Don't you want the sweet I promised you? It's right here in my pocket—"

Quentin's legs gave way. He caught himself against the wall, doubling over with dry heaves. The nausea and rage within him were such that he knew with sudden clarity what would happen if he walked through that door.

He flung back his head and howled.

Ingram's startled oath was muffled by the girl's scream of terror. Quentin crouched beside the window, waiting just long enough to hear the suite's outer doors slam and the girl's running footsteps down the hallway. Then he turned and leaped back through the window, his thoughts intent on one thing only.

Drink. Inebriety. Intoxication. The complete and total annihilation of all thought and feeling in the tender care of a bottle of whiskey. Even at this hour the Springs Saloon would still be open for business.

Chapter 16

"He hasn't come back, has he?"
Johanna turned at the sly insinuation in Irene's voice, letting the curtain fall from her hand. The rutted lane that led to the Haven's gate was as empty in late afternoon as it had been since early morning. Quentin was still missing, nowhere to be found in the house or the orchard or vineyard, not even in the woods where May had sought him when he'd failed to appear for lunch.

"It's so touching to see you worry over him," Irene cooed. "Just like the faithful wife."

The words struck more surely than any other insult Irene could concoct. Johanna stepped away from the kitchen window and met Irene's arch stare. "He is my patient, as you are. In fact, I have been neglecting you, Irene. I apologize."

"Don't apologize. I haven't had to listen to your boring speeches." She sat down at the kitchen table, draping her body over the chair in a languorous pose. "But it doesn't really matter, after all. I won't be stuck in this place much longer."

Johanna had heard this many times before, but for the past week Irene had been uncommonly quiet, even retiring—at least until last night.

Now she wanted to talk, and Johanna knew that she ought to take advantage of the opportunity. The other patients had all been seen today; merely waiting around for Quentin was a waste of valuable time.

Yet she was haunted by the fear that his absence was permanent. She'd told him of her plan to find another doctor for him, abruptly and without adequate explanation, chill as an alpine winter. Why should he stay, if she gave him no reason to do so?

She diverted her attention to the situation at hand. "Would you care to join me in my office and discuss it?" she asked Irene. "I'd very much like to try another hypnotic session, if you are willing."

"How predictable you are." Irene yawned. "Predictable, and stupid. You're so busy prying into people's heads that you don't even know what's happening right under your nose."

Johanna knotted her hands behind her back. "Would you care to enlighten me?"

"Why should I? You've always been so cruel to me." The older woman's eyes sparked with pleasure in her perceived power. "You've enjoyed torturing me. Well, now the shoe is on the other foot."

"I'm afraid I don't understand what you mean."

"Always that superior tone, as if you don't feel anything." Her voice began to shake. "Oh, yes, the great doctor. Just like God. So smart, so sure. Everything is so clear and easy for you. You look at people as if they were specimens in jars, and you can arrange them any way you like."

"Irene—"

"I'm sick of you and your hypocrisy! You're a whore underneath your starched collars. I know that you want Quentin Forster. But he won't have you, will he?"

White-hot anger bolted through Johanna. Irene shouldn't be affecting her this way.

"Go ahead, hit me again," Irene hissed. "I know you want to."

Johanna unclenched her fist and spread her hand on the table. "No, Irene. I realize that you're suffering. If you'll only allow me to—"

"You can't help me." The storm passed, leaving Irene panting and strangely rational. "But sometime soon you're going to find out what it's like to be helpless while other people take everything away from you, and there won't be anything you can do about it." She swept to the door. "As for Quentin," she threw back over her shoulder, "I saw him head for town late last night—after he was in your office going through your papers."

Johanna absorbed Irene's words. Quentin going through her papers? She wasn't shocked at the idea that Irene had done so, and had considered locking her office after the woman's outburst last night. But Quentin—

What had he said? *"If it concerns May's well-being, it concerns me as well."*

If he'd gotten into Johanna's notes about May, he would have read of her suspicions. And if he'd gone into town . . .

She nearly knocked over her chair in her haste to get up. She hurried to her room, changed her clothes and shoes, looked in on her father, and went out to the barn. No time to harness Daisy to the buggy.

May and Oscar were half-heartedly mucking out the cow's stall as she plucked the old sidesaddle off its stand. Oscar put down the shovel to help her. May watched, her gaze darting about and her expression pinched.

"Where's Quen'in?" Oscar asked. "May and I can't find him."

"That's what I hope to learn," Johanna said. She checked the girth strap and patted Daisy's withers.

"Are you going to town?" Oscar asked. "Can I come?"

"Not this time, Oscar." She smiled at May. "I'm going alone. I'd like you both to remain here, in case Quentin comes back while I'm gone."

May's shoulders sagged with relief, and Johanna realized that she'd feared being forced to return to Silverado Springs.

Not while I'm here, Johanna thought.

Or as long as Quentin was capable of interfering.

"Quen'in didn't read to us today," Oscar complained. He sensed Johanna's worry even though he didn't know the reason for it.

Johanna positioned an old crate she used as a mounting block and swung up into the saddle. "May, you're an excellent reader. Can't you read to Oscar this evening? I would consider it a favor."

May took a step toward her. "When will you be back?"

"No later than sunset. Can I rely on you to look after Oscar?"

May hesitated, glanced at Oscar, and nodded firmly.

"Sehr gut." Johanna guided Daisy out of the barn, May and Oscar trailing after. She waved good-bye and set off at a trot for town.

Silverado Springs buzzed like a jostled hornet's nest. A far larger than ordinary number of idlers stood on the street and porches, men and women who'd left their posts at store counters and desks to gossip over some new and exciting occurrence. Heads turned, as usual, when she rode in, but the stares lingered, and the hum of conversation stilled in her wake.

She didn't have to look far for someone to enlighten her. Bolkonsky stood under the awning of Mrs. Supp's dressmaking shop, deep in conversation with a man in an officious-looking suit. He glanced up, caught sight of her, and waved acknowledgment. Johanna dismounted and tied Daisy to the nearest hitching post.

Bolkonsky finished his conversation and came to meet

her. His smooth, handsome face bore the marks of recent strain.

"How are you, Johanna?" he asked. "Well, I hope?"

She saw no purpose in polite chitchat. "What is going on here?"

"We had best find a more private place to talk."

She folded her arms across her chest. "What has happened?"

"I'd thought you might have heard. Mr. Ingram was attacked and injured last night in the hotel."

"Attacked?" Her heart jumped. "By whom?"

"No one is sure—yet." He took her elbow and led her away from the prying eyes and ears of the locals. "Ingram didn't see his face. One maid at the hotel said . . . but that can wait."

Johanna remembered to breathe. "How badly is he injured?"

"He suffered a broken arm and a large collection of bruises. It could have been much worse, according to his report. But he was able to defend himself, and his attacker fled."

"A robbery?"

"Nothing was taken."

"I assume the authorities have been called in," she said. "Why was he attacked, if not in the course of a theft?"

"That is the question." Bolkonsky pursed his lips. "That is what the entire town is discussing. Apparently this has never happened before in Silverado Springs; it has deeply upset the residents. Since Ingram is a stranger here, no one can determine a motive for such an attack. And some of the speculation—" He stopped her and looked deep into her eyes. "It involves you, or more specifically, your patients."

Johanna forgot to breathe again. "What do you mean?"

"Some say—you know how these ignorant, small-town folk can be—that one of your patients might have come to town and attacked Ingram."

"That is ridiculous." She stepped back and turned in a small, agitated circle. "None of the Haven's residents would have done such a thing. When has any one of them ever come here and caused trouble?"

"Johanna," Bolkonsky said softly, "I agree with you. I know as well as you do the misconceptions held about the insane. But I have been listening to the gossip. Quentin Forster and one of your other patients caused a minor disturbance here several days ago. A matter of fisticuffs with local children."

Of course. Johanna hadn't forgotten. She'd known all along how that one incident could feed the fire of any prejudices the local folk already harbored.

"Oscar wouldn't hurt anyone," she said. "He was the one attacked. He merely defended himself."

"But he is certainly big enough to do damage if he wished, according to what I've heard. It's much easier for the ignorant to place the blame on outsiders than look among themselves for a culprit. And then there is Quentin—"

Quentin. The crux of the business. Quentin, who'd been missing all day. Who'd been worried for May. Who might have learned of May's father, and her acute misgivings about him.

"When did this attack occur?" she asked.

"Last night, well after midnight. A few drunks from the saloon claimed to have observed someone running away from the hotel, but no one clearly saw him, except a maid who was able to describe his general height and build."

Johanna didn't ask for the description. She felt cold all the way to her bones.

Why? Why should she jump to the same conclusions held by these unenlightened townsfolk? Quentin had exhibited occasional lapses into a darker state, a side of himself that hinted of undispelled pain and anger. He claimed, under hypnosis, to be a lycanthrope. He'd suffered periods of amnesia related to his drinking. He'd even admitted to concern for his own occasionally erratic behavior.

But he was not dangerously insane. He'd never acted overtly violent in any way—not with her, or the others. Surely reading of Johanna's suspicions about Ingram wouldn't be enough to send him tearing into town to attack a stranger.

But if that possibility were as ludicrous as it seemed, why was she trembling?

"What is it, Johanna?"

She shook herself from her bleak thoughts and met Bolkonsky's gaze. "If feelings against my patients are running so high, I must return to the Haven."

"Johanna—are any of your patients unaccounted for?"

"No." The lie came far too easily, but she felt free of guilt for the transgression. "I must be getting back."

"Why did you come to town, Johanna?" he asked, too insistently. "We still have the situation with May to resolve. You understand that in light of what has happened, Mr. Ingram is most anxious to leave Silverado Springs as soon as he is able to."

"We agreed upon a week at least, Dr. Bolkonsky."

"Did we?" His upper lip twitched. "I can make no guarantees, Dr. Schell."

His renewed formality came as a warning. She nodded and turned to collect Daisy. The pointed stares of the townsfolk made unpleasant sense, now. She could only pray that the residents of Silverado Springs were mistaken in their conjectures.

Once home again, she gave Daisy into a curious Oscar's care and began another circuit of the Haven's grounds, on foot, starting with the vineyard and ending at the orchard.

That was where she found him.

The half-conscious man slumped against a young apple tree was not the one she'd known for the past two weeks. He bore more resemblance to the stranger she'd rescued on

the lane to the Haven, clothes dirty and abraded, face unshaven, hair matted and tangled. He raised his head from
his chest to look at her through bloodshot eyes.

"Johanna," he croaked.

He had been drinking. She smelled it on him, but she
would have known even without the stench. It was amazing
that he could be in such poor condition after only a single
day of imbibing.

Unless his state had to do with other, less benign activities.

"Quentin," she said, shaping each word distinctly.
"Where have you been?"

He tried to get up and fell back, head rolling against the
tree trunk. "At . . . the saloon." He coughed out a laugh.
"Can't you tell?"

"Is that all?"

"I . . . don't remember."

Such a simple, terrible phrase. "Tell me what you do remember."

On the second try his efforts to stand were more successful. He propped himself against the tree, swaying.

"I went into town," he mumbled.

"Did you go through the papers in my office?"

"I wanted to find out about May."

"And you did."

He took a step toward her and paused to catch his balance. "I found out about her father."

Lecturing him on the impropriety of viewing private
documents was the furthest thing from Johanna's mind.
"And you went into town to do what, Quentin?"

"To . . . see him."

"Did you see him?"

"I think—" He clutched at his head. *"Don't. Please."*

He wasn't talking to her, she was certain of it. "What did
you do when you saw him, Quentin?"

With uncharacteristic awkwardness he spun on his foot

and staggered back to the tree, hugging it with both arms. "I went and got drunk."

"Something happened in town last night, Quentin, while you were gone."

His profile was stark and pale, cheek pressed to rough bark. "God."

Johanna came to a decision. She couldn't leave him like this, or allow both of them to remain unaware of what he'd done and unprepared for the consequences. Patient or not, she must continue to treat him to the best of her ability until this crisis was past.

"I would like to hypnotize you, Quentin—now. Can you walk with me to my office?"

He pushed away and started for the house, not waiting for her. She caught up and took a firm grip on his arm. May saw them first, and came running. Her face fell when she got a good look at Quentin.

"Quentin isn't feeling well," Johanna said, guiding him past the girl. "He needs to rest."

"Yes," May whispered. Oscar joined her, but neither made a move to follow them into the house.

Quentin fell back onto the chaise as if the short walk from the orchard had exhausted him. She made a more thorough inspection of his body for wounds or evidence of struggle, but found none. If he had been the one to attack Ingram, the other man hadn't left a mark on him when he'd defended himself.

If Quentin had attacked. If . . .

His half-dazed state made him even more susceptible to hypnosis than usual, and he went into a deep trance the moment she finished her induction.

"I would like you to do the best you can to answer my questions, Quentin. Reach into your memory, with no fear of what you may find."

His closed lids fluttered, but he made no answer.

"Let us start from the beginning. You went into town."

"Yes." His voice was flat, unemotional.

"To see May's father."

"Yes."

"Why?"

"I was worried about May. I read in your notes that he might have hurt her before she came here."

Johanna damned her own meticulous nature that demanded the recording of each thought and observation related to every patient within her care, no matter how based upon conjecture or guesswork. She doubly damned her carelessness in not locking those notes away.

"Did you think that May was in danger from her father?" she asked.

"I had to find out."

"And did you?"

Silence. She must approach the subject more cautiously.

"How did you find him?"

"You said where he was. I went to the hotel and found his rooms."

"When was this, Quentin?"

"After midnight."

That jibed with what Irene had said. "Was he there?"

Quentin's jaw tightened. "Yes."

"What did you observe when you found him?"

"He was . . . with a young girl."

Johanna became aware that her hands were fastened upon the arms of her chair. She stretched her fingers one by one.

"What was he doing, Quentin?"

"Forcing his attentions upon her."

She shut down her own feelings. "In what way?"

No answer.

"What did you feel, when you saw this?"

No answer.

"Why was it so important to you to protect May, Quentin?"

He turned his head sharply on the chaise's pillow, but still said nothing.

Obviously the ordinary method of questioning wasn't going to work, and she didn't have the leisure to experiment over days or weeks. Time for an entirely new, and potentially dangerous, tack.

"Quentin," she said slowly, "you once told me that you could change into a wolf."

He seemed to stop breathing.

"I'd like to see you do that now. Change for me, Quentin."

She had no idea what would happen, or even if he'd try to obey. She waited, knowing what she might have unleashed but prepared to face whatever might come.

Quentin opened his eyes. He looked across the ceiling, rose on his elbows, and lowered his gaze to hers.

"You called, Doctor Schell?" he said, smiling around bared teeth. "I've been waiting for you."

Oh, yes, he had changed. It was in the slight thickening of his features: the cruelty in them, the harshness, the narrow satisfaction in his eyes. They had lost every trace of warmth, their color like nothing so much as that of dried blood.

Complete antipathy. Utter loathing. Pure hate.

She knew this Quentin. She had encountered him before without even realizing it.

"Cat got your tongue?" he mocked. He swung his legs over the chaise. "I like you better this way, Johanna. Speechless."

"Quentin?"

"He's gone. You wanted him to change, didn't you?" He stood up, looming over her with curled fingers. "Well, he's changed. Now *I'm* here."

•　　•　　•

T*he moment had come.*
Fenris tested the feel of his body, slipping into it as easily as if he put on a coat. He'd worn it not so long ago, and had almost tasted Johanna's lips. He'd nearly gained control last night, and that evening when Johanna had so wantonly displayed herself. But Quentin had held on, pushing him back each time

Now *he* was in command. Never had he felt so liberated: in full daylight, his mind clear, and in the presence of one who could see him for what he was. No drunken haze inherited from Quentin's weakness. No waiting until the precise combination of emotion and drink and circumstance gave him the strength to escape.

The unwitting, luscious, naive Johanna Schell had let him out of his cage.

He looked her up and down, giving free rein to his lust. Quentin's lust as well, if that milksop would ever admit it. But Quentin was far away, helpless, as *he* was helpless during so much of their bitterly shared existence.

Quentin wouldn't be alive if not for him. But Quentin was afraid of living.

He wasn't.

"Surprised to see me?" he asked, walking slowly toward Johanna. "You shouldn't be. We've met before."

She held her ground, bracing one hand against the back of her chair. "Who are you?"

At least she wasn't so stupid as to believe he wasn't real. Not that her mind mattered to him in the slightest. Her body was what he wanted. He stripped her to nakedness with a thought, and in another had her panting beneath him, begging for mercy. Turning thought to action would take but a few minutes more.

"Who are you?" she repeated, more firmly. Her jaw was set, her gaze steady in an excellent approximation of courage. He laughed.

"Fenris," he said. He reached out and casually snapped off the uppermost button of her collar with a flick of a finger.

"Fenris," she echoed. "The monster Wolf, offspring of Loki and enemy of the gods, who remains chained in Asgard until Ragnarok."

"Not always," he said, licking his lips and watching her face as she realized his intentions. "Not today." He ran his finger down the center of her bodice, pressing between her breasts.

Her deep breath defied him. "Where is Quentin?"

"I told you." He grasped her elbow and jerked her toward him. "He's gone."

"Where?"

He tilted her head back, yanking the pins from her hair. "Where he can't stop me."

"You share his body."

"He squanders it." He tore off the second and third buttons of her bodice. "I use it. As I'll use yours."

Her pupils narrowed to pinpricks, swallowed in a sea of blue. "I understand," she said. "All the strange things Quentin has done, the behavior that made no sense—it was you."

"Stop wasting our time," he growled.

"When will . . ." She gave an almost inaudible gasp as he squeezed her breast in his hand. "When will he return?"

"When I'm finished. If I let him." He ground his erection between her thighs. "No more talk. Take off your dress."

She was stronger than he'd realized. Her resistance was a solid thing of bone and muscle, preventing him from relieving her of her bodice.

The resistance was what excited him. Making her admit she wanted him to take her was more exciting still.

"Release me," she demanded.

"Lying to yourself, Doctor?" He bent his head and

grazed her neck with his teeth, nipping just firmly enough to make her feel it. "You can't wait to find out what it's like to have me pounding my way inside you."

"You have no access to my thoughts . . . Fenris. What you propose is simply rape, nothing more."

The sheer coolness of her accusation filled him with rage. He twisted one of her arms behind her so that she couldn't move without pain. "It's Quentin, isn't it? You've been lusting after him like a bitch in heat. You think you can have him and get rid of me. It isn't going to work. Once I take you, he'll be that much weaker."

"Quentin's honor is more potent than your violence."

"Is it?" He laughed. "The honor that made him go to your room with only one thing in mind?"

"That wasn't Quentin."

"It was both of us. But I'm getting stronger all the time. And when I'm done, Quentin'll never show his face again. First I'll take his woman, and then the rest of his miserable life." He jerked her arm, forcing her to cry out. "Open your legs for me, woman."

"I will not." She stared straight into his eyes. "Do you know everything Quentin knows?"

He laughed in contempt. "More. Much more." He licked the underside of her jaw. "You pretend to be a tight little virgin, but I saw your body when you were with him, your tits all hard and your juices flowing. I smelled your lust. I smell it now."

"Does *he* know about you?"

She was distracting him with all her questions. "Shut up." He pushed her to the chaise and turned her so that she would fall on her back.

"You do intend to rape me, then," she said. "Now I know you are not Quentin."

"Quentin!" He flung her down and fell on top of her, holding himself just above with his braced arms. "Did he ever kiss you like this?"

He seized her mouth, hard, thrusting his tongue deep inside. She lay quiet under him, unresponsive. A howl of fury built up in his throat.

"Quentin would never kiss me like that," she said, when she could speak again. "He is a gentleman. I do not know what you are." Intermittent shivers rushed through her body, as if she were only half able to control them. "You have the strength to do what you like with me, but I doubt that you will find it entirely pleasant."

He raised his fist to hit her, saw the glint of fear under the stalwart façade, and let his hand fall. For all her brave display of fortitude, she was weaker than he was. Weaker, and not to be abused. That was the rule.

Quentin. Quentin did this to him. *Quentin's* rules still bound him. If he tried to break them, he would lose.

"Damn you," he snarled. "I will make you beg for it."

She touched him then, deliberately, spreading her fingers across his chest in a gesture that both invited and repelled.

"I have a better idea," she said with that excruciating, deceptive calm. "I'll strike a bargain with you. You want me—but not unwilling."

Oh, yes, he wanted her—now, as he'd wanted her from the very beginning, willing or unwilling.

"I'll give myself to you freely," she said, "if you answer my questions."

Questions, always questions. He leaned so close that her breath filled his mouth like wine. "Why should I bargain?"

"Because—" She paused, some calculation moving behind her eyes. "Because if you rape me, you'll be no better than May's father abusing that girl at the hotel."

The impact of her words sent his soul spinning like a top. For a moment he lost possession of his body, felt it slipping away from him.

Quentin was trying to take it back.

"No," he cried. *"Not yet."* He leaped away from Johanna and flung himself at the nearest wall, pounding his body against it until the pain convinced him that it remained in his power.

His body. *His.*

"Fenris?"

She stood by the chaise, unruffled, not even bothering to close the gap in her bodice.

Arrogant bitch. "A bargain," he said, hating and wanting so much that his bruised body screamed with the unrequited need to hurt in turn.

"You will answer?" she asked.

"Five minutes," he said. "And then—" He smiled and pointed at the chaise in a way she could not possibly misunderstand.

Chapter 17

Johanna let herself sag against the chaise, just enough to be sure that her body would not fail her, not enough for Fenris to sense her vulnerability.

Or her fear.

His thoughts were transparent on his altered face. She had prayed that hers remained hidden, and it seemed as if her prayers were answered. She held the advantage. Reason must always win out over savagery.

She had no doubt that Fenris was capable of savagery. That was what made the situation so remarkable, why fascination warred with fear and kept her mind racing.

For Fenris *was* Quentin. Not Quentin as she knew him, but another manifestation of his personality, ordinarily hidden from the world. She'd caught glimpses of him before, but now she had no further doubts.

And with his appearance came hope for the answers she had sought.

She had heard of such phenomena, read of them in books, rare though they were: incidences of two personalities sharing a single body, alternating ownership of it. In France there'd been the case of a woman named Felida. Two completely dissimilar women had existed in separate lives, total opposites in nature and ambitions. One, the original Felida, had been dull and gentle; the other, which her physician called her "second state," was flirtatious and wild. When one held ownership of the body, the other disappeared. And only the second personality knew of the other's existence or remembered the other's experiences. For Felida, whole periods of time—hours, weeks, eventually months—simply vanished.

Never before had Johanna the occasion to witness this bizarre syndrome for herself. It explained so much, yet her knowledge was pathetically deficient. If she could only speak to Fenris as she did Quentin, win his trust, she might find the way to heal Quentin's complex illness.

The key lay in this personality she confronted, in his mysterious origins—and in how much he differed from the gentle man she knew.

In at least one way he resembled Quentin. Her mention of May's father had been an act of desperation, based upon speculation and instinct. What Quentin hated, Fenris might also hate.

As what Quentin desired, Fenris also desired, without the inhibitions. And yet Fenris had been prepared to make a bargain.

"Four minutes," Fenris said.

She focused on him again, seeking Quentin behind that sneering mask. He was there, no matter how deeply buried he seemed.

"You were in town last night," she said, speaking as she would to any patient.

He wasn't fooled; his sharp white incisors flashed a predatory glint. "Yes."

"You attacked May's father, did you not?"

"Yes—once I got rid of Quentin." His lips contorted in disdain. "Is that the best you can do?"

"Why did you attack him?"

"I don't need a reason." He stretched, cracking the joints in his spine. "I enjoyed it."

He was lying. He had a reason. He, or Quentin.

"You said before that you know much more than Quentin does. What did you mean?"

"Can't you guess, Johanna?" Her name on his lips became almost an obscenity, laced with the threat of sexual perversions beyond naming.

"Quentin doesn't realize you exist," she said. "But you know everything he does, feels, thinks."

"Another brilliant deduction." Idly, he touched himself, outlining the heavy fullness of his erection. "He pretends I don't exist, to save himself. Stupid fool. If I weren't here, he would have died long ago. I keep him alive only for my own sake."

"You keep him alive?"

"He's a weakling and a coward."

"But you are not." She locked her gaze on his face and refused to look elsewhere. "You . . . do things he wouldn't. You are willing to fight, even harm others, as he would not."

He clapped his hands. "Bravo, Doctor."

Once more she mentally catalogued all she'd read about the condition sometimes known as "splitting of the personality," or "double consciousness." "You and Quentin share the same body," she said. "You cannot control it at the same time. But Quentin is the one who holds it most often. Is that not correct?"

Baleful light flickered in his eyes. "Until now."

"When you control your body, Quentin goes away. He can't affect what you do. He isn't even aware of your existence." More pieces of the puzzle fell into place. "But if he doesn't know about you, he can't consciously let you out.

When do you take possession, Fenris? What makes it possible?"

He took a step forward. "You're nearly out of time, Johanna."

"Answer my question."

"I come when he's afraid to act, when he meets what he
can't face. When he tries to escape into drink and can't hold
his liquor."

"When he gets angry," she guessed, "so angry that he
feels he may do violence."

"When he can't protect himself." His fingers curled like
claws. "Then *I* come."

"And what makes him so angry and afraid, Fenris?"

The ruthless mockery in Fenris's eyes subsided, replaced for an instant with confusion.

She was close, so close. A few more questions answered
and her supposition would be confirmed.

"When were you born, Fenris?" she asked.

He looked through her to some distant time and place.

"What is your first memory?"

His expression darkened, became so rigid that it looked
as though it might crack with a single twitch.

"The cellar," he said hoarsely.

"The cellar, where?"

"Greyburn."

Just as she had suspected. She subdued her excitement.
"How old were you?"

"Eight."

"Why did you come then, Fenris?"

"He called me."

"Quentin? Quentin called you?"

"To make sure he wouldn't die."

Her throat closed in on itself. "Why would he die?"

Fenris closed his eyes. "It hurt too much. He wanted to
kill—"

"What hurt, Fenris?"

He shook his head wildly. Johanna recalled that one session with Quentin . . . his childlike cries, speaking to someone from his past: *"If I don't do what he says—I won't—he
locks me up in here . . . then Grandfather brings the
ropes—"*

"You were beaten," she said, her voice thick to her own
ears. "Who hurt you, Fenris?"

"You know. *He* told you."

"His—your grandfather."

She hadn't thought it possible that Fenris's face could
grow more malevolent, but it did so now. Hate beyond hate.
The promise of punishment beyond the fires of hell itself.

"Yes," he whispered.

"He wanted you to hurt something, and you wouldn't."

"Quentin wouldn't."

"But you did?"

"I took the punishment." Fenris's lips drew away from
his teeth. "And I fought back."

She almost found it in her heart to pity the grandfather
who had created such a monster. Had Fenris taken revenge?

"Quentin knew about you then, when he called you for
help," she said. "Did he forget? What made him forget,
Fenris?"

"He forgot everything." Fenris backed up and slammed
his arms against the wall. "*I* remember. *I* suffered it all for
him."

And you hate him for it. Fenris *was* hatred—Quentin's
hatred and pain and terror. The memories he couldn't face.

"I'm sorry, Fenris," she said. "I'm sorry you had to suffer so much."

His gaze became terrifyingly lucid. "Sorry?" He threw
back his head and laughed. "You think you can help him,
don't you?"

"Help him—and you."

"I don't need help." He pushed free of the wall and advanced on her. "When the time is right, Quentin will disap-

pear. Only I'll be here." His feet made no sound on the floor. "Get used to it, Johanna. You're mine."

The backs of her thighs bumped against the chaise. Fenris's evil intent, his unfettered lust, poured over her like a dirty fog. Her flesh crawled with it.

Quentin's body would lie against hers; Quentin's hands would touch her, his weight move upon her. But Quentin would not be there.

Fenris had said she wanted Quentin. She did. Only Quentin. And he alone could save her now.

"Quentin," she said, searching his face. "I know you're there. It's time to wake up."

"It won't do you any good," Fenris said. "He's cowering in his little corner, and he won't return until it's too late."

"Quentin was the one who created you, and he can banish you as well." She lifted her chin and gave Fenris stare for stare. "It's not your time, or your place. Go."

Fenris flinched, as if her command had actually affected him. He shook himself and took another step toward her. One more and he'd be on top of her.

"Quentin," Johanna repeated. She reached out and pressed her palm to Fenris's cheek. "You have nothing to fear. Come back to me."

The unshaven skin under her hand twitched and jumped. Fenris opened his mouth on a scream.

"You lied," he roared. "I'll make you—"

He didn't complete his threat. It faded to a whisper, and the ferocious glint in his eyes went out like a snuffed candle. The transformation she'd witnessed so recently began to reverse itself as he surrendered his body to its original and rightful owner.

Quentin's eyes fixed on her in bewilderment, as warm as they had ever been. "What did you say?"

She knew instantly that he remembered nothing of Fenris's appearance, or what had been said since his other self had seized his body. He had spoken of "shadows" that haunted him, but those shadows had no name or personality he could grasp with his conscious mind. For him, it must seem as if he'd simply lost track of the conversation.

Fenris hadn't lied. Quentin was unaware that he lived a double life. He didn't know that he had attacked May's father.

Johanna's first impulse was to tell him everything. He deserved to know, and curing such a profound illness could not begin until he confronted the dark half of himself. She understood with a deep, unwavering insight that any cure must come from the deliberate reunion of Quentin's divided selves.

But how was such a thing to be accomplished? She had no experience to draw on, nothing but a few scattered cases to use as precedents. Fenris had been "born" in a time of great suffering, created by Quentin's own mind to bear the unbearable. She guessed that he had also emerged during the battle in India, the "massacre" that Quentin didn't consciously remember. And any number of times since.

Even so, she could not believe that Fenris was a killer. He must remain alive because he still served a purpose—a purpose that Quentin could not acknowledge.

If she told Quentin of Fenris now, she might be taking a terrible risk. He knew something had happened with May's father, but Fenris hid the true facts from his conscious mind. In his own way, Fenris was protecting Quentin from a more deadly madness—one that could destroy both of them.

Only by exposing Quentin's hidden rage, and the suffering in his past, could she eliminate the menace of Fenris's insidious presence. Only with Fenris's cooperation could she cure Quentin without shattering his sanity forever.

"What was your last question, Johanna?" Quentin said with a ragged smile. "I'm afraid I don't remember."

"It doesn't matter." She let her hand fall. "Our session is over, for now."

"Did you find out what you wanted?"

"Enough, for the time being."

He dropped his head into his hands, as if the dim light in the room hurt his eyes. "Did I . . . do anything? In town?"

"No, Quentin. *You* did not."

"You aren't lying to me."

She felt slightly ill. "No."

"And May—she's safe? You won't let anything happen to her."

"I promise you, Quentin. She will be safe."

"Then I think . . . I'll go and rest." He walked unsteadily to the door and turned. "I thought I might finally be over it—the drinking, and what comes after. I was wrong." He stared at the floor between his feet. "You were right, Johanna. There's nothing you can do to help me."

Her visceral protest stuck in her throat. He walked out of the room as if he didn't expect one.

She went to her desk, sat down, and attempted to take notes. Her hand only managed to make uneven ink blots on the paper.

Notes were unnecessary. She was all too sensible of her current predicament: two equally urgent cases, May's and Quentin's, strangely—and dangerously—interconnected. Fenris had attacked Ingram. He might reappear at any time if provoked—if May should be threatened again. And there was no telling how far he might go.

Why did Fenris, and Quentin, react so strongly to May's situation? Quentin had said that Ingram was "forcing his attentions" upon a young maid at the hotel. Fenris knew all that Quentin experienced. He had acted upon Quentin's desires. In his mind, May and the maid were one and the same.

Quentin would have understood the difference, but Fenris didn't care. He was a force immune to reason and negotiation, to all the civilizing elements that made Quentin who he was.

As long as Fenris continued to exist, Quentin must be watched, and kept close to the Haven. There were times she could not be with him—at night, and when she saw the other patients. That meant she had to believe that Fenris would remain dormant as long as Quentin was not provoked.

Restraining him by physical means was out of the question. And so, now, was sending him to another doctor. The responsibility was entirely hers. And if she could no longer call him her patient . . .

He remained her friend. She would lay down her life for him. She would save him, if it was the last thing she accomplished as a doctor.

Or a woman.

Resolutely she set aside her pen, gathered her notes, and hid them in a new place behind several heavy medical volumes on her bookshelf. She resumed her routine until dinnertime, visiting her father and the other patients and joining them at the table in the usual manner. Quentin remained in his room.

She tossed and turned that night. When she slept at last, vivid dreams swept her away on a tide of ever-changing images, both nightmarish and sublime. She found herself in Quentin's arms, turning her face up to his tender kisses, feeling his hands on her body. Between one moment and the next, in the manner of dreams, she was naked in his bed.

He stretched his length over her, murmuring endearments as he stroked her belly, her most intimate places. Her own voice emerged as a low moan of anticipation and need. She was about to be initiated into the mystery she knew only as theory: the supreme pleasure of sexual ecstasy, the joining of a man and woman in the act of love . . .

He kissed her. She cried out in pain, tasting blood on her lips.

Fenris held her; Fenris pushed her thighs apart and laughed in his victory. She fought him, raking his face and his chest with her nails, but he was immune to hurt. He pressed down, overpowering her, smothering her, possessing her.

"Quentin!"

The cry yanked her from the dream and halfway out of the bed. For a terrifying instant she couldn't move. Her nightgown was twisted around her body and wedged between her legs; the sheets lay spilled on the floor.

Hunched up against the pillows, she concentrated on catching her breath. Her skin was clammy to the touch, her heart leaping from beat to beat like a panicked doe.

Still halfway caught in the snares of her own mind, she crawled from the bed and felt her way to the door.

Quentin. She must see him, make sure of . . . what? That he wasn't the cruel and ruthless creature who laughed as he subjugated all her strength and confidence, and stripped her of herself? Or was it to prove she wasn't afraid?

She bumped into the walls of the hallway and flailed for the knob of Quentin's door.

Her clumsy movements would surely have awakened the heaviest sleeper. But as she reached Quentin's bedside she found him insensible, locked in a fathomless sleep.

In sleep, he was at peace. Fenris had no part of that face, those lips softly curved in some pleasant dream. She knelt beside the bed and gazed at him until the last remnants of her nightmare shredded and drifted away into the summer night.

This was Quentin. This was the man who had made such a vital place in the life of the Haven. The man who had held her in the dream, claimed her long before Fenris broke free to taunt and bully.

But no man claimed her. She belonged only to herself. She couldn't be taken.

She could *give*.

She leaned over the bed and kissed his brow, meaning it to end there. His skin was warm and slightly damp, tasting of male. One taste was somehow not enough. She kissed the outer corner of his eyelid, and then the high arch of his cheekbone. He sighed through slightly parted lips. She caught the last trace of his breath with her own mouth.

The dream wasn't over. She felt his arms come up around her, gently, neither constraining nor demanding.

"Johanna?" he murmured.

She tensed to flee, suddenly aware of where she was and what she did. The darkness was no hiding place. Quentin was awake. He held her. Not like Fenris, with the desire to seize and devour, but as if he had the most uncertain clasp on a miracle and might crush it with a twitch of his finger.

The decision was hers to make. She wasn't even sure how she'd come to this moment.

But she *did* know: She'd come to it step by slow, plodding step, just as she treated her patients in small, alternating increments of gratifying progress and frustrating reversal.

The dream was only an excuse. Hadn't it all been leading to this, from the hour she'd saved him by the lane? Hadn't she admitted her attraction at the beginning, no matter how much she fought it?

Quentin faced a terrible challenge. She'd vowed to see him through it, regardless of the cost. Fenris wished to drive her away from this man, who knew but half of himself.

She wouldn't be driven. But she must choose, now for all time: to remain apart from him, clutching at the last scraps of objectivity, or to forsake her principles and surrender to her heart.

Logic dictated the obvious answer. Logic, which had no more power to force her hand than did fear. But once she abandoned it, she couldn't turn back.

"Am I dreaming?" Quentin asked. "Are you here, Johanna?"

Muscle by muscle she allowed her body to melt against him. "I'm here."

He stroked the palm of his hand up her cheek and across her hairline, smoothing the stray wisps that had come loose from her braids. "Why?"

Answer him. Answer with the truth . . .

"I dreamed," she said. "Dreamed of you."

"What did you dream?"

"That . . . I was with you. Here, in your room."

"With me." His hand, stilled in its motion, moved again to cup the back of her head. But he drew her no closer. "As you are now?"

"Yes."

"I've also dreamed, Johanna," he said, stroking the pad of his thumb along the bridge of her nose. "But dreams do not always match reality."

As if she, of all women, were not fully cognizant of such facts. "Sometimes dreams reflect reality very well indeed."

"Or give us warnings." He let her go. Her skin felt suddenly cold in the absence of his touch. "Johanna, I think you'd better leave."

"You want me to go?" she said. "After all the—" She stopped herself, moved back to sit on the edge of the bed and began again. "You have, in the past, led me to believe that you are attracted to me. Was I mistaken?"

He sat up, and the sheets slid down to pool in his lap. She bit down hard on her lower lip.

"Why the change, Johanna?" he countered. "Why come to me now? You've been avoiding me." He smiled in self-mockery. "With good cause. I've behaved . . . less than admirably. Yesterday was just more proof that I'm not to be trusted."

"Yesterday you said that I couldn't help you—"

"You said it yourself, Johanna. I told you that you were right."

"I was *wrong*." She glared at him, trying to make him understand.

"I thought that I was no longer to be your patient."

"No. Not my patient."

"Then what, Johanna?"

That was the question, and now she had no choice but to answer. Answer *him*.

"Let me . . . let me show you," she whispered.

He turned his head. "Again, why now? Is it pity?"

She reared back. "Pity? Can you say such a thing, when—" She pressed her lips together. "I do not waste my time on pity."

"No." He met her gaze, and his eyes softened. "You're a curious woman, Johanna."

"It is a hazard of my occupation," she said. The nightgown was still damp with perspiration, and she realized that she was shivering. "Either you want me, Quentin, or you do not. I would appreciate an expeditious decision."

He laughed aloud. "Oh, Johanna, Johanna. Even now you can't stop playing the doctor."

"I don't play at anything," she said. "If that is your answer—"

His hand came to rest on her knee, burning through the muslin of her nightgown. "My answer, Johanna . . . is that I've always wanted you. From the very beginning."

A gush of heat rushed to the core of her body. "Then we need not talk any longer." She placed her hand carefully on his chest. It was bare, sleek with soft hair, and strongly muscled. The heat pooled between her thighs. "I am not afraid."

He seized her wrist. "Do you know what you're asking?"

"Is it so great a sacrifice on your part?"

"Not on mine." He eased his grip and ran his fingers up and down her arm. The sensation was delicious, but she tried not to let herself become distracted.

"You are concerned for my honor," she said. For all his joking and flirtation, he was no despoiler of women.

He was not. Fenris was another matter.

"I've known many women," he said. "I know what society demands."

"Of your aristocratic females, perhaps," she said. "But I am not a member of your society, nor am I attempting to make my way into an advantageous marriage."

He worked his fingers between hers. "You don't wish to be married?"

"We have had this conversation before, have we not? I have found that my work and marriage are not compatible."

"I'm sorry," he said.

"Do not pity *me*, Quentin. Do you think less of me, for making this offer?"

"No." He squeezed her hand. "You could never be less than honorable."

Her eyes began to prickle with incipient tears. "Then there is no obstacle—"

"What of your professional reputation?" His voice hardened. "I did not tell you before, but when I went into town with Oscar, comments were made regarding your possible relationship with male patients."

"I know. As they've undoubtedly been made in the past. I am not the first woman doctor to face such prejudices. But if they already suspect or prefer to believe that I am a loose woman of dubious morals, what we do now will make no difference."

"You must have plans for the future—"

"Yes. And I will continue with those plans. I am perfectly capable of discretion. What I do as a physician is entirely apart from what I choose as a person. A woman."

The bed shook with his silent laughter. "And to think I once asked you what you wanted as a woman, and doubted you'd ever allow yourself to find out."

"You have also made assumptions, Quentin," she said.

"I thank you—for your gallantry, and your desire to protect me. But I do not need your protection, nor that of any man. I can make my own decisions and weigh the consequences."

He was quiet for a long time. "You know that our relationship can never be the same if we go forward."

"I know." And she did. It was long past time for regrets. Neither one of them had much to lose by proceeding to the next logical step.

And she knew, in the center of her being where scientific discipline held no sway, that a more intimate connection between them would only strengthen her ability to help him. She'd always relied on intuition in her approach to treating the insane. She saw with complete clarity, for the first time in her life, that emotion was the very basis of that intuition. Her feelings for Quentin were an inextricable part of her.

Feelings she wasn't yet prepared to name.

But there was a final reason why the hour had come to let fall the barriers she'd constructed to keep them apart.

"You think you can have him and get rid of me," Fenris had said. *"Once I take you, he'll be that much weaker."*

If that were possible, the reverse must also be true. She had the chance to circumvent Fenris's plans here and now. He might return at any moment, but if Quentin was first, Fenris was disarmed. The act of love would be for mutual pleasure, not domination. And Fenris would lose some of his power.

Over her, and over his other self.

"I am as fully committed to seeking your cure as I ever was," she said slowly. "But we will do it together."

"Together." He held out his arms. She moved into them, feeling as though she'd been rescued from the midst of an icy desert. "This method of rational discussion is a strange, dry way to go about lovemaking. It's a technique I never thought to try."

"With all your other lovers?"

"Ah, yes." He rested his forehead in the hollow of her shoulder. "There is so much you don't know about me, Johanna."

"No two people can hope to know one another completely."

"I'm still a drunkard, and I don't know what I'm capable of when . . . I lose control. If you give yourself to me, you do more than risk your reputation."

It was the plainest warning he could give. He wasn't aware of Fenris, and still he was afraid for her—but he didn't reckon on the greatest danger she faced.

Losing her heart. Facing life alone when he left her, as surely he must—as Rolf had left her, and her father.

That, too, was her decision: to take the risk, knowing full well that the future was an unknown quantity. She'd already turned her back on a woman's traditional fate.

She wouldn't force Quentin to bear the burden of unreasonable expectations. She went into this with her eyes wide open. What happened beyond tonight was in the lap of the gods. And if she got with child . . .

She would cope with that eventuality if and when it came, as she'd always done.

Words were insufficient to persuade Quentin of her sincerity. The time for hesitation was past.

Deliberately she pressed her weight against him, bearing back down among the pillows. She laced her hands behind his neck, amid the wavy strands of his auburn hair, and kissed him on the mouth.

At last, he believed her.

Chapter 18

Now *Quentin was sure that there was more to sleep* than nightmares.

Johanna had come to him. She was in his bed, practically begging to be loved. And he hadn't the strength to deny her, even when he knew he should.

Even when he knew how unworthy he was.

Why now? What had changed? She'd never really answered that question. If he'd thought it was pity that drove her, after seeing him in such a pathetic state, fallen from his high resolves, his memory a blank . . .

But it wasn't pity. He sensed that she'd withheld the full truth about what had happened while he   drunk in town, but she wouldn't come to him if he'd committed any acts of violence. She was far too sane to commit her body to a lunatic.

Not Johanna. If she gave herself, it was with full comprehension, and of her own desire. She was as bold as any lady of the evening—unashamed, yet endearingly innocent at the same time; self-assured, yet betraying just a trace of feminine insecurity. Those very contrasts were what made her unique in all his wide experience.

He had known, from their first conversation, that loving her would be the premier experience of his lifetime. She'd give everything she had, for she knew no other way. And she'd chosen him to be her teacher in the arts of love.

But she was inexperienced, naive for all her intelligence. She needed guidance and a gentle hand.

She needed a lover who would take her so far, and no further.

Oh, it would be so easy to surrender to his own baser instincts and relieve her of the virginity she had so little use for. She was convinced that she'd accepted the potential repercussions of her actions. But he knew better. And he wouldn't let her destroy her life and career for a night's pleasure.

Not his pleasure, at any rate. All he'd done was to cause her trouble. Tonight, he'd bring her joy. And she wouldn't have to sacrifice anything but an hour's governance of her body.

As for her heart . . .

Wasn't it what he'd wanted, to break down that shell of cool restraint? But he'd never really believed it would come to this. He'd been so careful to avoid closeness with other human beings for the last several years. Was it because he thought Johanna was safe from his wiles that he'd dared so much with her, risked such intimacies?

If so, his scheme had backfired. Now he felt the heavy weight of responsibility. He might be weak, a coward and a scoundrel, but he had enough honor to keep her away from the crumbling brink of complete disaster. To regard tonight as a one-time miracle, not the beginning of a future that could never be.

As for tomorrow . . . it would take care of itself, one way or another. He believed in Johanna's good sense. And in his own instinct for survival.

She bent to kiss him again, and this time he met her halfway. He spread his hands across her back and kissed her as he'd always wanted to, without reserve or second thoughts: deeply, thoroughly, teasing her lips apart with his tongue and seeking inward. Her panting breath swept into his mouth.

Already he could feel her nipples like firm little buttons pressing his chest. She smelled exquisitely of woman, perspiration, and the unmistakable scent of desire. Her thighs straddled his, round and firm. Instead of shying away from the thrust of his manhood, patently outlined through the sheets that barely covered him, she rubbed herself against it.

He groaned. "Johanna," he said, "unless you want this to end very quickly, you'd better stop."

"Am I doing something wrong?" She sat up, her gaze sweeping from his face to his loins. Her hand found him, unerringly, and stroked, tugging the sheet below his hipbones. "This is the source of pleasure, is it not?"

"Yes," he said through his teeth. "Bloody hell—excuse me, Johanna." He caught her hand and lifted it away from him. "You're just too good at it."

She smiled. "Am I? I have been a student of human nature for a long time. And I know my anatomy—"

"It isn't all anatomy." He grabbed the edge of the sheet and pulled it higher as he sat up, afraid that if he didn't keep himself covered he'd find his way inside her. Before she could see his movement as a rejection, he cupped her hands between his.

"Do you know where the center of your pleasure is, Johanna?"

The darkness wasn't enough to hide the flush in her cheeks from eyes like his. "I believe so."

"Have you ever touched it yourself?"

The blush cascaded down her neck to the collar of her nightgown. "I . . . have never been one of those who holds that such activity is a form of abuse that can lead to blindness and insanity. But I have not . . ." She swallowed. "Not purposely."

He tried not to imagine how she might have done so accidentally. "Then you'll have to allow me to show you."

"Right now?" Her voice squeaked several notes higher.

"In a few moments." He slid his hand up her arm to her shoulder. "Relax, Johanna. This is supposed to be enjoyable."

"I know." She made a visible effort to loosen her muscles. "What is next, then?"

"This is also not a textbook lesson," he said, working his hand under the open collar of her nightgown. "There are no rules."

"No. Of course not." She held very still while he undid a few buttons and brushed his fingers down from her collarbone to the deep cleft between her breasts.

He'd thought of this countless times, holding her naked breasts in his hands. She was bountiful, richly endowed, any man's dream of abundance. She had no idea how desirable she was.

Slowly he covered her breast with his hand. She gasped. Her firm nipple rubbed against his palm. He curved his fingers around it, squeezing with utmost gentleness. She closed her eyes.

"It feels—"

"Tell me how it feels, Johanna."

"I can't." She breathed in and out rapidly. "I hadn't realized that my . . . that they could be so—"

"Sensitive? You have no idea, my Valkyrie." He pulled her forward, ignoring the warmth of her rump on his groin, and lifted her breast through the vee of her neckline. Cradling it between his hands, he lowered his head.

Her amazed cry was all he could have wished for. He curled his tongue around her nipple, wetting it thoroughly, and then began to suckle. She arched up against him. When he'd had his way with one breast, he gave equal attention to the other. By then Johanna was hardly breathing at all.

"Oh," she whispered.

"This is what they were made for, Johanna," he said, pressing his face between her breasts. "To be pleasured and to give pleasure."

If she meant to protest his dismissal of their biological function, she hadn't enough presence of mind to do so.

"You . . . enjoy—"

"Indubitably." To prove it, he caressed her again.

"Quentin?"

"Yes . . ."

"I have read about the experience of orgasm—" She kept her eyes firmly closed, as if to protect herself from embarrassment. "But I do not know what it's like. Can you explain it to me?"

He pulled back and muffled a laugh. "It's not something one can explain . . . especially from a man to a woman."

"Is it possible to achieve without actual intercourse?"

"Why?"

"Because I think . . . I think . . ." She opened her mouth and shuddered, rising up on her knees and falling back again. The impact on his erection was astonishing. Stars danced in front of his eyes.

"No," she said. "No, I . . . must have been mistaken. For a moment, I thought—"

Filled with an inexpressible tenderness, Quentin drew her close. "You'll know, Johanna," he said. He caught her face between his hands and kissed the tip of her nose. "And we aren't nearly finished yet."

Johanna was finally compelled to confess her ignorance. She hadn't had the slightest notion, for all her reading and observation, how wonderful sex could be. And Quentin had just begun.

It wasn't only the physical sensations, which of themselves were startling and indescribable. It was also the
closeness—physical and emotional—that was so much
more than the proximity of bodies.

She was eager to continue, but she contained herself.
She was no wild wanton to lose every last vestige of common sense, forget where she was and why. She wanted to
fully absorb every experience.

In case it never happened again.

"What is next?" she asked in a voice she hoped didn't
betray her enthusiasm.

"I'll show you." He set his hands at her waist and lifted
her easily, placing her on the bed beside him. He rolled over
to cover her with his body.

Johanna tensed. His position reminded her too much of
Fenris, and the feeling of helplessness she so despised. But
Quentin made no move to constrain her. He leaned on one
elbow and drew his fingers through her hair with his other
hand, working the braids loose.

"Trust me, Johanna," he said.

"I do." She allowed him to separate the strands of her
hair and spread it out across the pillow.

"Beautiful," he said.

"A very ordinary brown," she corrected.

"Let me be the judge of that." He kissed her, lightly at
first, and then with greater passion. Her arms moved of
their own accord to pull him down. He demonstrated the
amazing variations possible in a simple kiss, from agile use
of the tongue to subtle movements of strong, masculine
lips.

And then he showed her all the other places on her body
that could also be kissed.

He began with the other parts of her face: brow, cheeks,
chin, jawline. He suckled the lobe of her ear, provoking
waves of delicious shivers. She hadn't suspected how in-
credibly sensitive the flesh of her neck and its junction with

her shoulder could be, especially when he grazed it with his teeth and salved it with his tongue afterward.

Inch by meticulous inch he worked his way down her body. She almost cried out in anticipation as he reached her breasts and repeated his previous caresses. His mouth closed over her nipple, sucking and tugging in a way that sent lances of sensation shooting directly into her womb.

She felt . . . beautiful. Her breasts were beautiful, the slight roundness of her stomach, the full breadth of her hips. Each part he worshipped in turn. He kissed the gentle projection of her ribs and ran his tongue in teasing circles around her navel. All the while she felt him drawing closer to the place that begged for his attentions. Her breath rang hoarse and loud in her own ears.

He paused, giving her brief deliverance from the high pitch of excitement. Yet she didn't want him to stop.

"Please," she murmured.

"You aren't afraid?" he asked again. His voice was just as unsteady as hers. "I can slow down, if you like."

"No," she answered, half in a daze. "No."

"It was a very foolish question." He took her hips between his hands and kissed his way down her body again.

The first touch of his tongue to her femininity was a considerable shock. She felt as if she'd been struck by lightning, every volt of it focused on this one part of her body. She thought she might die in the next few seconds.

She didn't die. Quentin was an expert. He pushed his tongue into the soft, moist flesh, stroking and exploring. She clutched handfuls of sheet in her fists, wondering how she could bear it. How any woman could. And to think that some male physicians actually believed that females could or should not know this . . . this ecstasy.

A moan escaped her. Quentin's caresses became more urgent, as if he were propelling her toward the climax he'd promised she would recognize. Surely she was already there. But the feeling of sheer pleasure became one of rising, rising toward some immeasurable height, a Valhalla that only the blessed could know.

Quentin led her there, drew her to the edge, and then let her go.

She exploded, tumbled, spun to the bottom in a rush of light and joy. Quentin was waiting for her. She felt herself pulse against his mouth while he reveled in her delight.

Every limb weighted with gratified exhaustion, Johanna rested her head on the pillow and let the overwhelming sensations fade. At last she knew what it was to reach the ultimate physical completion. The feelings Quentin had aroused in her when he'd touched her breasts were nothing compared to this. She couldn't help giggling a little at her own naïveté.

"I don't believe I've ever heard you giggle before," Quentin said, rolling onto his back beside her. "You found it acceptable?"

"Acceptable? You can ask that when—" She paused, noting the gleam of bedevilment in his eye. The hopeless rogue. She reached for his hand. "More than acceptable."

"I am glad." He propped himself up on his elbow to gaze at her. "You have a certain natural talent yourself."

"But I've done nothing. It has been quite—one-sided, has it not?"

Quentin licked his lips. "I found it very pleasant, I assure you."

"But you have not—we have not finished." Even as she spoke, she felt a renewed ache between her thighs—the ache of emptiness, of a powerful need to be filled in a way only Quentin could do.

"Not everything must be done at once," he said. "We aren't on a schedule, are we?"

He was putting her off, she was sure of it. In spite of his initial acquiescence, he hadn't let go of his qualms. He held back from the ultimate expression of the desire she knew he felt. The bold stance of his admirable, rather awesome male part had not diminished in the slightest.

She sat up and slid her hand down his belly. "Maybe not," she said. "But now it is my turn."

"You needn't—" He gulped back his words as she reached the base of his manhood and stroked up with one finger. He was so hard, so silky, and so very fascinating.

"I have seen this before, of course," she said in her best professional voice, "but never one so, so . . . superior."

"Thank you," he said. "I think."

"And never in this state, I must confess." She wrapped her hand around him and drew it up and down experimentally. His body jerked. "How long can you maintain it, I wonder?"

"Not . . . very much longer," he rasped. "Johanna—"

"I'm not being too rough?" She smiled serenely and reversed the direction of her caress.

He groaned in answer. After a few moments of experimentation she found just the right rhythm. He gave up any effort to speak and closed his eyes.

She loved the feeling of pleasuring him as he had done for her. Still it was not enough. Her innate, driving curiosity remained unassuaged.

One thing remained to be tried. She adjusted her position so that she could bend over him without losing her balance.

Quentin's eyes shot open. He muttered an oath, his whole body going rigid as she proceeded with her explorations. His fingers caught in her hair. His breathing grew more and more uneven. At what she perceived to be the last possible instant, he pushed her away and swung his feet over the side of the bed, shuddering.

"I wasn't finished," she protested. "Come back here—"

"No." He turned about in one motion and bore her back onto the bed. "Not this time."

Her heart began to pound at half again its normal speed.

This was it, then. He lay over her, braced on his arms, the sleek and now-familiar shape of his manhood pressed into her belly. Her insides had become liquid with wanting him; her body couldn't be more eager to accept him.

He would enter, and thrust, and move within her. She knew what it would be like. She could imagine it so well that the excitement sparked all over again, threatening to burst out of control before he so much as breached her maidenhead.

"Quentin," she whispered. "I am ready. Now, *mein Herz.*"

He repositioned himself, nudging her legs apart. He slid into place like a key ready to enter a well-oiled lock. Just the smallest movement, the merest thrust . . .

And he withdrew, clumsy with unfulfilled desire. Johanna bit her lips to keep from crying out in frustration.

"Not today, Johanna," he said, turning his head from her.

"Why?" Tears collected in her throat—rare, unwelcome visitors. "Why?"

"It isn't your fault, Johanna. Never think that." He looked at her, all humor fled from his face. "I can't, Johanna. It isn't for lack of wanting you." He tried, and failed, to smile. "I've never wanted a woman so much in my life. But the time isn't right. You know it as well as I do. Too much is at stake, too much uncertain."

"But I explained to you—"

"I know. I wanted to share what I could with you, Johanna. While I still had the chance. But if there's ever to be—more between us, things have to be different. Don't you see?"

She folded her arms across her breasts, bereft, somehow ashamed. Though her body wailed protest and her emotions seethed with anger and sorrow, her intellect understood him completely.

One night wouldn't be enough. Not for her. Once they joined, she'd want him for all time. But such promises could not be made, such castles built, while Fenris stood by and waited to usurp Quentin's place.

She pulled the tousled sheets up to her shoulders and drew them tight. "I see," she said.

"Don't hate me, Johanna." He knelt before her, pleading with his eyes—this aristocrat, this fine and handsome madman who had loved her so magnificently. "I couldn't bear it if you hated me."

"Hate you?" *Mein Gott.* Hate him . . . how could she hate the man she loved?

A shot of ice water mingled with the blood in her veins. Love.

She smoothed her face to serenity and took his hand. "I could never hate you, Quentin. Not for any reason."

He lifted her hand to his lips and kissed it lingeringly. "My dear Valkyrie."

Her heart stopped and started again, heavy and sluggish. She turned her hand to cup his cheek.

"Thank you," she said. "Thank you for tonight."

Mute, he kissed her palm and rose from the bed. He flipped back the sheets and gathered her up in his arms, lifting her against his chest. In a few long, silent steps he carried her from his room to hers, and laid her down in her own cool bed.

"Sleep, Johanna," he said. He kissed her forehead and then her lips, almost chastely. "Sleep well."

S*he slept so well that she woke sometime after sunrise,* her body singing with remembered ecstasy after a night of glorious dreams.

Dreams that completed what she and Quentin had not.

She moved about the room only half awake, trying to hold on to the fantasies. And the memories. She saw herself in the mirror and wondered at this vision, this goddess she saw before her. She touched her breasts and remembered

how Quentin had caressed and suckled them. She pressed
her hand to her belly and imagined it filled with Quentin's
child.

That was not to be. Not so long as things remained as
they were. And she must take great pains to be sure that the
other patients didn't realize how her relationship with
Quentin had changed. But now she knew what she wanted
above all things in the world.

Once she'd told herself that the only way to be free of
her attraction to Quentin was to cure him. Curing him was
still the only route to happiness for them both. They had
gone beyond the safe association of doctor and patient, but
she had a greater advantage than any she'd possessed in the
past. She knew the full depth of Quentin's illness, and had
faced his inner nemesis without submitting to it. She had a
strong theory about how Fenris had come to exist.

And she had love on her side.

Love. It was much too new an idea to embrace fully. She
must grow used to it by stages, little by little, until it became one with her heart. Love, and all its attendant expectations.

She smiled foolishly at her reflection in the mirror and
began to dress.

With the perfectly valid excuse of keeping an eye on
him, she paused at Quentin's door on the way to the
kitchen. His belongings were in place and the bed was
neatly made, but he had already stepped out. To the woods,
undoubtedly, alone or with May. Once she'd started the
morning routine, she'd make certain of his whereabouts
and ask him to remain on Haven grounds.

Furthermore, she must prepare May for her escape to
Sacramento without alerting Quentin to the specifics of her
plans for the girl. With luck, Bridget would hear back from
her cousin soon, and she'd accompany May to a place
where Bolkonsky and Ingram wouldn't find her. Much
must be accomplished in the coming days.

Mrs. Daugherty was at work in the kitchen, making breakfast. When she saw Johanna she stopped her work and bustled forward with an envelope in her hand.

"Doc Jo!" she said, a little out of breath. "I have somethin' for you. Just an hour ago, that Dr. Bolkonsky met me on the road and asked me to deliver this." She scowled. "He said it was urgent."

That made it urgent for Johanna as well. She tore open the envelope. The letter was yet another request for her to meet him—not in town, but at a point halfway between the Haven and Silverado Springs. Once again he declined to visit the Haven, expecting her to come to him.

Nevertheless, she couldn't afford to ignore him. Keeping him satisfied was her best way of holding him off until May was gone.

She made her rounds to visit her father and the other patients, seeing to their immediate needs, and then asked Oscar to help her saddle Daisy.

"Have you seen Quentin this morning?" she asked as she took the reins.

"Nope. Not this mornin'." Oscar rubbed Daisy's nose. "May went out to look for him."

They weren't together, then. But Johanna refused to be concerned. May wouldn't venture far from the Haven, given her experience in Silverado Springs. And after last night, Johanna suspected that Quentin had as much to think about as she did.

"Oscar, you know the places where May likes to go. Would you find her and bring her home straightaway?"

"I will, Doc Jo."

"Thank you." She clucked to Daisy and set out for Bolkonsky's rendezvous.

He was waiting for her as promised, mounted on one of the best horses from the town livery. His animal's restless pawing reflected the anxious expression on Bolkonsky's deceptively handsome face.

"Johanna. I'm glad you came."

She drew Daisy up beside him. "You said it was urgent."

"Yes." His voice held a note of strain, and he kept looking back over his shoulder toward town as if he expected followers. "Something new has happened in Silverado Springs that I felt you should know about directly. Before someone else arrives to inform you."

Foreboding stiffened Johanna's shoulders. "Go on."

"Another man has been attacked," he said. "Last night, well after midnight. His body was disovered just outside of Silverado Springs. I am told the man was a local mine owner of some wealth, known chiefly for his cruel treatment of his Chinese workers. He was not well liked, so I hear—but someone resented him enough to kill him."

"He's dead?"

"Torn apart, I hear, though I have not seen the body."

A metallic taste coated her mouth. "And they suspect that one of my patients is responsible."

"Yes." He gave her a grave and sympathetic look. "I thought it best to warn you, so that you are prepared. After the previous attack on Ingram . . . the crowd was in an ugly mood this morning, and I fear—" He sighed. "I fear they may take matters into their own hands."

"Without proof?"

"What proof does a mob need? And there is more . . . two men from town claim to have identified a man lurking near the place when the mine owner was found. He bears, from the description, a striking resemblance to your Quentin Forster."

With as much stern discipline as she'd ever employed, Johanna prevented herself from showing any reaction. "I see."

"You do know where he is?"

"Naturally. It's all an unfortunate mistake. I thank you for your warning." She turned Daisy away, but Bolkonsky caught at her reins.

"My dear Johanna, I understand your dismay, but you can see now why it is necessary for me to take May with dispatch. She may be in danger from this—this madman, whoever he may be."

"But we agreed—"

"I'm sorry, Johanna. I'll be coming within the next few hours to fetch her. I would appreciate it if you'd have the girl's belongings packed and ready." He patted her arm. "I would prefer this to be as pleasant as possible, for all of us—without involving any outside authorities."

Bolkonsky had made just such a threat before. The last thing she wanted now was the local law sniffing about the Haven.

"Very well," she said. "I will do my best."

She sawed at Daisy's reins a little too violently, and the mare tossed up her head with a snort. She murmured an apology and kicked the horse into a gallop for home, not bothering with farewells. Let Bolkonsky look to himself.

As she must look to May and Quentin. All at once everything was falling apart, the reins of control slipping through her fingers. She had no notes or textbooks to consult, no protocols to fall back on.

Quentin—Fenris—was all but accused of being a killer. If, indeed, Bolkonsky was telling the truth. He was not a man to be trusted on any count, but she had to assume the worst. And May was in immediate danger.

So short a time ago she'd been filled with hope and happiness, imagining a future built upon love as well as science.

That future, and all she'd ever believed in, was crumbling before her eyes.

Chapter 19

Quentin *turned over in his bed, breathing in the scent* of Johanna's body. Her perfume saturated the sheets, filling him with fresh desire and the urge to roll about and rub the scent into his skin like the wolf he could so easily become.

Last night, after the loving, he'd run as a wolf—swift, sure, and silent. There was no other way to express the joy, the fullness of his heart. And the frustration of self-denial.

He'd done the right thing. He knew that. Johanna was still a virgin, free to give herself to another man without regret.

Or free to choose him, if by some miraculous turn of events fate granted him one more chance.

He got up and walked to the window, stretching in the shafts of morning sunlight until his bones cracked. Another chance. Was it possible?

Only if he wanted Johanna, a life with her, enough to change: not from man to wolf, but from drunk to sober, from ne'er-do-well to competent adult, from coward to hero.

He laughed at himself and pressed his forehead to the sun-warmed glass. The heroism was all Johanna's, if she could deliver him from his demons. But she couldn't do it alone. He must give up every trace of resistance and let her into his innermost heart, where she could drag his fears into the light. Where he must confront them unflinchingly, even those—especially those—he had never seen except as shadows.

How he hated choices. Easier to run. Easier until you found yourself bound by stronger chains than any in that dark, stinking cellar . . .

No. That dungeon was far away. Johanna was here, and now. Soon he'd see her, and all they'd shared would become his only reality. Soon he'd be a whole man again, able to love.

He mouthed the word and choked on helpless laughter. Quentin Forster, in love—with a distinctly unglamorous, too-serious woman well past her first youth.

An absurdity. Just like the rest of his life. Why should he be surprised?

Whistling with nonsensical happiness, he washed and dressed with extra care. This late in the morning, Johanna would be busy with the others, but Mrs. Daugherty was bound to have some leftovers from breakfast. He'd bide his time, visit Wilhelm and talk to Harper. He was surprised that May hadn't come looking for him, but somewhat relieved. May was too young to be aware of what had passed between him and Johanna.

Or was she? His good humor dimmed. May. What was to be done about her?

Trapped in indecision, he walked out the door and found Lewis Andersen waiting in the hallway.

The former minister shrank back as Quentin appeared, holding his gloved hands high like a shield between them.

"Did you do it?" he whispered. "Did you kill that man?"

"What?" His guts knotted. "What did you say?"

"Thou . . . thou cursed creature of Satan. Did you kill him?"

Quentin backed into the wall and felt blindly for its support. "Kill who?"

"The owner of the Red Star quicksilver mine—Ronald Ketchum. The actress told us about it. He was found dead, torn apart." He sucked his breath through his teeth. "You did it, didn't you? You are evil." His hands trembled. "You will not kill again. I will stop you."

Even in the midst of his horror, Quentin admired Andersen's courage. The man was hardly the heroic sort, yet he stood face-to-face with what he believed to be a monster. A killer. He had more grit than anyone knew.

"If this is true," Quentin said past the constriction in his throat, "you won't have to stop me." He took a step forward.

Andersen held his ground. He began to sing in a high-pitched, wavering voice—a hymn, "Soldiers of Christ Arise," that Quentin remembered hearing in his childhood.

"I won't hurt you," he said, taking another step. "I must find Doctor Schell."

"*Stop.*" Andersen produced a gun from inside his coat and pointed it at Quentin's chest. Where he had acquired such a weapon, or how he knew enough to use it, was a subject for wild speculation.

Quentin raised his hands. "Shoot, if you must," he said, floating within a bizarre calm. "I won't prevent it."

"But *I* will."

Johanna came up behind Andersen. She set her hand on his shoulder. "Give me the gun, Lewis."

"But he is a killer, spawn of the devil. I must—"

"You don't want to hurt anyone, Lewis. Even if what you say is true, he is entitled to representation before the law, is he not?"

Her calm, reasonable voice worked its usual magic on Andersen. The muzzle of the gun tilted down. Johanna pried it from Andersen's fingers and held the weapon as gingerly as if it were a poisonous snake.

"You would not listen before," Andersen said, never taking his gaze from Quentin. "You must listen now. He will come after you next."

"What makes you believe that, Lewis?"

His thin face puckered. "I *know.*"

"I have never given you cause to distrust my judgment, have I?"

"No."

"Then trust me now. Quentin will not hurt me. He won't hurt any of us." She looked into Quentin's eyes. "Whatever he may be, Quentin is not evil. No more than you or I."

"You will . . . keep the gun?"

"Yes. I must speak to Quentin now, but I shall not fail to protect myself. You would help me best if you'd gather the others and bring them into the parlor. Please fetch Mrs. Daugherty as well, and ask her to bring my father out of his room. It's very important that everyone stay indoors today."

Andersen bobbed his head. "Yes. Yes, I understand." He cast Quentin a glance composed of equal parts fear and loathing and scuttled backward down the hall, watching them both until he passed out of view.

Johanna released a long breath and stared at the gun in her hand.

"You won't need that against me, Johanna," Quentin said lightly. Better to joke than to run wailing in despair.

He hadn't known quite what to expect of their first meeting after last night's loving. Awkwardness, yes, and perhaps a little shyness on her part. A new familiarity between them. Possibly even her resolve that it should never happen again. Anything but this.

His latest, brief flirtation with hope had already come to

an end. Andersen had seen to that—Andersen and his accusations.

Accusations Johanna confirmed with the bleak, drawn expression on her face.

It was still a beautiful face, though the hair hung bedraggled about her shoulders and her forehead was moist with perspiration. He'd have to be dead not to appreciate it, however desperate his circumstances. Her face, her lips, her form from crown to toe were imprinted upon his hands and his lips and his heart.

He didn't dare embrace her, though his mind and soul and body demanded the solace of her arms. He didn't dare move at all.

"Andersen was telling the truth," he said. "Someone was killed last night."

"So I have heard."

"And you think . . . that I had something to do with it."

Anguish darkened her eyes to pewter. "When you left me—" Her voice faltered just for an instant. "Afterward, where did you go?"

"To the woods. And then back here."

"Do you remember every moment?"

Did he? Could he be certain he hadn't forgotten the forgetting itself? He remembered falling into bed, exhausted from his run, and then sinking into what he presumed was a deep, uninterrupted sleep . . .

"I didn't drink," he said, frantically sifting his mind for plausible alibis. "I knew nothing of this Mr. Ketchum before Andersen told me."

"He was known to mistreat his Chinese workers. As—" Her throat worked. "   as May's father might have mistreated her."

His lungs stopped working. "You said something happened in town . . . the night I got drunk. You never told me what it was."

"May's father was attacked and wounded."

"Oh, God." He fell back against the wall and clutched at his head. Trouble always followed in his footsteps, wherever he went, whispering of violence, of fear and hatred and suspicion. It had found him again, in this last and final sanctuary.

But in all those times past, the whispers had never been of murder.

He forced himself to look at her instead of cringing like a whipped dog. "Did I kill this man?" he asked, letting blessed numbness seep into his body.

She shook her head, too fiercely. It savaged his heart to see her so torn, so vulnerable. She was the very pillar of solid strength to everyone here, including himself.

He'd undermined that fortitude ever since he came to the Haven, hour by hour and day by day. Last night had shattered the remaining foundations of her life, and left her with nothing to be sure of.

"Johanna," he said. "Did someone see me do this thing?" He straightened, staring past her. "I'll go into town at once and give myself up—"

"*No.*" She raised her chin. "We know nothing yet. No facts, only rumor. But there is something I must tell you, something I recently discovered. I wish that circumstances permitted me to explain more gradually. I fear it may be difficult for—" Tears filled her eyes. "I am sorry, Quentin."

She led him into her office, still clutching the gun in a death grip, and closed the door.

Then she told him.

H*e didn't react at all.*
Johanna watched for signs of horror, denial, incredulity. None came. He listened to her account of Fenris's emergence, unmoving, as if she were describing a rather uninteresting acquaintance.

That was abnormal in itself, almost frightening. She

carefully edited her description of Fenris's advances upon her, but she doubted very much that he'd failed to guess what she omitted.

When she was finished, he gazed blankly at the wall and said nothing. Minutes ticked by. Precious minutes that she dared not waste, for May's sake as well as his.

Bolkonsky might arrive in a matter of hours. Oscar had not returned from his search for May, and if he did not come soon she'd go looking herself. Her original plan for the girl's escape was no longer viable; Bridget would simply have to spirit May out of the area while Johanna concocted a story that Bolkonsky and Ingram were bound to find wildly implausible. But she didn't dare risk facing them down with May still present.

Watching Quentin's face, Johanna mourned inside. She grieved for him, for May, for the man who had been killed, whatever his crimes in life. She grieved for what had been so briefly captured last night. She longed to touch Quentin, kiss him, and knew how impossible it was. Her organs had turned to water, filling her body like a reservoir apt to spill over into a flood of tears once she opened the gates.

That she must not do. Her brain must become as sharp as a scalpel, her heart as hard as marble.

"You never suspected this," she said at last.

"No." He turned his head toward her, but his eyes wouldn't focus. "Not this. I felt a shadow . . . the shadow I ran from. And it was always—" He laughed. "It was me all along."

She quenched the desire to comfort him with soothing words and promises she couldn't keep. "Not you, Quentin. A part of you, born at a time when you desperately needed help and found none."

"Fenris," he whispered. "It even has its own name. *He.*" He rose from the chaise and walked across the room, slow and halting as an old man. "All these times I've lost my memory—after the drinking—he's come out. That's what you're saying. He lives in my body with me. He takes over and does things—terrible things."

"So Fenris claims—and Bolkonsky. But there is no proof, Quentin."

"Except that two people have been attacked since I came to the Haven." He finally met her gaze. "And I don't remember. But someone saw me, didn't they, Johanna?"

"No one witnessed the attack on May's father. Fenris admitted it himself."

He closed his eyes. "Why? Why did he do it?"

"He wouldn't say. But I think . . ." She prepared herself to hurt Quentin again. "Your concern for May became something different for Fenris. You share a mind and a body. He felt what you feel, knew what you knew, but he was not constrained by the bonds of civilized behavior, or by the reason that tells us right from wrong."

"You mean that he did what I wanted to do, but couldn't."

"There is so much I don't know and can only theorize. I'm sorry."

"Your theories are more than reasonable." He sat down again, as if he couldn't remain still. "I never stayed long in any one place, because after a few days or weeks I always sensed something wrong. Sometimes it was just a hunch, a bad feeling in my gut. Rumors, the stares of people around me that told me that I wasn't welcome. Sometimes I heard stories. And once in a while, the law came after me." His voice became a monotone, devoid of emotion. "I didn't let myself think that my drinking did serious damage to anyone but myself." He smiled a chilling smile. "But you think that's what lets Fenris out."

"It's possible, but—"

"Just as it's possible that I killed this businessman last night."

"I do not believe . . . You said that you had no memory lapse—"

"I was asleep. Do you remember every moment when you're asleep, Johanna?" He raised his hands, crooked his fingers, stared at them as if they belonged to someone else. "Don't try to make it easy for me. I'm not a child. If a man died, it might very well have been by these hands." He pressed his temples. "You said that I created Fenris. *I* am responsible."

"No." She was losing mastery of this conversation, and she must get it back. "Quentin—I am convinced that we can reach Fenris. He is the hidden part of yourself. Somehow, you and I must find a way to communicate with him. Bring him into the light, and confront him."

"And until then?" He slammed his fist into the wall. "I can't stop what I feel. I can't even sense his existence. How can I prevent him from taking over and . . . attacking someone again? How many times have I hurt people in the past, and not known it?"

The tears built painfully behind her eyelids. "We *will* find a way. But now you must listen to me. Regardless of what actually happened, certain witnesses are claiming to have seen you in the vicinity of Ketchum's body. That was enough to rouse the town."

"You mean a mob." His gaze grew keen and alert. "A mob is coming to the Haven to get me."

"That is why we must take immediate precautions, for you and—"

"You knew about Fenris last night, and you still came to me. Why, Johanna?" His eyes glittered with unshed tears. "Why would you give yourself to a monster?"

"Because I—I . . ." How would it help, to tell him she loved him? Another burden for him to carry, another load of guilt and self-loathing, because in his own mind he didn't deserve to be loved.

"You were afraid of Fenris," he said with devastating insight. "Coming to me was a way to challenge your fear." He smiled, without bitterness or mockery. "I hope it helped you. I'd like to believe it did. I'd like to think we shared something other than sorrow, before I go."

"*Quentin.*"

"Don't deceive yourself. I must give myself to these people, to the law, before they come and destroy what little peace I've left you."

"That is out of the question. They may—"

"Hang me? I have heard that such things happen in this country. With justification, in my case."

"You have an illness. You are not a criminal."

"How can you be sure, Johanna? And what do you propose to do to keep me 'safe'? Bind me in chains so that Fenris can't escape again? Lock me in a padded room and push my food through the bars? Oh, no." He shuddered violently. "I'll take the rope, and gladly. It will end this farce I've made of my life."

"I will not lock you away." Tears ran down her face. She couldn't stop them. "You must go into hiding until things settle down. And it's not only you who is in danger. Because of what's happened, Bolkonsky has threatened to come for May this very day."

Quentin's body twitched, as if he'd experienced a sudden shock. "May. You have a plan to save her."

"I will not give her up to her father. Oscar has been looking for her, but I must have her ready to leave within the hour. You must go as well."

"I'll find her."

She swung on him. "*Go.* Do not make things more difficult—"

"Johanna." He spoke so gently, as if in the midst of sweet loving. "No one is better suited to bringing her back than I am." He smiled with tender sadness. "I have something to show you, something I should have shared long ago."

As she watched, uncomprehending, he began to remove his clothing. She couldn't avert her eyes. In her office, in full daylight, he was a thousand times more beautiful than he'd been in his dark bedchamber.

Her body woke despite the urgency of the situation, responding to the potent promise of his masculinity. *Lewis was right,* she thought dazedly. *Naked in the woods . . .*

The last of his clothing fell to the floor, and the outlines of his form seemed to shift and shimmer. Mist, the very color of his eyes, appeared from nowhere to gather about him like a magic cloak. It swallowed him up entirely.

Quentin vanished. All she saw at first, as the mist cleared, was a flash of sharp white teeth and russet fur. Then she realized what had taken Quentin's place.

A wolf. A wolf whose pelt was the shade of Quentin's hair, thick and sleek. A wolf with great triangular ears and a plume of a tail, immense paws, and slitted golden-red eyes.

He grinned at her. Quentin's grin.

She clutched at the back of her chair. His gaze was no beast's. Those were Quentin's eyes.

The wolf *was* Quentin.

His lycanthropy was real. His unconscious mind had told the truth. Lewis *had* seen him change into a wolf.

One less symptom of insanity to worry about. Or one more. Now he was three: wolf, Quentin, Fenris.

She laughed, muffling the sound behind her hand. The wolf—Quentin—no creature of fear but a beast as magnificent as the man—flowed toward her like liquid copper and nudged her other hand. His nose was warm and dry.

"The joke is on me," she said, wondering if she was making any sense. "Did you think this would make matters simpler?"

He lay down at her feet and rested his jaw on her foot. It was a gesture of love and trust she could not mistake. He was tame as a dog, utterly loyal, adoring her with his lupine eyes and the rasp of his tongue across her fingers.

Consigning one more secret to her keeping.

She plunged her hand into the thick guard hairs about his great neck and felt him tremble. "Quentin—if you still understand me—I . . . don't know what to say."

He slipped away. The mist enveloped him again. She was unable to observe the actual change, try though she might; the scientist was never long absent from her nature. He stepped, naked, from the dispersing cloud, retrieved his clothes, and dressed in silence.

"You need say nothing," he said. "I didn't believe that showing you this would make matters simpler. But it should make clear why I cannot remain."

"Because—" She tried to assemble words into proper sentences, drawing them into a line like a child's scattered alphabet blocks. They remained hopelessly disordered.

"Because I am not human," he completed for her. He sighed, and she felt his absolute weariness. "There are others like me throughout the world. We are stronger and faster than men, with senses a thousand times more keen. We are infinitely more dangerous if we choose to be."

"The nature of the wolf—"

"Is not what men have made it. We are neither cursed nor the children of Satan. The vicious cruelty men attribute to wolves is the product of fear and ignorance. There has been evil among the loups-garous—I have seen it myself—but no more than is found among men."

Question after question crowded Johanna's mind. How many cases of insanity might have been attributed to this very real ability? How did these loups-garous fit into the evolution of life and the human race, creatures Darwin had not even imagined? How had they remained hidden so long?

Not one of those questions was important.

"You are not a killer, Quentin," she said. She held out her hand. He brushed her fingertips with his own, fleeting as the mist that marked his transformation. "You are a wonder."

"If I have killed"—he worked his hands open and closed—"the fault is in me, not my kind. I am an aberration. But my abilities make me deadly. I can't trust my own body, and neither can you. If I don't stop myself, no one can."

"Then how can mere human law contain you?" she cried. "If you give yourself up to the authorities, what makes you believe that Fenris won't do anything to get you free again?"

"That's why he exists, isn't it?" He lifted his head. "Tell me, Johanna. Where can I go? Does the place exist where Fenris can do no harm?"

"Yes. But only if we make that place together."

"There is another option."

"I will not let you take it."

He laughed hoarsely. "I've never managed suicide thus far. Success is by no means assured."

"Fenris would stop you. *He* wants to survive."

"And there is only one who can match him, Johanna, whatever sort of creature he is." He thumped his chest with his fist. "He is *me*."

"Yet you haven't even met him." She strode forward until she stood nearly eye to eye with him. "You can't possibly fight what you can't see and don't remember. Without my help—"

"Have you ever cured a man with this disease, Johanna? Have you ever treated a werewolf? No," he said, forestalling her answer. "May needs you now. I won't put either of you in further danger."

She opened her mouth for another protest, and he silenced her with his lips. He kissed her as if it were the last time, hard enough to leave his impression seared into her skin. She held him as if by sheer physical strength she could prevent him from going.

But she was only human. He set her back and kept her apart from him. His endearing, crooked smile made a brief appearance and was just as quickly gone. "I'll find May and bring her back to you. If you need help after I'm gone, ask Harper. He's a capable man, and a real purpose is what he needs to be whole."

Johanna found nothing to say, not a single reasonable argument. Her legs began to tremble. Quentin guided her to her chair and sat her down in it.

"Good-bye, Johanna," he said. His breath hitched, as if he would say something more. "Good-bye."

Her vision blurred. She blinked, and Quentin was gone. Gone for good.

Chapter 20

"No." Johanna tried to stand, faltered, sat down again. "Quentin."

Someone banged on the office door. Oscar barged in, frightened and upset.

"Doc Jo?" he said. "I couldn't find May. I'm sorry." He pushed his hands deep in his pockets. "Mrs. Daugherty said to come get you. There's something going on in the yard. Lots of people. They look mad."

Gott in Himmel. The mob of townsfolk Bolkonsky had warned her about. Were they already here?

Her question was answered soon enough. A shout from outside came from the direction of the front gate, and it was not a cry of greeting. Necessity gave her the will to move. She hurried to the window and looked out. Possibly twenty men, and a few women, were gathered just beyond the gate. They swayed back and forth as one, like some huge, restive, hungry beast.

She knew what had to be done. Quentin would find May

and keep her from harm; Johanna's trust in him remained unshaken. It would be up to her to keep the mob at bay.

"Is everyone else in the parlor?" she asked Oscar.

"Yes. Mr. Andersen got us. He said to wait for you."

"Good. I want you all to stay there, and not move. Do you understand?"

"Are those people going to hurt us?"

Who'd told him that? she wondered. Andersen? Or had Oscar seen enough ugliness in his life to recognize it in the folk of Silverado Springs?

"Let's go to the parlor." She took his hand and led him down the hall to where the others waited. Andersen was pacing up and down the length of the room, rubbing his hands. Harper, beside her father in his wheelchair, gazed toward the kitchen, where Mrs. Daugherty waited nervously in the doorway. Irene, her expression half obscured by her garish face paint, perched on the edge of the sofa.

"What's going on?" Mrs. Daugherty demanded.

It seemed impossible that Mrs. Daugherty, with her ready ear for gossip, knew nothing of last night's incident, or of the townspeople bent on their version of justice. Yet she'd offered no warning. Johanna went to her side and spoke in a whisper. "You did not hear about what happened to the mine owner?"

"I haven't been in town since yesterday mornin'. I stayed with Mrs. Bergstrom last night, way up along the Foss stage route. She's alone now, and ailin', and I—" She pressed her lips together. "Why're them people here, Doc Jo?"

"There is no time to explain. I need you to help keep everyone calm and quiet." She addressed the others. "There is no cause for alarm. I would like you all to remain here, together, until I return. I am going to speak to the people outside."

"I know why they're here," Irene said shrilly. "They've come to get Quentin. He murdered that man in town."

Johanna was no longer surprised by the things Irene

knew. It was her own failure that she hadn't paid more attention to the older woman and monitored her activities.

One of many failures that were coming back to haunt her.

"I don't believe it!" Mrs. Daugherty said.

"*They* do," Harper said, pointing his chin toward the kitchen door. Everyone glanced at him in surprise. He, along with Johanna's father, was the only one who showed no outward sign of concern. "Is Quentin all right?"

"Yes." She looked at him more carefully, remembering Quentin's advice. "Harper, please give Mrs. Daugherty any assistance she needs."

"I reckon you're the one who'll need help," he said, getting to his feet. "I'll come with you."

"As you wish. The rest of you stay inside." She strode for the door and stepped out, Harper at her heels.

The people stirred when they saw her, setting off a ripple of low, hostile voices. She recognized several respectable townsfolk she'd spoken to or dealt with at one time or another, including the blacksmith and the butcher, but most of them were idlers who commonly hung about in the street, drinking and gossiping.

She thought of the gun she'd left on the desk in her office. Foolish; she should have hidden it, or at least brought it along.

And would you use it, Johanna?

"Gentlemen," Johanna said. "How may I help you?"

They obviously hadn't expected such a moderate response to their fearsome presence. The blacksmith looked about uneasily. Others shuffled their feet.

One of the men, a burly giant with a scar across his chin, stepped in front of the rest. She didn't know him, but it was clear that he relished his role as ringleader.

"You know why we're here!" he shouted. "You got all them loonies holed up in this place, and one of 'em killed Ketchum!"

Raised voices supported his accusation. Fists, some wielding farm tools, waved in the air.

"And you are Mr.—" She inclined her head in invitation.

"Mungo," he said with a belligerent sneer.

"I just heard of Mr. Ketchum's unfortunate death," she said. "I'm sorry that you have felt the need to visit the Haven under such circumstances."

Mungo scowled. "Don't try to protect 'im! We know who did it."

Johanna didn't allow her voice to waver in the least. "If you believe one of my patients committed this act, why have you not summoned the constable? I would certainly be glad to cooperate with the proper authorities."

"Don't think you can put us off with your high-and-mighty airs, woman," he taunted. "We al'ays knew something like this would happen, with crazies living near us. This man Forster caused trouble in town b'fore, an' Quigley saw 'im right near where Ketchum was kil't!"

"Nevertheless, until you bring a representative of the law, I will not permit you to bother my patients."

Harper stepped up to her side. "You heard the lady. Go on home, before you regret what you're doing."

"Loony!" Mungo spat at his feet. "We know all about you. We know about every crazy in this place. We c'n run you out and no onc'll stop us. If you don't bring Forster to us, we'll go in and get 'im!"

He started toward Johanna. Men followed in straggling twos and threes. Harper moved ahead of Johanna, readying for attack.

A streak of russet plunged between Harper and Mungo, striking the ringleader on the legs so that he staggered and fell. Johanna got a single good look at the wolf—bristling, fangs bared, eyes blazing with demonic fury—before it fell on the leaders of the mob.

Muttered imprecations became screams. Men ran every which way, seeking escape as hell snapped at their heels.

Mungo found himself gazing up into the open maw of a beast long thought to be extinct in California—except that no such creature had ever existed except in the darkest imaginings of men more clever than he. He shrieked and covered his face with his arms.

Johanna didn't dare cry out for fear of giving Quentin away. Harper dashed in front of her, seized Mungo's arm, and yanked him to his feet. The man didn't linger. He stumbled over his own legs in his haste to follow the others.

The wolf chased them as far as the gate, turned about once to look at Johanna, and leaped the fence with breathtaking grace. In a heartbeat he had vanished.

Harper returned to her side. "Lord have mercy," he whispered. "It's real, then."

She stared at him, wondering how long this state of perpetual confusion would last. "What is real, Harper?"

"You don't have to worry, Doc. I know I'm not crazy, and neither are you."

She had no energy left to pose sensible questions and interpret ambiguous answers. "You know?"

"I thought I'd seen all the wonders and terrors this world has to offer." He laughed under his breath. "A dog came by to see me, before I came out of myself. Least I thought it was a dog. He spoke to me—not like people, but the way other things do, sometimes. Later I had the same feeling around Quentin. Then the Reverend started muttering about men changing into wolves . . . I just sort of put things together."

Quentin was not the only remarkable man at the Haven. "And you accept this?"

"Don't rightly have much choice, do I?" He scratched his chin and looked down the lane beyond the gate, where the dust was just beginning to settle. "I don't reckon the folks from town will be back anytime soon. They'll have other things to gossip about for a while."

"No doubt. But after today, we can't make any assumptions." This entire conversation felt like a dream within a dream. She remembered what Quentin had said of Harper, urging her to rely on him. She badly needed his stolid dispassion. "How much do you know of what's been happening in town?"

"I keep my ear to the ground. Irene gossips."

And how did Irene know so much? That question must also wait until later. "There are many things I have been unable to tell you and the others. Are you aware that May's father has come to the Springs to take her from the Haven, with the help of a man named Bolkonsky, and that I have opposed this reunion for the sake of May's health and happiness?"

"I've watched May these past few days." He motioned to the place where the mob had stood. "It has something to do with all this?"

"May's father was assaulted in his hotel shortly before Ketchum was killed." She swallowed. "Quentin has been very protective of May."

He didn't ask if she believed Quentin had done the assaulting. "Why would Quentin go after this Ketchum?"

Explaining Fenris and her tenuous theories about him was not an option. "Matters have gone terribly awry, Harper. I ask for your trust . . . and I may need your help, if you feel able."

"Yes," he said simply. "Quentin's leaving the Haven, isn't he?"

She held back tears by sheer force of will. "He went to look for May. He must have found her, if he was able to—" She gestured wordlessly at the trampled earth. "May will be leaving as well, as soon as we can make her ready. Let us go inside."

Mrs. Daugherty stood sentinel by the kitchen door, clutching a cast-iron pan to ward off potential invaders.

"What happened?" she demanded. "First that man was

makin' threats, and then I see him an' his friends a'runnin' like the devil hisself was after 'em."

Thank God Mrs. Daugherty hadn't seen the wolf. "They thought better of their behavior. Has May come back?"

"I saw her in the parlor with the others just a moment ago, but they been mighty quiet since. Haven't seen Quentin." She followed Johanna into the parlor. "I thought someone should stand guard—"

She broke off. The parlor was empty except for Johanna's father, who was dozing in his chair. Johanna's heart clenched in panic.

"I didn't hear anyone leave!" Mrs. Daugherty protested.

"Please look through the house, Mrs. Daugherty," Johanna said. "Harper and I will search outside."

She rushed down the hall to the rear door, knowing that the others weren't in their rooms. Harper found Lewis at the edge of the garden, sitting in the dirt. Blood matted the thinning hair at the back of his head.

"Someone hit me," he said in faint outrage, accepting Harper's support. Johanna knelt beside him to examine the wound, which was rapidly developing into a goose's egg. He was lucky to have received such a glancing blow.

"I told them all to stay inside," Lewis said. "That . . . Quentin Forster brought May into the parlor and left again, but the girl had hardly been here a minute when that pernicious female, DuBois—she whispered to May and led her out the back door." He wiped at his soiled trousers and stared at the earth stains on his hands as if he would weep. "I tried to stop them. I followed them, and then someone struck me—"

"We'll find them, Lewis."

"But the wolf-beast—the mob—"

"They're gone. But I must find May." She took a clean handkerchief from her pocket and pressed it over Lewis's wound. "Hold this firmly in place. Harper will take you in, and I'll see to your injury as soon as I can."

She nodded to Harper, who supported Lewis to his feet. For once, Lewis did not reject the touch.

Someone had struck Lewis with the obvious intent of rendering him unconscious, or at least incapable of action. Irene had lured May outside, in spite of being told to remain in the parlor, after Quentin had delivered the girl safely home and gone out to confront the mob.

The confusion of the past few minutes would be an ideal diversion for one who wished to approach the Haven from the opposite direction unobserved. One who wished to remove a certain patient without interference.

Bolkonsky.

Dummkopf, Johanna swore at herself. "May! May, do you hear me?" She ran through the garden and turned toward the wood. She almost missed the book that lay facedown on the path to the orchard.

May's book, Elizabeth Stuart Phelps' *The Story of Avis.* She bent to pick it up and saw the footprints beside it, lightly engraved in the shade-moistened earth. Two sets of footprints, a girl's and a woman's.

Johanna followed their course like a hound dog with its nose to the trail. Just within the orchard itself a third set of prints, unmistakably male, joined the first two. They traveled together for a few yards more, and then the girl's disappeared.

That was where she found Irene.

The woman stood in the shade of an apple tree, holding a battered carpetbag against her chest. Her attention was entirely focused on the lane just beyond the orchard fence. May was not with her.

"Irene," Johanna said.

Irene's head snapped around. Her eyes widened in an expression of naked fear.

"Where is May?" Johanna demanded. "Where is she, Irene?"

"She's not here!" Irene stepped away from the tree, holding the carpetbag in front of her. "Go away. Leave me alone!"

"I know you took her out of the parlor," Johanna said, making no effort to quell her anger. "Was it you who hit Andersen?" She grabbed Irene's arm. "Where is May?"

"Gone!" Irene stretched her lips in a grotesque smile. "Gone to be with her father, and you're too late!"

"Was it Bolkonsky? You know him, don't you? He told you to bring May to him while the mob from town came after Quentin, didn't he?" She gave Irene a shake. "Tell me the truth!"

"Yes, I know Feodor!" She laughed. "You always thought I stayed locked up here like the others, because you never paid attention to me. You've always thought I was stupid, didn't you? But I knew everything that went on in town. I went at night. I watched, and I listened, and those country bumpkins never knew that the great Irene DuBois was among them."

Johanna let Irene go, stunned at her own blindness. The clues had all been there, had she chosen to see them—Lewis's complaint about Irene's visits to town, her new gown, her more frequent references to leaving the Haven, her unusual confidence. Johanna had never guessed that Irene was so superb an actress. All the woman's dramatic posturing had merely seemed evidence of her unyielding delusions . . .

"I knew when the handsome Doctor Bolkonsky came to town," Irene said. "I had my eye on him from the beginning. He was different, the kind of man I've been waiting for. I knew when you went to see him, and that he'd never be interested in *you*."

"Oh, Irene," Johanna whispered.

"He's been in love with me ever since he saw me on Broadway. He told me all about poor little May and what you were doing to keep her away from her father—the same way you tried to keep me from my true destiny. He needed someone to tell him what was going on here, and report to him. I agreed to help him get May away from you, and he promised to take me to San Francisco and set me up on the stage, where I belong." She tossed her head. "We just had to wait for the right time. You made it so easy—you, and Quentin!"

"It was Bolkonsky who sent the mob here, wasn't it? *He* stirred them up, and only pretended to warn me—"

"As I said, you made it easy for us. The people in town were already upset when they found Ketchum's body, especially after the attack on May's father. They were looking for someone to blame. Feodor told them that he was afraid your new patient, Quentin, had something to do with it. He was worried that you had lost control over your loonies. People listened to him—he's a doctor, after all!" She laughed. "The rest took care of itself. All I had to do was get May to come with me while you were busy. Quentin brought her back just in time, but she wanted to follow him when he left. I told her I could take her to him. Feodor's man was waiting for us outside."

The third set of footprints. "Bolkonsky wasn't here?"

"He's coming to get me." Irene's eyes glazed over with visions of her glorious future. "All the city will be at my feet, just like Feodor. You can't stop me now!"

Johanna followed her expectant gaze to the lane. Not for a instant did Johanna believe that Bolkonsky intended to take Irene away. A man such as he would have no personal interest in a haggard, aging actress. He'd merely used Irene as men had used her before, to serve his own ends.

Nothing about Bolkonsky was as it seemed. He'd deceived Johanna time and again—put the residents of the Haven at risk—as a ploy to return May to her father. He'd given her the news about the attack on Ingram, and planted the blame for Mr. Ketchum's death on Quentin.

Had Quentin been seen near Ketchum's body, or was that another of Bolkonsky's fabrications? Why was Bolkonsky so dedicated to Ingram's cause? Was it money, or something else she couldn't begin to imagine?

Putting such speculation from her mind, Johanna followed the male footprints as they crossed the orchard and continued on toward the wood.

"You won't find her," Irene shouted after her. "You've lost Quentin, too. You've failed, Johanna!"

Her triumphant words nipped at Johanna's heels, stinging with every step. Irene assumed she'd give up. Would Bolkonsky, and May's father, assume the same? Ingram had his business in San Francisco. He'd take May there, secure in his power.

Yet Bolkonsky had carefully avoided bringing in the authorities at any time in their dealings, preferring the use of subterfuge to steal May from the Haven. There must be a reason. Perhaps May's father had wanted certain secrets out of the public eye.

Secrets Johanna might attempt to expose, at the risk of her own professional destruction. But hadn't she already compromised her vocation, possibly beyond mending?

She passed out of the orchard and into the wild groves of oak and madrona. Her eyes caught a sudden change in the earth, and she stopped.

The ground was trampled here, marked by some struggle, and the man's footprints formed a mad pattern intermingled with the spoor of a wolf.

This was where Quentin had gone, after chasing the mob away. He'd followed May's captor, and caught up with him. But where were they?

Johanna knelt to study the tracks. May's footprints had also reappeared, as if her captor had set her down after carrying her for some distance. Johanna found a final set of prints, almost lost amid the others.

Those of a barefoot man, about Quentin's size.

Leaves rattled a few feet away. Johanna scooted about to face the sound. A man's blunt-fingered hand reached out from a cluster of bushes, to the accompaniment of a hoarse groan.

Johanna pushed aside branches. The man was a stranger, a big, nasty-looking character with a scarred face and shoes that matched the prints of May's kidnapper. Aside from a few scratches, he seemed unharmed, though he was just recovering consciousness. Johanna had no pity to spare for him.

"Where is May?" she demanded.

"Wolf," he muttered. His eyes opened, bloodshot and terrified. "Devil!"

She grabbed his shoulders. "Who took May?"

"Th' devil man!" He covered his eyes like a child hiding from a nightmare. "He'll kill me."

"Only if I do not." She tightened her grip. "Bolkonsky hired you to take May from the Haven, didn't he?"

"He'll . . . *kill* me."

Did he mean Bolkonsky or Quentin?

"You were to deliver May to Bolkonsky, weren't you?" she asked. "Where were you to meet him?"

"Let me."

She looked up to find Harper behind her, his ordinarily mild eyes glittering with a dangerous light. He crouched over the man, long fingers working.

"You answer the lady now, or I'll go get my friend the wolf and let him play with you," Harper said in a cold, flat voice. "Where were you taking the girl?"

The kidnapper's eyes went wide as saucers. "The . . . the old Miller ruin by Ritchey Creek." He snatched at Johanna's hands. "Please, don't let the demon get me!" He fell to whimpering gibberish about wolf-devils and repenting his sins. "If I tell you who really killed Ketchum, can I be saved?"

"Tell us," Johanna demanded.

"It was on Bolkonsky's orders. I didn't do it, I swear! I only lured him where . . ." He gulped. "We was supposed to tell everyone that your man killed him. I'll testify that it wasn't him, I swear I will!"

Johanna pried his fingers from her wrists and gave silent thanks. Whatever Fenris might have done in the past, he hadn't taken the mine owner's life.

She drew Harper aside. "Everything is all right back at the house?"

"As right as it can be. Mrs. Daugherty is staying with the others."

"Did you see Irene?"

"She was crying, over by the orchard."

Had she begun to realize that Bolkonsky would not be coming? "She has been meeting Bolkonsky without my knowledge. Since I opposed returning May to her father, Bolkonsky planned this clandestine abduction. Irene brought May out of the house while we were occupied with the mob, so that this man could take her. He didn't succeed, but May is still missing."

Harper met her gaze with perfect comprehension. "Quentin was here. You think he took her?"

"I don't know." She clasped her hands over her roiling stomach. "It is a possibility."

"He would have taken her to protect her from this Bolkonsky."

Quentin would have. But Quentin would also contact Johanna to let her know that May was safe. How long would it take Bolkonsky or May's father to seek the help of the law?

Brush crackled and twigs snapped. May's would-be kidnapper had stumbled to his feet and was making a clumsy attempt at escape. Harper started toward him, but Johanna held him back.

"Let him go. He's too frightened to be a further threat, and we haven't time to deal with him now."

Harper frowned after the man until he was out of sight,

then glanced at the ground at Johanna's feet. "Is that May's book?"

She bent to pick up the book she'd set down when she examined the footprints. The pages were creased and soiled. "She must have taken it with her when Irene lured her outside."

"May I have it?"

She handed it to Harper. He stroked the dirt-stained cover with reverent fingers, and she remembered his claims of reading men's pasts and futures in everyday objects.

If he thought that he could use some inborn magical power to help her locate May, she was not prepared to discourage him. Desperate circumstances called for desperate measures. And until this very morning, she had not believed in the existence of genuine lycanthropes.

Nor had she believed that she could falter in all her fine aspirations, all her high standards, all her confidence in logic and reason and her own well-trained abilities.

But she had.

"I must talk to Mrs. Daugherty," she said, trying to fill the terrifying void in her heart with words and plans. "She can go into town and listen for news. I'll ride to the place where Bolkonsky was to collect May. There is a chance he is still waiting. I may learn something of value."

"You shouldn't go alone." Harper shortened his stride to match hers as they walked briskly back toward the house. Irene had disappeared from the orchard.

"There is no time for argument," Johanna said. "It is much to ask, but if you can take care of my father and Oscar I will be deeply obliged to you. I will show you what my father requires. Lewis should be no trouble. As for Irene—"

"I'll keep an eye on her," he said. "When I find her, I'll put her in her room and keep her there."

"Thank you." She paused just beyond the back door to clasp his hand. "You are a good man, Harper."

"Without you and Quentin, I wouldn't be a man at all."

He squeezed her hand and let it fall. "Tell me what I need to do."

Within an hour she had laid out the bare bones of the situation to a fretful Mrs. Daugherty, including an account of the bizarre appearance of a wolf, and asked her to take the buggy into town to glean any news or gossip about Dr. Bolkonsky, May's father, or the aftermath of the siege on the Haven. Whatever the people of Silverado Springs might think of Johanna and the Haven's residents, they wouldn't hold Mrs. Daugherty accountable.

While Harper went in search of Irene, Johanna told Oscar that May had gone away for a little while, and that he mustn't worry. Lewis was in his room, but responded to her brief explanation with peculiar blankness.

She hadn't time to do more with him. She took Lewis's gun from her office, kissed her father on the forehead, and asked for Oscar's help in saddling Daisy.

The mare carried her at a willing canter to the meeting place Bolkonsky's henchman had described, but it was deserted. If Bolkonsky had been waiting, he'd either given up or been told of his plan's failure. With any luck—more than she deserved—he knew no more of May's whereabouts than Johanna did.

Avoiding the roads that would take her close to Silverado Springs, Johanna returned to the Haven. Harper came running to meet her.

"I think you'd better come with me right away," he said grimly.

She dismounted and followed him to the vineyard. The tableau that greeted her froze her in her tracks.

Irene was on her knees in the dirt, weeping hysterically. Lewis stood over her, holding a kitchen knife between his shaking hands. His head jerked up at Johanna's approach.

"Stay away!" he warned. He pointed the knife at Irene.

Johanna held up her hands. "Lewis. Put the knife down."

"Evil!" Lewis shouted. "All is evil. Don't you see? First

the devil wolf, and now this Jezebel, who has betrayed us all."

"No!" Irene shrieked. "Please—"

It was possible, in spite of the day's many disasters, for things to get worse. Johanna recognized that Lewis had reached the limits of his tolerance. He was on the verge of submitting to total madness, and there was nothing she could do to help him.

"You cannot hurt her, Lewis," she said urgently. "No more than you could hurt Quentin."

"I failed!" Lewis cried. "The beast is loose, because of me! I must rid the world of this whore of Babylon, who let them take the child—yes, I heard everything!" The knife began to dip, and he snapped it toward the sky. "She is like all the daughters of Eve, in league with Satan. Just like, like—"

"Irene is not the enemy," Johanna said. "Another man has taken May. We must find a way to get her back. That is all that matters."

"No! Evil must be wiped out, lest it swallow us all." He swung the knife in a wild arc. "I failed before—failed—but this time—"

" 'Let he who is without sin,' " Johanna quoted, " 'cast the first stone.' Are you without sin, Reverend?"

Lewis gasped, mouth working. "Without sin?" He fell to his knees. "She betrayed me. My Hetty. She lay with another man, and I sent her away. I sent her out to die." Water ran from his eyes and nose. " 'Thou hypocrite, first cast out the beam out of thine own eye!' " He pressed the point of the knife against his own chest.

Harper bolted toward him. Johanna dashed to Irene and dragged her away. With a cry, Lewis allowed Harper to wrench the knife from his hand. He fell prone upon the earth, his arms clasped over his head.

Johanna half-carried Irene back to the house and returned to the vineyard. Harper knelt beside Lewis, whose sobs had hushed to ordinary weeping. The madness was gone from his face.

"He'll be all right," Harper said. "I'll take care of him."

Johanna knew when she had run out of choices. "I will ask Mrs. Daugherty to take charge of Irene, but it will be up to you to keep Lewis quiet and hold things together while I am gone."

"To find May?"

"We will wait for Mrs. Daugherty's news," she said, "and then I shall decide what to do. But I need you here, Harper. I'll leave the gun with you, but I must go alone."

Harper touched the handle of the knife. "Me and Bridget will do what needs to be done."

Johanna had no doubt that he meant what he said. Fighting exhaustion, she tended Irene and went back to the kitchen to await Bridget's return. Everything within her screamed to ride out again, in any and all directions. She knew the utter futility of such a plan.

Three long hours later the buggy drew up in the yard and Mrs. Daugherty climbed out. Johanna met her at the front steps.

"I came back as quick as I could," she panted. "The town's abuzz with talk of the wolf. People who weren't here think the rest of 'em's crazy. No wolf's been seen in these parts in years." She shook her head, unable to believe it herself. "Some are saying the wolf must have kilt Ketchum, and they're gathering men to hunt it down."

No worse than Johanna had expected. "And Bolkonksy?"

"Well, it appears he and Ingram lit out of town this morning, just before the mob came. No one's seen 'em since."

So Bolkonsky must have left straight after "warning" Johanna about the mob. But he apparently hadn't summoned the authorities to search for May, which bought her a little time.

Time for what? She was no closer to being able to locate

Quentin than she'd been before. And she had assumed that
Quentin had May.

There was another explanation for those bare footprints
intermingled with May's. Fenris. He arose from Quentin's
mind when Quentin was threatened. What better time than
after the mob's attack to seize Quentin's body?

And if he had, what did he want with May? Were
Quentin's protective instincts enough to arouse like instincts
from Fenris's dark, twisted heart? Or had he some unfathomable, fell purpose of his own?

Johanna sat down in a kitchen chair and bent her head
low between her knees. This sickness and dread and terror
were only the beginning of her punishment.

She had transgressed. She had sinned far worse than
Lewis, with all his warnings of Biblical wrath, could imagine. Her deadly sin had been her arrogant presumption that
she understood the human mind and its frailties, that she
could cure illnesses that daunted far better doctors than she.
She had ridden high and serene on the crest of her own wisdom, her own faith in the infallibility of science.

Above all, she had forgotten the sacred trust of every
physician. She had allowed herself to fall in love, to become
personally involved, with a patient. The very weakness she
had deplored in other females had entrapped her. Had she remained pure, true to her calling, she would have kept a
closer eye on Irene and Lewis, protected May, dealt effec-
tively with Fenris, and found Quentin's cure. In her blind
passion, she'd thrown all that away.

Love had not healed, but destroyed.

"You need rest, Doc Jo," Mrs. Daugherty said. "I'll see
that everyone gets fed. You take care of yourself."

Hadn't she done too much of that already? The others,
even Harper, were counting on her to remain strong. She had
no right to indulge in hysterics or personal grief.

But she did need rest; she'd be useless without it. A little more patience might turn up the one piece of information she needed to make the next crucial decision.

After that, common sense be damned. She would find May and Quentin—or Fenris—if she had to search every inch of this Valley, and beyond.

"Thank you, Mrs. Daugherty," she said. She made her rounds like an automaton, went to her room, and fell face-down on the bed. And she wept. She wept until the pillowcase and the pillow beneath were soaked, so silently that no one came to inquire. Afterwards she washed her face, visited her father, and returned to her room to pace the floor through the long, excruciating night.

Just after dawn an unfamiliar young man came to the front door. Johanna rushed out to meet him, indifferent to her ravaged appearance.

It was obvious that he, too, had been up all night. "You the lady they call Doc Johanna?" he asked, scratching his dirty hair.

"I am. Have you something for me?"

"Sure have." He pulled out a sweat-stained, coarsely folded sheet of paper. "A man at the Bale depot gave me this an' told me to deliver it to you soon as I could get here. Paid me well—not the kind of man you cross." He shuddered. "Took me long enough to find this place."

Johanna snatched the paper from his hand. The words had been scrawled almost illegibly on a sheet of lady's stationery.

"You know that I have May," the words said. *"If you want her back, come to the corner of Jackson and Kearny in San Francisco tomorrow night. A man will be waiting to bring you to me."*

It was signed with a single letter: *F.*

Chapter 21

The place stank. That was the first thing he always noticed when he woke to another foggy San Francisco dusk.

All of the Barbary Coast reeked: of human sweat, rotting fish, stale saltwater, alcohol, cheap perfume, and broken dreams.

It was the closest place to home Fenris had ever found.

And so he ignored the offensive stench and established his territory here, in this boarded-up whorehouse in Devil's Acre, jammed between Jackson's bordello and a saloon where more than one unwary sailor had been known to suffer the loss of everything he owned—even his life.

He stretched out on the stained mattress and looked across the room with its peeling wallpaper and moth-eaten furniture. His wolf's eyes needed no light to see the girl huddled on the decrepit sofa he'd made for her bed. A blanket—relatively clean, for he'd stolen it from one of the better whorehouses—swathed her fragile form from chin to toe. Stray light caught the motion of her pupils as she stared back at him.

What did she think she saw?

Quentin had become the wolf to save Johanna from the mob. Quentin had followed May's kidnapper, set her free, and driven the man to his knees in fear.

But it was Fenris who took human shape again; Fenris who put the terror of damnation into the half-wit he'd chosen, on a whim, not to kill; Fenris who seized May and carried her off without any sort of plan, realizing only miles later what he had.

The means to bring Johanna to him.

Quentin would have taken May to protect her against those who'd harm her. Fenris had no such noble motives. But when he looked at the girl, as he did now, he did not wish her ill.

He almost pitied her. The mawkishness of it sickened him.

He arched his back to work stiff muscles and got up, reaching for his trousers. May watched him, unmoving. Afraid, with good cause. She'd seen him change from wolf to man; few humans witnessed such a transformation and remained unaltered.

Yet in all the time since he had caught her up outside the Haven and carried her away to the south—while he had stolen clothing and coins from unsuspecting farmers and bought tickets at the Bale depot for the next train to San Francisco—not once had she screamed or fainted or fallen into hysterics. She understood what he required of her. She became his meek companion, a mute little sister who wasn't quite right in the head. Fenris discouraged the curiosity and sympathy of strangers.

He'd rifled a lady's baggage at the depot and stole the materials to write his letter to Johanna. He'd paid a boy to deliver it to the Haven, promising retribution if the note didn't reach its destination by morning. The boy took his meaning, just as May did.

He and May reached San Francisco by nightfall. Fenris could have found his way across the city blindfolded; he knew every gambling den and house of ill repute from Murderer's Corner to Deadman's Alley. He and Quentin had shared San Francisco, but here Fenris truly reigned. Especially at night.

May had clung to him, the lesser of two evils, as he led her to his old haunts on the Barbary Coast. His derelict house remained as he'd left it, for no intruder had dared trespass in his absence. The citizens of the Coast knew *him* too well.

And he, Fenris, was still in control. Quentin hadn't the strength to return. He'd been defeated by the knowledge that he'd lost Johanna—and that he was not alone in his own body. He reached out blindly as he sought a link to his other self, a means of recognition and communication. Fenris pushed him back with hardly an effort.

Eventually Quentin would give up. Johanna wouldn't, so long as she believed that she could reach him. Fenris would teach her the futility of that false hope.

Two days had passed since she'd have received his letter—time enough to arrange for her absence from the Haven. He expected her this very evening.

Then he'd have to decide what to do with May.

He finished buttoning his trousers, reached for the chipped plate on the table beside the boarded window, and tore off a chunk of the sourdough bread he'd stolen from the baker's that morning. May's hungry stare was like the annoying buzz of an insect.

"You want this?" he said, holding up the loaf. "Take it." He tossed it toward the couch. She scrambled up to catch it, too late, and it landed on the grimy floor. She sat on the edge of the sofa, the blanket still wrapped around her, and looked at the bread as if it were a million miles out of reach. He waited for her to burst into tears.

She didn't. She raised her head and gazed at him, her pale face set in resignation.

"You aren't Quentin, are you?" she said.

Ironic that she should ask that question first, when she must have wondered *what* he was.

"No," he said mockingly. "I'm not Quentin."

Her brow furrowed. "I don't understand."

"You don't have to." He picked up the bread, brushed it off with his fingers, and thrust it into her hands. "Eat."

"I'm not hungry."

"You're a liar."

She shrank back a little, as if she expected a beating for her defiance. He was tempted to give her what she asked for, but his muscles refused to lift his arm.

Quentin. *Damn* Quentin.

"Eat or starve. I don't care." He turned his back on her and went for the half-empty bottle of whiskey balanced atop a broken armoire.

"Who are you?"

Her rash persistence surprised him, given her ordeal. He took a swig from the bottle.

"Fenris," he said.

"Fenris." She wet her lips. "You're not . . . a regular person."

He laughed at the absurdity of her understatement. "You're right." He leered at her, showing all his teeth. "I'm a monster. Just like Quentin."

"Quentin isn't—" Her protest subsided into a long, fluttering breath. "You and Quentin . . . are the same, aren't you?"

She wasn't completely stupid. "Don't go crying after him. You won't find him here."

She absorbed that in silence. "But he's not really gone, is he?"

"Shut up."

"Quentin is my friend. He always tried to help me."

He slammed the bottle down on the armoire. "I told you to shut up."

"*You* helped me," she whispered. "You saved me from that man, the one who wanted to take me back to my father."

Pain exploded in his head. "*I'm . . . not . . . Quentin.*" He strode toward her, hard and fast, bent on meting out swift punishment. She leaned back against the sofa, not so much as raising her arms to protect herself.

But in her eyes was the tiniest glint of spirit. It brought him up short.

"Will you hurt me, like my father?" she asked.

His headache worked to split his brain down the middle. "I'm not your father," he snarled.

"No," she said. "*He* pretended to love me."

He'd never heard such a voice, such aching acceptance and sorrow. The girl Quentin knew hadn't spoken of her past, not to him nor to Johanna. That girl had always been afraid.

Like the boy. The boy in the cellar, who'd cried out for help and found it.

Fenris clenched his teeth and fell to his knees beside the sofa. Something inside drove him to ask what he didn't want to know, didn't want to feel.

"What did he do to you?"

She closed her eyes. "He . . . he came to me when I was sleeping. He touched me."

Fingernails scraped against the bare floorboards, and Fenris realized they were his own.

"I don't want to go back," she said. "Please, don't make me go back."

He jumped to his feet. "You're not going anywhere."

"You don't have to take care of me. Quentin—"

"Quentin is a coward and a fool." He seized her chin in

his hand, deliberately relaxed his fingers so that he would not damage her skin and bones. "He couldn't even take care of himself."

Her eyes filled with tears. "Someone hurt him? His . . . his father?"

Grandfather. Please no more . . .

Fenris roared. He saw Quentin—himself—May—bound and helpless while one who should have loved and protected gave torment instead.

Killing rage replaced all semblance of thought. Tiberius Forster was dead, but Chester Ingram was not. The man called Bolkonsky was not.

The girl had become a wraith to him, like a half-forgotten dream. He started toward the door.

"Quentin?"

He stopped.

"Quentin, please come back."

Quentin heard. Quentin stirred in his prison, struggling to respond. He groped in darkness for his voice and his being. A shaft of light burst from an opening door.

Fenris flung his weight against that door, but not before Quentin saw him.

"You," Quentin said. "You're real."

The moment in which they faced each other was infinitesimal, but it was enough for Quentin to understand. Understanding was a new and powerful weapon, but he didn't yet know how to use it. He was paralyzed by horror.

Fenris heard the girl's tread behind him. "Quentin—"

"I'm here," he whispered in Quentin's voice.

Fenris howled. He slammed the door inside his mind and sealed it with a hundred massive locks forged by his furious will.

He couldn't kill Quentin, no more than he could kill a man already dead, or the girl shivering within her enshrouding blanket.

But Quentin couldn't stop him from eliminating Ingram,

because it was what they both wanted. It was the work for which Fenris had been born.

He turned to the girl, seeing her face as if through a sheer veil of bloodred silk.

"Wait here," he said with an icy smile. "I'm going to visit your father."

Johanna arrived at the San Francisco Ferry House on the evening's last boat and disembarked with the small group of passengers from Oakland. The others scattered to their various destinations, hailing hackney coaches or meeting friends, many chattering happily as if they looked forward to an enjoyable visit.

The sun was just setting, and already the night was damp and cold, lacking the Napa Valley's summer warmth. San Francisco's weather perfectly matched the chill in Johanna's heart. The coldness had settled in with the delivery of Fenris's letter, and hadn't left her since.

She'd done what needed doing in spite of her fears, arranging for Mrs. Daugherty and Harper to handle the running of the Haven and the most basic care of the other patients and her father. She hoped she would not be gone long enough to put a strain on Mrs. Daugherty's generosity, or compromise Harper's dramatic improvement. At least she had Mrs. Daugherty's assurance that the townspeople had lost their interest in revisiting the Haven . . . for the time being.

It hadn't been easy to lie to the patients, especially to Harper. Harper guessed that Quentin had taken May, but he didn't know that Fenris existed. She'd told him that she was going to meet Quentin in San Francisco and arrange for May's safe disposition. Mrs. Daugherty and the patients had been given a much simpler story. None of them knew the complexity of May's situation with her father.

But Harper wasn't satisfied. He'd held May's book, his

brow creased in worry, and told Johanna that Quentin and May were in serious danger.

She could hardly refute him, and she respected him too much to offer comforting platitudes.

She pulled Fenris's note from her coat pocket and read the scrawled address once more. She wasn't familiar enough with San Francisco to recognize the location, but someone at her hotel would be sure to know. She suspected that the place was in a very bad part of town.

She had no doubt that Fenris was waiting for her.

Squaring her shoulders, she flagged down the nearest hired hack and gave the driver the address of a modest but respectable hotel on Market Street, where she'd stayed for the lecture nearly three weeks ago. Once there, she strode to the desk with her single bag and waited impatiently behind another woman who was completing her registration.

After an interminable period, the woman turned from the desk and bumped into Johanna.

"I beg your pardon," the woman said, echoing Johanna's apology. They broke off simultaneously, and the woman peered into her face. Johanna felt a jolt of startled recognition.

"Dr. Schell?" the woman said. "Dr. Johanna Schell? It is you, is it not?"

Johanna took an involuntary step backward. "Mrs. . . . Mrs. Ingram?"

"Yes. Oh, it is you!" She beamed, and Johanna thought back to the last night she'd seen this unfortunate woman, haggard and terrified for herself and her daughter. "What an amazing coincidence to meet you here, of all places! And I was just making the arrangements to come to the Valley to see you."

She extended her gloved hand, and Johanna took it, praying that her trembling was not too obvious.

Mrs. Ingram. May's mother, who had disappeared for a full two years—communicating only through the occasional letter—who had trusted Johanna with her daughter's well-being when she could trust no one else. Her most recent letter had promised her return in the very near future, and she'd been as good as her word.

She had greatly changed. Her cheeks glowed with health and confidence; her eyes sparkled with genuine happiness. The happiness of a mother about to be reunited with a beloved child.

"I understand your hesitation in greeting me," Mrs. Ingram said, becoming serious. "I must have seemed a terrible mother to you, leaving my child as I did. My letters were hardly adequate, but I had reason for hiding my whereabouts."

Johanna found her voice. "Mrs. Ingram—I knew, when I accepted May, that you faced great difficulties."

"And I knew you would care for my girl and make her well." She squeezed Johanna's hand. "I knew the moment we met. But everything has changed. It has taken me two years, but I have the means of making certain that my husband can never threaten us again. I can pay you for all your good work, and May and I can live together in peace."

"I am . . . glad to hear it," Johanna said.

"I'm sure you have a great many questions, and I shall be happy to answer them soon. Are you in town on business? Perhaps you will allow me to accompany you back to the Haven." She smiled self-consciously. "It will be easier for her to meet me again if you are with me. I'm sure she's grown to love you, and I've been gone so long. Perhaps she blames me for leaving her."

Johanna swallowed. "Mrs. Ingram—"

"Forgive my chatter. My life has changed so, and it doesn't quite seem real as yet." She glanced toward the clerk behind the desk. "I must be keeping you. Please tell me—how is May? I can't wait to see her."

"May—May has improved, Mrs. Ingram. She has made

SECRET OF THE WOLF 333

friends at the Haven, and reads constantly. She's becoming a young woman."

Little truths to cover the big ones that could not be spoken, truths no better than lies. Lies would not protect Johanna, or undo her many mistakes. They would only spare this woman more suffering.

Mrs. Ingram closed her eyes. "I knew it. I have felt all these months that everything will be right at last. Thank you, Dr. Schell."

Johanna cleared her throat. "It seems that we are staying in the same hotel."

"As you see. I had planned to go to Silverado Springs tomorrow—"

"Might you delay a day or two? I have certain business to attend here in the city before I return. I have very good and reliable assistants at the Haven, but I agree that it would be best if we see May together."

Mrs. Ingram made a valiant try at hiding her disappointment. "Yes. I see. Of course I will wait on your convenience. A few more days can hardly make a difference." Her smile returned. "As it happens, it will allow me to put a few final details of my own plans in place."

"Very good." Johanna thought of Mr. Ingram, and wondered what resources this revitalized woman had found to give her such spirit to face him again. She hoped it was enough to thoroughly emasculate him.

But none of that mattered until she had May safely back.

"I'm very glad that things have turned out so well for you," she said, despising herself.

"Of course." Mrs. Ingram clasped her hand again. "Thank you. Thank you so much."

Johanna averted her gaze and waited until the other woman had gone up to her room. Only then did she register, leave her bag in her room, and hail a conveyance that would take her to Fenris's rendezvous.

"The Barbary Coast?" the hackney driver said, shaking

his head. "Bad place for a decent woman at any time of day. At night—"

"It is where I must go," she said. "Please take me there quickly."

"As you say, ma'am. On your own head be it." He clucked his tongue, helped her into the coach, and climbed up to the driver's seat. "Don't say I didn't warn you."

Johanna sank back into the seat and closed her eyes. The warning came too late.

A*ll he could see was fog.*
Quentin woke into his body with a sense of disorientation and icy metal against his fingers. He unclenched his fists from the ironwork bars forming a high, decorative fence that marked the boundaries of a landscaped garden. The garden of a large, handsome Second Empire house, with a slated mansard roof and lights burning in a pair of gabled windows on the second floor.

His vision cleared further, and he saw that the fog was not so thick as he'd imagined. It swirled between buildings much like this one, the dwellings of rich and prosperous folk perched atop a hill overlooking the city.

The city of San Francisco. Nob Hill, in fact; he recognized the neighborhood, though it was one he'd seldom frequented during his previous residence. He had no idea how he had come to be here—in the city, or at this particular place. He didn't know whose house this was, or why he'd been bent on trespass.

The last memory he could summon to mind was one of Changing from wolf to man in the woods near the Haven, May gazing at him in shock while her erstwhile kidnapper scuttled away. He remembered surrendering to instinct. Raw emotion. Despair. Anger.

He'd left the door open—

To Fenris.

He slumped to the ground at the foot of the ironwork fence and squeezed his eyes shut. How much time had passed? Hours, or days? What had this body done while it lay in another's control?

He opened his eyes and stared at his hands. They looked the same. There was no blood on them. His clothing was unfamiliar, not what he would have chosen. But when he'd Changed, he hadn't been wearing anything.

Fenris had dressed this body to suit himself. And come to San Francisco.

But Quentin had control again, for no reason that he could fathom. If anger and irrational emotion gave Fenris the edge, what had made him flee? Why had he brought Quentin to this place? To what had Fenris come?

And why?

Quentin pushed his palms against his temples. *Think.* His own intention had been to leave Johanna and the others and seek out some distant, isolated place where he could wrestle with his own demons—with Fenris—free of the fear of harming innocents. He'd delayed his departure long enough to scare off the mob and rescue May. He'd known that Bolkonsky or Ingram must be responsible for her abduction, but he hadn't thought beyond seeing her returned safely to Johanna.

Fenris had taken his mind before he faced an impossible decision. But what Fenris wanted was more a mystery to him than it had been to Johanna.

Johanna. She'd begged him not to go, to trust her to help him. Cure him. He couldn't think of her without an agony of desire and sorrow and love.

Fenris didn't love Johanna . . .

But he'd wanted her.

Yes. Quentin slammed his head against the iron bars. That was what Fenris was after—he felt it in his gut like the dregs of a nightmare. Johanna had come to *his* bed because of Fenris.

Because Fenris had threatened her, and she wanted to give Quentin willingly what Fenris desired to take by force.

If Fenris was everything Quentin was afraid to be, he would have remained at the Haven and seized what he wanted. He wouldn't have considered the consequences.

Unless something had restrained him, redirected his desires. Some*one*. If that person had been Johanna, surely she would have brought Quentin back. She had the skill, the courage, and the stubbornness.

No. The last he'd seen of Johanna was when she faced down the mob. He was sure that Fenris hadn't been near her since.

But who else could hold Fenris in check . . . except his other self?

Hope made Quentin catch his breath. Could he have been fighting without knowing it? Fenris had every advantage, with access to Quentin's memories, while Quentin remained in darkness. Until Johanna had told him, he hadn't known that Fenris existed. Now the implacable shadow had a name. A name was something to fight.

"Somehow," Johanna had said, "you and I must find a way to communicate with him. Bring him into the light, and confront him."

But this was not a matter of communication and confrontation. It was war. The battle was solely Quentin's—Quentin the coward, the ne'er-do-well, who had mustered up an inner core of strength to resist.

And he had to make use of it while he could. He had to learn what Fenris was doing in San Francisco, and then find a way to stop him. Expel him for good. Take back his life.

Win Johanna's love.

She'd never said she loved him. This was his great chance to prove himself worthy of her—worthy of the life he might create when Fenris was gone. Salvation. A new beginning.

Failure had only one consequence: oblivion. Death. That

was the final act Quentin Forster would commit should Fenris win the battle.

Do you hear me? he called into the depths of his mind. *I'm not running anymore, Fenris-the-shadow.*

An answer came—not in a voice, but as a memory. A memory of emotion, a red haze of rage, the scents of rot and hopelessness, the view of a face.

May's face. Quentin strove to grasp the memory and pull it closer. Like a weighted chain, it slipped from his hold.

But not before the memory gave up one last clue: an alley, a sign, a familiar streetcorner. The Barbary Coast. *That* was a part of the city Quentin knew, a den of iniquity that Fenris had shared with him all those times he'd wakened with no memory of his recent past.

That was where Fenris laired. And May was with him.

May. What did Fenris want with her?

Quentin pulled himself to his feet and swallowed the bile in his throat. *Run,* he commanded himself. *Save her.*

A vicious presence stirred, reaching, tearing, laughing. *You are Fenris. Save her from yourself.*

He stood very still, emptying his thoughts until his body and mind went chill and heavy. The presence fled. It could not survive—Fenris could not survive—where fear and anger were absent. Even love must be severed until Fenris was gone.

Love he'd already lost.

In cold-blooded dispassion, he turned and began to walk toward hell.

Chapter 22

J ohanna could almost imagine the stink of sulfur and brimstone.

The man who greeted her on the street corner where the hackney driver had left her was as seedy a character as any she'd met, wearing a patch over one eye and a sour, gap-toothed smile.

"You the doc?" he asked, scratching his flea-infested rags.

"Yes. Are you the man who is to take me to . . . Were you sent here for me?"

"Aye. I'm to take you to *him*. He's put the word out that no one in the Acre's to bother you." He leered at her brazenly. "Good thing. You wouldn't last a minute."

Johanna was not inclined to argue. Did Fenris have so much power here?

"C'mon," the man said. He set off down the ill-lit street, passing dance halls and opium dens, groggeries and dead-falls by the dozens. Shadows scurried and staggered from building to building: cutthroats, drunks, prostitutes, and thieves of every description. Some of them stopped to stare, a few graced her with catcalls, but none approached.

This was Fenris's kingdom.

She thrust her hand into her coat pocket and felt for the gun. Using it would literally be a matter of last resort, if May had to be protected. And even then she wasn't sure she could kill.

The person she'd be killing was the man she loved.

Her guide turned down an alley and Johanna followed, alert to every movement. The place to which One-eye brought her was a boarded-up house with cracked and staring eyes for windows. Even rats must avoid the place. There was just enough moonlight, filtered through fog, for Johanna to make out the door.

She turned to speak to One-eye, but he'd already slipped away. His services were no longer required, and she suspected that he had no desire to meet his master face-to-face.

The steps leading up to the door were fragile with rot, and Johanna moved carefully. To walk in unannounced would not be wise. Fenris was unstable, unpredictable. He might turn on May if angered.

Gott in Himmel, if he hurt her—

She knocked. The door creaked open. A single brown eye peered through the crack.

"Johanna?" May whispered.

"May!"

May pulled the door inward and rushed over the threshold into Johanna's arms. "You're here! You came to find me."

Peering past May into the lightless room, Johanna couldn't see anyone else inside. She smoothed back May's unkempt hair.

"Are you all right, *mein Liebling*?"

"Yes." A shiver worked its way through her thin body. "I'm all right."

"Let me look at you." She held May's shoulders and examined her. There were no signs of damage except a bit of dirt and a general dishevelment. Fenris hadn't hurt her— and he'd left her alone.

To remain standing on the doorstep, in plain sight, was the height of folly, but Johanna didn't wish to be trapped within should Fenris return. She led May just inside the door and half closed it.

"Where is he?" she asked, deliberately using the unspecified pronoun. She didn't know how much May had observed of Quentin's dual nature, or how well she had dealt with it. "He went out," May said. "To find my father."

So Fenris's absence was not unmitigated good fortune. "Did he say why?" Johanna asked.

"I think he wants to hurt him."

Himmel! What unspeakable ordeals had May been through since Fenris had taken her? She'd seen the man she'd thought of as a friend, a protector, become something grotesque and evil. How could she do other than retreat into fits of hysteria or catalepsy?

But she met Johanna's gaze steadily, her body straight and still. Trusting. Waiting. Expecting Johanna to make everything better again.

She didn't understand that her physician had discovered the depths of her own weakness and folly.

"We must leave, immediately," Johanna said. "Is there anything you need to take from this place?"

May didn't move. "What about my father?"

It was not uncommon for the children of abusive parents to maintain an attachment, even love, for those who had mistreated them. But May hadn't wanted anything to do with her father. Did she want to protect Ingram, or was she hoping he'd be removed permanently from her life? More likely, she was simply confused, torn by conflicting needs and desires. Who could blame her?

Johanna could see May to a safe place and go to the police. It was a certain death warrant for those men who went after him, for Fenris was more than human. He'd kill without compunction. "I'll get you to safety," she told May, "and then I'll do what I can."

May buried her face in Johanna's bodice. "Please don't leave me alone."

"Oh, she won't leave you, Miss Ingram," said a familiar, masculine baritone. "At least not yet."

Johanna turned, pushing May behind her. She knew that voice, though his face was in shadow.

Bolkonsky.

He walked through the door and kicked it shut with one well-shod foot. In the semidarkness, his pale hair flowed like tarnished silver to his shoulders. The gun in his hand had the same dull sheen.

"I wish we had met under less unfortunate circumstances, Johanna," he said, tipping his hat with his free hand. "How was your trip to San Francisco?"

Johanna reached into her pocket. Bolkonsky cocked his gun. "Please hold your hands away from your sides," he said. "I'd rather not be forced to shoot you."

She obeyed, stunned at the hatred she felt. "You will not take her. I will not let you."

"So you've said many times, in one fashion or another," he said. "When my man didn't arrive with the girl at the appointed time, I knew something had gone wrong. Eventually I learned why."

"You went to a great deal of trouble to take May from the Haven," Johanna said coldly. "Did her father hope to spirit her away with none the wiser? Did you both think I'd give up so easily?"

"Your stubbornness is almost admirable. But it doesn't matter now."

Johanna eyed the door behind him. What she needed was a diversion, one that would allow her to grab her gun.

"Why doesn't it matter?" she asked, shuffling a step forward. "You cannot expect me to remain silent. I can make things very uncomfortable for May's father. Ingram may be powerful, but, as you said, I am extremely stubborn."

"You're hardly in a position to threaten," he said pleasantly.

"I do not fear for my reputation, professional or otherwise, if sacrificing it means saving May. And if you intend to use that"—she nodded toward his gun and moved another step—"you'll hardly draw attention away from your patron, or yourself."

"You're right. And if it were my intention to take May to her father, I might even be concerned. But that was never my true object, Johanna."

She checked her subtle forward motion. "What?"

"My dear girl, have I managed to surprise you? How delightful." He smiled. "The focus of all my efforts—my seeking of your acquaintance and that of May's father, my pursuit of the girl, everything I've done since we met—has been another of your patients. Can you guess which one?"

The face of each of the Haven's residents flashed through her mind in the space of a second. It could be any one of them, except possibly Oscar—each had his or her own past secrets even she didn't know.

But, without so much as a single iota of corroborative evidence, her intuition told her the answer.

"Quentin," she whispered.

"Excellent. You're a bright woman, for a human."

The hair rose on the back of her neck. "Who are you?"

"Quentin knows me. We're old friends."

Behind him, the door groaned. Bolkonsky leaped about, graceful as a dancer. Johanna reached into her pocket and pulled out the gun. Bolkonsky thrust out one arm without even looking at her, knocking the gun from her hand. Then he hit her in the chest, and all the air poured from her lungs. She fell to her knees, gasping, just as Bolkonsky yanked the door open to reveal the man on the other side.

"Quentin!" May cried.

Johanna peered through the black spots that crowded her vision. Quentin stood in the doorway, hands at his sides, staring at Bolkonsky. Quentin, not Fenris. The difference was plain to her heart, if not her eyes. She had no voice to call out a warning.

"Quentin," Bolkonsky said. "It's been a long time."

"Stefan Boroskov," Quentin said, dull surprise in his voice. His gaze found Johanna, and May just behind her. "Let them go."

"I think not." Bolkonsky—Boroskov—retrieved Johanna's gun, tucked it under his coat, and gestured with his own weapon. "Come in, old friend. We have so much to talk about."

Q*uentin had expected disaster, but hardly of this* magnitude. He could ill afford the luxury of astonishment.

He walked into a room half-familiar in its rank decay, and came to a stop between Johanna and Boroskov. His thoughts were reluctant to focus, but this was the time above all when he must remain master of his mind.

That brittle clarity was all he had with which to face one of his family's oldest enemies.

Stefan Boroskov, who he'd last seen in England five years ago. Boroskov, with Johanna and May. Quentin knew how May had come to be here—Fenris had brought her. Johanna had surely followed in search of one or both of them. But Boroskov . . .

"Now that we're all together," the Russian said, "I think we should have formal introductions. If you please, Quentin?"

He ignored Boroskov and spoke to Johanna. "This was your Bolkonsky, wasn't he?"

"Yes." She tried to convey some message with her eyes that he couldn't interpret. "That is what he called himself."

"And I never suspected." He turned back to his enemy. "How did you contrive that, Boroskov? You stayed away from the Haven, but I should have smelled you."

"You didn't notice the scent of cologne about Johanna's person?" he asked. "I've found that it masks subtler odors wonderfully well."

"You have execrable taste in cologne."

"Ah. I'm wounded to the quick." Boroskov touched his heart. "Yes, to Johanna I was Feodor Bolkonsky, fellow practitioner to the insane and mentally afflicted, spokesman for little May Ingram's bereaved father."

"Who is he?" Johanna demanded, her gaze fixed on Boroskov. She moved to Quentin's side, her shoulder brushing his. The contact sent his pulse spiralling. "Why has he done this, Quentin? What does he want with you?"

Of course. Boroskov had tried to kidnap May, but the girl wasn't what he wanted. His failure had been temporary. His real prey had come to him.

"Such a curious human," Boroskov commented. "Perhaps you ought to explain, Quentin, before she grows faint with confusion."

Quentin laughed, the movement hurting his chest. "Johanna? You don't know her, Boroskov."

"But I do. Please, the introductions."

Quentin bowed with heavy irony. "Johanna, may I present Stefan Boroskov," he said, deliberately omitting the Russian's title. "His family and mine have been acquainted for many generations. He is . . . like me."

Johanna understood. "A loup-garou," she said. She reached behind her to touch May's arm.

"Ah, she knows!" Boroskov said. "My informant at the Haven did not."

"Your informant?" Johanna put in.

"Irene DuBois. She gave me information about you and the Haven even before I first contacted you, my dear doctor. We loups-garous have certain . . . talents. I would have learned all I needed to know even had Irene not been so easy to manipulate. Because of her eagerness to cooperate, and her considerable acting talents, I was able to conveniently arrange my various distractions." He clucked at Johanna. "You didn't keep your records and notes locked away. Not at all wise."

"That explains—" Johanna began. Her expression hardened. "You promised to take Irene away in exchange for her help in kidnapping May."

"Among other things. But those are mere details. Of course Irene didn't know of Quentin's nature, nor my own. Yet you and May do. Who else among your patients has guessed, I wonder?"

"None," Quentin lied. By now at least two others did, but he wasn't about to jeopardize them by suggesting otherwise. Boroskov despised humans, and would not tolerate a perceived threat of any kind. "Did you think I'd go about advertising it?"

"Who knows what a drunkard might do in his cups? Did you ever cure him of that, Johanna? But I digress. You were about to elucidate our relationship, Quentin, when I so rudely interrupted."

Quentin grasped at the change of subject. "Of course." He turned to Johanna. "The Forsters and the Boroskovs have been . . . at odds for many years. Five years ago, Stefan and his brother attempted to kill my brother, Braden, the earl of Greyburn, in a treacherous fight, hoping to capture the leadership of the loups-garous. The Boroskovs lost, and Braden sent them home with their tails between their legs. He chose not to kill them, though it was his right to do so." He smiled, showing his teeth. "Apparently it was a mistake."

Boroskov shook his head. "I don't know how much you've told her before, Quentin, but I fear you haven't made matters any less confusing for our doctor. You see, my dear girl, he has not defined the political complexities of our society, to which few humans are privy. He has also neglected to mention the reason behind his family's hatred for mine."

"Milena," Quentin said. "His sister and Braden's former wife, who betrayed and blinded him before she herself died."

As he expected, Boroskov's face contorted in anger. "Was *murdered*. Alas, that I don't have time to explain the truth, Johanna."

"Your society," Johanna said to Quentin, as if Boroskov hadn't spoken. "Are there so many of you?"

"We're scattered, but there are still a few hundred families working to preserve our race," Quentin said. "Within human society, we live as humans. Away from it, we have our own rules, our own way of life. It is not always an ideal existence."

"For good reason," Boroskov said. "We are superior, and yet we live like whipped curs, hiding in our dens. And that is why, decades ago, your grandfather and my father developed the great Cause of attaining dominance over humanity.

Quentin's muscles seized up. *Grandfather.* The presence seething below the surface of his thoughts took strength from his instinctive reaction. "That may have been your Cause," he said with an effort, "but it was never my brother's. He wished only to save our kind from extinction."

"Your brother turned from the path set by those stronger and wiser than he," Boroskov said. "He perverted the Cause into something paltry and wretched."

"He defeated *you*."

"Temporarily, yes. But his lack of ruthlessness is one of his weaknesses, and the reason why I am here now."

"Why are you here, Boroskov? What do you want with me, and Johanna?"

Boroskov tilted his gun toward the floor. "You may well

wonder. In these past few years of following your progress, you've never shown any sign of remembering."

"Following me?"

"Oh, not personally. Not until the past six months. I had trusted human servants, aware of our secrets, tracking your movements and sending back their observations. You were so caught up in your own miseries that you were oblivious to their presence."

Quentin recalled a hundred times when he had ignored the sense of being watched. It was a pathetic werewolf indeed who could not detect a human follower. But he had little self-respect to lose.

"You are about to ask why I had you followed," Boroskov prompted.

"The question had occurred to me." Quentin glanced at Johanna and subtly pushed her behind him. May was quiet as a mouse. "You said I showed no signs of remembering. Remembering what?"

"That is part of my story. Patience." He waved Johanna and May toward the dilapidated sofa. "Sit down, dear doctor, and take the child with you."

Johanna looked to Quentin. He nodded, and she led May to the couch. She did not sit.

"Your brother, Braden, inherited the Cause without understanding its true purpose," Boroskov said. "We shall never know how much your grandfather, the previous earl, told him. Perhaps he died before he could reveal all his plans." He shook his head. "The arranged marriages between our scattered families, to restore our blood to its former strength and numbers, was only a small part of his Cause. In time, your grandfather and my father intended that our people should take their rightful places as rulers of the world."

Quentin laughed until his belly knotted in pain, and laughed harder still at Boroskov's expression. "World conquest? When most of us can't even meet every five years without squabbling like infants?"

"Because Braden cannot rule as a leader must. But the former earl and my father made a pact, to develop a means of ensuring that the true Cause would not be subverted. And that is where you come in, Quentin."

"Of course," Quentin said, catching his breath. "You want to use me to take revenge on Braden, or force him to step down. Surely you can't believe I would cooperate."

"I am disappointed in you, my boy," Boroskov said. "Nothing nearly so obvious." He met Quentin's eyes in a direct stare, werewolf to werewolf. "You were to play a very special role in our future plans. And from my observations, you may be what we had hoped for."

"Me?" Quentin's throat was too raw for laughing, but he managed a rasping chuckle. "I was never good for much of anything—certainly not for your Cause. I got away before Braden could pin me to some female of his choosing." He wiped at his eyes. "Did you want me to take Braden's place?"

"Hardly. That role is mine. But you will be at my right hand."

"You have a very strange sense of humor, Boroskov."

"I am not laughing." He adjusted the fit of his glove, dangling his gun from one finger. "I told you that your grandfather and my father made a separate, secret pact. They knew that our goal of conquest would not be an easy one, or swift. It would take many generations to achieve. And over those generations, we would require soldiers who would be trained and willing to commit whatever acts we might deem necessary in pursuit of our goals."

"Soldiers," Quentin repeated.

"Soldiers stronger and faster than any human. And ruthless, disciplined from childhood to obey their leaders without question."

"Murderers, you mean," Quentin said, struck with a sudden chill. "Assassins."

"Quite. When the time came, such specially trained detachments would be sent into the field to remove select human leaders, businessmen whose assets would become our own—any who might conceivably stand in our way. But first we had to learn how to create such a special 'army.' Your grandfather, and my father, chose one each of their offspring upon whom to experiment."

Quentin couldn't respond. He saw the cellar, smelled the sweat of his own fear and blood. Grandfather . . .

"They chose their subjects as young children, to allow for the greatest tractability of character. There was a risk that the subjects might be damaged in the attempt, so your grandfather chose you as the most expendable."

Quentin's teeth ground together with an audible crack.

"Your instruction was begun when you were a boy," Boroskov said. "You were to be broken to your grandfather's will by any means necessary, become indifferent to murder and absolutely obedient.

"You see, my brother—you were meant to be a killer."

J ohanna *felt for the seat behind her and fell into it. May* gave a soft whimper.

Quentin was a statue, staring at Boroskov as if the Russian had bespelled him with his evil.

"You do remember something of those days, don't you?" Boroskov asked, almost gently. "I see it in your eyes. Your grandfather's methods were harsh, no doubt, but necessary. I have none of his notes on his procedures, but I can guess what he did."

"The cellar," Quentin whispered, as if he didn't realize he spoke. Johanna rose to go to him, but Boroskov pointed his gun in her direction.

"No. Your usefulness is past, my dear doctor. No more coddling. He is mine, now."

"You are wrong," she said. "He belongs to himself."

"Cling to your illusions if you must," he said. "You, too, know of his sufferings, do you not? You have discovered many of his secrets. But you cannot imagine what it is like to be one of us. I will be—I am—closer to Quentin than any other living being. For I was my father's selection as one of the new army."

Johanna met his gaze and understood. If Quentin's form of madness had been born in the tortures he'd endured in his grandfather's cellar, then Boroskov's came from the same source.

"Yes, my father trained me," he said. "I did not break. I grew stronger. I saw what had to be done. But somewhere, somehow, Quentin's instruction faltered. He broke free of his grandfather's influence in his adolescence, and for a time we believed he was a loss to us."

Johanna took another step toward Quentin, disregarding Boroskov's threat. "You are not a failure, Quentin."

"No, he is not. When he ran from England, from the skirmish his brother won over me, I knew he had begun to recall those things he'd tried to forget. The training he'd rejected. His deep and binding brotherhood to me."

"No," Quentin croaked.

"Why deny it? You feel the truth already. Yes, you escaped your grandfather. When you came of age, you joined the Army and went to India. Even then I was watching you, and waiting. I was not disappointed. It was there that your grandfather's careful work began to bear fruit." He smiled sympathetically. "Do you remember the time when you single-handedly rescued your men from ambush by the tribesmen? You killed eight of the enemy, they said. They called you a hero, but they were afraid. You were something they had never seen before—a berserker, who did not leave the field until every foe was dead."

"God," Quentin said, his face stark with horror.

"The necessary instincts were coming to the fore—to kill your enemies without mercy. But you were undirected. You did not yet have a cause that bound you. You returned to England, and led a meaningless life of pleasure and forgetfulness. But that came to an end when I arrived at Greyburn to challenge Braden."

"I was a coward."

"No. You felt drawn to me, to what we shared. You had begun to sense what you were, felt the stirring of your blood at the sight of violence. So you ran. But you could not run from your destiny. It followed you here, to America. My men reported the many times your training rose unbidden, to put the humans in their place."

"I killed," Quentin said hollowly, making it a question.

"No. But you created enough havoc to prove that you had what we required. Each time you moved on, losing yourself in drink, as if you could escape what you knew you were destined to be. Each time, the warrior within you could not be restrained. All it needed was discipline, and a master to temper your violence. I will be the one to complete what your grandfather began."

Slowly Quentin's expression relaxed, and he looked at Johanna with full comprehension. It was as if everything he had wrestled with became clear in an instant. Just as it had for Johanna. Her heart ached for him.

"Why did you involve Johanna and May?" he asked.

"When I first followed you to San Francisco, I was prepared to seek you out. But you proved surprisingly elusive, until I was able to track you to the Napa Valley. There, I learned of Doctor Schell's new patient, and obtained informants who could give me the information I needed—most notably Irene DuBois. From her, I learned of Johanna's other patients, including May.

"It soon became clear to me that you had indeed located a haven, a place where you might find the help you sought, the support that would make it easier for you to resist. I had to pry you loose. Miss Ingram's situation presented the ideal opportunity to disrupt your life at the Haven, and pull Johanna's attention from you. I had Irene look through Dr. Schell's notes, and she told me that May was essentially in hiding from her father, a wealthy businessman in San Francisco."

"You forced Irene to obey you?" Johanna demanded.

"He could do it, Johanna," Quentin said, his voice betraying no trace of emotion. "Our kind have mental abilities humans do not. He could make her do as he chose, and erase her memory of the events."

"Indeed, but force was hardly necessary," Boroskov said. "I merely turned her thoughts from certain subjects, and encouraged her in others."

Johanna filed that astonishing fact aside for further examination, one more among a hundred others. "So you used May to get at Quentin," she addressed Boroskov.

"I approached May's father in San Francisco and told him that I knew of his daughter's whereabouts, if he wished her back. He did. He trusted me as a learned doctor, who could restore his daughter to him without inconvenient fuss or awkwardness."

"It didn't quite work out that way," Quentin said.

"No, but it doesn't matter. I achieved what I intended. I diverted Johanna from her work with you, kept both of you off balance and worried about May while I perfected my plans. Irene DuBois was most useful in reporting on your actions, with very little persuasion from me—she was quick enough to believe me smitten. She also had scant love for either of you." He sighed. "But you, apparently, had become quite enamored of each other—an annoyance at first, but it proved to be a factor in my favor." He cocked a brow. "Did you really believe, Quentin, that Johanna could save you?"

"I always believed in her."

"But that wasn't enough, was it?" He turned to Johanna. "When it was obvious that you would not let May go, and Quentin was no further along in being detached from you and the Haven, I arranged for the death of the mine owner, and saw it blamed on Quentin. A simple thing to manipulate the ignorant humans in Silverado Springs."

"I didn't kill . . ." Quentin began.

"No. You may take credit for Ingram's beating, but not Ketchum's death. While the mob came to the Haven, I had one of my men abduct May. I knew, from Irene's reports, that you would inevitably follow to rescue her, and once you were out of Johanna's sphere of influence it would be easy enough to trap you. Though my man failed, you are here. You took May, and I followed." He addressed Johanna. "A pity you had to involve yourself further. I rather liked you, dear doctor."

"You won't hurt her," Quentin said. "Not her, or May, or anyone else." The change in him was subtle, but Johanna recognized it. He seemed to grow, gathering his strength, preparing for bedlam.

He was being threatened. Those he cared for were in peril. Inside him, Fenris was awakening. Fenris, who *was* the very thing his own grandfather had tried to create. Fenris, who might be a match for Stefan Boroskov.

"If you cooperate, I'll have no need," Boroskov said. "I do not worry that the doctor will expose us. No one will believe her—they will merely think her infected with her patients' madness. And May is merely a child."

"If I do as you tell me, you'll let them go," Quentin said.

Boroskov shrugged.

"And if I don't cooperate, you'll kill them."

"Johanna, perhaps. The girl I may simply return to her father."

Quentin lunged at the Russian. "You scum—"

"Yes." Boroskov's eyes lit. "Yes. Let it go, Quentin. Remember who you were meant to be." He held out his hand.

"Come, my brother. Take what I offer. You have no place in the human world, or in that of your brother. You are not the weakling you've believed yourself to be. You are one of the true, new blood of the werewolf race, the hope of our people. Your future is in my hands. *Our* future."

Johanna watched in horror as Quentin took Boroskov's hand.

Chapter 23

He'd forgotten who he was.

He hung, suspended, between two wills, two souls. One cried out for release, for a peace he had never known; the other screamed in triumph, sensing final liberation from all the chains that had bound him.

Only one anchor offered itself. He clutched the extended hand.

It anchored him to the present as memories crashed about him like a storm. The first time Grandfather had taken him to the cellar, a few months after Mother's death, and explained what he was to become. The years of beatings, starvation, promises of dire punishment he'd kept hidden from Braden and Rowena—yes, even from his twin, who thought she knew everything about him. How he'd fooled them, laughing his way through hell.

Sometime, in those years, Fenris had been born: to take the punishment, to endure the pain—and, in the end, to turn against his tormenter.

Alien, terrifying images spun in an endless loop through

his mind. Grandfather's face, grim and merciless, leaning over to administer his brand of "discipline" . . . his expression dissolving into astonishment. And fear.

Victory. Grandfather never took him to the cellar again. The beatings didn't stop, not entirely. But the terror did. Eventually Grandfather died, and he'd thought himself free. The memories faded. His other self had little reason for existence, and went into dormancy. Whatever he had once known, or guessed, of Fenris was buried under layer upon layer of protective armor.

But he remained haunted still. He looked for escape in every sort of harmless debauchery available to a young man of good family who possessed a generous income. He gained a reputation as a rake and gamester, ever amiable and full of high spirits.

Those spirits had led him to join the Queen's Army as a subaltern on the northwestern frontier of India. He'd sought adventure, and found violence instead. And his other self, so long asleep, woke to kill when he could not. Details of the battle he hadn't remembered formed an explosion of bloodred, smoke gray, and smothering black behind his eyelids.

He'd awakened in the hospital and, after his swift recovery, was prompted to resign his commission. Boroskov was right; he'd been a hero who'd saved his troops, but what he had done was too terrible for his comrades and officers to accept. He'd never known why, until now.

Fenris was responsible.

So home he came, to take up the threads of his civilian life, running occasional errands for his brother the earl and otherwise losing himself in the pursuit of pleasure. Everyone knew that the honorable Quentin Forster hated any sort of conflict.

Then the year of the Convocation had arrived—that grand meeting of the world's werewolf families on Braden's Greyburn estates in the far north of England.

Boroskov had disrupted the proceedings with his challenge to Braden. And when Braden won the fight, Quentin ran. Ran all the way to America, and had never stopped running.

Because Fenris could no longer be forced back in his dark corner. Because the memory lapses had already begun, and the implacable urges, half recalled, could no longer be borne.

America offered no sanctuary. The Other was always with him. But he blocked the awareness that would have led him to recognize what he was becoming.

"You know, don't you?" Boroskov said. "You see that I speak the truth."

Quentin heard the voice as if he were under water, on the verge of drowning. It was seductive, commanding, and the coward within wanted nothing more than to give himself up to its master.

He disregarded the coward's whimpers and sought the one who would fight, no matter what the odds.

Fenris. Fenris, who was Boroskov's ideal killer, except that he would never obey any master. Who would turn on the one who tried to control him?

Fenris would save them both.

But something snapped inside. It was as if the restoration of Quentin's memories sapped Fenris's strength—as if their absence alone had been the foundation of Fenris's very existence. He stirred, roared, writhed in impotent fury.

And vanished.

"Quentin!"

Johanna. He pushed his way toward the lightless surface high above him, let go of Boroskov's hand, and grasped the other that plunged so fearlessly into the seething waters.

He opened his eyes and looked into hers. She smiled, warm and brave.

"How touching," Boroskov said.

Quentin realized that he'd made a crucial mistake. One

glance at Boroskov's face told him that the Russian knew he'd won his internal struggle.

Quentin's only secret advantage, however dangerous, was Fenris. And Fenris was gone.

"I thought, for a moment, that you had come to your senses," Boroskov said. "But I see you will need further persuasion."

"Boroskov," Johanna said. "You said that you had been intended by your father to become one of these assassins, like Quentin."

He glanced at her through half-lidded eyes. "What of it?"

"You were tortured, as he was."

Quentin followed her line of thinking and despaired at her hopeful ignorance. Stefan Boroskov was not one to be reasoned with, drawn from past suffering to recognize the source of his own evil.

Boroskov laughed. "Ah, Johanna. Let me guess . . . you wish to persuade me that I, too, can be relieved of my sorrowful burdens. What will you do, place me under hypnosis and assure me that I can be cured of my madness?"

"You didn't choose who you were to be, did you, Stefan?" she said, her gaze locked on his. "Your father chose for you. He betrayed his own son."

"And he paid for this so-called betrayal," Boroskov said. "I killed him when I came of age, and took his title and all he owned. But he taught me much, and his goals were worthy. They are now mine."

"And so you have become what he was."

"I have become more than he ever was. And I will succeed where he did not."

Johanna shook her head. "No, Stefan. There can be no peace in such a victory. If you'd only let me help you—"

"Enough!" He swept out his hand, and Quentin barely had time to intercept the blow. It sent him stumbling, but he

caught his balance and placed himself between Boroskov
and Johanna.

"Never touch her again," he said.

"That is your choice." Boroskov smiled at Johanna. "My
dear doctor, you have proven yourself a failure in rehabili-
tating your patient, and I suspect you know it. But you can
save him yet." He negligently twirled his pistol. "I have the
power to force Quentin to bend to my will. It is one of the
superior skills the greatest among loups-garous possess,
and I'll use it if I must. But I would prefer his cooperation,
to spare myself a waste of time and resources.

"Convince him, Johanna. Convince him to do as I command, and you will be allowed to leave with the girl. I have
no further interest in your affairs. But if you do not succeed—" He shrugged. "I don't think I need elaborate." He
pushed past Quentin and seized May's arm before either
Quentin or Johanna could react.

"Now," he said, gesturing toward a doorway at the rear
of the room, "if you will kindly go through that door." He
aimed the gun at Johanna until Quentin obeyed, and she
followed, casting anxious glances at May.

The door led into a black hallway and to more closed
doors, one of which Boroskov kicked open with his foot.
The room was as lightless and dank as the rest of the house,
its sole furnishing a soiled mattress scattered with a heap of
blankets.

"I'll leave you two alone now, to make your tender
farewells. You have two hours. The girl will come with
me —in the off chance that you get the notion to take an un-
scheduled trip."

Quentin growled, stricken with the savage fury that
should have summoned his other self. Fenris remained
silent. "If you hurt her," he rasped, "so much as a hair on
her head, you'd better kill me."

"As I said," Boroskov replied, dragging May toward the
door, "that is entirely up to you." He bowed to Johanna and

walked out. A lock clicked into place, and Boroskov's foot-steps, accompanied by May's stumbling counterpoint, re-ceded down the hall. A minute later Quentin heard hoofbeats, the jingle of harness, and the clatter of a carriage driving away.

Johanna went to the door and rested her hands against the scored wood and peeling paint. She had no hope of breaking the lock. Quentin might have the strength, but what good would come of that? Boroskov had them trapped as surely as if he'd barred them in a cage.

And there was nothing she could do about it.

Nothing.

"Where is he taking May?" she whispered.

"To his henchmen, no doubt, for safekeeping," Quentin said. His voice emerged from the darkness, somewhere in the vicinity of the mattress. "He won't harm her. He has no reason to."

She struck her forehead against the door once, and then again. Quentin was at her side before she could strike again.

"Johanna."

She turned. Quentin looked at her, such transparent compassion on his face that her body bowed under the weight of her emotions.

Shame. Fear. Anger. At herself most of all. Johanna Schell, the great and innovative doctor who would show the world how the insane could be healed. It had all become one vast joke.

Worst was the hopelessness that stripped her of even the desire to continue fighting.

"Well," she said, her voice cracking. "What now? I have not a single suggestion to make to you. Shall we draw lots to see who shall live and who shall die?"

He remained where he was, as if he feared to approach her. As one might fear to approach a lunatic. "Don't blame yourself," he said in a raw whisper. "You're not responsible."

"Am I not?"

"I brought all this down on your head, Johanna, and on May's. *I.* My own selfishness—"

"And my insufferable arrogance. Now we shall spend the time Boroskov has left us discussing which one of us is more contemptible." She walked to the mattress and sat down. "Perhaps that is his plan: divide and conquer. Not that I should ever be the least threat to him—"

"You heard him, Johanna. He'll use you as a way to get to me."

"And May as the means of forcing both of us to do his bidding." She rested her head in her hands and began to rock. "I am sorry. So sorry. So sorry—"

"Stop it." Quentin knelt before her and took her hands, pulling them away from her face. "Don't leave me now, Johanna."

Was he afraid that she was descending into madness? She wished it were possible. Possible to let go, dismiss reality, and resign every responsibility for her life. She felt like collapsing into Quentin's arms and wailing like a child, begging for him to make it all better.

Even May hadn't done that. May had kept her head and her courage, and look what she had received as a reward.

She, Johanna Schell, was supposed to be the strong one. No longer. All her illusions were cracked apart like the last of her mother's china figurines, destroyed by an angry patient. Like a mind that had borne too much.

"I never thought I'd see the day when you felt sorry for yourself." Quentin forced her chin up. *"Look* at me, Johanna."

She had no choice. He compelled her with his eyes, with his voice, with his will. Above all, with his heart.

His gentle, generous heart, warped into a monster by

pain. Fenris was nowhere visible in his gaze, in spite of all that provoked him. Where had he gone?

"Johanna," he said, stroking her chin with his thumb. "I brought you and May into this. I was selfish—selfish in wanting the peace your Haven offered, though I knew my mere presence was a menace to everything I valued. I refused to consider the dangers once I had . . . grown to care for you. And I never dreamed that Boroskov was part of the danger. If I could only go back—"

"I was arrogant," she interrupted harshly. "I thought I had perfect mastery over the situation with May. I was so sure I could cure you, even share your bed without making a single compromise." Tears dripped onto her sleeves. She thought they must be hers. "I thought I had all the answers—and this is where they've led us both."

He rested his forehead against hers. "We are pitiful creatures, are we not?"

She looked for mockery in his eyes and found none. His smile was heartwrenchingly calm.

"You've . . . given me a chance at something I didn't have for most of my life, Johanna. Faith in myself and in my ability to rise above what I'd become. Hope."

And what worth has it now? she wanted to rail at him. *What worth has anything?*

"We can't fight him," he said. "He's too strong. He has skills I do not. And I . . . I can't kill." He kissed her lips with a feather-touch. "I won't allow you or May to pay for my debilities. When Boroskov returns, I will tell him that I'll go with him—after I've watched him release you and May."

She shook her head wildly.

"I assure you that I won't let him use me."

"You mean that you'll die before you become his assassin."

"Yes. You know it's right, Johanna. I can't be unleashed on the world, as unstable as I am." He skimmed his knuckles across her cheek. "If I can stop Boroskov for good—any sacrifice is worth it. He's my kind. It's up to me. And if I succeed . . . I'll have redeemed myself."

"And escaped one more time," she lashed out. "Never having had to face life squarely. An easy end to all your suffering."

"You said you didn't have the answers." His voice grew distant, as if he were withdrawing into himself. "This is mine. You must be the one to go on living, so that you can help people as you were meant to."

"I can help no one."

"You can. I know you, Johanna. You're too strong to give up. Not even for me." He began to rise. "I'm sorry."

She grabbed his hands to stop him. "I am not strong!" she cried. "I want to do what I wish, only what *I* wish. The world can go to hell. I want to be happy—" She wrapped her arms around Quentin's neck and kissed him hard on the mouth.

The room disappeared. The stale scent of the mattress, the cold dampness of the floor and the walls, vanished.

Happiness was not hers to own. Perhaps even hope was beyond her reach. But she could snatch what small joys were to be had in this terrible place.

And when she left, she'd take a part of Quentin with her.

The part he had held back the first time.

Now she'd have all of him.

She tugged at the bottom of Quentin's rough shirt, barely glancing up to see his response. The pupils of his eyes had grown very large, engulfing the color.

"Johanna—"

"No talking. No words." She kissed him again. He responded ardently, recognizing, as she did, how little time they had left. He would not deny her.

She lay back upon the blankets, and he knelt over her. He stroked his hand from the top of her bodice to her skirts, cupping his fingers against her womanhood. Her body reacted instantly. He found the hem by touch alone, watching her face, and drew her skirts up around her thighs.

Hard and fast was how it must be. Johanna's breath grew short. She gripped Quentin's hands and met his questioning gaze.

"Yes, Quentin," she said. "Yes."

"I've wanted you, but not like this," he murmured. "I wanted to love you the way you deserve to be loved."

"I don't know what I deserve," she said. "But if you ever cared for me, give me something to take away."

In answer he brushed his fingers up the length of her stocking, seeking bare flesh. Her unadorned, knee-length drawers posed no barrier to him. He opened them and touched her moist skin.

She arched up into his caresses. The memory of the last time flooded into her mind, joining with the present. She feared that her body's completion might come too fast, before she could feel Quentin moving inside her.

"Don't . . . wait," she begged.

He whispered unintelligible endearments and joined her on the mattress. He parted her legs with his hands, raising her skirts to her waist.

Too slow. She didn't want his tenderness now, only to be possessed, claimed by him forever. She seized the front of his shirt to bring him closer and all but tore at the buttons of his trousers. He was hard under her fingertips. She set him free and held him between her hands.

"Do you wish to make us both suffer?" she demanded fiercely. "Do you?"

He closed his eyes with a groan and flung himself down upon her. The drumming of his heartbeat pierced her bodice, the flesh and bone beneath to mingle with her own heart's frantic pace. His skin was burning where it touched her, the cloth of his trousers deliciously rough on her flesh. His hips found their natural cradle between her thighs, and just as she rose to meet him she felt the clean, swift thrust of his entry.

Nothing had prepared her for this. There was an instant of discomfort, and then a sweet ache more beautiful than anything they'd done before. He moved, withdrew, then thrust again. Fire filled her womb. She throbbed in time to his motions, each pulse drawing him deeper.

He kissed her lips and her chin and her cheeks, murmuring her name like a nonsensical rhyme. She clenched her legs about his waist. Abruptly, with stunning ease, he lifted her from the mattress and carried her, still impaled, to the nearest wall. He held her there, his strong hands cupping her buttocks, and thrust again and again, making her feel what it was to be in another's power and willingly submit.

It was that surrender that finally pushed her over the brink. Her body and her mind ceased all resistance. She gasped and pressed her head back against the wall as the waves of pleasure came. Still he did not finish, not until the pulsing had stopped and she went boneless in his arms. Then, with one last great thrust, he found his own completion.

He kissed her and let her slide to the floor. When her legs trembled in reaction, he swept her up and carried her back to the blankets, drawing her into his lap. She felt raw and fragile and lost in bliss.

Bliss that couldn't last. It had no more substance than the fog outside these walls, no more solidity than sand on the ocean shore.

Like sand, it slipped through her fingers and was gone. But it left in its wake the hard, bright knowledge of what must be done.

She was afraid. Fear had been an abstract concept before this moment, no matter how much she'd thought herself capable of it. Never before had so much been at stake.

If she failed in this, it would mean Quentin's sanity, if

not his life. It might mean letting loose a creature prone to violence few men could envision, and relinquishing Quentin's chance to fetter Boroskov.

She didn't know if she could do what her plan demanded. Her deficiencies had become all too clear, and all too deadly. She must be far more daring, more cool-headed, and more skillful than her best image of herself, let alone the flawed woman she'd turned out to be.

Her mouth went dry, and her heart beat so loudly that Quentin must have heard. He shifted her about and held her face steady between his hands.

"What is it?" he asked. "Did I hurt you, Johanna?"

"No." She swallowed. "There is something I must tell you, Quentin."

The slightly dazed look left his eyes. His mouth tightened. "Tell me."

"I love you."

H*e laughed in startlement, and saw Johanna's face.* She was serious. More than serious; she was giving him the most precious gift she had.

Johanna—his grave, beloved Johanna, gazed at him as if he were someone worthy of love. As if they sat in a rose-scented bower, and he were the gentleman he was born to be, she the brave and true lady her soul and spirit made her.

"Johanna," he said, choking back ridiculous tears. "God."

"I know it's hardly a suitable time to make such a declaration." She wriggled from his hold and stood, shaking her skirts down around her ankles as if she dismissed what had just passed between them. "In light of what we've just done . . ."

"Do you know what we've done?" he asked. "I've been with other women, yes. But none of them—not one of them—" How could he tell her that he could take her a hundred times more and not get his fill of her? She made him feel formidable, sure of himself, the man he might have been.

Might have been, but was not. Johanna carried that Quentin away with her and sent the familiar craven Quentin back in his place. The man who was so very good at running.

The man who couldn't speak the words she wanted to hear.

Her back was turned to him, head high, spine erect. The pliable, passionate woman slipped from her body like a ghost. What remained was not Doctor Johanna Schell but some brittle reproduction held together by filaments of habit and sheer pluck, a doppelgänger who spoke with Johanna's voice in a parody of her competent manner.

"Forgive me," she said. "It was foolish of me to speak as I did, but I was not sure I'd get another chance."

"Johanna," he whispered.

"We need not dwell on it any longer. In fact, we must put it behind us now if we are to save ourselves." Her shoulders rose and fell. "I have an idea, Quentin. A dangerous idea, and so much of it depends upon you. I do not know if I am capable of what is necessary."

He stood up, took a few steps toward her, stopped at the stiffening of her body. She took another deep breath. "You've said that you wish to go with Boroskov and find a way to overcome him. But I believe there is a chance to defeat him, here and now, by confronting him with what he would never expect to see."

Dire premonition turned guilt and grief to icy lumps in his chest. "Fenris."

"Fenris." She turned to face him, her expression blank. "Boroskov knows nothing of him, though your other self is the embodiment of what his father, and your grandfather, desired to create."

"Something evil, murderous—"

"But Fenris is a *part* of you, Quentin. He has your were-wolf abilities, as well as the very traits of character that make him an equal to Boroskov in ruthlessness and lust for power. Don't you see?"

"I see. I see very clearly."

"Then . . . we have no choice but to enlist Fenris's help in defeating Boroskov."

The last remnants of the ephemeral well-being that had come with their loving drained from Quentin's body. "Yes," he said. "Get Fenris to fight in my place, because he is the last thing our enemy will be expecting. The only problem with your otherwise excellent idea is that I've already tried it. I can't make him come."

"You've tried to summon Fenris?" She frowned. "But you've never truly met him, only sensed his presence—"

"Just before I found you and May and Boroskov, I woke up in another part of town with no memory of how I'd arrived in San Francisco. It hasn't been long since Fenris was here. But now—he is *gone*."

Her eyes darkened. "How can this be?"

"Oh, I'm not free of him. He still perverts our joint existence as he wishes it to be. I'd rip him out of my soul if I could."

"That is what you cannot do." She held his gaze unblinkingly. "I know little of this, Quentin. It is beyond my meager experience. But I think that you must find a way to accept him as part of yourself."

"Part of myself? Should I let him use and discard you, and destroy everything in his path? Is that what you want me to be, Johanna?"

Her jaw clenched. "No. But you can't simply erase him. He won't let you. You and Fenris are two halves of what was meant to be a single whole. Neither one of you is . . . complete without the other. And now he has the means, perhaps the only means, of saving us all."

Her theory made a bizarre kind of sense. He felt the merciless logic of it, though his insides turned to ice. Fenris, the lost piece of the puzzle, the final answer.

"Even if you're right," he said, "why should he help us? What has he to gain?"

"It is true that he's said that he intends to displace you, Quentin—just as you want to erase him. That is part of the risk. The greater part. But you will not be alone." He caught a glimpse of her heart in her eyes. "We shall contact him through hypnosis. I will be with you. But *you* must be willing to let him out, under our control. Yours and mine, together. You must truly face him for the first time in your life."

He sat down, too numb to remain on his feet. "You think that I can influence such a monster?"

"Fenris has no friends, no brothers. If you convince him that he is more than your brother—if you embrace him rather than reject him . . ."

Quentin smiled through his terror. "Embrace?"

"His needs are yours, Quentin. He must be acknowledged, for he was your creation, and he suffered on your behalf."

"My creation, born of my cowardice."

"You were a child. You were not to blame. But now you know Fenris exists, and why."

And only Fenris could kill Boroskov.

Quentin slammed his fist into the wall, feeling it give under the blow. "He'll be our hired assassin," he said hoarsely. "But the blood will still be on these." He raised his hands and rotated them slowly. "I'll become what he is."

He waited for another facile answer, but none came. Her eyes welled up with the tears she must have been fighting all along. She crumpled in on herself. The counterfeit Johanna Schell became a vulnerable young woman who questioned everything she'd ever believed worthy and strong and true in her own nature.

It struck him with the full force of revelation that this was her greatest fear, that she lacked the skill to do what she proposed; not that he didn't return her feelings or rejected her love, but that she would ultimately fail them both.

He turned his face to the wall, unable to hide his emotions. He ached to hold her close and assure her that it would be all right. To tell her that he loved her.

But he couldn't. And with that realization came a second revelation, too overwhelming to deny.

Words of love and empty platitudes were not what Johanna needed from him now. What she required most was the strength, the fortitude, the self-reliance that was so much a part of her being. She needed to remember that she was a doctor of great skill and bravery.

By admitting her love to him, by loving him, she had relinquished the very qualities she most needed to win the coming war. If he denied her this chance she'd never regain the spirit and assurance to continue with her work. She would be ruined in every way that mattered.

To do what she asked, he must hold fast all the way to his soul. No running, no slipping away. The surrender he must make was to his deepest self and the memories that had created him.

He had to do it for her. For Johanna.

He stood up and strode toward her, stopping mere inches away.

"Very well," he said roughly, "Let us proceed."

"No." She bowed her head. "I was wrong to suggest it. I recognize that I am no longer fit—"

"Fit?" He took her by the shoulders and made her look at him. "You think that you are fatally flawed, don't you, Johanna? You've made too many mistakes. You've misjudged. You don't trust yourself, and you don't expect anyone else to trust you, either. You have your theories, but you have no confidence in them. You're just going to . . . give up."

Her body trembled violently. "You don't understand. If I'm wrong—"

"Have you suddenly lost all the skills you had when I first came to the Haven?"

She stared at him. "No, I—"

"You still know how to hypnotize me, I presume."

"Yes."

"That's how you'll call out Fenris, so that I can face him."

"Yes, but—"

"We don't have much time. You'd better get started."

She pulled free, jerking up her chin with a touch of the old spirit. "I cannot be within your mind, Quentin. I can only begin the process. In the end, you must fight three battles—with Fenris, with Boroskov, and with yourself. You must ally with Fenris to win over Boroskov, become the guiding intellect behind Fenris's hatred. Without you, there can be no victory."

"Without you, we haven't a chance in hell." He grinned. "But damned if I don't love a challenge."

Chapter 24

Johanna's heart broke into a thousand pieces and slowly, bit by bit, reassembled itself. It bathed in the healing warmth of Quentin's grin, took strength from the enormity of his faith in her, grew until it stretched the walls of her ribs and expanded beyond the mere physical boundaries of flesh.

The gift of his trust held her heart safe, like a magical coffer made of precious gold and priceless stones hidden in a cave on the highest mountaintop. She'd asked that he be strong, and he was—strong in the face of fear she knew as well as she did her own. His great courage lay in his willingness to confront his fear, and challenge her to do the same.

She'd been sure, for so long, that love was a luxury she could ill afford. When she let down her guard, it had happened just as she predicted: Once she opened the gates to emotion, she could not close them again. Out spilled the fear, the doubts, the indecisiveness, the despair, weaknesses that stripped away the unassailable façade of Dr. Johanna

Schell. The rational moorings upon which she'd built her life snapped and sent her crashing down into bedlam.

That Dr. Schell had been extinguished, and the new creature born out of the ferment was blind and deaf and nameless, searching desperately for identity in the midst of chaos, prepared to grasp at any anchor. She was close to becoming the very thing she most despised: dependent and helpless.

Looking into Quentin's eyes, she recognized the truth. His only hope was to acknowledge and unite both halves of himself. She was no different.

She must summon her doctor's skills to give Quentin the chance he needed, but she could no longer rely on the old definitions of competence. Rationality was not enough. If she rejected her emotions, her fear, her love, she would be fighting with only half a weapon. Dr. Johanna Schell had not disappeared; she had merely evolved.

Love *was* her anchor. Love for this man, who'd turned her life upside down, who'd begun to heal a physician who hadn't learned how to heal herself.

Overcome with gratitude, Johanna stretched up to kiss him. He stepped just out of reach and averted his face before her lips touched his.

It hurt. She couldn't guess which of her many shortcomings, or his regrets, made him withdraw. But what might have been a devastating blow was a minor bruise she could and must bear. Love remained steady and sound, unaffected by anything Quentin Forster, Fenris, or Boroskov could do or say.

"Please sit down, Quentin," she said evenly. "If you are ready, we will begin."

Aware that Boroskov might return at any moment, Johanna ushered Quentin into a trance as quickly as she dared and, with a whispered prayer, called Fenris out of the darkness.

It was like shouting into a chasm miles deep. Minutes

ticked by. Johanna tried every trick she knew, and still Fenris didn't answer.

Quentin had warned her that Fenris was gone. She didn't believe it. He was waiting, holed up like a hibernating bear, dangerous to wake and biding his time for his own incomprehensible purpose.

Then she remembered what Fenris wanted more than anything in the world except permanent mastery of Quentin's body. She had asked Quentin to try to accept Fenris as a part of himself. How could he do so if she refused to accept Fenris the same way?

Accept him, even submit to his lust. Another risk she had to take.

"Fenris," she said. "I know you hear me. I am waiting for you. I need you. I need *you*, Fenris."

Quentin jerked.

"Come to me," she coaxed, her voice filled with promises. "Help me."

The muscles in Quentin's face suddenly shifted, swiftly completing the subtle but distinct change to the coarser features of his other self. His eyes snapped open and focused on her.

Her comparison of Fenris to a hibernating bear was apt indeed. He lunged up from the mattress and stalked toward her, every line of his body shouting violent intent.

"You want *my* help?" he snarled. "I still have some use to you, now that he's had you?"

She could only guess what it had been like for Fenris to experience Quentin's life as an observer, watching and unable to interfere as she lay with Quentin at the Haven, seizing control only to lose it again before he could complete his goal.

"Yes, Fenris," she said, refusing to flinch. "You know of Boroskov—"

He grabbed her by the arms, almost lifting her from her feet. "I know everything. You gave yourself to the weakling. But I brought you here, didn't I?" His fingers bit into her sleeves. "Now you're in trouble because of *him.* But when I save your pretty little neck, you plan to get rid of me, don't you?" He gave her a shake. "Don't you?"

Of course. He hadn't been so far "gone" that he'd failed to hear her discussion with Quentin. The only defense she had left was to make him understand.

"Haven't you always defended Quentin from his enemies, and yours?" she asked, ignoring the pain. "You and Quentin share a fate, just as you share a body. You can't escape what happens to him."

"You're calling me a coward?"

"Quentin said you were gone, even when he tried to find you. You ran from Boroskov, didn't you? You buried yourself deep, because you know that what Boroskov wants is worse than anything Quentin could do. Worse than anything you could be."

He let her drop. "Boroskov is like me," he said. "Why shouldn't I ally myself with him?"

"Because you won't be anyone's slave. Because you know he'll eventually destroy you. Because he embraces the evils that you endured for Quentin's sake."

"Words. Boroskov wants power. I want the same thing."

"No. You want the pain to stop."

"And when it stops, I'll be gone. There won't be anything left." He bared his teeth, but the gesture was ruined by the quivering of his mouth. "Quentin will have you. I'll have nothing."

Fenris the monster was gone indeed. Now she heard the voice of the boy he had been, callow and immature, desperate to find some meaning in his hellish existence.

Begging to be loved.

It wasn't cold reason Fenris needed, but intimacy. Not animal lust, but true caring. Like Quentin. Like herself.

She had to love Fenris as she loved Quentin in order to set him free.

She closed the space between them and lifted her hand to his cheek. "When I see you, Fenris, I don't see Boroskov. I see Quentin. I see what both of you share. I see the man I love."

He stared at her. "You're lying."

In answer she did as she had done with Quentin not so long ago. She drew his face down to hers, and kissed him.

T*he kiss was given, not taken. And it was devastating.* Fenris froze in shock. Johanna pressed against him, and he felt the heat of his rage drawn from his body through the gentle parting of her lips.

Without the rage, he didn't know who he was. Johanna had summoned him forth against his will, against every instinct of self-preservation he had learned in childhood.

Something was happening inside him, an unfamiliar transformation he couldn't comprehend. It frightened him. He didn't let Johanna see his fear, but lifted her high and kissed her in return, hard enough to remind her who was master.

Even in that he lied to himself.

He put her down and looked around the room. Boroskov was coming, he could sense it. But he had Johanna. He could still win.

"I'll save you," he told her. He threw his weight against the door, and the rotten wood cracked. Another blow tore it from its hinges. He seized Johanna's upper arm and pulled her out into the hallway. "Boroskov won't find us again."

Her weight dragged against his arm. "We can't leave, Fenris. You know we can't, for May's sake."

He spun about and snarled at her defiance. He could force her. He was so much stronger than she was. But she was strong in a different way, and he'd never seen it until now.

"You know everything Quentin knows," she said, making no attempt to free herself from his grasp. "He has been running all his life, and you've helped him by hiding his own darkness away where he's never been forced to face it. Now he must recognize you, Fenris, and you must help him make a stand against Boroskov. For the sake of you both."

"Not for me—"

"Yes, Fenris. For you." She turned her hand to cup his arm in a tender touch. "Quentin needs you, but not in the way he once did. He needs you to be whole, as you need him. Your division was never meant to be. It's time for the rejoining. Time to begin living again."

He didn't want to hear her. "You love *me*," he insisted.

"'Yes. As I love Quentin. But I can't choose, Fenris. Not if you are both dead. Neither one of you is strong enough to defeat Boroskov alone. You and Quentin must confront him as one, or he will win."

"*Quentin* will win."

"Trust me, Fenris. Look into my eyes, and know that you can trust me."

"*No.*" He yanked away from her, but she caught him and held him fast.

"Let Quentin out, Fenris," she said, her cheek pressed to his chest. "Let him share your body, just for a moment, and I'll show you that there's nothing to fear."

He closed his eyes, feeling Quentin within him. Quentin was aware, already sharing Fenris's consciousness. But he could not come out unless Fenris let him.

Fenris knew how to take control from Quentin, but not how to release the Other without losing himself.

"Let me help you," Johanna said. She took his hand and began to speak low, like a mother to her child. He hardly heard the words. But in his mind a door swung open, and his rival, the weakling, the one he'd always despised, walked through.

They stared at each other, reflections in a distorted mirror. Quentin was smooth and handsome and refined, everything Fenris was not. He flinched and crouched as if he might flee at a whisper.

"You're afraid," Fenris said contemptuously. "You're always afraid."

"Yes," Quentin said. He held up his hand. It was trembling. "But you're afraid, too."

"I'm stronger than you are! I'll win. *I'll* take Johanna."

"Maybe you could. But you won't win her heart, Fenris."

"She loves me!"

"She has a great heart. And she loves what we can become. Together." He smiled raggedly. "I could have met you long ago, Fenris, but I was a coward. Johanna taught me to be brave. She has shown me that you are a necessary part of me, as I am necessary to you."

"I don't need you."

"You can go on living half a life, Fenris. You might even take my half away from me. But Grandfather will have won. Grandfather and Boroskov. They created you as much as I. More than I. They made you into a killer. You were helpless, just as I was. But you aren't helpless any longer."

Helpless. Fenris choked on a howl.

"Make your own choice, Fenris," Quentin said. "Let us defy Grandfather and all his schemes. Let us do battle . . . together." He held out his hand. "You are my strength, the part of me that survives and goes on fighting. Without you, I can't defend the woman we both love."

"I don't . . . need you!"

"You don't know how to love, Fenris, or how to stop hurting people. I'm the side of you that can live in the world and search for a little happiness." He breathed in and out, his face very pale. "You *are* me."

A sound like thunder crashed between them. The air in the no-place where they stood filled with the scent of the Enemy.

Boroskov.

•　　•　　•

Reality rushed in like a great ocean wave, slapping Quentin back to consciousness. Fenris disappeared from his inner sight, and he found himself standing in the center of the main room, his hand extended.

Empty.

Johanna wore a look of dazed startlement, her gaze moving quickly from him to the door. Boroskov was coming. Quentin could smell him, as Fenris had done, but there was no time to prepare. Shoes drummed hollowly on the outer porch, accompanied by the clanking of metal.

"Fenris?" Johanna whispered.

He shook his head, and then Boroskov stepped inside. He bore in his hands a pair of manacles and a length of chain.

"I trust you have come to the right decision," he said, closing the door behind him.

"Where is May?" Quentin demanded.

"Are you ready to submit to me?"

Quentin stared straight ahead. "Yes. Let them go."

Johanna made a wordless sound of distress. Her scheme hadn't succeeded. Fenris had refused the joining Quentin proposed, and Quentin knew why.

He hadn't wanted it enough. His words might have been steady, even sincere, but his heart and his mind were screaming denial: *Don't let the monster in.* How could Fenris not recognize his imposture?

"You must realize that I can't simply accept your word," Boroskov said. He lifted the manacles. "You will wear these until we are securely on the next ship bound for Russia. The girl is in the hands of my associates, and will be released in twenty-four hours. Doctor Schell may leave now, with the understanding that May pays with her life if she visits the authorities."

Quentin stared at the chains, his tongue thick in his mouth. "Why should I trust you?"

"Because the alternative is immediate death for those you profess to love. Oh, I know you can break these chains as easily as I, but you won't do so. And when we are back in Russia, it will be my pleasure to complete the instruction your grandfather abandoned."

"No," Johanna said.

"Hold out your hands," Boroskov commanded.

"Let Johanna go first," Quentin said.

Boroskov jerked his head toward the door. "Go."

Johanna didn't move.

"Go!" Quentin shouted. His head seemed to split apart. "Get out!"

"You have five seconds," Boroskov said.

Johanna grabbed Quentin's rigid arm. "Fenris! Will you let yourself be put in chains all over again? Will you submit to Boroskov's torture? Who will save *you*, Fenris, when the pain begins?"

Quentin tried to shake her off, but the agony in his head redoubled. The smell of Johanna's skin intoxicated him like a drug.

"I love you," she said.

Boroskov pushed her aside. Chains rattled. The absurdly smooth kid of Boroskov's glove touched his wrist, followed by the rough chill of metal.

Senses dimmed. All he could see was red, within and without, and he knew he wasn't alone inside his skin.

Fenris had arrived. Like a hot wind, he swept everything before him. He controlled, but he allowed Quentin to share what he knew and saw. The two of them no longer faced each other in some zone of truce created in his mind, but looked out from the same eyes.

They met Boroskov's gaze and smiled.

Boroskov stepped back, as if he sensed the change. His nostrils flared. He snatched at Johanna, but she scrambled out of his way.

The temporary confusion was enough for Quentin and

Fenris. They struck fast and hard, snapping Boroskov's head back with the force of their blow. Before he could recover, they leaped onto him, pinning him to the stained floor.

Boroskov gaped. "Quentin?"

"I'll win this time, Boroskov," Fenris said, holding Quentin mute. "Do you submit?"

"Who are you?"

Fenris prepared to roar out his name. Quentin, feeling his identity slipping away, resisted with all the desperation of his most ancient terrors. His revolt froze the body he and Fenris shared. Boroskov kicked up with his legs like a bucking horse and threw them off. They stumbled and fell.

Who are you?

Quentin—Fenris—Quentin. The time of decision had come at last. Two wills locked in implacable combat, forsaking their brief and tenuous alliance. Only one would survive.

Distantly, through the din of their clashing thoughts, they heard Johanna's exclamation of alarm and warning. They smelled the new intruders just before they burst into the room: Harper in the lead, bearing a wooden beam like a club; Oscar right behind him, fists raised; and then Irene and Lewis Andersen. The Haven's residents crowded through the door, and Boroskov lunged out of their path.

"Harper!" Johanna cried.

The former soldier advanced on Boroskov, beam at the ready. "You all right, Doc?"

Irene forced her way past the wall of Oscar's bulk and stood before Boroskov, her face bare of paint and her body drawn up high.

"You," she hissed. "You betrayed me. You deserted me—"

"Get back!" Johanna shouted.

Boroskov sent Irene flying across the room with one blow. Lewis Andersen ran to tend her crumpled form.

Harper lifted the beam, and Oscar came to stand beside him.

"You bastard," Harper said. "You aren't going to hurt anyone else."

Boroskov laughed. "Rescued just in the nick of time," he said. "Your mad humans, dear Johanna, have more fortitude and resourcefulness than I would have suspected." He snatched the beam from Harper's hands as if it were a twig. "A few more deaths on your conscience will make little difference, will they, Quentin?"

Unable to act, to move, even to breathe, Quentin saw the end of everything he had come to love. He was incapable of speech, but it didn't matter. Fenris would hear him.

If only one of them could have this body for the years to come, it must be the one who could save the others. If Quentin—if all he knew as himself—must die, so be it.

His fear vanished.

"My life is yours, Fenris," he said. *"Take it. Stop Boroskov."*

His heart—Fenris's heart—jarred to a stop and then started up again at double the pace.

Free.

Quentin felt what Fenris felt as he charged at Boroskov, ripped the beam from his grasp, carried him with the weight of his body up against the wall.

"You . . . won't . . . win," Fenris panted, his hand grinding into the Russian's throat. But he did not strike to kill.

Give me your strength, he asked Quentin. And Quentin gave it, all he had, even to the last shred of his identity.

Fenris took it. And this time, miracle of miracles, the sharing was complete. Together they knew the fierce joy of a new power filling muscles and organs, flesh and bones, mind and spirit—a sense of completion they had blindly sought all their lives. They knew courage blended with hope, strength matched with restraint, anger channeled by discipline and resolve.

Fenris stared into Boroskov's eyes and summoned up the mental gifts of the werewolf breed, the gifts Quentin had never been able to find within himself. He drove into Boroskov's mind.

Boroskov met him, will for will. But Fenris stepped aside with animal cunning, let Boroskov's mental counterattack slide past, and plunged deep into the Russian's memories.

All the memories. Pain. Torment. Darkness. Punishment for disobedience, pleasure for cooperation. Day after day, night after night. Father's face. Grandfather's. Masks of sinister purpose and merciless brutality.

Kill. Kill. Kill.

Chapter 25

Boroskov *screamed. Quentin felt the jolt of sudden* abandonment as Fenris left his body.

His body.

He fell against Boroskov like a puppet with cut strings. The Russian continued to scream, clawing at the wall behind him. With sheer stubborn determination, Quentin worked his numb hands to life and pinned Boroskov's arms to his sides. He sensed Johanna very near, the others watching in astonishment. He didn't let them distract him. He held onto Boroskov until the Russian's flailing stopped. His screams faded to whimpers, and then nothing.

The silence was so intense that Quentin could hear the sounds of people moving in the streets outside, drawn by the commotion. Cautiously he released Boroskov. The Russian slumped to the ground, blank-eyed. Spittle ran from the corner of his mouth.

"Quentin?" Johanna said.

"I'm here."

Johanna knelt beside Quentin and touched Boroskov's throat. "He's alive," she said, "but unconscious."

"Yes. And I don't think he'll be waking soon." Quentin closed his eyes and breathed out slowly. "Is everyone all right?"

"Yes," she said. "I've already checked on Irene—she'll be badly bruised, but nothing is broken. She was very fortunate." The straight line of her lips promised a long list of questions for the Haven's heedless residents when this was finished. "We must find out what Boroskov did with May. She could still be in danger."

"We'll find her," he said with absolute conviction. Real confidence, not the false bravado that had sustained him for so long. He reached for her hand and squeezed it gently. Boroskov couldn't have taken her far."

"And Fenris?" she asked, for his ears alone.

"He came when we needed him," he said. "You were right. He was the one who finally defeated Boroskov."

"Was he?" Her eyes, so beautiful even now, demanded more from him, a deeper truth.

Such truths were no longer to be feared. Quentin searched his heart and found all the fear shrivelled up and bereft of power. Just as the memories, freed from Fenris's mind, could no longer distort his life, though it might take him years to fully reconcile himself to him.

"*We* defeated him," he amended. "Fenris and I. But only after I realized that I had to make my surrender complete. I had to trust him with everything I am. As I trust you."

"You accepted him at last," she said, stroking his hand. "You let him out. And yet he did not kill Boroskov."

"No." Quentin smiled—no bitterness or mockery, only a sense of peace, almost too new to seem real. "He used powers I lost long ago, if I ever had them. He met Boroskov on his own ground—on the ground we shared, all three of us. And then he—" He paused, trying to put the impossible into words. "He joined with Boroskov, and gave me back myself."

"He . . . joined—"

He touched his temple. "Fenris is gone, but he's not. What he was is still in me—the parts I needed, just as you said. The parts that make me a whole man again. But the rest—it's Boroskov's, now."

He could see she didn't understand. He didn't truly understand it himself. Fenris had willingly flung his being into Boroskov's mind, and the two had become one.

Fenris had not killed Boroskov. He'd left him hopelessly mad.

"Perhaps one day I can explain," he said. "Suffice it to say that Boroskov will not be a threat to anyone, human or otherwise. Fenris will stop him."

Johanna shivered, her scientific curiosity left without answers, and she looked at the Russian. "I judge him to be in a cataleptic state. We cannot leave him here."

"It will be necessary to confine him to some place where he can be cared for—and watched, in the rare event that I am mistaken."

"An asylum," she said, sadness in her eyes.

"But not the Haven."

She glanced away. "I could not care for him, in any case. I am not sure if I am qualified to see patients again."

He cupped her chin in his hand and turned her toward him. "Johanna—don't you know that I—we—couldn't have done this without you? I never would have found the courage to recognize the darker part of myself, or the memories that created it, if you had not shown me the way. You made it possible."

"You give me far too much credit," she said with a faint, self-deprecating smile. "I have learned that we doctors do not cure our patients. We merely help them, just a little, to cure themselves—if we are very lucky."

"You're wrong, Doc."

Harper came to crouch beside them, looking from Johanna and Quentin to Boroskov and back again. "None of us would be where we are now, if not for you."

Johanna's eyes sharpened. "How *did* you come to be here, Harper? What possessed you to put yourself and the others in danger by following me?" She looked beyond him to the remaining three patients. Oscar was perched on a broken chair, kicking his legs and looking quite unperturbed by the recent action. Amazingly enough, Lewis Andersen sat beside Irene, half supporting her. He was brushing himself off with a once-pristine white handkerchief, glancing about the filthy room with visible distaste. Irene gave a loud sniff, and he belatedly passed the kerchief to the actress, who blew her nose into it. His narrow upper lip curled, but he did not draw away from her. Something had changed with Lewis during Quentin's absence.

"It's a long story," Harper said, addressing Johanna's frown with a wry nod. "You remember when I told you that I get visions from things belonging to people, things they've touched. I took May's book right after she was kidnapped. I had lots of things of yours, Doc, and I had this—" He pulled a woman's ring from his pocket and pressed it into Quentin's hand. "I saw Irene with it, not long after I came out of my long sleep. I don't know how she got it. She dropped it and ran away, guiltylike, when she saw me, and I picked it up. Knew it was yours right away." He shrugged in embarrassment. "Sorry I kept it so long. I had a feeling I'd need it."

"I'd wondered what had become of it," Quentin said. "I'd thought it was gone forever." He kissed the ring and slipped it onto his little finger. "Thank you, Harper."

"You're welcome." He glanced at Johanna. "I couldn't just let you come out here alone, Doc, knowing what'd happened. So right after you left, I started concentrating on these things. And I could see where May was. I could see you, and Quentin, only he didn't feel right." He cocked his head at Quentin.

"Another long story," Quentin said. "You were saying?"

"Well, I got enough of a sense of where to look that I talked to Mrs. Daugherty and asked her if she could hire some help to see to the others while I was gone. But Miss DuBois overheard, and she asked me if I knew where Bolkonsky was." He glanced at Boroskov. "She was in a right taking. Didn't do any good to tell her no. She insisted on coming along, said she'd follow if I didn't let her. And then Andersen found out, and he said he wasn't going to let either one of us go without him—though he did a right lot of scrubbing and praying before we left."

Johanna rubbed at her eyes. *"Mein Gott."*

"Then, well . . . Oscar wouldn't be left behind, either. He's strong, so I thought he might come in handy. Lewis donated some money he'd saved, and we took the train and the ferry to San Francisco. Then I just followed what the visions told me."

Quentin exchanged glances with Johanna. Both of them knew that Harper and the others had only the vaguest idea of the danger they'd rushed into. But even leaving the safety of the Haven had been a great act of valor for people who had feared and distrusted the world, or themselves. An act of valor, and of selfless loyalty.

"You should not have done it," Johanna said thickly. "But I thank you for your concern." She brushed at her cheeks. "Mrs. Daugherty is still at the Haven with my father?"

"Of course," Harper said. "She warned me that if we didn't all come back in a few days, she'd get the law involved."

"That is not necessary." Johanna rose. "We will go home as quickly as we can, as soon as we find May—"

"I can help," Harper said. "I still have her book in my pack. She'll be all right."

Johanna shook her head, her eyes suspiciously bright. She gave Quentin an intensely private glance, acknowledging that their conversation was not over. "Lewis?"

The former reverend gave up his attempt to clean his blackened gloves and rose from the couch. "Doctor?"

"We must find May, and I will need Quentin's and Harper's help. Will you look after Irene and Oscar if we take you to a hotel where they can rest?"

Andersen stood very straight. "'The Lord is my strength, in whom I will trust.' I can, Doctor Schell. Simply tell me where to go."

"Thank you." She smiled at Irene and Oscar. Irene sniffled, but her habitual hostility was as absent from her face as the garish paint. Oscar sang a nursery song under his breath.

"Are we going home now?" he asked.

"Very soon." She drew close to Quentin again, and his constant physical and mental awareness of her rose to a higher pitch. He felt a little of Fenris's irrational desire to drag her off to a dark corner and ravish her, but also the patience to wait. Their time would come.

"I'm afraid you will have to use the manacles on Boroskov," she whispered. "If we leave him here until May is safe, will he escape?"

"No."

He could see that she was still adjusting to his new self-assurance, but she didn't question him. "Very well. I'll take the others outside, and wait for you. Then we shall escort Lewis, Oscar, and Irene to my hotel and go in search of May."

Quentin hid a smile of love and admiration. His dear, headstrong Johanna. She couldn't help but take command. She might have suffered a few doubts in the course of this day's work, but she'd rally in the end. She was too strong to do otherwise.

Just as she'd made him strong with her love.

"I'll be right with you," he said. As she turned to gather the patients, he caught her and pulled her into his arms. In full view of their gawking audience, he kissed her soundly.

"For Fenris," he said. "And for me."

Q*uentin held nothing back.*
Every one of his inhuman senses worked in perfect harmony, as they hadn't done in years. It was almost ridiculously easy to follow Boroskov's trail to the place where May was hidden. He had no need of Harper's psychic abilities.

If not for the girl, he would have left Johanna and Harper behind. But they needed to be a part of this, and so he let them follow.

The old warehouse, at the edge of the Barbary Coast, was guarded by a small army of Boroskov's henchmen, who looked ready to put up a nasty fight. The Russian wouldn't have left so many if he had been as confident as he pretended. But even in this he'd miscalculated.

Quentin felt no reluctance to face them, no fear of what he might do once unleashed. Nor was he inclined to explain to them their master's incapacitated condition. He knew a more efficient way of gaining their surrender. His anger, and his strength, were under his complete command.

He didn't bother to Change. He pushed Harper and Johanna behind him, expecting their obedience, and stalked his prey with bared teeth and a hard, predatory stare.

Boroskov's men couldn't have known what he was, but they recognized danger. Like the mob from the Springs, they shifted and muttered among themselves, brandishing knives and pistols as if those alone could hinder a were-wolf.

They had no hope of stopping the reborn Quentin Forster.

The assortment of thugs, footpads, and ruffians kept up their bluff until he was within spitting distance, and then the first of them broke and ran. One fired his pistol; Quentin effortlessly dodged the bullet. Another three split off from the group and dashed around the nearest corner.

Of those who remained, two might have been quite a challenge for an ordinary man. Quentin dispatched one of them with a handy facer before the fellow knew what was coming. The second lunged with a wicked, long-bladed knife, and was rewarded with a dislocated shoulder. The pitiful remnants of Boroskov's army thought better of their erstwhile loyalty and took to their heels.

May was loosely tied up in a small office inside the warehouse. If she'd had a personal guard, he'd heard the commotion outside and made himself scarce.

The girl stared at Quentin in astonishment, struggling against her bonds.

"You came!" she cried, gamely fighting back tears. "I knew you would. I knew—" She paused. "Quentin? It is you?"

Quentin snapped the ropes with a flick of his fingers and lifted her into his arms. Johanna and Harper rushed to his side.

"It's me, little one." He kissed her forehead and passed her into Johanna's arms. "You're safe. We're all safe."

Johanna hugged May and met Quentin's gaze over the girl's head. Her eyes blazed with pride and affection.

"Yes," she said. "We are whole again." She set May back and wiped the girl's tears with her thumb. "And there is more, *liebchen*. Your mother has come home."

•   •   •

The first promise of dawn lay upon the eastern horizon when they arrived at Johanna's hotel. The three they'd left behind were waiting in the lobby: Lewis and Irene in a matching pair of armchairs by the window, Oscar sprawled and snoring across one of the hard settees. A jubilant greeting followed, but it was not to be the happiest.

Johanna went to fetch Mrs. Ingram herself. Quentin never learned what passed between them, but May's mother came flying down the stairs in her dressing gown, and a moment later mother and daughter embraced in a flurry of endearments and joyful sobs.

Quentin couldn't steal so much as a second alone with Johanna. But he watched her—he never tired of doing so—and saw her mingled sadness and pleasure in the family reunion. His heart swelled with the same mixed emotions. She had much to be proud of, and much to let go. He swore to make up for every one of her losses.

"Reckon that's the prettiest sight I ever did see," Harper said, coming to stand beside him.

"Yes," Quentin answered. "I reckon it is." But his eyes were only for the sturdy, practical woman who gravely received Mrs. Ingram's breathless thanks.

Harper smiled. "You have a lot of catching up to do, brother."

"And a lot of living," Quentin agreed. "For both of us."

"In that case," Harper said, "I reckon we'd better get started."

The gate to the Haven stood open, as if in welcome. On every side the vineyard, woods, and orchards held steadfast in spite of the travails of men.

Mrs. Daugherty came out onto the porch, shading her eyes and looking ready to let loose with a terrific scold.

Oscar ran ahead of everyone and charged up the stairs, bursting with news for the housekeeper.

Johanna stopped at the gate and let the tears come. Quentin put his arm around her and nuzzled her hair.

"Glad to be home?" he asked.

"No," she said, wondering if this tendency to weep at the drop of a hat was a temporary affliction. She sincerely hoped so. "I'd much rather be back in San Francisco, battling monsters."

He chuckled and kissed her temple. "I wonder."

Mrs. Ingram cleared her throat and came forward to join them. May clung to her arm, as she'd done ever since mother and daughter had been reunited in San Francisco. The girl was radiant, as if her recent experiences had shocked her out of the remnants of the old troubles. Johanna could not envision her suffering from hysteria ever again—as long as she was given a chance to grow up well outside her father's pernicious shadow. Mrs. Ingram intended to do just that.

May wasn't the only one to benefit from adversity. Lewis Andersen seemed to have experienced an epiphany during his confrontation with Irene in the vineyard. Although he remained fastidious and vigilant, he had actually removed his gloves during the ferry and train ride home. He had been seen to smile, with nary a word of sins or sinners. Instead, his quotes from the Bible were those of hope and inspiration.

Though he continued to regard Quentin with nervous suspicion, he didn't seem inclined to expose Quentin's secret to the world. Gradually he was allowing himself to touch and be touched—especially with Irene, who was sober and quiet and changed in ways Johanna expected to find most remarkable.

What precisely had changed Irene remained to be explored, but Johanna suspected that she, too, had been forced to see herself clearly for the first time in many years. Johanna hoped to make Irene's transition to reality as painless as possible. She and Lewis might be sufficiently recovered to leave the Haven in a matter of months.

As for Quentin . . .

She glanced up at him shyly, amazed all over again at the strength of her passion. She tried very hard not to let him see it. She'd accepted his support on the journey home, needing it more than she had any other man's, glad enough to let herself be a little dependent for a few brief hours.

But she did not deceive herself. The Quentin who stood with her now was not the one who had left the Haven a mere few days ago. Oh, the alterations were subtle enough: They lay in his unflinching carriage, the challenge in his eyes, the assurance in his walk—the way he spoke, as if a real future existed, and the way he gathered everyone he cared for under the cloak of his protection. He was no longer afraid.

His past might still haunt him for a time, the memories Fenris had restored to him. He had become neither perfect nor incapable of guilt and regret. But now he would be able to deal with that past and accept it, just as he'd accepted Fenris.

Did he still need her? Was it too much to ask, that he should wish to remain with someone who reminded him so much of the obstacles he'd overcome?

Quentin had his own life to seek, a family waiting to embrace him, a nonhuman heritage to explore. She would not keep him from the future he chose.

But within her heart was a kernel of hope. They had shared so much. If only they could share the rest of their lives . . .

"It has been a long time," Mrs. Ingram said. "Isn't it strange, how things have come full circle, and yet that circle has led us to a better place." She smiled at her daughter. "A wonderful place."

"Indeed," Johanna said. "It has been a long two days. Shall we go inside?"

Mrs. Daugherty hurried down the steps, Oscar trailing along beside her like an overgrown pup. "I was so worried, wonderin' what you was all up to in the city!" She clucked her tongue. "You all look fit enough, but I hope you never do it again!"

"Believe me," Quentin said, grabbing her work-roughened hand for a kiss, "I hope the same."

"Oh, you." She blushed and gave him a mock frown. "Doc Jo, your papa's fine. He asked for you, and I said you'd be back soon."

"Thank you," Johanna said. "Thank you, Bridget. I don't know what I would have done without your loyalty."

"Go on." She turned back to Quentin. "There's a feller here to see you—been here since morning. I told him I didn't rightly know when any of you'd be back, but he said he had to wait." She smiled knowingly. "Said he'd come all the way from New Mexico Territory, tracking you down for your sister."

"Rowena?" Quentin said, his face reflecting startled joy.

"That's the name. He's waitin' in the parlor. Just about eaten us out of house and home, too. So the rest of you better come on in and get your supper!"

"Yes," Johanna said, stepping aside. "Go in. Mrs. Ingram, please make yourself at home. I'll join you directly."

The others dutifully followed Oscar and Mrs. Daugherty up the stairs, leaving Quentin and Johanna alone.

"Rowena," Quentin said. "I can't believe it. Rowena found me here?"

"Your sister? I thought your family was in England."

"She came to America shortly before I did, for reasons I'll explain when I can. We kept in touch for a while, but then I—" He bowed his head. "She's probably been sick with worry."

"Then you must talk to this man immediately." She pressed his hands. "And I must go to my father."

"Yes." He hardly seemed to see her, his thoughts centered on those he had known long before Johanna. "Yes."

She went up the stairs ahead of him, her heart bursting with happiness for Quentin and a sorrow she couldn't acknowledge.

Her father sat in his wheelchair in the parlor, gazing at the wall with a slight smile on his face. He blinked and turned his head to look at her as she entered the room.

"Johanna," he said. "It's good to see you."

"And you, Papa." She knelt before him and took his hands. "I missed you."

"That's my Valkyrie," he said vaguely, touching her hair. "How is the new doctor working out?"

He meant Quentin, of course. He probably hadn't even noticed that so many of the Haven's residents had been gone. Johanna was grateful for that small favor.

"He may not be able to remain, Papa," she said gently, playing along with his assumptions. "He's been called to see to his own affairs in another part of the country."

"A pity. I liked him very much. A personable, intelligent young man."

So much like the old Wilhelm Schell. She rested her head on his knees. "Yes, Papa. I . . . liked him very much, also."

"You are sure that you cannot persuade him to remain? Our work is so very important here."

Yes, it was. For all her doubts about her own competence, her desire to surrender the responsibility forever, she knew Papa was right. She couldn't take the easy way and give up everything she and her father had worked to establish. To do so would betray what she and Quentin had found, in themselves and each other.

But she didn't wish to go on alone as she'd done for so long, independent and free of personal ties. She knew what it was to love. Quentin was the lost half of herself. She needed him as he'd needed Fenris.

She had to tell him. Outright, with none of the usual protections against hurt and disappointment. She must find exactly the right moment, and pray she didn't trip over her own tongue.

As for the Haven, she had also given that careful consideration on the trip back to the Valley. Though Quentin would eventually be cleared of guilt in the matter of Ketchum's death, suspicion about the Haven's residents would not so easily be dispelled. Now that May was leaving, Harper was cured, and Irene and Lewis had made such progress, it would be much less difficult to start again elsewhere, perhaps in another state. Begin another Haven, to help whoever needed sanctuary in a complex and sometimes frightening world.

A world Johanna would never view again with the same eyes. Or the same heart.

She spoke to her father of this and that, the trivialities that so often filled his once brilliant mind. She took comfort in such things, as he did. She brought him his tray, helped him eat the dinner Mrs. Daugherty had prepared, and took him to his room to rest.

Then she went to face Quentin.

May was just leaving the parlor when Johanna found him there. She saw on his face that he'd been making his farewells to the girl; sadness and pride mingled in his cinnamon eyes.

He glanced toward the kitchen, where May had gone to join her mother. "May will be leaving us soon," he said. "Her mother tells me that she has assembled certain damaging information about Mr. Ingram's personal and business practices that will make him very unlikely to interfere with her decision to take May to Europe. It's something of a miracle, how things have changed for both of them."

"Indeed." Johanna sat on the chair nearest the fireplace

and folded her hands in her lap. "It is far more than I could have hoped."

"But things have changed for all of us, haven't they?" He sat down on the sofa opposite her. "I sometimes wonder if I'm dreaming. And then I look at you, and realize there is such a thing as heaven on earth."

She shivered as if with fever. *Now. Tell him now.* But she was as tongue-tied as she'd feared, driven mute by his tender words. All that would come to her was a single stuttered question.

"What . . . what had the messenger to say of your sister? Is she well?"

"Better than well." He leaned back, watching her with a secret smile. "The little vixen has married—an American, no less—and I didn't even know it! Another long and complicated story, which she promises to tell me in detail when we meet again. But she's never sounded happier. I confess that she almost doesn't sound like herself at all. And she tells me that my brother's family in England is well, his two young children growing like weeds. They're all on excellent terms now . . ." His smile faded. "We've been too long apart. She said she's had men searching for me for over two years, since I stopped writing. I owe my family a great many explanations."

"There is . . . nothing to stop you from tendering them in person," Johanna said, managing a smile of her own. "Your sister found you at the right time."

"Yes. I'm myself again—more myself than I've ever been."

"Then you should not delay going to her."

He gazed at her with that long, unblinking, predator's stare that Fenris had bestowed upon him. "Do you want me to go, Johanna?"

No! Not without me . . . She swallowed the cry. *No need to become hysterical, Johanna. Calm, calm and prudence.*

"I want you to be happy," she said. "You have so much

to reclaim, Quentin. All the things you left behind, in England—your family, your heritage—"

"My old ways as a rake and ne'er-do-well?" he said. "Oh, yes. The second son, returning home to become a burden on his family."

"You would not be a burden on anyone," she said, her throat growing thick with passion.

"Except upon you."

She surged to her feet. "You were never a burden. You were my patient, and then my friend. My dear friend."

"Only a friend, Johanna?" He rose with deliberation. "As I recall, you told me that you loved me."

This was the moment. *Speak.* Her mouth was so dry that she could hardly swallow.

"You promised me, Johanna, that you'd see me through to a cure. Are you going to abandon me now?"

"You are no longer my patient. You have not been, since we—" She caught her breath, her face unbearably hot. "In any case, you have made remarkable progress, crossed the most difficult threshold."

"But I'm not cured, you know. I have all of Fenris's memories, as well as my own. Ugly memories." He wasn't joking any longer. "I must learn how to forgive myself. I don't know if I can do it alone."

She refused to let him belittle his own extraordinary accomplishments. "You are strong, Quentin, or you would not have survived."

"Not that strong," he said, walking toward her. "Not strong enough to leave you." He knelt at her feet. "You see, I love you, Johanna."

He loves me. He . . . loves . . . *me.* Her entire body vibrated like a metronome, and her mind went utterly blank.

"Patients often think that they love their doctors. It is a common—"

He sealed her lips with his finger. "But you just said I'm

not your patient, Johanna. Can't you make up your mind?" He sighed and shook his head. "Let me help you."

Giving her no time to prepare, he leaned forward and kissed her. Deeply, passionately, with everything he was and could become, with Fenris's ferocity and Quentin's gentleness.

"I have a proposition for you, dear doctor," he said, when he let her up for air. "Be my wife."

"Quentin—I want you to know that I . . . I—"

"You might as well take pity on me." He smiled, the old smile laced with both wickedness and a new resolve. "I've been waiting to love you in a proper bed ever since that night in the Barbary Coast."

Rampant desire made it impossible to concentrate. "I have been trying to tell you, but I am not very good—" She wet her lips and croaked out a laugh. "Quentin, I need you. I do not wish to go on without you by my side. I love you."

He gave a crow of triumph and kissed her again. She laced her arms around his neck and hugged him as if he might vanish if she dared let loose. Was she dreaming?

"You know—" she gulped and started again. "I am merely human. How will your family accept—"

"My family cares about me, and they'll love you for the remarkable woman you are." He bared his teeth. "I assure you that they will."

"But you must want to return to England."

"America is my home now. My old life is over."

"You . . . understand that I am a doctor." She laughed again, nervous and jubilant. "I am not much of a cook. Nor a housekeeper—"

He took her face in his hands. "My Valkyrie. I would never ask you to give up your great gifts for healing the mind." He kissed her hands, one by one. "I know very well that you can get along without me. But together—" He swung her off her feet and twirled her in a dizzy circle. "Beware to anyone who stands in our way!"

They kissed, and danced about the parlor like a pair of dervishes, until Johanna's hair came loose and they both looked as though they'd just left the bedroom. Johanna didn't even bother to straighten her frock.

This was not madness. She loved, and was loved by, a man who expected, even demanded that she embrace her gifts, just as he embraced his. He'd never regard her as anything but an equal. A friend, a helpmate, a lover.

She knew she'd have cause to doubt herself again. So would Quentin. But they would no longer be alone in fighting their battles. She need not be strong and sensible and responsible every moment of every day; Quentin could be those things for her.

As she would be for him.

"At least one matter is relatively straightforward," she said, summoning up the breath to speak. "I have already considered that it would be best for the Haven's residents to relocate to a place far from Silverado Springs, where we can start afresh. You said that your sister lives in New Mexico. We should be able to sell my uncle's remaining land for a good price. Surely there is land to be bought and room to build in the Territory. I will have to talk to the others, but—"

"Does that mental machinery of yours ever cease its work?" he teased, kissing her on the nose. "Of course, my Valkyrie. I've passed through the Territory, once or twice. It's a wild country, but there is still room for men and women to grow. We'll find our place there."

"You won't mind sharing our lives with my patients?"

"Not at all. As long as we have a little time to ourselves." He gave her a delightful sample of what he had in mind for their private times. Johanna found her thoughts turning with increasing persistence to her bed down the hall.

But she still had obligations. "I must say good-bye to May and Mrs. Ingram. And there's your messenger—"

"Not quite yet. You didn't answer my question." He dropped to one knee again, and took her hand between his. "Will you marry me, Johanna?"

She felt the smile on her face growing and growing until it became a ridiculous grin. "It seems a perfectly rational thing to do."

He jumped up, caught her about the waist and whirled her around and around with such a caterwauling that Mrs. Daugherty, Irene, Harper, Lewis, Oscar, May, and Mrs. Ingram came to watch in amazement.

Johanna only laughed. If she'd gone a little mad, it was a price she was willing to pay.

AUTHOR'S NOTES

Secret of the Wolf is a work of fiction. As an author, I love to explore intriguing story ideas that may or may not necessarily reflect my own personal beliefs or those of current specialists in a given field.

In *Secret of the Wolf*, Johanna Schell is an early "psychiatrist" who used the relatively new science of hypnosis to help her patients. The modern concept of the trance state was made popular by Franz Anton Mesmer in the last quarter of the eighteenth century. Mesmer advocated the concept of "animal magnetism." The Marquis de Puysegur was the first to describe the three central features of hypnosis. But it was James Braid who, in 1843, coined the word "hypnosis," and he wrote many papers on the subject as well as using forms of hypnotism in his medical practice. In 1845, James Esdaile performed his first operation under hypnosis, or "hypnoanesthesia." However, as the nineteenth century progressed, hypnotism fell out of favor and most physicians considered its therapeutic use a stumbling block to acceptance by the medical community.

In the mid-nineteenth century, a French country physician, Ambroise-Auguste Liebault, began using the method to treat various illnesses in his rural patients. He wrote a book that was largely ignored, and it was not until a colleague, Hyppolyte Bernheim, paid him a visit in 1882 and adopted his methods that hypnosis was revived as a respectable therapeutic tool.

Johanna is ahead of her time in this respect, since she and her father continued to develop medical applications of hypnosis during a period when it was out of fashion.

Today, hypnosis is used to treat many kinds of disorders and remains a somewhat controversial type of therapy. More controversial, however, is the concept of "suppressed memory" and "Multiple Personality Disorder." There are wildly divergent views on both subjects.

Some psychiatrists, psychologists, and specialists are advocates of the concept of "suppressed or recovered memory," in which a person—usually a child—will "hide" a traumatic experience from the conscious mind. The theory is that such hidden memories may be uncovered through hypnosis and other forms of treatment. In *Secret of the Wolf*, Quentin possesses such memories. Some mental-health specialists believe that the act of uncovering these memories will help effect a cure. Others strongly believe that "recovered memories" are often implanted by the therapist, or are simply an amalgam of wishes, beliefs, and actual memories.

Some advocates of the suppressed memory theory believe that traumatic childhood experiences can result in Multiple Personality Disorder, or MPD, which is now called Dissociative Identity Disorder (DSM-IV.) The brain "separates" itself into at least two personalities with different functions, which allow the child to deal with the unbearable. Others claim that the additional personalities do not really exist at all, but are the products of the therapy itself.

The concept of MPD/DID was born in the seventeenth century, when Paracelsus recorded the case of a woman who claimed that another personality stole her money. In 1812, Benjamin Rush described several cases that fit the modern definition of MPD/DID. The case of Mary Reynolds, in 1817, was described by Silas Weir Mitchell as one of "double consciousness." Later in the nineteenth century, a number of physicians and psychologists, including Eugene Azam, reported cases of two or more personalities sharing the same body. Interestingly enough, the early cases were nearly always a matter of only two personalities; it was not until the twentieth century that cases of true multiples were uncovered.

Post-traumatic Stress Disorder, a recently named phenomenon, is displayed by the character of Harper in *Secret of the Wolf*. In the nineteenth century, the condition was variously known as "soldier's heart," "railway spine," traumatic neurosis, nervous shock, and various forms of neurasthenia and hysteria. During WWI, it was called "shell shock." Today, entire fields of study are devoted to PTSD, its causes, symptoms, and cures. As with the other conditions mentioned above, there is considerable debate about the specific parameters of PTSD.

I neither advocate nor refute these theories in *Secret of the Wolf*. They are used in a fictional sense to tell a story.

Because these subjects are so controversial and many-sided, I offer a selection of sources for further information. A full spectrum of opinion on these subjects is represented in the following.

Disclaimer: *Susan Krinard does not in any way advocate or recommend these websites and/or books as representing her personal beliefs, the current state of mental health research, or the "truth or falsehood" of hypnotherapy, suppressed/false memories, or MPD. Susan Krinard does not advocate the services of any practitioner or organization mentioned, or linked to, the following websites, nor is she responsible for website content. Viewers should visit at their own risk.*

Websites

History of Psychiatry and Mental Health Treatment

http://psy.utmb.edu/research/psyepi/course/1concept/history/
history.htm
http://www.psychnet-uk.com/training_ethics/
history_of_psych.htm
http://www.geocities.com/Athens/Delphi/6061/en_linha.htm

Hypnosis

History of Hypnosis
http://ks.essortment.com/hypnosishistory_rcdg.htm
http://www.infinityinst.com/articles/ixnartic.html
http://www.hypnotherapy.freeserve.co.uk/History%20of%20
Hypnosis.htm

Hypnotherapy.

http://www.altemativemedicinechannel.com/hypnotherapy/
http://home.earthlink.net/~johnsonsaga/hypnotherapy2.html

Suppressed / Recovered Memory and False Memory Syndrome

http://www.brown.edu/Departments/Taubman_Center/
Recovmenm/Archive.html
http://www.skeptic.com/02.3.hochman-fms.html
http://www.mhsource.com/pt/p991137.html
http://www.vuw.ac.nz/psyc/fitzMemory/contents.html

MPD/DID

http://www.dissociation.com/index/Definition/
http://www.religioustolerance.org/mpd_did.htm
http://www.psycom.net/mchugh.html
http://www.csicop.org/si/9805/witch.html
http://www.usc.edu/dept/law-lib/law-center/usclaw94/
saksart.htrnl
http://www.ac.wwu.edu/~n9l40024/CampbellPM.htmi
http://www.golden.net/~soul/didpro.html

Partial Bibliography

Berrios, German and Porter, Roy, eds. *A History of Clinical Psychiatry: The Origin and History of Psychiatric Disorders.* New York: New York University Press, 1995.

Bliss, Eugene L. *Multiple Personality, Allied Disorders and Hypnosis.* Oxford: Oxford University Press, 1986.

Brown, Peter. *The Hypnotic Brain: Hypnotherapy and Social Communication.* New Haven, Conn.: Yale University Press, 1991.

Dean, Eric T., Jr. *Shook Over Hell: Post-Traumatic Stress, Vietnam, and the Civil War.* Cambridge: Harvard University Presss, 1997.

Ellenberger, Henri F. *The Discovery of the Unsconscious.* New York: Basic Books, Inc., 1970.

Gauld, Alan. *A History of Hypnotisim.* Cambridge: Cambridge University Press, 1992.

Grob, Gerald N. *The Mad Among Us: A History of the Care of America's Mentally Ill.* Cambridge: Harvard University Press, 1994.

Hacking, Ian. *Rewriting the Soul: Multiple Personality and the Science of Memory.* Princeton, N.J.: Princeton Paperbacks, 1995.

Jackson, Stanley W. *Care of the Psyche: A History of Psychological Healing.* New Haven, Conn.: Yale University Press, 1999.

Morrison, James. *DSM-IV Made Easy.* New York: The Guildford Press, 1995.

Reid, William and Balis, George. *The Treatment of Psychiatric Disorders, Third Edition.* New York: Brunnner/Mazel, 1997.

Sargant, William. *Battle for the Mind: A Physiology of Conversion and Brain-Washing.* Cambridge: Malor Books, 1997.

Scull, Andrew, ed. *Madhouses, Mad-Doctors, and Madmen: The Social History of Psychiatry in the Victorian Era.* Philadelphia: The University of Pennsylvania Press, 1981.

Shay, Jonathan. *Achilles in Vietnam: Combat Trauma and the Undoing of Character.* New York: Simon & Schuster, 1994.

Shorter, Edward. *A History of Psychiatry: From the Era of the Asylum to the Age of Prozac*. New York: John Wiley & Sons, Inc., 1997.
Stone, Michael H. *Healing the Mind: A History of Psychiatry from Antiquity to the Present*. New York: W. W. Norton & Company, Inc., 1997.

Best wishes,

SUSAN KRINARD
skrinard@aol.com
http://members.aol.com/skrinard/

P.O. Box 51924
Albuquerque, NM 87181